The
Fallen
Snow

Stone Cabin Press | Washington, DC
First Edition – December 2012
www.thefallensnow.com

Publisher's Cataloging-In-Publication Data
(Prepared by The Donohue Group, Inc.)

Kelley, John J. (John Joseph), 1965-
  The fallen snow / [John J. Kelley]. -- 1st ed.

  p. ; cm.

  ISBN: 978-0-9884148-0-8

  1. Gay military personnel--Psychology--Fiction. 2. World War, 1914-1918--Veterans--Psychology--Fiction. 3. World War, 1914-1918--France--Lorraine--Fiction. 4. Self-realization--Fiction. 5. Lorraine (France)--Fiction. 6. Appalachia (Va.)--Fiction. 7. Historical fiction. I. Title.

PS3611.E554 F35 2012
813/.6

12 13 14 15 16 10 9 8 7 6 5 4 3 2 1

To the Brushy

Death had gone after youth that year,
and like all stunned survivors they treaded
gingerly among the ruins.

~ Elisabeth Hensworth ~

For in the stillness of snow
All things are possible.

~ Samuel L. Barrett ~

1 - Joshua

He wasn't sure how long the woman had been watching him. But her stare was deep, and her hair ghostly white. That was all he could tell with his head lowered. He didn't dare meet her gaze.

When he had dozed, there'd been only a couple of passengers outside the Elkton depot. Now there were over a dozen, hovering near. They'd want to talk to him, like the folks in the Baltimore station and at the diner before it.

He pushed off the bench, rising as best he could. The wood platform ran the length of the building. Men were smoking at the end nearer the town. But the other side was empty, and dark. It would do.

The first steps were the hardest. The cold didn't help, though it was more than stiffness. More like his leg muscles had to relearn the motion, as though they'd forgotten their purpose. Maybe that was why he'd felt the compulsion from the time he'd awoken at the field hospital. He had to keep pushing lest he find himself trapped, or paralyzed. Or left for dead.

Movement came easier now. A man edged back, eyeing the scar along his scalp. The man's son, no more than ten, looked too. His gaze fell to the collar insignia and division patch, coming to rest on the ribbon. The younger ones always studied the uniform, seeing it more than him, which was just as well. But the boy said nothing, nor did the father. Another step and he was free of them.

Without his cane.

He glanced toward the bench. The cane was there, resting against his duffel. He wasn't going back now.

Continuing on, he scanned the predawn sky. The night was moonless, or at least he couldn't find it. There were stars though. At the end of the platform he could see them better. A soft glow bathed the farm across the tracks. The smell of cow manure was strong. Beside the station sat a lumberyard. He could smell the felled trees too, a warm woody scent destined to fade fast.

The nearest trunks were thick, four or five feet in diameter. Probably from the Blue Ridge, unless they'd cleared the whole length by now. Maybe some were from the western ridges, brought in on the Chesapeake & Western line. Logs from Hadley might be among them.

The thought stuck. It had never crossed his mind, though eighteen months was long enough. The loggers were efficient. A crew could clear an entire slope in a few months, and there were scores operating across Augusta County. Hadley wouldn't escape their reach forever.

Would Mom have mentioned it? The ridges were his element, not hers. She hated the mountains. Still, it would have been news. Surely she'd have made note.

He looked up when he heard the whistle. A freight train barreled along the far track, not slowing. The thunder rose to a feverish clamor. Just a train, that was all. No grenades or gunfire. No shells or gases. Yet his body made no distinction. He heard the ringing in his ear and felt the tightness in his chest.

He fled home, as he had each night on the front.

An orchard of hardwoods blanketed the land. By now prominent oak, chestnut and hickory would have cloaked the ridges in deep reds and muted yellows. Beneath their twisting canopy, he could wander for hours among hay-scented ferns, through sprinklings of mountain laurel, witch-hazel and dogwood. Stands of birch and spruce clung to high northern niches. Groves of hemlock shielded rocky streams below.

He remained there, safe along the wooded slopes, even after the train had passed. When he could breathe again, he opened his eyes. He wiped his neck, feeling the slender chain beneath his palm. His hand grew damp.

At his bedside in Toul, Claire had tried to explain the night sweats. "Your body is mending. You will be fine, mon ami," she had whispered, as if her words could make it so.

But he wasn't fine. He'd have to face them alone. And they'd want things from him. They'd want the old Joshua. It's what they'd expect.

The chill sank clear to the bone. Shaking it off, he turned. Passengers had begun to shift. The eastern sky was lighter. It wouldn't be long now. He should get his duffel and move nearer the tracks. Boarding would go easier that way.

He flexed his leg then made his way back up the platform. His gait was steadier now, but that was only half the battle. The rest was harder, much harder. So he dropped his shoulders, and he kept his head low.

2 – Sergeant Reynolds

"You look lost, men," a booming voice interrupted.

Joshua looked up from the scrap of paper. "We are," he admitted. "We're here for instruction, but I can't make this out . . . Sergeant," he added, noting the stranger's stripes.

The man touched the note. "Ah, battlefield triage. Walk with me. I'm headed there myself." And with that he launched.

Tommy nudged Joshua so he scrambled forward, weaving through medical personnel along the busy hall.

At the corner the man swung about. "I'm Sergeant Reynolds, though you can call me Aiden for today." He looked them over. "I take it you just arrived."

Tommy spoke. "We transported in from England yesterday. 82nd Division. Our lieutenant dispatched us while the others pack up. We're joining the British for training. I'm Private Thomas Jones. Back home they call me Tommy."

"Good to meet you, Tommy." The sergeant's eyes lit upon Joshua. "And you would be?"

"Private Joshua Hunter, Sergeant," he stammered.

The man grinned. "If you insist. Though I'm new myself, at least to the army. Just transferred from the Foreign Legion now that the states have joined the cause." He smirked. "Been waiting on orders, though, so I guess the gears are still grinding. In the meantime I'm helping a friend. Were you told about today?"

Joshua glanced at Tommy. "Not a thing, Sergeant."

"Figures. Though it's pretty simple. There aren't enough medics on the front. With units arriving each week, a few of us suggested teaching basic field dressing to a cadre of soldiers passing through. Command allows it as long as we don't hinder operations." He grew serious. "Listen up today. This isn't about trench foot and lice. You've heard your fill of that already. This is about battlefield wounds, keeping yourself and your buddies alive when all hell breaks lose. You'll hear more in the instruction."

As they resumed walking, Joshua studied the sergeant. His dirty blond hair was cropped close, and his narrow waist flared into broad shoulders. Though not huge, the man owned the space he occupied, which explained his own jitters.

A nurse emerged from a room ahead. She lilted over and planted a peck on the sergeant's cheek. "Bonjour, mon ami!"

It was one of the few phrases Joshua recognized. One night over cards, a crusty ship crewman had shared conversational tidbits, as well as more bawdy expressions.

The sergeant clasped the spry brunette's hand. "Ma belle," he breathed. Then he introduced them to Claire Laurent.

Joshua dipped his head. "Bonjour, mademoiselle."

Her dark eyes embraced him. "Well done, Monsieur! But hardly necessary. I speak English quite well."

"I don't know much at all. French, I mean. That was about it."

"You will. People learn as they need." She touched the sergeant's wrist. "Though Aiden here thinks his smile is enough, and he's usually right." The sergeant shrugged, and she laughed. She started to go on, but caught herself. "The others are waiting," she chastised.

"Then let's join them," said the sergeant.

The nurse sauntered back toward the doorway, and Tommy followed. The sergeant walked with Joshua, tossing him a wink as they stepped inside.

Joshua joined Tommy beside the men gathered at the rear of the makeshift classroom. Then he turned to watch the sergeant make his way to the front.

3 – Brothers

Joshua tried to sleep, but jagged memories tripped him up. Near Harrisonburg the fingers of morning began tapping his seat, so he resigned himself to watching the blur of passing fields. An hour later, as the train churned away from Mount Solon, the porter announced the final stop at Stokesville.

He planned his departure. In the shadow of a hill, he rose to retrieve his cane. Then he flexed repeatedly, hoping to ease the knots from his thigh.

The effort fell short, leaving him unsteady and struggling with the heavy duffel. He dropped his arms to his side when he sensed the presence beside him.

"I got it," an old man muttered, yanking the bag free.

As Joshua moved to follow, a frail hand clasped his wrist. It was the man's companion, the woman from the Elkton depot. Her blue eyes were piercing.

"It's over, honey. I can only imagine the hell you've seen, twitchin' like you were. But the war can't harm you no more." She squeezed tight. "Let it go, child. Providence has brought you home."

He shuffled forward. Only on the platform did he find his voice. With a nod to the woman, he thanked the man, who brushed off the gesture.

Wary of inviting further sympathy, he took stock while the passengers cleared. The mountain coach didn't leave until noon. For now he needed something to eat, a toilet and an out of the way place to work through the stiffness. Mom would worry enough without fearing he'd gone lame.

A café across the street would suffice for the first two. He clenched his jaw and grabbed the duffel.

*　　　*　　　*

He'd nearly finished his biscuits and gravy when he noticed the wagon at the station. He watched his brother bound up the platform steps and disappear behind the depot building. Already taller at the time of his leaving, Scott had grown in his absence. As he ambled back into view, Joshua waved through the glass.

Scott jumped down and trotted over. "Josh!" he yelled a bit too loud as he bolted through the door.

Joshua stood, only to be swallowed in a hug. "The leg!" he yelped, pushing back before it buckled.

"Sorry, brother. I didn't think." Scott turned to the waitress. "Scrambled eggs and coffee, please ma'am?" He shed his coat, planted himself in the opposite chair, then looked up.

"You've grown," Joshua offered. He didn't know what else to say, having counted on more time. At least it was Scott. They could get under each other's skin. But they had never burdened each other with expectations.

Scott flashed a grin. "Not such a little brother anymore, huh?" His eyes traced the scar. "You look like hell."

"Rough trip . . . couldn't sleep on the train." He tugged at his cap. "What are you doing here? I said I'd take the coach."

Scott cocked his head. "You know Mom wouldn't hear of it. She kept fretting over you in the cold then stuffed in a buggy with strangers. She wanted Dad to come fetch you in the truck. Dad got riled. Said he had two pallets to deliver. He kept barking at how you could take care of yourself.

"I let them bicker a bit before I piped up. Got me out of school, but put me on the road before dawn. If Butterscotch hadn't known the way, I'd have ended up in the creek."

"Still going at it, are they?" Their parents could raise holy hell over anything, or nothing at all. Apparently Scott was running interference these days.

The waitress appeared with Scott's breakfast, which he attacked with a vengeance.

Joshua finished his remaining bites. A patch of sumacs across the tracks caught his eye. He lost himself in it, watching blasts of red emerge from the melting frost.

Scott was waiting when he returned. "Josh," he muttered, "something's not right with Dad. He came home from the doctor a couple months back spitting nails. Ever since he's been on my tail, like I can't do nothin' right. He even suggested I quit school to start in the quarry full time, though Mom nipped that in the bud."

He leaned in. "I'm not exaggerating. He's worse than ever. I can handle his snapping. But he looks old all of a sudden. I heard them arguin' one morning. Mom was furious he wouldn't go back to the doctor."

Joshua tried to follow along, but grew dizzy. His temple throbbed. "Mom didn't mention it."

"You know they never tell us anything," Scott whined. "Besides, Mom was worried about keeping your spirits up. All her letters were rosy. You were on the front, for chrissakes. And by the time this came up . . . well, we thought you were dead. One day we get word you're missing. Then some nurse writes, saying you're alive but can't write. Mom's been on pins and needles."

Joshua studied his brother as he spoke. Scott was no longer a kid. He might not be all grown up, but his face hinted at more. Only two years his senior, Joshua felt ancient. Best he could muster nowadays was relief borne out of exhaustion.

He'd take what he could get. The tide had turned. If the Germans surrendered as hoped, Scott would be spared. Lord knows he'd have been only too eager to follow.

Scott didn't look relieved, and he sounded downright dejected. "She hasn't been herself for months. None of us has." He fidgeted. "The flu was the last straw. They closed school, canceled church services. It came so fast. I was sick as a dog last month, though I snapped back quick. But you remember Deek, Katie's cousin in Churchville? He died the week I was laid up."

Joshua felt the ground give way.

Scott tumbled with him. "Oh, God. I'm sorry. You wouldn't have known." He downed a gulp of coffee then slumped back in his chair.

They sat in silence.

Joshua realized his brother had been a dam ready to burst, eager to talk like before. Not wanting to disappoint, he summoned old habits. "I wondered how Hadley had fared. The flu swept the front too. Claire, the nurse who wrote, she said scores of men died while I was unconscious. When we landed last spring, the entire company came down with something. But it was different then. Nobody died."

He paused while the waitress refilled the coffee. "I'm glad you're better. It's a real shame about Deek. He was mighty nice."

"Smart too. Hardly seems right. I was still weak so Mom wouldn't let me go to the funeral. She said Katie couldn't stop crying. Katie got sick as well, but she had it pretty mild." He fiddled with his spoon. "Josh, she's confused. She wants to know why you stopped writing, keeps asking me like I know."

With that, Joshua's brave face fell. This was only the start. The questions would keep coming, both spoken and silent. And none of his answers would satisfy. He couldn't tell them. No one could ever know.

"I don't care, Josh, really I don't. You never promised her anything. Just thought you should know, that's all. She's coming by today. Mom insisted."

"Course I want to see her," Joshua blurted. "There was just so much. The drills, the rotations, the battle." He tensed, his body feeling what his mind forgot.

Scott appraised him. "And you, are you okay? That's a nasty scar. And what's with your leg?"

Joshua ran his finger along his scalp. "Just a graze. I don't rightly remember how. As for the leg, the doctors say it was pretty much shredded by the rubble."

He found it strange. It was easier to talk about his wounds. They were straightforward, visible. Folks understood broken bones. He could show someone a scar. Yet it was the endless spinning in his head that tore at him. No one would want to hear of that, even if he could bear to talk about it.

"They say I'm lucky to be walking, but Mom can't know that. I'll need you to stop so I can kick around a bit. I don't want to be awkward when they see me, you hear?"

"Sure, Josh. Whatever you need."

What he needed? The question had wracked his brain since the hospital. He had to claw his way back. That's all he knew. Scott couldn't help there. Nobody could. So the offer stood, and he forced a smile. "Show you my thigh later, if you think you can handle it?" As kids, they used to try to make each other squeamish. His leg was nothing compared to the bloated cows crushed in the flood, back when he was twelve.

"Bad, huh?"

Joshua sighed. "Yeah. Though not a word to Mom. No descriptions . . . nothing."

He didn't tell Scott the rest. Claire said the only reason they hadn't amputated was because they found him late, days after the initial wave of casualties.

In triage they wouldn't have saved it. They might not have treated him at all. He'd been so bloody and pale the soldiers who found him had at first thought him dead. But the debris that crushed his leg had pressed it in place too, staunching the bleeding. The delay had kept him from becoming another amputee, if not a corpse.

No, there was no use talking about it. He intended to walk normal. The drive to be whole was weak. But it was the one thing he had going.

"We should head on," he breathed.

Scott eased back from the edge. "Suppose so. I promised Mom we'd head straight home so we're already running late." He grinned. "I brought Dad's old guitar along. Been picking at it a while now, getting the hang of it too. Maybe I'll play when we stop."

"Dad's guitar?"

Scott shrugged. "That's what I said when Mom told me. It was in the attic, bundled up in a quilt. Dad went off on me when I asked him for a tune. But later on he said I could have it, long as I don't play near the house."

Joshua shook his head. That was as near to encouragement as

you could find in the Hunter household. He knew all too well.

And what was with Dad? He sounded as fiery as ever. How sick could he be? Still, if Scott noticed, there might be something to it.

"You ready?" Scott asked, buttoning his coat.

He glanced outside. The frost had melted into a slushy mess. "Yeah . . . ready as I'll ever be."

4 – Awakening

At the front of the room Tommy threw his hands up. During the chart instruction, he'd crept forward to see. Now they were pairing off for exercises, and he'd been approached before he could make his way back.

Joshua glanced to his left as a bud joined the nearest man. He'd begun to scan the room when he felt the tap on his arm.

"There's an odd number so you'll need a partner."

"Sure, Sergeant."

"Besides, you'll get more practice. I've had some experience with all this."

Joshua nodded. He could only imagine all the sergeant had seen while in the Foreign Legion.

The medic spoke. "Now we're going to let you have a hand with the procedures. In each exercise one of you will act as the injured man while the other treats the condition. Then you'll switch. Obviously, this will take imagination. None of you have broken bones, and we're not stitching anyone up today.

"Nevertheless, picture yourself in the field, performing the steps under the worst circumstances. When you reach the front, you'll encounter devastating situations, sometimes in battle, at times with no warning at all. But with knowledge and focus, you'll be able to care for a man until a medic arrives or until they reach a clearing station."

He flipped the chart back to the beginning. "So let's begin."

Over the next few hours, the medic walked them through various scenarios. They applied tourniquets, crafted slings, even practiced moving the wounded. The nurses wandered among them, handing out supplies and answering questions.

Joshua tried to get things right. But while the sergeant was quick to give pointers, he tended to ham things up as well. At one point he flailed when Joshua pressed his arm to staunch a simulated shrapnel wound. "*Remember, it'll hurt like hell,*" *he explained. Later he purposely grazed Joshua's abdomen while placing a sling around his arm, tickling him.*

The familiarity unnerved Joshua, though he slowly warmed to the attention. After a while he even reciprocated. When the sergeant kept turning to chat with Nurse Laurent during a head wound exercise, Joshua proceeded to wrap the gauze across his mouth.

She erupted in laughter as the sergeant snapped back.

Joshua unwrapped the strand. "Sorry, Sergeant."

The sergeant winked. "I suppose I deserved that."

"Alright, men, let's wrap things up." The medic chuckled at his own pun. "We'll take a short break. But I want everyone back in fifteen minutes."

Nurse Laurent gathered the gauze, still smiling. "Good work, Joshua!" she offered before moving on.

Joshua eyed the sergeant. "You're not a good patient."

The sergeant laughed. "That's for sure. I'd be horrid, which is why I make a point of not becoming one. You, on the other hand, would make an excellent medic. You pick things up fast. I swear you had that tourniquet tied before the medic even explained it."

"Practice, I guess."

"Really?"

"Nah. Just something from when I was a kid. You wouldn't want to hear of it."

He felt the sergeant's gaze. "Actually, I would."

Joshua glanced up as Tommy headed out with the other men. "It was a childhood incident. I'm not sure how I knew."

The sergeant sat back, making it clear he wasn't moving.

Put on the spot, he relented. "Well, I suppose I should start at the beginning. I was born in Alabama but raised in Virginia, a little place called Hadley. My dad has a ledge quarry up above town. It's nothing special, but it backs up to the prettiest mountain forest you'd ever want to see.

"When I was little, my kid brother and I used to play along the ridge, like it was our own private wilderness. We were supposed to

stay close, but we always ventured deeper. We'd scramble about, then come running when Mom yelled up.

"So this one autumn day, Dad was out delivering a load of stone when Mom had to head to town for some groceries. Mrs. McCullough, whose husband works for Dad, was supposed to keep an eye on us. But she's old and tends to hit the bottle in the afternoons. She wasn't one to pay too much attention.

"I was nine and convinced I didn't need anyone watching me. It wasn't long before I hit on the idea of hiking over to Hawk's Peak, this outcrop of rock you could glimpse from my brother's room. We'd never seen it up close, though we'd fantasized about climbing it forever."

"Adventurers," the sergeant teased.

"I suppose. I wanted to go by myself, but it was drilled in my head never to leave my little brother. Scott followed me everywhere anyhow. So we waited 'til Mrs. McCullough yelled up to check on us once, then took off.

"Now that I think about it, the trek out was pretty quick. Once you're under the old trees, it's fairly easy going. When we reached Hawk's Peak, we started combing through the rocks. I found a big chunk of coal I wanted to bring back. Then we sat and looked over the valley a while.

"We lost track of time, I guess. The day was warm, and we were having fun. I didn't realize it was late until the colors started to glow. So we jumped up . . ."

"Your brother fell?"

"Heck no! The cliff was too steep so we never even tried. But what happened was even scarier. We had just started back. I was in front, running best I could with the coal. I remember being worried Dad would get home before us.

"Suddenly I heard a rustling. Scott cried out. I swung around to find him lying on the ground, sprawled among a patch of ferns.

"I stepped toward him, thinking he'd tripped. That's when I saw it."

"Saw what?"

"A mountain lion, off to the side, staring. He'd knocked Scott clean off his feet."

"Damn."

"Yes, Sergeant. I froze at first. We'd always been told the big cats were gone, hunted down or pushed out by settlers. But the old timers, they said mountain lions still stalked game in the backcountry. A man in the valley once claimed to see one, but everyone said he was crazy. Guess he wasn't so crazy after all, least about that.

"So the lion growled at me, then slunk over toward my brother. I threw the chunk of coal hard as I could . . . hit the cat square in the head. He let out an awful scream.

"I was shaking so hard. I just knew the mountain lion would maul us both. But he didn't. He shot up the ridge, and it was like he'd never been there at all."

"And your brother?"

"Well, I kept looking up, convinced the cat would come back. I didn't see the blood 'til I was right over him. His face was scraped from a rock. But that was nothing. The gash below his elbow was what frightened me. He'd been lying on it so I hadn't seen it at first."

The sergeant touched his arm. "You alright?"

He let go of the image. "Sorry. I used to have nightmares about it. Everything is kinda fuzzy after that. Scott started sobbing. I ripped my shirt and wrapped a strip where it was bleeding real bad then another above his elbow. I even managed to pick him up.

"When I started home, I couldn't keep my balance along the ridge. Finally I ran straight down. Tried to anyhow. I kinda slid down into the hollow before stumbling over the creek. The rocks were slippery, but I made it to the road. I couldn't have carried him to town, though. By then I could barely stand. Scott had passed out. He was white as a ghost. I thought he was dead."

"But he wasn't?"

Joshua shook his head. "No. A man happened by on a horse. He raced off with my brother. I chased after them, bawling my eyes out. When I got to town, the doctor was with him. He said Scott had nicked an artery, but that he'd recover.

"And he did. He healed up fine. There's a scar on his forearm, but you'd hardly notice it. Scott barely remembers that day, though I sure do. Dad took a strap to me. I'd have gotten worse if I hadn't been so bruised already."

He picked at a gash on the old oak floor. "Guess I deserved it."

"You were only a kid, and you saved your brother's life."

"Maybe." He stood up, embarrassed.

The sergeant rose beside him. "Not maybe . . . definitely. You were brave. Quick thinking too. He's lucky to have you as a brother."

"I suppose."

The sergeant was studying him when Joshua looked over. "I imagine you were scared of the forest after that."

He pondered a moment. "Maybe a little, but not for long. See, the ridges have a rhythm. I just had to learn to listen. Now I pay heed when I wander, but I'm never frightened."

The sergeant nodded. "That's a wise perspective."

Joshua felt warm under the sergeant's gaze. He wanted to say more, but Nurse Laurent was approaching.

She eyed the sergeant. "Is everything alright over here?"

The sergeant sighed. "Yep. Private Hunter here was just recounting acts of youthful bravery. He's a natural, you know."

"I noticed. Not easily distracted like some people. Perhaps he'd make a good doctor, too."

Joshua squinted. "You're a doctor?"

The sergeant shook his head. "No. I am most definitely not a doctor." He noted Joshua's confusion. "It's a tedious tale."

"So? You got me to talk."

"That I did," the sergeant quipped. "Let's just say I'm interested in medicine and leave it at that." He glanced at the door, where men had begun to filter back in. Then he looked to the nurse. "Do you need me?"

She nodded.

Joshua was ready when he turned. "Thanks, Sergeant," he said quickly.

The sergeant smiled. "We're almost done. When we finish, I'll find you and Tommy."

"Sure, Sergeant," he replied, still puzzling why when Tommy returned.

5 – Hadley

The wagon squeaked a broken rhythm as they set off. Hadley wasn't easy to get to from anywhere, but from Stokesville the logging road along the river was faster than the Parkersburg pike. Plus it avoided the toll.

Joshua studied the looming mountains. The leading ridges had been bare for as long as he could remember. Proceeding through the gap, he began to see more recent carnage. Acre after acre of virgin forest from his youth now lay littered with piles of slash. The river valley had been clear-cut, along with surrounding knobs and ridges. A sign announcing the new national forest mocked them, as there was no sign of renewal.

Scott glanced over. "Forest rangers have been all over Hadley as of late. Seems they're trying to purchase the whole lot before the loggers. It hasn't gone over well."

"I can imagine. Anyone greet them with a rifle yet?"

"Not that I've heard. Then again, they haven't cornered Dad. He's still snarling at how Richmond sold us out."

Joshua could hear it now. From geologists who lied to partners who threw in the towel to politicians who derailed a train before it ever ran, Dad had a litany of reasons why they occupied a rickety house on a broken ridge instead of the mountain estate he'd promised Mom. The quarry kept them afloat, but it wasn't the booming coal mine he'd once touted.

Not that it had ever made sense to Joshua. They'd already had a huge house, back when he was little. He could recall Dad on a tractor, moving across a big field. He'd been watching from the porch, a wide one running all around the exterior. To hear Mom talk, her father's farm had been near perfect. But Joshua preferred the mountains. The remaining ones, that is. The mess around them didn't count.

To the north he glimpsed the Tuckerman mine, the last working coal mine in the area. A bit later the slashed hillsides gave way to old mountain farms, some dating back a century. Scott stopped as promised, pulling alongside the tiny chapel at the base of the draft. He grabbed his guitar and walked over to a cedar beside the weathered fence.

Joshua watched him pull out a satchel of chew. Mom considered tobacco a vice, going as far as forbidding Dad from partaking. Nevertheless Scott had acquired the habit years earlier, after finding a box of snuff by the creek. His brother was a good egg, but could be stealthy when he wanted to be.

When Scott lifted the satchel in his direction, he shook his head. He'd taken to cigarettes while in France. Since the injury the scent of tobacco in any form made him queasy.

He forced the cane into the duffel as best he could. Then he ambled to the grassy patch where the Presbyterians held potlucks in the summer. Bits and pieces of tunes drifted his way as he worked the kinks from his leg.

Awaiting his service discharge, Joshua had walked the hills north of Toul nearly every day. He'd even wandered into the village once, before bumping into memories. After that he'd opted for deserted fields above town. Though the walks had done little to clear the muddle from his head, they had aided his physical recovery. Near the end the doctor who'd performed the surgery had even visited.

"Had to see for myself," he'd explained. "I didn't think you'd pull through, much less walk. If not for Nurse Laurent, we wouldn't have saved your leg. It seemed too far gone." The doctor had pursed his lips. "Count your blessings, son. You've been given a second chance."

The only blessing Joshua had seen was an expedited discharge. It had come the next week, along with a citation praising the acts of a stranger. Now he was losing the hospital as well, numbness the only lasting impression of his weeks there.

All the lost and fuzzy days furthered a sense he was but a ghost passing time. Claire said when he'd first opened his eyes he'd stared in silence at the bulky fixture above his bed. Later, crying out for Aiden, he'd so startled the nurse she'd nearly dropped his bedpan.

The following morning Claire had rushed over from the clearing station, bringing Aiden's Saint Christopher medal. Joshua had been wearing it when they found him.

He recalled holding it. "I don't know. I'm sorry," he'd mumbled, unable to find the memory within.

Questions haunted him. Why did he have the medal? Why had no one known where he was? Answers never came, just a blur of sensations. *Billowy waves of fog, a flash of gunfire, blood-flecked seedlings.* Once he had dreamt of a German soldier on a forest floor, writhing in pain. But there was never enough to string it all together. And it was hard to know what was real and what was imagined.

Only one moment was clear, the image in his head when he awoke. At the misty edge of a dusky field, Aiden was speaking while a medic hovered in the background.

That was all.

Next he knew incessant ringing had given way to the muted sounds of the hospital, as if he'd been snatched away and dropped into a broken body. He had no recollection of the collapsed bunker where they'd found him.

"You alright?" Scott interrupted, leaning his guitar against the fence. "You've been muttering to yourself."

"It hurts like the devil. Cursing, I guess." He moved toward the wagon. "It's better now. Let's get on home."

"You sure?"

"I'm fine," he insisted, climbing up. He nodded at the guitar. "You play well."

Scott's face lit up as he scrambled to join him.

They talked more as they neared town. Scott said worries over a slowdown were countered by rumors of a renewed push for a rail line. He spoke of the mild autumn and lingering fears over the flu.

When they reached Hadley, it looked sadder than Joshua remembered, a mere speck getting smaller. They passed clapboard shanties, some abandoned. They passed the Bucks' diner and the

Daltons' cash store. He looked for Katie through the open door, but saw only Mr. Dalton, unpacking boxes.

At the far end, a service banner hung over the Morrisons' porch. Unlike the rest of Hadley, the Morrisons were of the mountains, their kin having settled the ridges generations earlier. Though they knew the old ways, they'd accepted the scraggly town that had sprung up like a weed beside them. Before the war their son Nathanial had even been the star pitcher of the valley league. Nate's younger brother Pete was friends with Scott.

Drawing near, Joshua saw a gold star pinned atop the blue one on the field of white. A bouquet of sunflowers lay wilted on the rail beneath it.

Scott filled him in. "Word came two weeks back . . . killed in the Argonne forest. Pete's taking it hard. Poor Mrs. Morrison's plumb bereft. She keeps claiming he'll turn up, like you. Mr. Morrison added the gold star over her objections. Guess he thinks it'll help her come to terms."

Joshua kept vigil as they passed. Though the curtains were drawn, he could feel the pain within. Mrs. Morrison had always been tightly strung, but who could blame her now?

Beyond town they passed beside hemlocks crowding the stream, its gurgle rising to greet them. Scott guided Butterscotch over the bridge and up the incline. Joshua tilted his head at the first bend, scouring the jagged face above. He glimpsed their house just before they entered the forest. And there, in the rust red glow of the gnarled oaks, he contemplated another mother awaiting a son's return.

6 – On the Porch

Elisabeth took the pot off the stove then hurried onto the porch. There was still no sign of the boys, but the afternoon sun had tempered the chill so she lingered. The stew could be reheated if need be.

Plopping onto the swing, she eyed the peeled paint on the arm. Some women took snuff in private or sipped from a flask hidden on the back stoop, like Mrs. McCullough across the way. Elisabeth Hunter dug at her worries while gazing down the ridge toward town. If you ignored the hacked up hillside, the view was pleasant enough. Such were the perks of a quarryman's wife.

Her gaze drifted closer, to the cloth moving slow in the breeze. The service banner had taunted her daily for over a year. She'd come close to removing it the week prior, but had grown superstitious at doing so before Josh was home. Besides, as she'd told the ladies at church, she wanted him to see how proud they were.

The remark was true, of course. What she'd failed to mention was the nagging guilt each time she saw it. Had she and Wayne driven him away?

Other boys had joined . . . drafted. Josh had volunteered shortly after graduation, clear out of the blue. So she couldn't help but wonder, never quite shaking the suspicion.

Josh was the more temperamental of her sons. Though eager to please, he could be moody and defiant, which infuriated Wayne. Then again, Josh and his father had never seen eye to eye, both as stubborn as all get out.

By the time he'd reached his teens, Josh had withdrawn from her as well. She wanted to chalk it up to him becoming a man, pulling away as boys did. But Josh had a tendency to spurn everyone, even classmates. He'd be glum for days, up in his room buried in a book or out wandering the ridge. When Elisabeth would prod, he'd snap out of it for a time. But she never knew where his mind went, and was never convinced his returns were anything more than temporary appeasement.

Then there was Katie Dalton, the closest thing he'd had to a girl. Who knew his intentions there? She had sights on Joshua for certain, which Elisabeth didn't mind. Katie was sensible and came from a solid family. The two were good together, compatible. Even Wayne, notably oblivious of such things, once commented she had a knack for pulling Josh from his shell. Poor thing. She'd been as blindsided as the rest of them by his enlistment.

Initially Elisabeth had been encouraged by the young couple's correspondence. But though Elisabeth's letters had continued, the notes to Katie had ceased during his time in France.

Elisabeth wondered why, her imagination running wild as always. Had he fallen in love overseas? She knew it happened. Seemed everyone knew of some relationship forged in the heat of the moment, at home and abroad. Times were tough. People grew desperate for attachment.

She wasn't blind to the ways of the world. One couldn't blame folks for seeking comfort. But running away with your passions wasn't God's plan. Spontaneous liaisons destroyed the spirit and always ended badly. Most youth didn't care, not these days. They wanted it all now. It was disrespectful, unhealthy. Her boy Josh had never been like that.

Still, she wondered. Truth be told, it might come as a relief. Perhaps he had feelings for that nurse who'd written? Elisabeth had found the letter, though brief, strangely intimate. *Claire Laurent . . .* sounded French.

Elisabeth was grateful the woman had taken the time to refute the official notice that Joshua was missing. After that torture, the news had been a godsend. But as relief faded, questions had emerged. Wayne dismissed her fretting. Yet each time she read the letter, something tugged at her.

She glanced down, finding herself digging again at the scarred wood. She rattled off a prayer, another plea for grace. Lord knows she needed to abandon her bushel of worries, else she'd best start sitting on the opposite end before the whole contraption crashed down around her one fine afternoon.

Josh was coming home! She gripped the arm tight. Wayne would scold her something fierce if he came up to find her weeping. Frantic, she glanced about, her gaze settling on the sweetbay over the rail.

Its blooms had browned in the recent frost. Though the leaves weren't far behind, a few remained defiantly green.

The local ladies had laughed at the foolishness of planting a southern specimen so deep in the Virginia ridges. "It'll die in the first cold snap," Olympia Dalton had declared at a Daughters of the Confederacy gathering shortly after Wayne planted it. Only Eloise Pipken had appreciated its significance. The sweetbay was Elisabeth's last connection to Adeleine, a stone's throw from Eufaula.

Wayne had brought the sapling back from a visit to her father's grave. Though sheltered along the southern flank of the house, winter blasts had taken their toll. It never brimmed with the creamy blossoms of her youth. Yet it held on, producing a handful each summer. A single waft of the vanilla scent could stir images of her mother, forever young in her mind. The association soothed her, if only for a while.

She recalled Wayne lugging it aboard the train, and how he'd locked horns until the flustered steward relented. Her husband's gruffness had its merits, even if some couldn't see them, her elder being one.

Before she got wound up again in that particular knot, Wayne appeared on the lane. He appeared almost chipper so she hoped it was a good day. There were so few lately.

She drew a deep breath as she moved to the top step.

Wayne trudged up the bluff to the patchy yard. "Sakes alive, Eli! You look pretty as a picture standing there."

She bounded down, and he reached for her. A peck on her cheek became a full kiss on the lips. He could still charm her with his randy spirit, even with the doctor warning the cancer would take him within a year.

"Bullshit!" had been Wayne's curt response. "I'll outlive that bloodsucker," he'd snarled to the nurse, leaving Elisabeth to smooth things over. He was back at the quarry the next morning, and every day since. Once his mind was set, there was nothing more to say. So she pretended not to notice his hacking when it came and didn't speak of the growing hollowness in his cheeks.

They broke their embrace, his hand lingering on the cusp of her face. "I suppose you want to wait for the boys."

"I can whip up a plate. You left right after Scott pulled out. Imagine you're starved by now."

"I grabbed a couple biscuits, so I'm good. And they ought to be home anytime. Is Katie coming?"

She sighed. Just when she got accustomed to his growling, he'd find his manners. "She's stopping by with her mother. After not hearing from Josh, she wasn't sure. But I said it'd be fine."

"Don't the girl realize he's been busy fighting the Huns, then holed up in some damn hospital?" The final words caught in his throat.

"Honey, she knows that. She's just young. Her whole family's reeling. Losing Deek shook them up something horrible." She scoured the hillside for the wagon. "Too young for the war, taken by the flu. It's like we're all under siege."

Glancing back, she saw fear in his eyes. She'd said the wrong thing again. She clasped his hand, "Our boy's coming home! Eloise sent her youngest up with two cherry pies. We could spoil ourselves while we wait." She tugged him toward the steps, hoping to elicit a grin.

He obliged. "Pie, huh? Hmm. Now that you mention it, maybe I am hungry."

*   *   *

Elisabeth heard the wagon first. Dropping her fork, she rushed outside.

Wayne caught up then moved ahead as she slowed, watching

their approach. She stopped on the steps when she saw the scar. Wayne looked back from the lane, puzzled.

The wagon drew to a halt, and Joshua nodded to his father. His movements were deliberate as he descended. When he stumbled, Wayne reached to steady him. Joshua bristled then grabbed for his duffel.

Brows furrowed, Wayne stepped back.

Joshua turned.

Wayne went to shake hands but stopped upon seeing the bag. Hugging was out of the question. Wayne hadn't coddled the boys since they were infants, and only rarely then. So they stood, off kilter, each awaiting the other's move.

Elisabeth shook her head. Separated by an ocean and a war, only to pick up right where they left off. She wanted to scold them, but knew better. Back when she used to, it had made matters worse. So she said nothing, watching them fumble another exchange.

She drifted closer. Joshua was pale and gaunt, his stance haggard. The young man who'd bounded onto the train eighteen months earlier was nowhere to be seen. When she saw the cane handle poking out of the duffel, her heart sank. His letters from the hospital had been so vague. The nagging worries bubbled anew.

How bad were the injuries? Were they lasting?

Joshua looked over. He was alive . . . it was enough. She flew the final steps.

"Mom," he breathed.

She hugged him tight, and a tear escaped.

"Don't cry. I'm here."

She stepped back, wiping her cheek. "I know."

Wayne tried again as they made their way to the house. "How was the trip?"

"Long," Joshua replied. "I'm stiff. Damn near froze on the Elkton platform."

"Then let's get you inside. Your mother made some stew."

"Save me a bowl," Scott called out.

She watched him unhitch Butterscotch. "Thanks, son."

"No problem," he yelled, moving toward the shed.

"Hurry. There's pie as well. Mrs. Pipken made a couple."

He glanced back. "What kind?"

"Cherry. Your favorite."

"Mine too," Joshua chimed in.

She smiled, but her frown returned when she saw him on the steps. The ascent was quick, but the movement off, clumsy. Wayne noticed too and held the door.

The gesture startled Joshua. "I'll need a few minutes," he mumbled.

She followed his uneven progress up the stairs inside.

"You comin'?" Wayne scowled.

"Sure am. Just moving at my leisure, old man."

They exchanged daggers before Wayne softened, holding out his hand. They knew how to needle each other good, but now wasn't the time.

7 – Home

Joshua dropped the duffel and tossed his coat upon the bed. He imagined crawling in after it, but resisted the urge. Instead he pressed his eyes shut then moved to the window.

Nothing had changed.

A hundred paces over sat the McCullough's shanty. Between their homes, broken ground trickled down toward the quarry. He studied the craggy lip a moment before turning his attention to the rear.

Beyond the clothesline and a patch of yard, the forest rose clear to the ridgeline. He knew the layers of foliage by heart, having checked the weather countless mornings over the years. Today was typical for late October. The chestnut and hickories were mostly spent while maroon leaves clung to the twisted oaks, fighting a losing battle. In a few weeks only an army of skeletons would remain.

Older than Hadley, other than the Morrison place, the homestead consisted of a handful of structures first built for a start-up mining operation. In addition to their home and the outhouse, there were three shanties. Some years back Dad had hauled one below the quarry to store explosives and cutting tools. Another housed the McCulloughs, while the smallest had been gutted to serve as a stable for Butterscotch and an open shed for the truck.

He could still recall the day they moved in. Dad had guided the horse up the steep grade. Scott had been on Mom's lap, pestering her to no end. He had simply sat in awe, marveling at the oaks on either side of the lane. So thick and twisted, they had seemed like something from a fairy tale.

Inside the house, he had climbed the stairs, finding the afterthought of a room tucked beneath the steep pitch of the roof. Later that evening Mom had put him to bed in the larger room along the back. He remembered waking, terrified by wild sounds on the darkened ridge.

The next morning they'd found him curled up inside the tiny room. After that a battle of wills had played out, his desire for his safe haven clashing each morning with Dad's need to squash his defiance. The whippings and wailings had continued for days until Mom intervened. When Dad relented, he'd sworn never to move the bed again. For his part, Joshua never asked.

Truth be told, the room *was* small. The bed barely fit, though some time later Mom managed to squeeze in the base of a narrow hutch for use as a dresser. A few items rested upon it – an oil lamp, a crude woodcarving of a bear, arrowheads from the hillside. On the far end sat a globe, a gift from Mom when he was seven, after she'd observed his fascination with it at the church bazaar.

When he'd turned twelve, he'd nailed a makeshift shelf and mirror above the hutch. The shelf held a collection of National Geographics and a tattered copy of Robinson Crusoe. The mirror had fostered study of another type, his face . . . everyday, in private, scrutinizing for hints of a beard.

Over the years the room had proven sufficient. It had, after all, held all his boyhood dreams. If pressed, he might admit resentment at having to share Scott's wardrobe. But aside from that singular inconvenience, the nook had always given comfort.

Except for today.

His thigh had tightened again so he propped himself against the bed. Massaging it hurt like hell, as the scar tissue remained sensitive. But forcing the pain released the tension. So he kneaded his palms deep as he could until the welcomed tingling began. At the hospital he'd once asked if he might damage it, provoking hearty laughter. "Do whatever it takes!" the doctor had explained. "You can't harm it any worse than what's already been done."

He glanced at the doorway. He could linger until Scott finished up. With an ear to the stair, he scooted over to the globe. An ink spot over Hadley marred the yellow shape of Virginia. He tapped the dot, sending the globe into a slow spin. The continent gave way to the pale blue Atlantic. Europe arrived quickly, and he pressed down near the coast of France. The training camps of St. Valery-sur-Somme were close in his mind as well, more immediate than the room he'd occupied most of his life.

Falling back was easier than moving forward.

*   *   *

Tommy was talking but Joshua didn't hear, distracted by the sergeant's interaction with Nurse Laurent. The two of them had retreated to the corner, partly obscured behind shelves of medical supplies. The nurse looked peevish, pacing back and forth. At one point the sergeant offered his hand, which she brushed aside. It had been clear they were close, but he hadn't suspected romance. Perhaps he'd been wrong.

"What were you talking about?" Tommy was asking.

"With the sergeant?"

"That's what I asked, wasn't it?"

"Oh nothing. He asked where I grew up. Then Nurse Laurent joined us. She said something about him becoming a doctor, but I didn't understand."

"It would explain why he's here today. Well, that and her."

"And you, with the love of your life back home, noticed?" he teased.

Tommy bristled. "I can still look. You're not blind either. She is a cutie."

"Bright too. Saw she had to fix your splint, you clumsy ox."

"Hey! I didn't sign up to be a nurse. And quit changing the subject. So you're saying you like her brains, are ya? Be sure to mention that to Katie in your next letter."

Joshua glanced about, fishing for a comeback. Sergeant Reynolds and Nurse Laurent emerged from the shadows. Across the room the medic cleared his throat. Off the hook, he shifted his attention.

"Let's get started," the medic announced.

The men complied in silence, as if the talk of blood and broken bodies had sobered them.

"*Thank you for your attention today. While you may not be ready for surgery, you've learned valuable skills. Now Nurse Laurent is going to share some final thoughts. So be sure to give her your full attention.*"

The nurse slipped off her gloves then moved to the center of the cadre. "*First of all, I want to say how impressed I am. You picked things up so fast! I'd be honored to work alongside any of you.*" *She nodded to a man up front.* "*Except you, Private Miller. You need more practice.*" *The man blushed, and she laughed.* "*I'm teasing. You were exceptional.*"

Joshua observed the men's reactions. Nurse Laurent was fascinating. Despite her small stature, she carried a gentle authority. He had noticed all day. She seemed to know herself and what she was doing. The men responded in kind, treating her with respect.

She had gained their confidence. And now, having put them at ease, her tone grew serious. "*We at the hospital would like to hope the skills we introduced today would prove unnecessary. Yet as Medic Smith said at the start, it is likely you will someday need them.*"

A few men nodded.

"*Nevertheless our final topic does not require any physical skill.*" *She glanced at the sergeant.* "*For that reason we hesitated including it, given our short time. Still, we decided it was appropriate to draw lessons from our experiences, lessons no medical text or army manual can teach.*"

Her gaze swept the room. "*There is no easy way to say this. But at some point, you might find yourself in a situation, one in which you have to . . . have to face . . .*"

She seemed to lose her train of thought. Her gaze fell, and she drew a deep breath.

When she looked up, she began again, more tentative. "*I became a nurse because I wanted to help with the war effort. I wanted to be near, to be there for brave men like all of you.*

"*So I did. I studied. I trained. And now I am a nurse.*" *She sighed.* "*A new nurse, still with much to learn.*

"*The work is hard, and the hours long. But it is rewarding.*

Dedicated men and women surround me, offering encouragement. So while my duties may overwhelm and at times sadden me, this is my refuge. A hospital can be a place of hope. Lives are saved here. Men recover here."

She paused. "I fear it will not be the same for you. The front is different. When a man is maimed in the field, the war rages on. Battles don't cease for ambulances. Medics cannot rush across no man's land. Yet that is where men are struck. It is where men often die . . ."

Her voice quivered as her eyes again found the sergeant.

This time he stepped forward. "What Nurse Laurent is saying is that despite our efforts today war remains a bloody hell." His expression hardened. "A bloody hell for which nothing can truly prepare you."

He motioned to the group. "Look at the men around you."

A few men scoffed.

"Go ahead! Look at them. These are your comrades, your brothers. Yet neither you nor any of them will leave this war unscathed. For a fortunate few, the war will shake you to the core. For others, it will leave scars that never heal." He lowered his voice. "And as for the rest, well, the war will kill you."

The room grew still. No one spoke of dying, not directly. Death was a taunt tossed about in drills . . . scrambling on your belly so as not to lose your head, attacking to destroy the enemy. No one talked of individual mortality.

Yet the sergeant did. "So what do you do, knowing that to be the case? How do you face it? Do you look to God? Do you look within? Or do you banish the thought, as if nothing can touch you?"

He shook his head. "Well, I don't have the answer. But I do know one thing. Pretending doesn't work. You have to prepare for the unthinkable. You must face it before it is forced upon you, or it will shatter you when it strikes."

Joshua remembered to breathe. He broke his gaze. Tommy was riveted. Nurse Laurent had retreated, slipping behind the medic.

The sergeant continued. "You have to face the possibility, if not for yourself, for your buddies. And here's why. Because if you are the fortunate one. The one the shell misses. The one who escapes the gas. Then you must take care of the others. At that instance your presence can mean the difference between life and death for your fellow men, for your platoon, even yourself. But if in that moment you fail to keep your wits, the skills you learned today will mean nothing."

Joshua's attention drifted back to Nurse Laurent. The color had drained from her face. Her eyes glistened, then a tear slid down her cheek. As she brushed it away, he saw a flicker, a sparkle from her exposed hand.

His heart skipped. Nurse Laurent was married.

Or widowed? The possibility stunned him, though he supposed it shouldn't. War had waged for years, ravaging France. The number of deaths was staggering.

Imagining her pain, he felt his own eyes water. He snapped his gaze back to the sergeant.

Where he was caught. The sergeant had been watching as he spoke.

Joshua blushed. Men didn't cry, not in public. Never in the army. He stiffened, following the cadence of his voice.

He began to hear the words. " . . . you must be strong, and use that strength to carry your men in whatever manner they require." The sergeant released Joshua for a time, but returned with his closing words. "Trust your instincts. Never defeat yourself. And above all protect your brothers!"

By then Joshua had secured his mask, but the thoughts lingered even after the medic dismissed them.

Tommy punched his shoulder. "You holding up?"

He jolted. "Yeah, just thinking."

"I hear you. Nobody talks like that. I wouldn't even let Mary bring it up. So don't be getting all mushy on me. I'd hate to have to tell the men you've gone soft."

Joshua gave him a look.

"I'm kidding. I'd never tell McKenzie it got to you."

"You damn well better not," Joshua growled, only partly in jest. Phil McKenzie could pick for days at any perceived weakness.

"Guess you owe me then," Tommy added with a smirk.

"Whatever you say, Babyface."

Tommy fumed. "You know I hate that. I oughta . . ." His voice trailed off as he glanced over Joshua's shoulder.

The sergeant's voice boomed behind him. "Everyone has a nickname, Tommy. What's yours, Hunter?"

Tommy answered before he could respond, "It's 'Wolfie.'"

The sergeant laughed. "'Wolfie!' What's the story on that?"

Joshua fished for the explanation. "Something about the way I fight," he shrugged.

Sergeant Reynolds looked unconvinced.

"It's his eyes," Tommy jumped in. "One day back in basic, we were conducting hand-to-hand drills. Joshua got paired up with this guy twice his size, Buster Higgins. And Buster was wiping the floor with Josh."

"I was holding my own!"

"Not at first you weren't," Tommy insisted. "But then Buster started teasing him. And Josh, well, he kinda snapped. Phil McKenzie, the fellow who gave most of us nicknames, said Josh took on the 'stare of the wolf,' or something like that.

"Whatever it was, it worked. Josh hauled off and leveled him. Wouldn't let up either. Took three of us to pull him off. After that it was set. By week's end even Buster was calling him 'Wolfie,' which meant I got stuck with 'Babyface' though Josh is younger."

Joshua looked up, captured again by the sergeant's gaze.

"So are we alright, Wolfie?"

He felt flustered. Clearly the sergeant was talking about earlier. "Yes, Sergeant. I'm fine."

"Good," the sergeant replied. Then he rubbed his chin, hesitating. "Listen, I managed to snag a scout vehicle so Nurse Laurent and I could spend some time alone. We can drop you by the barracks if you want."

"Thanks, Sergeant!" Tommy accepted. "Are you and she?" he

added, letting the question hang.

The sergeant crushed his opening. "No, Private. We just go way back. Nurse Laurent is heading home. Close as she can anyhow. She's transferring to the Lorraine sector, the hospital at Toul, so we won't be seeing each other for a while."

Tommy repaired the breach. "Yes, Sergeant. I understand. Well, we'd much appreciate the ride."

The sergeant looked over to where the medic was speaking to the nurses. "I suppose we should pry her away before she's pulled into a crisis." He let Tommy lead then glanced over. "You ready, Wolfie?"

Minutes later, Joshua was crouched in the damp bed of the Model T. The sergeant was making good on his promise to take a winding route. A shower had passed, and a warm wind whipped across his face. He closed his eyes, breathing in the heavy scent of clover.

Opening them, he saw Nurse Laurent's hair before him, tussling in the breeze. Just then she tossed her head back, all signs of her earlier distress erased. "I should cover up, but it feels so good," she sighed. "I'd begun to think winter would never end."

Sergeant Reynolds glanced across at her, then back at Joshua. "What are you looking at, Wolfie?"

Normally the nickname bugged him. He felt the men were mocking him, like a tag for an annoying kid. But with the sergeant he didn't mind. "Just taking it all in. We've been on the go since we landed. First chance I've had to look around."

"You should. It's a huge world, and France is one of its gems. Besides, it's always best to keep your eyes peeled. You never know what'll surprise you."

The nurse whipped her scarf at his face. "And you need to keep yours on the road, Aiden. This is my day," she chastised.

The sergeant touched her ear. "I'm all yours," he teased, provoking a shriek of laughter.

Joshua listened to their banter a bit then gazed about. Tommy was observing the fields, lost in thought. Overhead, an unseen hand shredded a wispy cloud. He didn't know what lay ahead, but being there felt right. Of that he was certain. Perhaps he was stronger than he believed. For a moment he felt invincible.

*   *   *

The door slammed downstairs, yanking him back.

He looked into the mirror. Blotchy skin and the gash along his scalp confronted him. He ran his fingers through his hair, mussing it. He needed to hide the evidence.

The movement shifted the chain above his collar. He went to remove it, but heard Scott's footsteps on the stairs.

Time was up. He had to face them.

8 - Expectations

Joshua made it through a bowl of stew and half a piece of pie before the chatter around the kitchen table grew tense.

At first Scott had talked up a storm. Though shy with strangers, he had a knack for spinning local gossip into funny tales. Joshua peppered him with questions, anything to keep from having to talk himself.

In time, though, attention turned his way.

Talking about his travels was easy enough. He described pines rising from the red clay hills of Georgia. He recalled the expanse of ocean glittering in moonlight as they shipped over.

Mom asked about Europe so he shared impressions of England from their brief stay. He described the French countryside and the tall steepled churches in each village. He avoided any mention of the devastation near the front.

Dad aimed in that direction, inquiring about logistics and the daily routine. But it wasn't until Scott started in about the weaponry that he bristled.

"Did you use grenades?" Scott asked, testing the waters.

"Some."

"Ol' McCullough claims they're the trench busters winning the war. But I said the automated machine gun would be my weapon of choice. What about you?"

"I used a rifle," Joshua breathed, wiping his hands on his pants.

Scott puzzled over his reply. "Like hunting up on the ridge? With all the new firepower, I'd have thought they'd given you something bigger."

Joshua's temple throbbed. "I was in the infantry. And it don't much matter anyhow. They all leave a bloody mess."

He lowered his head. Scott hadn't meant any harm.

"There'll be no talk of that today." Mom rested her hand on his shoulder as she placed another slice of pie before him.

"I just . . ." Scott started before her glare silenced him.

Dad saw his opening. "It'll be good to have you back in the quarry. Ol' McCullough does what he can, but his back's about shot."

Joshua knew Dad would start in soon enough. He just hadn't expected it so soon. "Not sure you're better off with me. I'm still a might banged up."

"I saw your limp, but you're getting around. Long as you can plant weight on it, you can handle the work."

Joshua scrambled. "It's better, but the doctor said to watch it."

That's all it took to set him off.

"Doctors don't know a damn thing!" Dad erupted, pushing back from the table. "That quarry out there feeds this family. You aim to stay under this roof, you best get that through your head."

Joshua seethed. He didn't feel much these days. When he did, it came as fear and rage. With his father, those had always come easy.

Behind him, a pan slammed against the counter. "And they'll be no fighting either!" Mom brought the rest of the pie over, shaking her head. "There's time to sort that out later. Right now Josh needs rest."

Dad fumed. "I've got a backlog now. If I lose those orders, we'll all be aching. So Josh better be getting off his backside soon. Be damned if a son of mine is gonna sit up here feeling sorry for himself."

"I plan to work! I just can't handle the quarry, not yet. Hell, it . . . it takes everything I got to stand," he stammered.

The admission left him weak. Sweat dampened his brow. Looking up, he saw the pain on his mother's face. She'd been caught in the middle again.

"What can I do in the meantime?"

Though never comfortable with the explosives, he'd been helping since he was twelve. Ol' McCullough handled the bulk of the stone cutting, but Joshua knew the basics. Mom had taught him the books. He was good with his hands too. One summer he'd fixed the sheds and repaired the stone culvert where the lane crossed the spring.

"What I need is another man digging stone," Dad growled. But under Mom's steely gaze, he eased back. "There is a farmer over in Head Waters. He's looking to have a fireplace built, says he'll hire a good man. I'm delivering his stone in a couple weeks. You might ought to speak to him."

"We'll see," Mom interjected. "I want Josh rested. I won't have him worked plumb ragged."

The attention was suffocating. Couldn't they leave him be? The ringing in his head returned. He closed his eyes.

"You alright, son?" Mom asked.

He reopened them. "Just tired."

She was eyeing his neck. "Those your dog tags?"

"It's a . . . just a buddy's." He evaded her reach. "He didn't make it." The casual betrayal stung.

She pulled back, clinching a fist against her chest. "Bless his soul," she whispered.

Joshua braced himself. He should have removed it.

Mom might be patient about the quarry, but she'd have a few choice words over a son of hers donning a saint medal. She was convinced Catholics were out to destroy the world. Joshua knew the sermons too, well versed in the theatrics of Preacher Clark. But he'd never bought into the menace of saints as Mom had.

Besides, the hysterics over the idolatry would only be the start. Other questions would follow. There were no answers for them. Not ones she'd accept, nor anyone else for that matter.

The knock on the door saved him.

Scott, wisely hunkered down over his pie, bolted over. He swung the door open to reveal Mrs. Dalton, standing formidable on the porch. Katie hovered a step back, lips pursed as she ran her hands down the front of a pale cream dress. She glanced up, her gaze finding Joshua.

"Afternoon, Mrs. Dalton . . . Katie," Scott greeted them.

Mom joined him, "Afternoon! Please come in!" She nodded to Mrs. Dalton.

Joshua rose awkwardly under watchful eyes.

Mrs. Dalton extended a stiff hand. "Your mother's pleased to have you home, young man," she said with pointed detachment.

"It's good to be home." he replied, dipping his head. He struggled for something to add. "I sure missed your roses. Are they as beautiful as always?"

Joshua had tried for years to ingratiate himself to Mrs. Dalton. The only safe topic he'd ever found was her prized roses. Anything more unleashed a barely concealed scorn.

"We've had better seasons. Aphids nearly devoured my Dainty Martha's. But how kind of you to ask," she added dryly.

Behind her Katie was deflecting Mom's fawning. "Mother found the lace in Richmond. We have it in the store now," she explained, touching the stitching on the collar.

Having exhausted the potential for pleasantries with Mrs. Dalton, he turned to Katie. "Hi," he breathed. "How are you?"

"I'm good. And you, Josh?" Katie asked, eyeing the scar.

She looked fragile, and he could empathize. "I've been better, but I'm here," he answered, offering a shy grin.

Katie relaxed, flashing the same warm smile he recalled from their childhood. It felt as reassuring as it had all those years ago.

Dad rose from the table. "Get them some pie, Eli!"

Mom ushered them over. "Yes, do join us. We have plenty."

Katie hesitated until Joshua nodded.

He glanced out the window as they situated themselves, dismissing the twinge of guilt. Things were different now. They had to be.

*   *   *

Later, up in his room, he studied the burnt orange glow upon the ridge. He'd made it through the first day.

Nothing had changed with Dad, but seeing Katie had gone better than he could have hoped. Surrounded by family, they'd managed a brief, amiable conversation.

After a time his energy had ebbed, prompting Mrs. Dalton to put an end to their visit. Under her harsh gaze, he'd given Katie a stilted hug at the door. She'd beamed at his promise to come calling.

The light was fading so he made his way to the duffel. When he leaned over, the Saint Christopher medal swung free. Rising with a handful of undershirts, he glimpsed it in the mirror.

He'd best deal with the matter now.

Setting the shirts atop the hutch, he removed the chain from around his neck. He laid the medal in his palm and caressed the worn surface, recalling the first time he saw it against Aiden's muscular chest.

It did no good to remember.

Opening the top drawer, he retrieved a cigar box stuffed with trinkets. He lifted the lid and placed the medal inside. With a heavy sigh he shoved the box to the back of the drawer. Then he swept the undershirts into the void left behind.

9 – The Hunt

Crouched upon the front porch, Joshua gave the new boards a final sanding then ran his hand along the grain. It would do. He felt about for the rag before realizing it had tumbled partway down the steps. When he stretched for it, his thigh seized up so he rolled over. The muscle relaxed quick enough, but he'd need a moment.

The rotting boards beneath the railing had bugged him since his return. Being inside felt constricted, too many thoughts trapped in too little space. Each morning he'd found himself wandering out to the swing in spite of the cold. There he'd linger, studying the valley below and the tree line above. For lunch he'd join Mom inside and then help her with tasks. Yesterday he'd filled the coal bin and snapped a bushel of beans. Afterwards, he'd walk into town to see Katie.

It wasn't much of a routine, but it passed the time.

Each evening Dad would return from the quarry, drag himself to the supper table and then on up to bed. If Joshua timed his comings and goings right, he'd miss him altogether. On those days, his only interaction was hearing the hacking down the hall as his father readied for work. No one spoke of it. The matter lay untouched, like so many others.

He could tell Mom was worried. Joshua saw her furrowed brow as she went about her business.

Scott went to school and did his chores. He took care of Butterscotch and toted his guitar most everywhere. But he seemed blind to anything else.

It was as if they were travelers on different journeys, mere strangers sharing a roof each night before moving on.

At least the roof didn't leak, unlike everything else. In the past week Joshua had tackled larger projects - fixing the faucet, beefing up the sagging back stoop, and now dealing with the rot on the porch.

The door squeaked behind him.

"Looks good, son," Mom offered with a glass of water. "But are you sure you ought to be crawling around on your leg?"

He shrugged. "It's holding up."

"Well, if you say so. Lord knows the ol' place needs attention." She wiped her hands on her apron. "Your father noticed. He'd tell you himself if you went upstairs."

"Dad's home? I didn't hear him this morning, but figured I'd been asleep."

"Orders have slowed as of late, so he'll be staying home Saturdays as he needs from here on."

"Oh." He reached again for the rag, pondering the comment. Dad had worked six days a week for as long as he could remember, even when there weren't any orders. Why would now be any different? He looked back, half a mind to ask.

Mom was headed back in. "You should go and see your father," she repeated as the screen door slammed.

Sitting up, he tossed the rag aside. And say what? Dad would only bring up the quarry again, angering them both. Talking with Dad meant arguing, but Mom never saw it that way.

Across the yard Scott emerged from the shed, rifle in hand. Joshua acknowledged him when he reached the steps.

"Looks like you got them pretty well in place. Why not come help me bag a gobbler? Thanksgiving's coming, and I'm not having much luck."

"It might help if you got to them before noon."

Scott frowned so he eased up. "You have to be patient," he added, retrieving the rag once more. "I have to paint."

"Come on, Josh! We haven't hunted since you got home. I'll grab your rifle."

His heart caught. "No!"

Scott stepped back. "Fine. I was just asking."

Joshua watched his brother retreat toward the shed. Scott had never been one to push. He might stew for weeks, but he'd never ask twice. "I could tag along," he called out. "I'm just not much in the mood to hunt."

Scott glanced over his shoulder. "What about your painting?"

"It can wait. Leg's cramping up anyhow. Might do me good to stretch it out."

"Alright, I'll grab the ammo," Scott replied, his gait betraying his gruff tone.

*　　*　　*

Joshua was relieved they didn't talk as they hiked up the ridge. Not only was he stiff, but he'd also underestimated the challenge. Despite the chill, he began to sweat.

Still it felt good returning to the woods, the experience more varied than the dusty lane into town. The weathered trees stood nearly bare in the sun, and dried leaves lay thick underfoot. Early on, he glimpsed a scurrying fox. Atop the ridge they paused to watch a bear, his coal black coat stark against an ocean of rusty ferns.

After he passed, they eased down along the northern face. There, approaching the exposed boulders marking the fault, Scott drew to a halt. "You holding up?"

"Mostly."

"It'll be rougher below. That's where I've been seeing tracks, the only place I've seen any this year."

Joshua wiped his brow. "Maybe I'd better hold back then."

Scott laughed. "That'd be fine. Surprised you made it this far. Any other tips for me?"

Joshua shrugged. "Move in slow, slower than you think. It won't do any good to barge down. The noise will only spook them. And wait 'til you're in position before you start up with your calls." He finished with a smirk.

"What?"

"You'll only get one shot."

Scott bristled. "That's why you should have brought your rifle. But I'll keep that in mind." He took a few steps. "You gonna be right here?"

Joshua looked about, noting the spikes of green peaking above the boulders. It had been years since he'd seen the spruces. "I might wander a bit, but we can meet back here. I'll expect you to have a gobbler."

"Yeah, well, we'll see about that." Then he was on his way.

Joshua sighed. Worn from the climb, he ached from head to toe. Would he ever feel right again?

Was no use dwelling on it so he glanced about. He watched a squirrel nose among the leaves, then eyed the canopy, studying the weave of branches. The air was so still he could hear the gurgle of the creek below. Scott had his work cut out for him on a day like today. He turned to scour the lower hillside, straining to locate his brother.

The flash of memory startled him.

Lying among seedlings on soaked ground. A wave of fog rushing in. He yanked at the strand, but the image slipped away, fading as suddenly as it had appeared. The only thing that stuck was the fear. His heart was racing . . . as was he.

He lurched along the steeper incline, pushing through the pain. Reaching the fault line, he entered the maze of boulders. The crunching leaves underfoot gave way to soft ferns. After a couple of false turns, he found the old path. A moment later he emerged among the spruces, the bold green defiant against the gray sky.

Tucked somewhere among them was an old stone cabin. Scott and he had first stumbled upon it as boys. Playing along the ridge, they had wandered through the boulders and onto the hidden ledge. He recalled how they wove the cabin into their game of *Cowboys and Indians*, claiming it as a fort.

As a boy, he'd accepted its existence without question. But now it baffled him. Why would anyone build a cabin here?

The stone chimney appeared through a gap. He aimed for it, encountering a fallen spruce. As he scrambled over, his leg cramped. He fell to one knee, gasping for air. Then he rose, drawing deeper breaths.

There it was, battered but standing, a tiny refuge with a single door and a handful of windows. Stone structures were rare in the county. Nestled between ancient fault lines, this one was all but forgotten.

Too tired to ponder the matter further, he limped to a sunny spot beside the door. Leaning against the uneven surface, he joined the silence. Warmth penetrated his body.

He closed his eyes, entering a light but restful sleep.

The earth rotated. He felt a shadow cover him, and the cooling stone. Yet he remained, content to drift.

Some time later he heard a shot below, followed by a triumphant whoop. He cracked a smile. Apparently Scott could manage when he put his mind to it.

He pushed off the wall, then rubbed his thigh. The cramp had eased. He noted how the light had shifted. A narrow shaft now illuminated stones along the lower corner. One had a rougher surface, unnaturally so. It was etched.

Stepping close, he kneeled. The letters were uneven, but legible. *For Anna*, it read. He sighed . . . as if the cabin weren't peculiar enough. He reached for the stone.

Scott's distant shout broke his trance.

Joshua rose and trudged back through the spruces, retracing his route. Only after he cleared the boulders did he respond. "Coming!" he yelled along the ridge.

10 – Tommy

Crossing the patchy field to join Tommy, Joshua's gaze fell to the hodgepodge of grasses and weeds covering the hardened soil. The land had lain fallow for a long time. Still, he studied the undulating surface, noting a few dried husks. Apparently wheat had once been harvested.

The captain, irritated by the British focus on trench warfare, had ordered construction of a makeshift target range. "We won't end this blasted war hunkered down in the trenches," he'd growled. "Division expects us to take the fight to the Germans. So, damn it, we'll train ourselves!"

Joshua agreed with the sentiment. Down with the flu the week prior, a British chap at the infirmary had told him all he needed to hear about the trenches. Stories about filth, illness and putrid food didn't frighten him. Yet he'd shuddered at the man's tale of gunfire in the night, waking covered in blood from his buddy beside him. The man said he'd only survived the raid by thrusting his bayonet into a German soldier who leaned in close, assuming he was dead.

The image had settled the matter for Joshua. Some men might feel safer in the trenches; but he'd just as soon take his chances in the open, battling across no man's land.

Since they'd joined the British, such mental games weighed heavy on his mind. He supposed it was only natural. The unit ate, drank, drilled and slept with the war just over the horizon.

After their training they'd likely integrate into existing lines, though word had it General Pershing wanted more than to fill depleted British and French divisions. America was demanding its own stake on the front, intent on being equals in driving the Huns from France.

Joshua liked hitching his role to a larger purpose. So much of his day was spent following orders – charging up hills, cleaning his rifle, inspections and so forth. Relating the mundane to a greater cause helped him cope. Other men said all they wanted was to make it back alive. He wanted that too, but needed more. He ached to know his efforts would count, that it was all worthwhile.

The preparations took all his focus, sapping his energy. Only at night did his mind wander. Sometimes he thought of home, though not as much as he'd expected. Though he dreamt of the ridges, the affairs of Hadley seemed too distant.

More often than not, he'd drift off while reflecting upon the day. There was always some dispute among the men, nerves fraying and tempers flaring. He avoided the major eruptions. Tommy watched his back, and he Tommy's. For that he was thankful.

But when all was said and done, company bickering didn't hold his attention. Dealings beyond the unit were what intrigued him. Joshua liked the British instructors. When he could, he'd observe their units as they conducted drills or went about their duties. While at the infirmary, Nurse Laurent had crossed his mind as well. He pondered her life caring for men from the front.

That, in turn, brought to mind Sergeant Reynolds . . . Aiden. Then again, he thought of him anyhow, curious where he'd been assigned.

He wished they could have talked more. Something about his manner made Joshua feel he could ask him anything. He even imagined telling him his fears, which was nonsense since he never shared them with anyone, even Tommy. Yet he pictured it anyhow, the idea seeming natural in his head. Perhaps it was the interest Aiden had shown. That must be it, he concluded, not letting himself consider the matter further.

He recalled the sergeant's advice to take note of his surroundings, appreciating experiences as they came. He smiled. Maybe that's why he'd been scrutinizing a dusty field beneath a blistering sun.

"What's got you grinning?" Tommy shouted as he approached. "Thinking of Katie again?"

Tommy ribbed him constantly, having decided from the start that he and Joshua were closest in situation among the men. Arriving at

Virginia's Camp Lee the same day, they'd been shuffled into a unit being shipped down to Georgia. The only volunteers in the group, they were younger than the conscripted men. Both hailed from rural communities, he from Virginia and Tommy from a Pennsylvania farm. And though Joshua wasn't engaged as Tommy was, each received weekly letters from a hometown girl.

Joshua had to admit Tommy's presumption was mostly right. Besides, he liked Tommy. They were friends. "Maybe," he replied from habit. It was easier.

"I can't get Mary out of my head either. Back home we used to sneak off to an old barn in a field like this one. Damn sure wish she were here now!"

"You'd put her to work setting up targets?" Joshua teased.

Tommy leered. "Nah. I'd have to take a break."

He rolled his eyes. "It's good I'm here to cover for ya."

"At least you know your place." Tommy glanced away, then shook his head. "Who am I fooling? It isn't that so much. I'd just give anything to hold her a while."

Joshua nodded. He admired the honesty but had no response.

"You know how it is, when you hunger for your gal, needing to touch her," Tommy went on. "Like you with Katie."

Joshua gaze fell again to the lumpy ground. "Yeah, I miss her sometimes."

Did he feel that way? Was that how it was supposed to be?

"Well, guess we should finish up," he dodged. "I'm gonna start on the other end."

"That'll work, if you can drag 'em by yourself. Holler if you need a hand."

"Sure," he mumbled, retreating to the cluster of targets. He hoped he could manage alone. Tommy sometimes needed assurances he wasn't equipped to provide.

He gave the nearest one a tug. It was stop and go at first. But once he found the right grip, he managed.

As he worked, he considered Tommy's assertion that Joshua's intentions mirrored his own. He was used to it. People always assumed they knew his feelings, yet their expectations never added up in his own head. For one, he didn't pine for Katie the way Tommy longed for Mary.

Admittedly she'd been a constant in his life since he was ten. When she'd arrived in Hadley, she'd been so skittish, a city girl thrust into the backcountry. As her house was along the way, he and Scott had accompanied her to and from school. Assigned the seat beside her in class, he'd taken to watching after her. On many a day he'd eaten lunch with her, encouraging her when she seemed low.

Even after shedding her shyness, she'd stuck with him. But they weren't all at each other, not like some of their classmates. She liked walks, so he'd asked her to join him. They'd find an open hill or quiet spot where they could look out over the valley. She was bright and made astute observations.

Joshua studied people, trying to make sense of them. But where he saw individuals, Katie imagined relationships. On occasion she was even right. She'd been the only one who figured out the widowed principal was smitten with the music teacher, musing about it months before their engagement.

Joshua was oblivious of such matters. He hadn't even realized Katie liked him at first, not in a serious way. They hadn't kissed until a few months before he left. He recalled her wondering aloud what it would be like as they walked during a winter thaw. Mulling the matter in silence, he had turned to face her under the covered bridge in the valley. It had been brief and awkward, but she hadn't seemed to mind.

After that they'd been a couple, kind of. Katie had shared the incident with a friend. From there word had gotten around. When Scott blurted the news at home a week later, Mom had accepted it as confirmation of a long-held suspicion. Mrs. Dalton had sharpened her already abrupt demeanor. On the other hand, Mr. Dalton had begun speaking to him. It hadn't seemed to matter one way or another to Dad. As for himself, well, he'd had his doubts. But he'd only ever shared those with Scott, and then only vaguely.

Joshua felt their expectations, but didn't understand them. He liked Katie. He cared for her a lot. But he sometimes thought about that kiss, pondering if he could have avoided all the fuss if he'd taken her to Buck's for a soda instead.

Still, he could picture her at the station the day he left, hovering near. "I don't want you to be all alone, Joshua Hunter," she'd whispered as the train pulled into the station.

"Don't you be afraid," he'd replied. Then, choking up, he'd added, "I'll miss you." For a moment he might have understood.

But then the train had arrived, and the moment passed. Mom had hugged him. He'd shaken hands with Dad. Scott had lifted his bag, tossing a mock salute. From his seat Joshua had waved once before turning to watch the valley open before him.

A branch snapped in the woods, dissolving the memory.

Hunting instincts kicked in. The break was too sharp for a bird. Joshua paused from dragging the target. He turned, expecting a wild boar or other animal. A few domesticated breeds roamed free in the area. Once he'd even seen a cow wandering through camp at daybreak.

The dark woods contrasted with the bright field, but he could see shapes. His heart quickened at the sight of a soldier beside a large oak, then eased when he recognized the AEF uniform. He couldn't make out the man's face.

Acting casual, he sized up the situation. Tommy was behind him. Across the field, Nico and Smitty were still busy marking the firing lines. Clearly someone else had joined them.

Who would sneak up to spy on them? McKenzie might pull this kind of stunt, but he was taller than the figure in the trees. Maybe the corporal was making sure they weren't dragging their feet. That made the most sense, so he returned to pulling the target into place.

When the soldier still hadn't announced himself a minute later, Joshua made up his mind. Before returning to retrieve another target, he walked over to the one nearest the tree line. Pretending to adjust it, he listened for movement.

Not a sound. He was being watched, but why? Growing weary of the charade, he turned to face the stranger.

"Hello?" he asked, sounding more sheepish than he'd intended.

A familiar laugh echoed back as the soldier edged nearer. "You're sharper than your buds at the other end."

"Sergeant Reynolds?"

"Yeah, it's me. Private Hunter, right?" he asked. "Wolfie," he added, softer.

"Yes, Sergeant. What are you doing here?" he sputtered.

The sergeant shrugged. "Looks like someone's orders came through." Then he stepped into the sunlight.

11 – Thanksgiving Morn

Joshua jolted awake, disoriented. The room was dark, save for moonlight. A narrow shaft bathed a vase of asters so he focused on it, a trick he'd taught himself at the hospital.

The present seeped back. It was Thanksgiving. Katie had left the flowers with Mom while he was down in Head Waters. The portly farmer, afflicted with a bad back, had hired him. Joshua was to start on their fireplace first thing Monday.

His breathing eased as he studied the slender blue petals. They seemed too delicate for late November, even a mild one. But there they were, tattered but blooming. No doubt Katie had been drawn to them for just that reason. She had a big heart for injured souls and lost causes.

He sighed. Surely he fit the first category, if not the latter.

The moonlight shifted, sending a glimmer off the bevel of the mirror. It dappled softly, casting pearls across the wall. He kicked the blanket aside, letting icy air sweep over him. Though sleep was done, he dropped his head back onto the pillow. There was nothing to do except wait for dawn.

He considered the dream briefly before dismissing it. It was typical of ones in the hospital, the images so vivid as to seem real . . . *a forest, flashes of gunfire, screams.* Though less frequent now, they persisted, stubborn reminders that the will he exerted each day held little sway over the night.

Still, the discipline was necessary. The war was over. Moving on meant leaving it behind.

He was trying. He'd seen Katie most every day, calling on her at home a few times but more often than not meeting in town. They'd sit on the bench outside Buck's diner, chatting.

They talked of small things. Katie would let him gripe about his leg, or his father, offering encouragement where she could. Some days, sensing his mood, she'd share anecdotes while he sat in silence. She had asked if he was taking on too much too soon. Yet he imagined she was pleased at the prospect of him working, heartened to see him taking steps.

Even Mrs. Dalton had been more agreeable since the first awkward visit. She'd gone as far as to commend his duty the day Preacher Clark asked him to stand while he read the award citation during Sunday service.

All the hoopla had bothered him. The war hardly seemed God's work. Still, he'd accepted the congregation's praise. It was bound to get easier. People would forget soon enough, letting him to fade into the background. Until then, he had to convince them he was fine.

The bedroom was brighter now. A pair of crows lit on the eave, providing a distraction. He studied them from the bed before moving to the window. They flitted to the woodpile and then on to the frosted trees above. Eventually they darted up the ridge and out of sight.

Soon after, he heard movement in his parents' room. Their door opened, and Mom's soft footsteps padded toward the stair. Dad's coughing erupted before she reached the bottom.

Joshua slipped on pants and a shirt. He massaged his leg, then ran his fingers through his matted hair. He traced the scar, shrugged and went on down.

She was propped against the counter, staring out the window.

"Mom?"

She straightened up, still facing away. "You're up early."

"I couldn't sleep. You alright?"

She turned, revealing bloodshot eyes. "Yeah. I, um . . . I'm just not sure where to start." She gathered herself. "Son, I want a nice Thanksgiving."

"It will be, Mom. It'll be fine. Let me help."

"You're already a help, more than you know. Heck, you've been taking care of things I stopped seein'. I meant to ask Scott to repair the porch months ago. But it slipped my mind. It's just, well, it just didn't seem all that important I guess." She rotated back toward the window.

He felt guilty. All he'd done was adopt old habits. She was in pain, and he hadn't any idea what to do. He never had.

"There's got to be something," he persisted.

She sighed. "Well, everything's mostly prepped. I've planned us a real feast. Scott's gobbler is in the oven. I finished the stuffing last evening and can snap the beans quick enough. After that I'm baking sweet potato pie like my mother used to make.

"Mostly I just need to wake up and pull it together. Coffee will help with that." She reached for the percolator. "Looks like you could use a cup too."

Joshua watched her fill the pot.

"Come to think of it, could you bring in more wood so we won't have to fetch any later?" She paused, choosing her words. "Your father's been working hard. He gets chills nowadays. It'd be a load off my mind if he didn't have to do too much."

"I'll get it now." He retrieved his coat from the entry closet then knelt to lace his boots.

"Son," she whispered from above, startling him. "There is one thing."

He rose. "Yes, ma'am?"

"I want today to be special . . . memorable. Try talking with your father. He worried when you were gone, more than he'd ever let on. I know it's hard for you two, but if you could make an effort."

Her pleading left him feeling small. He nodded.

She touched his cheek. "Thank you, son. Having you home, having all of us here together . . . that's what I'm thankful for, today and everyday."

"Me too," he breathed, wanting to feel it. Then he stepped into the raw morning air.

12 – Chuck

Katie was waiting on the porch as he approached. Obscured by the cedar in front of one of the empty shanties, he paused to observe her. She plucked a few dead ivy leaves from the trellis then checked her appearance in the window. A knitted gray sweater covered her lavender dress. She fiddled with the collar and adjusted the barrette holding back her dark bangs. Always sensible, she had dressed for the outing hinted at earlier in the week. While she hadn't revealed details, she'd suggested it would be a bit of a hike.

The day was blustery, but not cold. High clouds moving in from the southwest hinted at rain. The days had grown shorter, but there was plenty of time for an outing. He'd kept his promise to Mom during the family meal and needed a break. Scott had bolted before the table was even cleared, grabbing his guitar on the way out.

Dad had vanished upstairs soon after. He'd been tolerable during the meal, even asking about plans at the Johnson farm. Even so, he'd snorted when Joshua said the old man had hinted there might be work after the fireplace, suggesting it was a ploy to get his best effort. As he'd put it, "Don't go counting on that. Country folk do for themselves. They don't put stock in needless extravagances."

As far as Dad's digs went, it was tame.

Katie peered up the street, forcing him to scramble so as not to be caught spying. She waved upon seeing him, and he began to trot. Aside from his awkward gait, it felt almost like a visit before the war.

She bounded down to greet him. "You look chipper. Your color's back, and your hair's filling in."

He beamed. "You as well, very sharp. I like your hair pulled back."

"Mother says I've been hiding my eyes for too long so I'm trying." She shrugged. "I don't know. I'm never going to be like Carole."

"Who'd want that?" he shot back, provoking a shriek of laughter. "Joshua Hunter, that is mean!"

"But what you were thinking, right?" he teased, knowing it to be the truth. Katie had once confessed Carole Lundy was a source of envy. She'd grown up fast and fashionable, leaving Katie feeling awkward.

"Not at all. Carole's nice. I just can't pull off a look like she can. That and I'm not a buxom blond," she added with a smirk.

"No one wants you to be," he replied, catching her eye.

She held his gaze. "Oh, I don't know about that. But thanks."

"I thought I heard you two," Mr. Dalton interrupted, opening the screen door. "What's so funny?"

"Nothing, Pa. Joshua's just teasing me."

"Now you be nice to my girl, young man. But keep her smiling. Laughter's good for the soul."

"Yes, sir." He didn't mind talking to Katie's father. He never eyed him with suspicion like her mother.

"Would you like some dessert? Katie made a delicious pumpkin pie. Better than her mother's," he whispered, "though let's not mention that to Olympia."

Joshua read Katie's expression. "No, sir. But thank you. I'm plumb full. Mom prepared a nice spread today."

"How are your folks holding up, Joshua? I understand your father's been under the weather."

Joshua figured Mr. Dalton knew as much as he did, possibly more. "Yes, sir. He's a bit tired of late but getting along."

Mr. Dalton's brow furrowed. "Well, tell your mother to let us know if you need anything, anything at all."

"I'll be sure to mention it, sir."

"You do that. It's been a rough couple of years for Hadley. We all ought to look after each other a little better." He turned his attention to Katie, who'd grown antsy. "So you two are heading out, are you?"

"Yes, Pa, going for a walk while it's still warm. We'd best be on our way."

"Alright, alright. Don't want to hold you up. You sure you don't need a hat? We're due for some rain."

"Nah, Pa. We won't roam too far. I'll keep an eye on the horizon."

"Then fly free, my little dove. You two be good now."

"We will," she promised. She rushed up to give him a peck on the cheek, then trotted back down, giving Joshua a yank.

*   *   *

Katie kept mum on their destination, chatting about nothing in particular. They followed the creek toward the river for a bit, not taking the fork up to Hawk's Peak as he'd feared. He wasn't sure he could have handled the steep trail. But when they crossed to the other side a bit further along, he grew puzzled.

"You'll know soon enough," she answered his unspoken question.

They ducked under a strand of barbed wire, joining an overgrown lane leading into the hollow. It wasn't until they emerged from the forest a short time later that it made sense. There, nestled between the two ridges, a narrow field of yellowed grasses basked in the afternoon sun. A couple of flatbed wagons were parked askew at the far end, with the horses tied to a collapsed shed. The ruins of a house sat off in the trees behind it. Scott was propped up against a barrel on one of the wagons, strumming his guitar. Strands of "For Me and My Gal" wafted toward them.

Katie issued her warning with a smile. "Now be nice. They're mostly Scott's classmates, but a few familiar faces are here as well. Everyone's been asking about you, even Carole."

"If Carole Lundy's here, I'll be on my best behavior," he teased, letting her move ahead.

"You'd better be," she chuckled. "It isn't Lundy anymore. Tim Campbell up and married her last spring."

Katie was wise not to have told him of the gathering. But they were here now; he might as well make the best of it. He recognized

Scott's buddies. And sure enough Carole was hanging onto Tim as always. Other classmates from the valley school hovered around them, opening up when he and Katie drew close.

Saying their hellos, he noticed Pete Morrison on his own by the wagons, watching Scott play. Joshua wondered how he was dealing with his brother's death, but lost the thought as the gang surrounded them.

"I see you're with Katie," Chuck Taggart commented a few minutes later, shoving a tin in his direction.

"Yeah, she drug me out here." Joshua glanced over to where she stood, cup in hand, chatting with the girls.

Chuck smirked. "What would her mother say? Imagine it'd be rather embarrassing for the queen of prohibition."

"Katie has a mind of her own," he defended.

"That she does. I rather like her spunk." Chuck lifted his cup. "To Katie!"

Joshua took a sip. The burn was sharp. "Whoa!"

Chuck's auburn beard glistened as he laughed. The joker had joined his father's logging operation after graduation. Years earlier he'd begun supplying moonshine from cousins over in West Virginia. As far as Joshua could tell, the only thing state prohibition had achieved was pushing locals from malt brew to pure grain.

"It does have a bite," Chuck confessed. "Though I rather like the oakiness. There's a whole nother keg in a spring up the ridge a ways. Men from the crew are out hunting. We'll need it if they come. They down it like water."

"Damn!" Joshua gasped. It had been months since he'd had spirits, and it hadn't been one eighty proof. He thought of Montmartre as the warmth filled his veins. With a flourish, he swallowed a gulp. Liquid boldness might help the afternoon flow.

"That's more like it," Chuck urged, chugging from his own cup.

"So did you set up this little gathering?" Joshua asked.

Chuck nodded, waving as another youth wandered up.

"Why here?"

Chuck shook his cup. "You mean beside the obvious?"

"Yeah . . . beside the obvious."

"I wanted to check it out. This old farm's been abandoned near forever. My dad's trying to purchase it. Well, he and some partners. It's a huge tract. This is but a sliver." He lowered his voice. "Not simply for the timber either. If it goes through, they'll have mineral rights. The seller owns a big chunk of the opposite ridge too, over beyond your place."

"I know . . . the Garth parcel. The government doesn't already own it?"

"Nope, though they'd sure like to. Dad caught wind of the opportunity recently. He's tired of playing small-time while the big logging operations rake in the dough, so he's joined with some out of state investors. They say they can gin up support for extending the rail line. Heck, they think semi-anthracite coal still has a future in these parts. Damn fools." He glanced at Joshua. "No offense to your father."

Joshua shrugged. "Seems to me it's water under the bridge. He just likes to growl."

"That's for damn sure. Still can't believe he won't let us log those acres above your place. He cussed us up one side and down the other for even suggestin' it." He took another swig. "Ain't no matter anyhow. Dad's partners have connections with the governor. They're convinced they'll be up and running in a few years. Who knows? Maybe they'll find something to mine.

"Dad's steering clear of that. He just wants a foothold. There's enough timber to keep us busy while they fiddle. Prime too, some of the last virgin forest in these parts. Government can't touch it if the owner won't sell.

"I took a little walk last week. Found some real giants up there, older than those oaks above your place." He motioned at the field. "We aim to start a sawmill here next summer."

So this was how it started. Joshua studied the ridges on either side, imagining the loss. He followed the fault lines up through the bare trees, thinking of Scott's gobbler hunt. "I take it the parcel includes the cabin?"

The question stumped Chuck 'til he noted Joshua's gaze. "Oh, you mean that little stone one in the spruce cradle. I didn't think anyone knew about that. Then again you've been all over these ridges, haven't you?" He grinned. "Yeah, it's included. Matter of fact the owner's father was the man who built it."

Joshua recalled the etched stone. *For Anna.* "He lived there alone?"

"Nah, never lived there at all. But my dad remembers him, says he was an odd one, some wealthy bugger from back east. He grew up in these parts, or maybe it was his wife. Not sure which. He showed up in Hadley the year Dad finished school. Mostly kept to himself, but he hired Dad to haul supplies up to the spruces. After that he gave him odd jobs from time to time, though he pretty much built it by hand.

"Dad said the man worked on it nearly a year, straight through the winter. He spent weeks scouring the creek beds, picking out particular stones. When he finished, he vanished quick as he came. Never came back as far as anyone knows.

"He never touched the land. Dad offered to log it. No doubt the larger operations did too. But he held out. When he dropped dead from a stroke earlier this year, I guess the son realized he had quite a chestnut squirreled away up here."

By then Joshua had located the spruces below the clouds shrouding the peak. The stand was tucked back and easy to miss. "Wonder why he built it?" he mused.

"Crazy with grief, I guess."

Joshua squinted. "How so?"

"Well, Dad said the man was a quiet one. But one day he kinda broke down. He spilled some sad saga about an accident that killed his wife. Apparently he'd left the son with her sister before scurrying off for Hadley. He told Dad it was the house his wife had always talked about, said he built it for her." Chuck shook his head. "I suppose he was looking for peace."

It took a minute for the silence to register. Joshua looked over to find Chuck staring up, somber. The joker had dropped his mask.

The reveal was short-lived. Chuck leaned in close. "The bugger may have been mad, but he paid good money when no one else was hiring." His eyes twinkled. "Heck, maybe Dad would've followed my uncle over to Pendleton County if the work hadn't gotten him through a lean year." He toasted his cup toward the ridge and took a final swig.

Joshua lifted his as well. "To Anna," he whispered. Then he downed the rest of his moonshine, watching the spruces disappear within the sinking clouds.

13 – Elisabeth

Elisabeth paused from cleaning the porcelain platter.

The meal had gone well. Wayne had been in good spirits, and the boys talkative. Josh had even mentioned the new job. Though still ruffled, Wayne had held his tongue. For his part, Josh had taken the high road as well, listening to his father rather than fighting him.

But now with Wayne resting upstairs and the boys out, the silence summoned the shadowy thoughts of recent days. Wayne would deny it, and he did when given half a chance. Still, the truth was plain . . . he was getting worse.

Was this what her future held, left alone like this? She gripped the platter tight. After gravitating around her husband for so long, the thought of drifting free shook her to the core.

Faith only took her so far. There were practicalities to consider. Mending shirts had once been a way of bringing in a little extra, easing them through the lean times. But it wouldn't sustain her.

She couldn't run a quarry, and she'd be damned if her sons were going to. Wayne still talked like it was a legacy, some great family business to pass on. But this whole venture had turned his stubborn determination to bitterness. Now it was killing him, she was convinced of it. She wouldn't wish their existence on her worst enemy. Why in God's name would she force it upon her own sons?

Even if she wanted to leave, who would buy it? They'd sunk their all into it, investing too much upfront, then squandering the rest to pay off the partners when they bailed. She'd fought Wayne on that, a battle she'd lost. Now she was trapped, sure to face the consequences on her own.

Wayne would just as soon shoot a ranger than sell to the government. She didn't dare cross him on that, which left the logging companies. There was plenty of timber above. Wayne had refused to cut it, still harboring some fantasy. "I'll build you a castle someday," he used to tease.

She shook her head. There were no castles in her life, and her knight had fallen. Besides, she'd once been told their relatively small parcel might not be worth it to the loggers. Of course George Dalton might be wrong. From what she could tell, no twig was too small. Perhaps she could sell the timber and keep the land, living out her days on a barren ridge.

Then again, maybe she would sell out to the government and board a train to Adeleine. But it wasn't like she could head back to the farm. She'd return a disgrace.

She rocked in place, imagining the looks of pity. Dear God, why hadn't they stayed? They had been happy there.

The admission was the final straw. She slammed the platter against the lip of the basin. It shattered spectacularly.

Wayne stirred upstairs. "I dropped a plate," she yelled up.

Just another glorious mess. She drew a breath and studied her hands for cuts, finding none. Then she crouched to gather the larger shards. At least this could be remedied.

It wasn't all Wayne's doing. When he'd first brought up the idea of a mine, she'd swallowed her concerns. Lord knows why. Maybe she'd wanted to support him, like a good wife. Wayne had wanted his own path, not her Pa's.

She pursed her lips. That wasn't it, not entirely. Wayne was brash, but he'd have listened to her. She'd chosen to say nothing. Perhaps she'd been afraid. Fearful he'd resent her, or leave her, though he'd never given cause for doubt. None at all.

Rising to retrieve the broom, she glanced out the window. There was coal on the ridge, lustrous seams that looked promising until they broke apart and vanished farther down. The old timers knew that. Even the Tuckerman mine up in Rockingham County barely stayed afloat. Still, Wayne had kept pushing. It's what he knew. When his pressure couldn't form coal, he'd latched onto the idea of a quarry instead.

Why had they rushed so? Why hadn't she trusted herself?

She shuddered. It did no good to dwell. By the time she'd found her voice, they were in too deep. Though she had raised hell when the partners bailed, by then their bed was made. Now they were doomed to rot on this damned ridge.

As she finished sweeping, she breathed a prayer. There was hope. There had to be. What other choice did you have but to believe there was?

You had to make your own luck, and she was trying. She'd let it be known she was seeking real sewing, not just mending. Word was getting around, even reaching the valley. Last week she'd finished a couple of dresses for Otto Meeks' daughter, Ellie. Poor farmer, left to raise a girl on his own after his tramp of a wife absconded with some drifter.

Elisabeth intended to get by, and she'd do it without clutching at her sons the way some women did. She'd set out to raise men, not gelded handmaidens for her lean years.

She sighed. The job wasn't done yet. Joshua was home, but he remained elusive. Katie was a godsend, sticking with him like she had. Maybe the time apart, hellish as it must have been, had opened his eyes. Pa used to say life had a way of catching up and smacking you 'til you paid heed. He'd been right.

Then again, Mother's death had done more than hit. It had nearly destroyed them. Even after they clawed their way back, they'd never really spoken of it. There had never been good enough reason, the look in his eyes too painful. So she'd relegated any discussion to small tokens – Mother's favorite foods, funny anecdotes, memorable days. They had fiddled with the edges, avoiding the heart of the matter.

Bittersweet memories were better than nothing, she supposed. She shook her head. Maybe memories just fed the grief, even as they ate you up inside.

She didn't know. What she did know was you needed the touchstone of loved ones. Family kept you going, moving in God's grace. It was worth every sacrifice. It was worth enduring the awful hole when they were gone.

Joshua needed a rock in his life. God bless him, her boy ought not squander what lay before him. He'd best do right by Katie, and do it soon.

As for Scott, he was a work in progress. His eagerness to prove himself a man was slowly giving way to a measure of real maturity. Once he finished school, it'd only be a matter of time before he moved on. Truth be told, the thought didn't bother her as much. Spared her bouts of darkness and Wayne's temper, Scott seemed to float through life like a leaf in the creek, bouncing off the boulders. He'd find his way to the surface no matter the whims of the current.

She loved her younger son, but she didn't fret over him like her elder. She and Joshua were cut from the same cloth, prone to doubt and blue moods.

Though she worried now, his absence had been worse. When he'd gone it was like she'd lost a part of herself. At least if Josh married Katie, he'd stay near. That'd be a comfort.

Wayne hollered from upstairs. She ignored his tone. It was just a lot of bluster to say he needed her. This time he was thirsty, angry at not having water at the bedside.

"I'll be right up," she yelled. Sure enough, the glass was sitting on the bannister, right where he'd left it. She emptied the dustpan and made her way over. He could scowl all he wanted. Her husband carried an angry boy inside, acting up whenever he was frustrated. She could handle it. She had for years. It was the silence he'd leave behind that scared her.

14 - Katie

The ground flew beneath his feet as cheers propelled him down the field. A booming voice sliced through the din. "It's going long, Wolfie!"

He pulled ahead of the defender. Glimpsing the ball, he jumped. It flitted off his fingertips. Slipping to earth, his foot caught. He stumbled, clutching madly. The pigskin landed in his grasp just as he hit the ground.

The swarm of teammates overtook him as he picked himself up. He basked in their cheers.

As he trotted back upfield, Tommy moved alongside him.

Joshua glanced over. "I caught it! A touchdown!"

Tommy grabbed his arm, easing him to a halt. "I know. Great catch, buddy. But are you alright? You're acting kinda strange. That was a big hit earlier."

"What?" The field behind Tommy tilted off kilter.

Tommy waved his hand. "Look at me a sec. Buster laid you out flat at the start. You remember that, don't you?"

Joshua stopped fidgeting, the words sinking in. Tommy looked concerned. "A little," he admitted.

He recalled lying on the ground, heated words over him. Then he'd jumped up, claiming he was fine. He could take a hit. Was that what Tommy was talking about?

"Come on. Let's walk it off." Tommy guided Joshua to the side as he shouted over to the others.

Sergeant Reynolds appeared. After Tommy left to rejoin the game, he placed a hand on Joshua's shoulder. "Let's take a look, Wolfie."

"Sure." He felt giddy. Sergeant hadn't used his nickname since his first day with the unit, out on the target range.

"Follow my finger," he directed, holding it in front of Joshua before moving it off to the side.

Joshua snickered. The exercise seemed silly. He glanced back. Sergeant's eyes were hazel, and beautiful.

"Thanks. But try to focus." He touched Joshua's head, feeling his neck. "Does this hurt? Any pain at all?"

"Huh?" Had he spoken aloud? "It's tender. Guess I am a bit dizzy."

"I imagine. You have a concussion, Wolfie. Let's head to camp and get some ice on it. How's that sound?" Aiden turned him around and started walking.

"Sure, Aiden, if you say so." The sergeant's arm felt good around his shoulder.

Aiden smirked. "Guess you know my name after all. Only took a blow to the head to use it."

*   *   *

"Guess it's good we came, seeing as you're smiling." Katie nestled against him, and he wrapped his arm around her small frame. The moonshine had snuck up on them both.

He gestured toward the makeshift field where a few boys had begun to scrimmage. "Watching reminded me of the time I got a concussion in a company game. I played better, even scored. Who'd have figured?"

"Maybe you let go, trusted your instincts."

"Don't know about that. My instincts are pretty messed up."

She sat up, looking him in the eye. "I don't believe that. You've got more drive than any boy I know. You set your mind to something, and you do it. That's a gift."

He plucked a blade of grass. "I'm nothing special, Katie. You don't know . . ." The words drifted away. Her faith in him could be suffocating.

"I know *you*," she insisted, poking at his side. "That's all I need to know."

He sighed. She knew parts, but ultimately he stood alone. Still, she had a way of making him feel he was good, or good enough. "Thanks," he said, watching the next play. The less said the better.

She rested against him until the game ended. By then Chuck's crew had arrived. A couple of burly men lugged the fresh keg from the tree line while another man, scruffy and lean, lingered along the wooden fence, a shotgun by his side.

Katie spoke again. "I remember your concussion. It was before your last letter."

There it was, tactful. It wasn't even a question, though she deserved an answer. "Things got confusing," he muttered.

She stared ahead. "I imagine. You were headed to the front." She tensed. "But you're back now."

"Yeah." He thought of the distractions rippling through his head. "Making my way back."

"Good," she breathed. "Just know that I'm here." She rolled her head in a lazy arc. "And woozy at the moment. I'd better walk around." She started to rise.

The cold ground had left his leg tingly. It'd start to ache if he wasn't careful. "Maybe I should join you?" he suggested.

She offered her hand with a smile.

*   *   *

They walked to where the old lane petered out into mud at the base of the ridge. The breeze picked up, sending leaves raining down through the trees.

A herd of deer passed in silence above. "Carole's expecting," Katie whispered. "She couldn't wait to tell the girls."

She wouldn't meet his gaze, but accepted his hand.

They retraced their steps in a stiffening wind. By the time they reached the field, the thickening clouds had thinned the gathering.

"We should head back too," Katie suggested.

"Maybe Scott'll join us if he hasn't already left."

"Over there," she pointed.

Guitar in hand, Scott stood with Pete behind the wagons. They circled around to avoid the men, who were jostling as they took swigs from the keg perched on the edge.

Scott looked up as they neared. "I wondered if Katie would convince you to come."

"I just didn't tell him," she grinned.

Joshua shrugged then shook hands with Pete.

"Hey Josh . . . Katie," Pete drawled. The lanky teen had always been quiet. Today he seemed downright sheepish.

"I'm sorry about Nate," Katie offered. "Your family's been in our prayers."

He shifted his weight. "Real sorry about your cousin too."

Joshua squeezed her hand.

She glanced down at Scott's guitar. "I was beginning to wonder if I'd ever hear you. Wish we had heard more."

Scott blushed. "I hadn't planned to play in front of everyone, but figured I'd give it a shot."

"After a shot of moonshine, you mean?" Katie teased.

Scott cracked a smile. "Something like that."

Pete turned to Joshua. "Are you working in the quarry?"

"No. Been kicking around the house mostly. Though come Monday I start a job over in Head Waters, building a fireplace for an old farmer."

Pete looked puzzled.

"The leg still gives me fits," he explained. "Mom doesn't want me hobbling around with explosives."

"Well, I imagine your dad's glad to have your help however you're able."

"Yeah," he replied. It was easier.

"I'm over at the coal mine now."

"The Tuckerman mine?"

"Yeah, started this past summer. Just pickin' up shifts, but it's work. The guys gave me shit at first. Now I'm getting the hang of things. Half of it's just getting used to being underground."

"I didn't know they were hiring, struggling as they are."

"Mister Tuckerman took a liking to me, said he admired my

persistence. I bugged them every week for a month, even after they told me to get lost. Figured no one's hiring anyhow so what's the harm in asking."

"That's good news, Pete. I'm glad you got hired on."

"Me too. It's a trek, but I stay at my uncle's place when I'm working. Mom worries, 'specially after Nate. But she's doing better, I guess."

Pete didn't sound convinced. Joshua wondered about Pete as well. He'd always idolized his brother. "Maybe I'll see you around town sometime, when you're not over at the mine."

"Hope so," Pete replied.

A rifle blast rang out. Pete flinched.

Joshua nearly dove, but caught himself. He spun around.

"Hot damn!" a hulk of a man whooped. "You hammered it, you bastard."

The shooter attempted a bow, but lost his balance and staggered forward. As the rifle swung free, Joshua felt the projection sweep across them.

The scruffy man snatched the barrel. "My turn," he announced, stepping into position.

In their absence the men had placed rocks atop the wooden fence. Now the preening had begun. Joshua knew how bravado could explode into cockfights. After a night of drinking, men in the unit would come to blows over next to nothing. A gun in the mix could prove deadly. He should get Katie out of harm's way.

"What's got you all bug-eyed, bud?" the big man bellowed in his direction.

A second shot rang out. Twigs rained down from a hickory at the edge of the woods. Joshua felt his blood race. The scruffy man cursed, prompting guffaws from the other men. "I think it hit up over the ridge, Sammy!" one taunted.

His face burned. He thrust Katie's hand aside and started around the wagon.

The big man barked again. "What are you looking at? We're just having some fun. No need to get your knickers in a wad."

Joshua charged forward, but stopped when he saw Chuck.

"It's fine, CJ!" he yelled, approaching from the lane with a girl in tow. "That's my buddy Josh. He's alright."

The big man held Joshua's gaze. "He don't look alright. Looks bent outta shape over my men letting off steam."

Chuck swung his arm around Joshua, gripping his shoulder. "Nah, he's good. Josh here just got back from the war," He cast a sideways glance. "This is CJ, Josh. One of Dad's foremen."

Joshua's temple throbbed.

"He sure don't talk much, does he?" The man tossed a smirk to his buddies. "You must have got lots of practice laying out the Huns. So what do you have against a little target shoot?"

He hawked a big wad of tobacco. "Then again, maybe you weren't all that good. I noticed you gimping around with your girl."

The contempt squelched the laughter.

Joshua pulled free of Chuck. The scruffy man dropped the rifle to his side, taunting him with a sneer. Scott placed his guitar in the wagon and edged over. Pete and Katie stood motionless, worry etched on their faces.

Nausea wafted over him like the stench from no man's land. The fools thought this all meant something. A voice inside said to walk away, but he strangled it. Focused on the big man, he reached for the gun. "Well," he snapped when the scruffy man failed to hand it over.

The big man nodded. The scruffy man released it and stepped back.

Joshua sized up the rifle. It was a Winchester like the one he grew up with. A stiff breeze pelted his face as he raised the barrel. His heart pounded.

Channeling his fury, he fired three rounds in quick succession.

His breath came in shallow gasps as the shots echoed in his head. He let the barrel fall. The demons were purged for the moment.

He didn't bother looking up. Rocks were easier than men. There was no smoke or fog or screaming to confound a man's perception. The only mistakes today would come from idiots with too much moonshine and too little sense.

He handed the rifle to Chuck. "I held my own," he said. Then he glared at the men. "Don't go shooting your heads off. It isn't pretty."

The rush faded, leaving him weak. He sensed Scott at his side. Katie moved toward him. Pete slumped against the wagon. Seeing him, Joshua felt the stab of his words.

"I'm sorry," he breathed to Katie.

She tugged at him. "Let's go."

Joshua nodded then stepped to the side of the wagon. "Pete," he whispered.

Pete lifted his head.

"Go back with us?"

Pete jolted as if he'd seen a ghost. Then he moved to join them.

*   *   *

Chuck caught up to them as they reached the woods.

"Chuck . . ." Joshua began then stopped. The damage was done.

"CJ's an ass, that's all. Now I know he's a mean drunk to boot. Dad should never have promoted him. Even sober, he's a son of a bitch."

"Yeah, but . . ."

"Let it be. There ain't nothing to gain mullin' over a bully. Besides, I'm glad Katie brung ya. It's good to have you back."

"Thanks, Chuck," Katie said.

"It was good seeing everyone," Joshua added. "It's just . . . oh, nothin'." He couldn't explain.

"That's right, bud. It don't mean a thing." Chuck backed away. "I better get going. Gotta run Mia home."

He started to turn, then hesitated. "What am I thinking? Why don't you take the second wagon, Pete? I was gonna leave it for the crew. But, hell, they can get drenched for all I care. It ain't covered, but you'll get back quicker."

Pete stepped toward him. "Sure. I'll hitch her up."

"I'll help," Scott offered.

Joshua took a step, but Scott raised his arm. "Just wait. We'll handle it."

Katie pulled him back. "You two go ahead. We'll be fine."

"I'm sorry," he repeated after they'd gone.

"Stop with the apologies. They were being fools, swinging a shotgun around like a toy."

"I should have gotten you out of there. Instead I made it worse." He avoided her gaze. "You're always defending me."

She made him look. "Because I feel safe with you. I always have."

He couldn't help but laugh. Somehow she believed in him. He followed the impulse. "You want to do that forever?" he blurted.

She pulled back. "What do you mean?"

He had to be strong. "You know what I'm asking. Will you marry me?"

Her eyes widened. She said nothing at first, then her smile broke like a ray of sunshine. "Yes! Of course I'll marry you." She threw her arms around his neck.

He ignored the pain as they rocked gently. Squeezing his eyes shut, he heard the branches creak above them.

He'd left his final prayers in France, but sometimes he still hoped. There, beneath the swaying oaks, he hoped he could make her happy.

15 – Heading to Lorraine

Tommy's head drooped for the third time in as many minutes before bobbing back up. His eyes fluttered open.

"You alright there?" Joshua teased.

Tommy shrugged. "Trains always put me to sleep."

"Even cattle cars?"

"Apparently so." He sat up and looked around.

Joshua joined him in scanning the spartan rail car, one of dozens on the troop train, each packed with men. This particular one was covered. Shafts of light streamed through an open doorway and two cutouts. Calling them windows would have been too generous. Among the first aboard, they'd found themselves jostled into the interior as men piled in behind them. Seeing no chance of positioning themselves near the exposed sections, they'd scrambled for space along the sides. Tommy had managed to squeeze in, but there wasn't room for them both.

"You want to switch?" Tommy asked.

Joshua laughed. "I'm fine. I think you'll need the wall."

Sitting cross-legged on the dusty floor, he had at first strained to glimpse the countryside. Finding it impossible, he'd pulled the French phrase book from his duffel. He figured if he memorized a few expressions each day, he might have a sense of conversations among the French soldiers along the front. No one knew how much interaction they'd have, but he wanted to be prepared.

Tommy gestured at the booklet. "Guess we shouldn't have been so quick to assume we'd serve alongside the British?"

"Wasn't just us. Those weeks getting familiar with the Enfield rifle seem kind of a waste now."

"Hey, the gents gave us plenty of bayonet practice. That'll be of use. I'm hoping to get a Chauchot, though. An automatic rifle might come in handy defending myself while you're scurrying across no man's land, scouting and sniping."

"I don't know if that's gonna happen. It was just a few days of training."

"Like they're not going to make use of the best shot in the company. You think they mistakenly sent you on exercises with the British scouts? Corporal says they have plans for you, Wolfie. You'll be a sniper by the time we reach the front."

"I suppose," he acknowledged. Things did appear to be pointing that way. The British had spoken highly of his skills, calling him stealthy in the field and an uncanny marksman. He had their manual as well. Perhaps he'd be better off studying it instead of the French, but he wanted to learn the language. Reciting the phrases comforted him. He always heard Claire's gentle voice in his head. "Do you think we'll see Claire in Toul?" he asked aloud.

Tommy looked puzzled. "You mean Nurse Laurent? I hadn't considered it. Is that where she was transferring?"

"I think so," he said, feigning hesitation. He knew it to be the case; he could remember everything about that day.

"Well, I don't plan on seeing a nurse, or any medical staff, if I can help it. And you shouldn't either, whatever the intention. You have Katie."

Joshua blushed. Tommy was still marrying him off, and Joshua still played along. "I'd been wondering is all. Pretty sure Sergeant Reynolds said she'd be at Toul."

"Well, you can always ask him if you have the nerve. I'm not striking up a conversation. He might take my head off."

"Sergeant Reynolds is no worse than any other first sergeant. He just wants us to get things right."

Tommy shook his head. "Listen Wolfie. That might be so. But you aren't going to find a lot of agreement from the other men. Those glimpses, those times we saw 'Aiden.' Well, they might have been nice and all. I'm sure he's as fine a fellow as you'd want to meet outside the war. But the fact of the matter is he's been an ass since the captain promoted him. I swear even the lieutenant tensed when he wandered through the other day."

"Well, we have to be ready for what's ahead. Sergeant's seen a lot."

Tommy shrugged. "A lot of death, you mean."

Joshua shifted uncomfortably. Tommy was on edge, like all the men. They knew they'd face the enemy soon enough. If not at the front, the Germans might bring the fight to them. The Huns had been advancing all spring. Just in the past week they'd launched an offensive north of their current route.

"I shouldn't have said that," Tommy admitted. "It's just maybe the sergeant's seen too much. I can't imagine spending years on the front, only to turn around and ask for more. I'd be a mean son of a bitch. But he ought to understand. We're giving all we've got." Tommy stopped venting long enough to catch his breath. "Wolfie, I know you respect him. I do too. And I'd like nothing more than to whip the Germans and end this war. We all would. If we did, we might even see Aiden again."

Joshua nodded. Tommy had a point, but he couldn't help but defend the sergeant. Aiden seemed a loner, even among his peers. Yet he was confident and strong, traits Joshua didn't possess. Joshua always felt like the odd man out, even when he excelled. Maybe it was envy, but he couldn't get the sergeant out of his head.

Tommy began to droop again, the breeze unable to compete with the midday sun baking the train car. "Go ahead," Joshua suggested. "Grab some shut eye."

Tommy relented. "Wake me if we get a chance at an opening. I promised Mary I'd write her about the sights. Right now there's not much to say. I might as well tell her to climb into her father's corn crib to see what it's like."

"Will do," he promised before reopening the phrase book.

*　　　*　　　*

After a while the rocking motion slowed. They came to a stop, but he let Tommy be. It didn't seem worth the bother as the men crowded the openings even tighter. A few started spitting broken

French through the cutout. Straining to hear, he noticed a small hole along the side. Though merely a blur in motion, at rest it offered a sliver of view. He dipped his head and peered out.

He could make out a village square lined with shops. A cluster of women in black stood outside a store. As he watched, one stepped into the street and lifted her veil, revealing a delicate face. She called out, motioning toward the train.

Joshua couldn't hear, but his suspicion proved right. A young boy, maybe eight, meandered into view. A little girl followed, clutching his hand. As they tottered near, the woman yanked them to her side. She picked up the little girl and rejoined the other women.

Even from their brief exposure to Abbeville, the scene was familiar . . . an absence of men, scores of women in mourning. How many children of France would grow up without fathers? Could the two in the square even remember a time without war?

He found it hard to imagine, but then it struck him. The states had weathered the same in the not so distant past, losing nearly a generation of men.

Mom's father had died of natural causes, but Dad was a child of the Civil War. His father, a soldier in the Vermont Brigade, was killed at the Battle of Cold Harbor less than a year after Dad's birth. He hadn't even had a proper burial, his body lost forever in a Virginia swamp. Joshua wondered if the loss was what later drew Dad south. Of course, he didn't know. Dad never talked of his past. It had been Grandmother who'd shared the family history.

The whistle blew, startling him. Tommy stirred then nestled back into place. Joshua wondered if he'd sleep as sound on the front.

They had been back underway only a short time when men in the center of the car began shifting about, clearing a path. Seconds later, he heard the sergeant's voice. Both he and the lieutenant appeared, stopping a few feet away. Apparently the sergeant had switched cars during the stop, probably to find the lieutenant.

They were in deep discussion. The lieutenant stood largely silent, listening as the sergeant laid out plans for their arrival. They discussed the weapons exchange and billeting for the night. Then the sergeant brought up the schedule of drills, most on their own, a few joint exercises with the French as could be arranged. It was important to start fast, he explained, since it was unclear how much time they'd have before rotating into the lines. The lieutenant nodded. All in all the conversation sounded routine. They probably had discussions like this all the time, though typically away from the men.

As they continued, Joshua studied the sergeant. He had strong features – a square jaw and prominent nose. Even in profile, Joshua could feel the power of his gaze. When he grew excited or irritated, the energy rippled through his body. And his hands flew into action whenever he emphasized a point.

Watching him was mesmerizing. Aiden was handsome . . . masculine.

Joshua tore his gaze away. He fidgeted, as if caught. No one was paying attention, the men nearby listless from the motion or busy in their own conversations. Tommy remained fast asleep.

He turned his focus to the dirty floor, burying the feelings. It was a practice he'd perfected . . . automatic, instinctive. In a minute he'd convince himself it hadn't happened, like always.

Soon enough he recovered. He eavesdropped on the New York contingent nearby. They were arguing over prospects for the Giants after last October's painful series loss. He listened for a while and then glanced back at Tommy, who was nearly slack jaw. Any more relaxed and he'd probably snore.

Joshua felt the presence an instant before he heard the voice. "How're you holding up, Wolfie?" the sergeant whispered as he crouched beside him.

He smiled in spite of himself. "Good, Sergeant." He looked at and then beyond him.

The sergeant noticed. "The lieutenant went back up front. I wanted to check on you. You looked bothered."

"It's nothing, Sergeant. Just a bit cramped."

"Not for much longer; we're nearly there." The sergeant glanced about then plopped down beside him. Their shoulders touched for an instant when he leaned over. "I heard good things about your training with the scouts. They say you're a natural. How'd it feel?"

"Good. Once I knew what was expected, I did alright. It isn't all that different from turkey hunting. You have to be silent to get in close."

The sergeant chuckled, his shoulder again pressing against his. "Well, you have more than that going for you. Half the men in the unit grew up hunting, Wolfie. They aren't acing target practice."

Joshua felt the sergeant tense so he turned to face him.

Aiden's expression had turned serious. "Being a scout is risky enough, but that's just the beginning. Becoming a sniper takes discipline, not only the skills but mentally too. The guilt can weigh on a man. It's different than battle, Wolfie. A sniper hunts men." His eyes locked. "Are you ready for that?"

The bluntness surprised him. Nobody asked those kinds of questions. It never occurred to him anyone would. A soldier followed orders, always, without hesitation. The sergeant himself emphasized the point in every drill. Still, he had asked. Joshua looked around, considering the matter. He tried to picture a man in his sights, unaware, going about his business. Could he pull the trigger?

He bit his lip. "They have snipers, don't they? They'll be looking for us."

"Yes, they will. Better trained than ours probably. The Germans killed a lot of good men when things first bogged down. They were ready before we were."

Joshua looked at Tommy, still deep in slumber. This time he didn't hesitate. "I can do it, Sergeant."

"Alright, Wolfie. I believe you. I just thought someone should ask."

"Is the lieutenant making me a sniper?" he asked, confused.

"The lieutenant doesn't have much say in this. They'll be using men from across the units. Ultimately it's up to the colonel, possibly the French as well, at least for a while. And we'd have to find you a decent spotter, likely outside the company." He smirked. "Of course that British major said you didn't seem to need one.

"The long and short of it is before they decide, they'll ask me if you're ready. So you come to me if you have any doubts. You understand, Wolfie?"

"Yes, Sergeant. I understand."

The sergeant looked around the car and at Tommy, then again at Joshua. It seemed he wanted to say something more, but he rose abruptly. "I'd better get back to the lieutenant."

"Sergeant," he began.

"Yes?"

"Thanks." He hesitated, realizing he didn't have anything to add. He'd just wanted him to stay.

The sergeant winked. Then he turned and wove his way through the men.

16 – Churchville

Joshua hobbled up the incline from the quarry. Between the chill and the lifting, the twitch in his thigh had reawakened. Despite his assurances to the contrary, the leg remained weak. He might not have lasted all day.

Up top he saw Scott emerge from the shed and angle toward the house. He considered calling out, but decided against it. He might as well enjoy the moment before provoking his brother.

His eyes traced the ridge. The sky was deep blue, and the day was shaping up nicely. Too bad he wouldn't be able to enjoy it.

Scott was inside by the time Joshua reached the yard. At the porch he stomped hard before removing his muddy boots. He dropped them at the top of the steps.

"I was about to come after you," Mom scolded when he opened the door.

"Sorry. Ol' McCullough's back is acting up again so I did the bulk of the loading. They're nowhere near finished." He looked at Scott. "Dad says he's gonna need you this afternoon."

Scott slammed his mug down. "I knew it! I spend half my time studying and the rest in servitude. Can't a fellow get a few hours to himself?"

Mom cut him off. "Enough of that. You've had it good since your brother came home."

"It's just I was meeting some of the guys today."

"It's just nothing." She pointed at Joshua. "You, upstairs now. The Daltons are expecting you. Scott can take you down in the wagon." She turned back to Scott. "And you'll head straight home, young man. No lollygagging. And that guitar stays upstairs."

They knew better than to push when she was in a mood.

"I'll hitch up," Scott muttered.

Joshua let him pass then climbed the stairs. At least he'd be able to rest his leg on the ride into town.

He pulled off his work shirt and rinsed in the hall basin. In his room he found it waiting on the bed, confronting him.

He retreated to the top of the stairs. "Mom," he yelled. "Where's my suit?"

She stepped into sight, wiping her hands on a dishcloth. "The moths got to it. Your uniform's the best I could do on short notice. I ironed it for you."

"What about Scott's?"

She shook her head. "You know he's taller now. It won't fit. The uniform will do fine. Mrs. Dalton even suggested it."

"But I'm not in the service anymore," he groused, wondering if he could inspect the suit for himself.

"Once a soldier, always a soldier. Now time's a wasting. Get dressed, Josh."

He cringed. The last thing he needed was to be paraded around again. He'd damn near suffocated the Sunday Preacher Clark announced his return, what with the ladies clutching and the men glad-handing him.

Scott had returned by the time he descended.

"You look handsome," Mom observed.

Scott shrugged and gulped the last of his coffee.

She adjusted his collar. "Now have a nice time. I'm sure they're good people. Katie says they can't wait to meet you."

He found the prospect less than assuring. "Let's go," he said, letting Scott lead.

They rode in silence, and Scott picked up the pace near town. Katie and her father were on the porch, but Mrs. Dalton was nowhere to be seen.

Scott gave a friendly wave as he pulled to a stop. "You owe me," he snarled, tossing him a mock salute.

Katie met him on the front walk. She flicked a piece of lint from his shoulder. He questioned her with his eyes.

"It wasn't my idea," she whispered, confirming his suspicion.

The screen door slammed, and he heard Mrs. Dalton above.

"Are we ready?" A large hat adorned with silk roses made an appearance before she leaned over the rail. "Now that's a handsome young man!"

Mr. Dalton trotted down. "I'm ready when you are, dear." He winked. "You do look good, Joshua."

They piled into the automobile, and Joshua found himself holding a large tin of teacakes. Katie held his arm while Mrs. Dalton rattled on with her husband. She leaned back periodically to comment on their progress. "A lot of good it did washing it," she complained along a particularly muddy logging route. "That's better," she added when they reached the farm road along the valley floor.

The homes came more frequent as the lane widened near Churchville.

Mrs. Dalton adjusted her hat. "Do we have time?"

Mr. Dalton pulled out his pocket watch. "We might."

She glanced back, fluttering giddily. "You didn't tell him?"

"No, mother," Katie assured her. "You said you wanted it to be a surprise."

Joshua tensed. He looked to Katie. "What surprise?"

Even as he asked, Mr. Dalton came to a halt before a vacant storefront. "There she is!" he announced.

Joshua looked up to see the stenciled lettering for *Dalton Cash and Carry*.

"That surprise," Katie responded. "My parents are opening a new store."

Mrs. Dalton's excitement bubbled over. "We've been working toward it so long! We acquired the land last spring, and my sister introduced us to the man who built their house. Now we're nearly done!"

"It's nice," Joshua said. He tried to match her excitement but fell short. "Congratulations!" he added with more gusto.

Mrs. Dalton failed to notice, swept up in her moment. "I want to go inside, but suppose we should wait" she twittered.

"It'll be dusty," Mr. Dalton advised, "and the others will be waiting."

"You're right. There'll be time later." She glanced back. This time Joshua was ready, nodding with enthusiasm.

A few moments later they entered a curved drive before a large white foursquare with a deep porch. Mr. Dalton maneuvered the auto beneath a cluster of grand oaks, rolling to a stop among the other vehicles.

"Mr. and Mrs. McGuinty are our hosts," Mr. Dalton explained over his shoulder. "Their families have been in Churchville for generations. Dottie, Mrs. Dalton's sister, introduced us when we first approached the town council. Their word carries weight, which was essential. The other grocer in town was quite underhanded in trying to thwart us."

"A despicable man," Mrs. Dalton scowled. "Most unchristian."

"But that's behind us now," Mr. Dalton interjected.

"Yes," she agreed, sparing Joshua the tale.

They climbed out and approached the house. Mrs. Dalton appraised them on the porch, adjusting Joshua's collar. "Suffice to say we owe them a debt of gratitude. They've taken an interest in Katie and wanted to meet her fiancé."

"Yes, ma'am," he replied, the furious energy surrounding the day finally making sense. He wondered why Katie hadn't just told him, but he knew how Mrs. Dalton could be. She had probably just followed her mother's instructions to a tee.

Mr. Dalton knocked, and Katie touched his hand. "Isn't the wreath lovely?"

He nodded, mentally tracing the strands of cedar sprinkled with ribbons, chestnuts and acorns. After a delay, a vibration of footsteps raced toward the door. It swung open to reveal two boys jockeying for position. A maid in the entry hall and a man from the side parlor scurried close behind.

The man arrived first and corralled them back. "Sorry, Emma" he said to the maid, a portly black woman with silvery hair.

"That's alright, Mister Karl. Children are gonna be children."

She turned and gave a weary smile. "Please come in," she motioned. "William and Betty Jean McGuinty welcome you to their home."

Mrs. Dalton stepped in to remove her wrap, and Katie followed suit. Even with the mild weather, the old woman seemed overwhelmed with garments by the time Mr. Dalton added his topcoat to the pile. "Nothing here, ma'am," Joshua shrugged, wondering if she needed help as she made her way up the center stairs.

The next moments were a jumble of names, nods and handshakes as Mrs. Dalton introduced him to the guests assembled in the parlor. Though futile, he tried to remember a few. Mr. McGuinty was the model of an ancient patriarch, saying little but dominating the room with his mere presence. His son, Karl, had retrieved his two boys from the door. Karl's wife Nancy was a boisterous woman whose voice sliced the din like a buzz saw through hard chestnut.

Mrs. McGuinty entered a few minutes later, fresh from directing operations in the kitchen. She quickly cornered Katie and him. Wearing an expression of perpetual distrust, she peppered him with questions. The brief chat was more interview than conversation. Still, it seemed to go well.

"A quarry," she observed at one point. "Men would do well to have hard work in their youth. No wonder the war didn't frighten you. Most young men today are so timid."

Joshua pretended not to notice the glance toward her own son.

"And this gem was waiting upon your return," she concluded, her eyes lighting in genuine affection. "Our Katherine." Mrs. McGuinty didn't reach over to pinch her cheeks, but he wouldn't have been surprised if she had.

"Yes, ma'am, I suppose I was," Katie demurred.

"Well, any man worthy of Katherine is a friend of ours. Welcome, young man. Now the name is Hunter, right? Joshua Hunter?"

"Yes, ma'am. Thank you for having me."

A harsh cackle from her daughter-in-law erupted across the parlor. Mrs. McGuinty sighed. "I'd best go rescue your parents, young lady."

"She certainly likes you," he observed when she'd gone.

Katie shrugged. "She never had a daughter, and doesn't exactly see eye to eye with Nancy."

"So I gathered."

"I know this is all a bit much. Mother wouldn't let go of the idea once Mrs. McGuinty suggested meeting you."

"It's fine."

They observed the mingling in the parlor for a time before she looked over again. "Pa is going to want to talk to you about the new store."

Joshua stiffened. "Oh."

"I know I already blindsided you once today. Just hear him out." She tugged at him until he relaxed.

"I will."

"Good." She glanced about. "Will you be alright on your own? I want to find my aunt. Uncle stayed home. He's not much up for parties this year, what with Deck. But Dottie promised Mother she'd come. I imagine she's in the kitchen."

"You go ahead. I'll be here."

He made the best of it, chatting with a few guests, all of whom rotated in the McGuinty constellation through some past or current intervention. When Emma announced dinner, they dutifully assembled in the stately dining room.

He found his assigned seat across from Katie. Her parents were near the middle, along with Dottie. The buzz saw daughter-in-law beckoned her boys to the far end, near their grandfather's post. The younger, maybe all of five, climbed into his chair. His blue eyes took in the entire room before coming to rest on Joshua's uniform, where they remained most of the meal.

And what a meal it was. Mr. McGuinty offered grace in a booming bass before the first course of sweet pickles and oyster stew. The main course consisted of roast turkey with giblet gravy. Heaping bowls of candied sweet potatoes and plump peas appeared, as did baskets of steaming rolls. Fresh fruit arrived next, followed by a dessert of Christmas pudding. Mrs. McGuinty concluded the meal with a toast over cranberry juice, enjoining all to keep the faith despite the hardships of the year.

By the time the meal ended, Joshua had reached his fill in more ways than one. While the others meandered back to the parlor, he gathered a few dishes. On his second trip, Dottie met him at the door of the kitchen.

"Same ol' Joshua, only bigger," she teased. "You were always a help when we'd come up to Hadley. But I won't have that today. Now you give me those and go join the others."

Her tired eyes belied her good-natured ribbing. "I'm so sorry about Deek," he blurted. "My brother told me soon as I got off the train."

"I appreciate that. I surely do. But God has his plans, and it isn't for us to understand why." She squeezed his arm. "He brought you home, and that's a blessing. So you shoo now. Get on back to Katie. We have this all taken care of."

She vanished, but her words lingered. What plans? He recognized the trap, and cursed it. He managed a few steps before the swirl of movement and noise from the parlor repelled him. Growing dizzy, he slipped through the mudroom and out the rear door, stumbling onto the narrow stoop.

The fresh air was a relief, as was the silence. He pressed against the railing, drawing deep breaths. People were so hard. They all wanted something, needed something, needed him to be something. He couldn't keep up.

After a time he looked about. A split rail fence ran along the rear of the yard. Beyond it a field dotted with haystacks stretched to a distant line of trees. Foothills rose on the horizon, and puffy gray clouds now marred the afternoon sky.

He stared at the nearest one, mustering the nerve to return.

Two figures breezed around the corner, streaming by him. Apparently the boys had escaped the confines of the house. He watched them race to a pile of discarded lumber. The older one tugged at a busted frame, broke off a jagged piece, then carted it to a nearby patch of mud. There he emptied a sack of wooden soldiers and plopped down.

"Mom said not to dig up Grandfather's yard," the younger one warned, examining a toy airplane as he lingered near the woodpile.

"It's just mud. No one's gonna know unless you snitch."

The little boy turned warily toward the house. His eyes widened. As at the table, the uniform mesmerized him. He lifted the toy airplane and ran forward, swooping down in a mock dive. Repeating the action, he drew closer. After several iterations, he arrived at the base of the steps.

The boy kicked at the grass before whispering a shy hello.

"Hi," Joshua replied.

The boy looked up. He pointed. "What's that, mister?"

Joshua glanced down at his chest. "It's called a ribbon."

"What's it for?"

He sighed. "They say I was brave."

The boy said nothing for a moment, eyeing his toy. "Did you fly an airplane?"

Joshua shook his head. "No. I wasn't a pilot."

"Oh," he breathed, disappointed. "I want to fly when I grow up."

"I see." Joshua nodded toward the other boy. "Good idea. It's not as messy."

The boy smiled. "That's my brother Tommy. I'm William."

"Hi William. I'm Joshua. I had a buddy named Tommy."

"Over there?"

"Yep, over there. In France."

William nodded, gears turning. By then the older boy had risen and was moving toward them.

"Hey mister!" he shouted.

"Hey yourself," Joshua replied, bracing for more questions.

"That pretty girl out front was looking for you."

Joshua bounded down the steps. "Well, I guess I'd better join her then." He patted the younger boy's head. "You keep your brother outta trouble, William. And watch for nails in that woodpile."

"Yessir," the boy replied, flitting away.

Joshua knew he was in trouble when he saw her pacing on the porch.

"There you are! Mother sent me after you. Where have you been?"

He shrugged. "I needed to stretch my leg a bit. It was only a few moments."

"She was all ready to announce the engagement!"

He charged up the steps. "It's not a big deal. We don't even know them."

"I know them!"

"Then let's go in." He caught her hand before she could turn away. "Come on, Katie."

"One moment you were there, and the next you were gone."

"Katie, I was out back! The boys were in a woodpile. I got onto them."

She shook her head, but her tone softened. "You mean the demon duo found trouble again?"

"They aren't all that bad. The little one's kind of cute."

"Won't be for long if he takes after his brother. Our children won't be wild, Josh. Not if I can help it." She opened the screen. "Let's go. Mother's waiting."

The announcement was well received, but Joshua could tell Mrs. Dalton wouldn't forget. Maybe it was for the best. Why waste all those years of well-honed disdain? At least now they could return to familiar territory.

The conversation with Mr. Dalton later on was harder. He'd always given Joshua a fair shake. When he stepped away from the gentlemen and their cigars, he was kind.

"I imagine your father wants you at the quarry," he began.

"Yes, sir. He'd like that."

"Your mother tells me you help with the books too."

Joshua was cautious. "She does mostly, but I know how."

"Well, as you can imagine, taking on a new store is a lot to manage."

"I imagine so."

Mr. Dalton sighed. "Truth is, and I trust you'll keep this in confidence, we won't be keeping the store in Hadley. Our lease is coming up, and frankly it hasn't panned out as we'd hoped. That town is dying, Joshua. I know you can see that."

Joshua nodded. People didn't say it aloud, but the truth was plain.

"In the end it may not matter. God willing, we'll be settled here. And we'd like Katie close." His gaze met Joshua's. "This isn't charity, son. Shopkeeping's a profession. I'd teach you all you need to know."

Joshua scrambled despite the heads up. "I appreciate the offer, sir. I, um . . . I need to finish up the job I took. And I'll need to think it through."

"And talk to your family," Mr. Dalton added.

"Yes, sir."

"Family's important, young man. Family's everything."

"Yes, sir," he repeated, sensing it was expected.

17 - Wolfie

Joshua heard ground give way behind him, followed by dirt clods dribbling down the wooded bluff. Buster had lost his footing again.

He looked to Tommy. With his face covered in face paint and mud, all Joshua could see was his eyes. They were filled with irritation. He could hear Tommy's thoughts . . . Corporal made you the lead, so lead already. The daylight raid was risky enough without Buster's lumbering giving them away.

He checked their progress. Nico was close behind. Buster wasn't even halfway up. There wasn't time. Joshua sliced a hand across his throat.

Buster's eyes narrowed, but he held position.

Joshua glanced up. No men had appeared so they were still a go.

Continuing the climb, he saw the church belfry come into view. What was left of it, that is. Half had been blasted away, and the steeple was gone. Near the top they dealt with thorn bushes, the added cover not worth the nuisance. Crawling through without rustling them was damn near impossible. They had no choice but to inch along. Too fast and they'd be discovered. Too slow and Smitty's team on the far side risked exposure.

Finally they reached the crest. Slipping his helmet off, he peered over. Two men with shovels. Beyond them sat the church, a chuck of wall missing. A clean shot, if they got past the men.

They waited. As he and Smitty had hoped when plotting the raid, the men weren't on watch. They'd begun a shallow trench, preparing for nightfall. Still the men faced them. If Smitty sacrificed his team to provide a distraction, the win would be hollow.

Nico crawled up between them just as an opportunity appeared. The duo dropped their shovels and turned in unison, listening to a man out front.

Joshua pointed to Nico. "Ready" he mouthed. When the men

took a few steps, he made his move. Nico followed. Racing silently they overtook the men from behind, tapping them with their rifles. The men turned in shock.

"You're dead," Joshua whispered. For a second he thought the second man might yell, breaking the rules. But then he saw the corporal with the clipboard over to the side. The kills had been noted.

Tommy joined them. Together, they scurried through the broken wall. Inside they navigated the rubble from the collapsed roof. The ribbon lay draped across the altar, as they'd been told.

Tommy snatched it. "Yes!" he yelled. Silence was no longer necessary. They'd met the objective.

They swung open the entry doors, surprising others from the defending team. "Wildcats!" Nico yelped, swinging the ribbon high. Two corporals by the trees broke into grins. Even Sergeant Reynolds cracked a smile.

A minute later Smitty led his team and a handful of their own kills from the woods. Despite the more heavily defended approach, even they'd managed to chip away at the enemy positions. The defending unit hadn't considered a day raid, so busy preparing for the night. Not a single man had been lost. It had to be a first.

Gathering them in the shade of the bombed-out church a few minutes later, Sergeant Reynolds acknowledged as much. Addressing both units, he heaped more praise in ten minutes than he'd given since joining the company. "Don't expect the Huns to run by your clock or follow your map. A daylight raid with a limited number of men is risky as hell, but can work if executed well. You must always be on alert. There is no downtime. No safe place. This is war, men."

He called out Smitty and Joshua by name. "Bold thinking like yours today will lead us to victory in the coming months."

Tommy nudged him. "Atta boy, Wolfie. We may win the competition yet."

Not everyone was happy. "Send him out with scouts a few times, and he thinks he's a tactical wiz," Buster snarled as they made their way to the temporary camp along the river.

Joshua said nothing, having learned to ignore him.

Nico's defense came as a surprise. He and Buster were always in cahoots. "Let it go, Buster. You know you would have given us away. Wolfie just made the call."

Buster sneered. "And I'm making one now. To hell with this crap smeared all over me. I'm heading to that pond we saw this morning."

Tommy glanced about. "You sure you oughta?"

"You heard the corporal! That was the last of it, least 'til dawn. Then another day of wallowing in the mud. Don't know why they had to march our asses way out here to begin with. So the Germans held this patch of forest for a few months at the start of the war. Like I care. A couple of bombed out buildings." He shivered. "Ooohh. It's all so much scarier now."

The other men wandered ahead, but McKenzie held back. "I'm in." He jabbed at Tommy. "What about you, Babyface? I know you want to. But you can run on along, Wolfie." He laughed. "Sergeant's pet."

Joshua exchanged glances with Tommy. He'd have left, but then he didn't need to fit like Tommy. Even so, he'd promised to stick by him. "I'll go. What are we waiting for?"

The rest of the men were proceeding up the draw. A couple hundred yards behind, another unit was moving up. If they were going to sneak off, now was the time.

Without a word they slipped over the crest. That's all it took. Nico and Buster exchanged glances. McKenzie smirked when he caught Joshua's eye.

He knew he'd been goaded into coming, but three days of competition drills had taken their toll. Between the grime and the bugs, he'd hardly been able to sleep. He found himself rushing, anticipating the water.

* * *

The pond wasn't natural. A run had been damned off at the corner of an old pasture, forming more of a mud hole than anything.

Still, the surface glistened in the sun, beckoning. Ten minutes and they'd be on their way.

He and Tommy moved onto the slope along the side. With the earthen dam seeping from neglect, the pond was lower than normal, maybe a couple feet. Across the middle the water turned sorghum brown. Lilies covered the edges. Weeds littered the narrow bank.

"What are you waiting on?" McKenzie called out, already stripping. He tossed aside his boots then removed his shirt in a single motion.

Nico raced him. He unbuckled his belt and dropped his pants.

Joshua glanced back, wondering if they'd been seen. He looked again at the pond. There was a chain below him. Thick and rusty, coiled up partly in water and partly in weeds. The links disappeared beneath the lilies.

"Come on!" Tommy hissed, removing his shirt. Nico was down to his skivvies, waiting on McKenzie. Buster had removed his boots.

Crouching down to unlace his own, he could see better. The chain continued into the deep, but not on the ground. It was suspended, like it was attached to something. He followed the line to the other side.

The chain was there too, underwater, but visible between lilies near the bank. Hobbling closer didn't help. The water was too dark to see the center.

He glanced up. Nico and McKenzie were jostling each other, laughing. They weren't intending to wade in. He could tell they would jump.

It was all instinct after that. They started to run, Nico in the lead. Joshua sprang forward, tackling him as he leapt. He felt McKenzie clip his calf.

"What the hell?" Nico yelled. He popped up, brushing grass from his torso. He rubbed his shoulder. "Trying to break my arm or something?"

McKenzie lay sprawled in the mud along the bank. He got to his feet, limping off to the side. "I think the wolf is back," he muttered.

Joshua rolled over. He started to rise.

Buster pounced, pinning him to the ground. "No, just a mad dog. And someone needs to put him down hard!" He raised his fist.

Joshua covered his face. Tommy shouted but was in no position to prevent the pummeling.

Someone else was. The sergeant appeared from nowhere, grabbing Buster's fist and twisting his arm around. "Now you're going to calm yourself, soldier. Right now! You hear?"

Buster winced, nodding. The sergeant held tight as he rose.

"Now step away," the sergeant ordered. Buster complied.

The sergeant looked down at Joshua. His eyes were on fire, but his tone was even. "You get up too."

Joshua scrambled to his feet, casting a sheepish glance at Tommy. They all had to think he was crazy.

The sergeant's fury exploded. "What a bunch of lame ass fools! Not even an hour ago I'm singing your praises. And now this? You think this is a game?" He looked at Nico. "Like you're sneaking onto the ferris wheel at Coney Island. You think you're twelve again?"

Nico looked at the ground.

"I asked you a question!"

Nico snapped to. "No, Sergeant!"

"Well, you sure act like it." His scowl condemned them all. "This war needs men, not a bunch of kids off playing in the woods. Because the boys who think like that are all rotting out in no man's land. Or will be!"

His eyes drilled Joshua. "I thought you were smarter than this." He glanced at the others. "Are you smarter than this?"

There was a hesitation. The sergeant cocked his head.

"Yes, Sergeant!" they barked in unison.

"Good."

The sergeant took a deep breath. He stomped around for several seconds, shaking his head, getting in their faces but saying nothing.

Eventually he calmed. His gaze rose to the hazy sky then fell to the pond. He spoke to Nico. "Been a long six weeks since you landed, hasn't it?"

Nico failed to answer, but the sergeant let it slide. He shifted his focus to McKenzie. "No leave like some of the other units. No women either. That right?"

McKenzie stiffened. "Yes, Sergeant."

The sergeant again faced Nico. "You are already naked, I guess." He sighed. "Have at it, soldier."

Nico dropped his shoulders and took a halting step.

"What are you waiting on?"

Nico peered over the bluff.

"If you're gonna do it, then do it. Jump."

Joshua jolted. Something still wasn't right. "No, Sergeant!"

The sergeant spun around. Behind him Buster stifled a smirk.

"What did you say?" The fire had returned.

"I said 'No, sergeant.'" He pleaded with his eyes then shifted his gaze to the bank, toward the chain.

The sergeant furrowed his brow. He turned toward the pond. At first he didn't see, but Joshua could tell when he did. He took a step and dipped his head.

Jumping down onto the bank, he brushed past McKenzie. At the water's edge, he crouched. When he rose, he looked back.

Joshua gave a nod toward the opposite side.

The sergeant again followed his gaze. He squinted at the water then studied the bank. Reaching down, he pulled a long stick from the weeds. He motioned with his palm. "Back up."

McKenzie scrambled up from the bank. No one else made a sound.

The sergeant waded out, dipping the stick into the water.

He eased forward, waving the stick slowly beneath the surface. A couple yards out it struck something. Pulling back sharply, he waited. Then he leaned over, peering into the deep.

"Get down here, McKenzie."

McKenzie took a tentative step.

"I said get down here. We don't have all day."

McKenzie leapt onto the bank. He entered the water as the sergeant retrieved the chain from beneath the lilies.

Together they pulled, a light tug at first, followed by a stronger yank. The slightest of eddies whirled in the center.

"Higgins! Hunter! Over there!"

Buster was confused, but Joshua understood. He led the way to the far side.

They pulled in unison, moving toward Tommy. Joshua watched the water. More eddies, then an object broke the surface. The edge of a blade. Then another, followed by a row of spikes. Tommy's mouth opened. He could see better.

"Again!"

This time something broke free. The whole contraption snapped forward before sinking into the mud.

Additional tugs brought it to the edge of the bank. They rose, taking it in. Between them lay a series of plowshares and wide hay rakes. They'd been mounted to a sheet of metal, all the blades and spikes facing up.

They joined Tommy in the grass.

Nico grew pale. "I would have . . ." he breathed, but didn't finish the thought. McKenzie looked like he might puke.

"Good eye, Wolfie," the sergeant whispered. Then he addressed them all. "And that, men, is a booby trap, a little gift from the Huns. A crude one, but it would do the job." He clinched his jaw. "Just a swimming hole. What could go wrong?"

He kicked Nico's boots. "Now get your asses to camp before the lieutenant catches you."

With that he was gone, leaving them alone in the field.

They said nothing as Nico and McKenzie dressed. They would say nothing all the way back. But as they retreated, Joshua stole a final glance. The menacing blades, honed with care, caught the light. Yet beyond them the pond sparkled, beckoning still.

18 - The Stone Cabin

Joshua charged up the ridge, planting his cane like a walking stick. He avoided a large outcropping near the top, but still found himself hobbling over a few jagged spots. It wasn't as painful as he'd expected.

Moving onto the northern face, he was surprised to see the fault line so close. The more direct route had indeed proven easier. Begrudgingly, he admitted the cane might also have helped.

Bringing it had been a last minute decision. After the stuffy service during which Preacher Clark announced the engagement, he'd needed to escape. Relying on a prop was weak, but his desire to see the stone cabin had won out. He didn't want to be worn ragged this time.

He trudged through a patch of mountain laurel and onto the steeper slope near the fault line. Reaching the boulders, he wove his way though the stone maze. Beyond them the ground was blanketed with spruce needles.

The air grew still. Soft light filtered down.

He paused to observe the stand. The oldest trees stood sentry at its heart, guarding the cabin. He moved toward them, glimpsing the chimney just as he penetrated their ranks. When he reached the fallen giant from before, he slumped against its trunk.

Silence enveloped him.

He studied the dense branches against the pale sky. Then his gaze fell to the second line of boulders farther along. Chuck had called the niche a spruce cradle, and the description fit in more ways than one. Not only did the ledge shelter the spruces, but one felt safe among them.

Calmer now, he began to circle the cabin. His earlier impressions had been correct. The basic stone structure was sound. The wood components were free of rot, though the upper jamb of one window had pulled free, causing a sash to hang loose. Several panes were also cracked. Neither repair would be difficult.

He noted only one serious flaw. The fallen spruce must have clipped a rear corner. Its glancing blow had snapped the wall cap, allowing the rafters to sag. Stones littered the ground, calling attention to the breach.

He pulled aside the rotted section of spruce before finishing his sweep. Returning to the front, he approached the door. A tangle of wire secured the knob to the trim. He untwisted the rusty strand then pushed gently.

The door failed to budge, having frozen tight within the frame.

He shoved again, harder. This time it swung open. A squirrel confronted him with a raspy bark then bolted up the wall, exiting through the exposed corner.

Stepping inside, he surveyed the interior. It was brighter than expected and, other than a smattering of old cones, empty. A whisper of ashes swirled a pattern across the simple hearth, indicating the fireplace had once been used. The windowpanes, though caked in dirt, offered glimpses of the surrounding trees.

With a few repairs, it could be habitable.

Maybe I could just stay here.

His heart stumbled upon the ragged truth, breaking the spell.

He retreated. Pulling the door shut behind him, he fell back against it.

"Please," he begged, not sure to whom.

He waited.

After a time, he pushed off. The world was tugging him back. Why had he even come?

He'd taken a few steps when he again observed the stones beneath the rear corner.

This time he followed instinct. He shuffled over, propped his cane against the wall and then fell to his knees. Ignoring the tightness in his thigh, he gathered them. Perhaps he could linger a while. After all, there was work to be done.

19 – Aiden

Sunlight flickered across Joshua's face as the truck breezed through the wooded dale. They passed fields overgrown and orchards unkempt. Though the abandoned farms were eerie, they hinted at things normal.

Leaving the support area before dawn, it had been too dark to see. Now, with the haze of the front rising ahead, he drank in the summery sights as if he could save them for later.

He'd been like that lately. The days were long and harsh. But in rare quiet moments he'd find himself struck by common things – wind whistling at night, rain gusting in a storm, sausages sizzling on a griddle. He knew the clock was ticking. Some units had already rotated up. Their time was coming.

"You up for a pint?" the sergeant asked, interrupting his thoughts.

Joshua furrowed his brow. The road would be as empty heading back as it had been on the way out. Curious, he bit. "I guess."

He glanced back for a hidden stash among the crates of rifle sights. "You pulling my leg, Sergeant?"

"I asked, didn't I? The drill's not 'til tomorrow, and I'm starved. There has to be a pub in one of the nearby villages. Besides, it's your birthday, right?"

"How did you . . .?" Joshua stopped, realizing he'd only get another cryptic response. "Yes, Sergeant. I'm nineteen today." He ventured a grin. "If you order it, I don't have a choice."

"Hold on then!"

Joshua grabbed the frame as the sergeant swerved onto a side road.

After the turn, the sergeant leaned over. "Aiden," he whispered, like it was a secret.

Joshua nodded. "Aiden."

Sergeant Reynolds, Aiden, was a mystery. Stern and impenetrable since joining the company, the men either feared him or hated him. Or, as Joshua suspected, some of both.

With his battle experience, it had made sense when the captain named him first sergeant. But he'd chafed egos among the officers by taking full advantage of the position, staging exercises more elaborate and grueling than anything the British had conducted.

Joshua had heard him discussing the matter with a fellow sergeant shortly after their arrival in Lorraine. "Respect won't come easy. We have to prove ourselves to the Allies," he'd said.

As the division prepared to integrate with the French along the Woevre front, Joshua could only hope he was right.

By all accounts their particular company was ready. They still awaited some vaguely promised reward from having won the regimental competition the week prior.

The objective of tomorrow's drill remained a mystery. But it would involve everything from a full-scale assault to hidden sniper teams, which prompted their current errand. The regiment had been expecting rifle sights for weeks. Irked by the delays, the sergeant had traded a few favors for extras in the adjoining sector.

That was like the sergeant. He knew how to get things done, but rubbed some the wrong way. It wasn't only officers he'd bruised. He was prone to blistering critiques, dressing down men who failed to meet his impossible standards. "Lives are on the line, and you just killed your buddy," he'd yell if a man hesitated during a key mission.

Truth be told, the sergeant's fury scared Joshua too. He hadn't forgotten the fire in his eyes that day by the pond. If he hadn't met him at the triage training, he might have doubted the gesture now. But he knew the sergeant was more than a disciplinarian drilling them every waking hour. At times Aiden had gone out of his way to remind him – greeting him at the range his first day with the company, attending to him after the concussion, approaching him on the troop train.

Apparently that Aiden was back for a while. So Joshua settled back for the ride. He intended to enjoy the visit.

Entering the village twenty minutes later, they passed military vehicles outside a café. Aiden never slowed, his eyes darting about as if seeking someplace particular among the narrow cobblestone streets. Just as they seemed destined to pass clear through town, Joshua glimpsed a hanging sign for "Le Bar de Loup" at the end of a cluster of shops.

Aiden saw it too. He pulled alongside an old fence beyond the row of buildings. "This'll do," he said simply.

As they made their way to the pub, Aiden continued to glance about. "We can sit back there," he suggested, pointing to a cluster of outdoor tables behind the pub. "Don't want to lose our sights to another unit."

The unease puzzled Joshua. Absent the hum of the automobile, they could hear the thunder of distant shells.

Was it guilt? Joshua sure didn't feel any. The war could wait. Leaving support for a few hours was already the best birthday he could have hoped for. The prospect of a meal and a draft left him nearly giddy. His only concern was the opportunity slipping away if the sergeant changed his mind.

Unlikely as that might be, he reacted. Leaping the mangled iron fence, he grabbed a seat along the wall. "Here, this way we can both keep an eye out."

Aiden's frown dissolved. "So we can." Then he swung over the fence to join him.

*   *   *

"Deux autres bières, s'il vous plaît!" Aiden called out, catching the sullen waitress before she disappeared again.

The conversation had flowed as smooth and light as the amber Aiden continued to order even after their meal, some creamy concoction with carrots, onions and a bit of pork. Though Aiden hadn't said much, he'd peppered Joshua with questions about nearly everything – Hadley, his family, even his impressions of men in the unit.

Joshua, for his part, basked in the attention. Talking to the sergeant was easy, natural. Aiden might be ice cold day to day, but he could be charming when he melted.

"You seem happy," Aiden observed when Joshua paused for a gulp of warm ale.

He looked around. "I am. I mean we're sitting here. Beer. Good food. Thanks for ordering. And to think Nurse Laurent said you avoid speaking French."

Aiden cocked his head. "I know you notice me, Wolfie. But do you remember everything too?"

Joshua shifted. It was true. The sergeant fascinated him. He could recall every encounter, clear as day.

Aiden let him off the hook, not waiting for a response. "I do speak more French than I let on. You don't join the Foreign Legion and not learn the language, at least passably." He laughed. "I pretend when I'm with Claire. I don't have to do as much talking then, yet I still get my drinks." He took a gulp of his draft. "She probably wants us out of here," he muttered.

"Nurse Laurent?" Joshua asked, baffled.

"The waitress. She keeps glancing out here like she wants us gone."

Joshua looked about. "We are the only ones."

"I meant generally." He set his beer down. "Villages like this have been caught in the war seems like forever. They evacuated the ones outside Verdun when the battle started. Most civilians made it out. Good thing too. Their houses were shelled. Streets were blown to bits. Bodies were left where they fell, buried only by more fighting.

"Villages hundreds of years old were taken then retaken over the course of days, weeks, weeks that stretched into months. In the end the front barely shifted. But the towns are gone. All that remains is rubble and ravaged fields. Claire's home above Toul is no different. German fortifications slice right through the middle."

Joshua sat up. "Remenauville? McKenzie mentioned it the other day. He said it was all busted up, hardly nothing standing."

"Yes. Yet her mother thinks she's coming home someday. But

with all the shells, the mines and the poisons . . . well, there'll be nothing left to return to, even when it all bloody hell ends.

"Can you imagine how it is for them? France may be glad we're here. They'll line the streets in Paris for the Fourth next week, cheering us like we're back home. But these villagers probably resent us as much as the Germans. To them, our being here simply means it isn't over."

The bluntness took him aback. "But we can change that. It's why we're here. That's what you tell the men. It's why you're here too, isn't it?"

The sergeant stiffened. "Private," he began, then shook his head. "Wolfie. I'm not sure I ought to be doing this. I've never done anything . . . social, with a man in my command. I can't afford to lose the men's respect." He weighed his words. "You're absolutely right. We're here for a noble cause."

The rebuke stung. What could he have done wrong?

He felt the sergeant studying him. "It's not like I'm gonna say anything," he blurted. "You asked me if I want lunch, and now we're talking. You asked me! You bring me here and ask all sorts of questions, yet I still don't know anything about you. I just want to know you too!" He downed the rest of his beer.

The sergeant laughed. "So there is a voice in there when you let it out, isn't there? Like the other day by the pond. Now that's what I expect from a sharpshooter."

Joshua bristled.

The sergeant leaned in. "Wolfie, look at me."

He complied.

"You're right. I keep tugging, but not giving much back. I'm cautious. Always have been, especially around the men." The waitress made an appearance, and he motioned for the check. His hands were shaking as he fished coins from his pocket. "This is different for me," he said after she'd gone.

Joshua nodded, trying to understand. "It's fine, really."

Aiden's smile returned. "You in the mood for some plums? I've been thinking about them since we passed those abandoned farms.

Some had orchards."

It was Joshua's turn to laugh. "Sure," he said.

"Good." Then the sergeant rose like nothing had happened. Still, he faced him as they neared the truck. "I'll answer your questions, Wolfie . . . promise. I'll tell you what I can."

*   ＊   ＊   ＊*

The orchard sat a couple hundred yards off the road, beyond a barn. Aiden rolled to a stop and glanced about. Satisfied no one was around, he opened the throttle and sped by the makeshift barrier.

Joshua chuckled. It felt devilish, like the time he and Scott had snuck into the boarded up tavern shortly after state prohibition. The liquor had been cleaned out, but it hadn't mattered. They'd simply wandered around the darkened interior. Back home he still had a shot glass from beneath the bar, a trophy of the illicit deed.

Rolling to a stop behind the barn, they tumbled out and made their way through tall grasses to the fruit trees. The branches were heavy with a pale yellow fruit.

Joshua plucked one and sniffed it. He could tell it was a plum, but the musky sweetness was new to him.

"They're called mirabelles," Aiden explained. "Best dessert I ever tasted was made with them, a tart. It was shortly after I arrived in France. Now I crave them every summer."

"Are they ripe?"

"It's early, but some are. Look for deep yellow ones, and ones flecked with red. Come August they'll be dropping from the trees, their nectar sweet as honey. Even now they'll be better than any plum you've tasted. I'd love to take some back, but we'd better not. Let's grab some and head to the barn." He pulled off his cap and moved to a nearby branch.

A few minutes later, they entered the cool shadows of the barn. They climbed to the upper level and found an open perch. Joshua nibbled at the first plum. The skin was tart, the flesh juicy and sweet. He licked the syrup dribbling down his wrist.

Aiden tossed a pit out the opening. "Good, isn't it?"

"Delicious," Joshua agreed.

"I always thought blueberries were my favorite fruit. My sister and I used to pick them on Long Island when we were little. But if I ever go home, I want to bring some mirabelles." He sighed. "Maybe I'll start an orchard or something."

"Where's home?"

"Oh, if I only knew. New York City. Boston. It was London for a while." He tugged at the chain around his neck. "My mother's insufferably Irish. She mailed a Saint Christopher medal after I joined the legion, but it didn't come with instructions."

"Where's your family now?"

"Boston for the moment. But I won't be going there."

"Why not?"

"Because I can't. My father made that clear. Besides, I'd want to see my sister. Sarah's in New York so maybe I'd head there."

"Did she marry?"

"No. She's in a hospital . . . an institution." He took another plum from his cap. "Sarah came down with meningitis when she was twelve, hasn't been the same since. She can't talk anymore. Plus she has nightmares and horrible tantrums.

"Mother tried to care for her, but she kept getting worse. My father found a place for her. We were in Manhattan at the time, so he had connections." He devoured another plum, gazing across the field. "My father has lots of connections."

Joshua turned to let his legs dangle out. "I'm sorry about your sister." He hesitated. "Is that why you and your dad don't get along?"

Aiden plopped down beside him. "No. That came later. I wasn't happy about Sarah. But it crushed my mother seeing her like that." He flung the pit toward a tall oak, just missing a low branch. "Sarah's why I wanted to be a doctor though. I had this idea I could heal her, that I'd find a way to make her better."

"So how did you end up in France?"

Aiden shrugged. "Ego, I guess. Some perverse sense of revenge. At the time I said it was for the money."

Joshua looked over, unable to mask his confusion.

"I was angry. My father stopped paying for medical school, and I wanted to prove something . . . to him, maybe to myself too. So I joined the legion. Then I landed, sank, nearly drowned." He shook his head. "I was way in over my head. But the war has a way of straightening you out, if it doesn't kill you first. I made a few friends. Saved money too, enough to go back to school."

"So why didn't you?"

Aiden rose, lost in thought. He stepped into the shadows.

"Why didn't you go back?" Joshua asked again as he moved farther away.

Aiden turned to face him. "Because I'm good at this. I know what it takes to win battles. I can teach men how. So many have died, including men I cared about. If I leave before it ends, I'll have let them down. I have to stay until it's finished."

"And your sister?"

Aiden drew a deep breath. "I can't save her. She's too far gone." He looked down. "She doesn't even know me now."

After that he grew silent.

Unsure what to say, Joshua ate another plum and studied the orchard. The trees glowed yellow in the late afternoon sun.

He felt Aiden kneel beside him, near enough to touch. He grew flush, but didn't bury the feelings. Not this time.

Aiden locked eyes when he turned. "I notice you too," he breathed. Then he sprung up. "We should get back."

Joshua rose, dizzy from the rush.

Aiden brushed his hand. "Wolfie?" he began.

"Yes?"

"The company's getting leave after tomorrow's drill, passes to Paris. They've been preparing them since the competition. We'll be moving up when we return. I asked Claire to come, and she received permission." He faced him again. "I'd like you to join us, but nobody can know. You'd have to avoid them."

Joshua's heart pounded. He started to speak, but Aiden shushed him.

"Please don't say anything. Just think about it. The men will all take the morning train. We'll be on the 2:20. If you choose to come, you can meet us at the station."

20 – Dinner with the Daltons

Elisabeth couldn't recall ever seeing a sky so orange. In spite of the cold, she tilted her head out the truck window for a clearer view. The hue deepened as she watched, providing a bold backdrop to the bare trees along the lane.

She started to point it out to Wayne, but his scowl dissuaded her. It was a shame. He looked handsome in a suit, yet hated wearing one. She'd made the latest alterations in the blind so as not to provoke him. Fortunately she had an eye for fit.

Wayne had put on weight over the years, but he was shedding pounds now. Last time he'd joined her at service, folks had even complimented him. Except Eloise Pipken. Having buried her father the year before, she knew the signs. When pressed later, Elisabeth's frown gave up the truth before she uttered a word.

At the base of the ridge, they crossed the creek and made the turn toward town. The sky before them was purply blue now, but the orange still glowed behind. She glanced back and smiled. Pa had always appreciated a good sunset. He used to venture onto the porch whenever he noticed a particularly beautiful one. He'd have liked this one.

Turning forward, she realized Wayne was watching her.

"What?" she asked.

"They're not a lick better than us."

"The Daltons? Honey, I know that. No one said they were."

"Then why'd I have to get all gussied up? Why'd you have Scott wipe down the truck? We buy provisions from them, Eli. I don't have to impress them."

She sighed. "They invited us to dinner in their own home. Their daughter is marrying our son. I thought it would be nice." She ran her hands across her skirt, smoothing out the flowery print. "This is nice, isn't it? I used to wear it to the dances in Eufaula. I was surprised it still fit. Do you remember?"

He pulled to a stop in front of the Daltons' home. "I thought it looked familiar," he muttered before opening his door. She waited as he walked around the back.

"What time is it?" she called out.

He pulled out his watch. "Quarter after five. Why?"

She fumbled with her shawl and climbed out. "We're early, that's why. Olympia asked us to come at half past."

"I'm starving. Do they always eat at this hour? If I'd known, I could have worked 'til dark."

"And then we'd be late. Besides, I imagine they do dine later than most folks, what with the store." She glanced at the house to make sure they hadn't made a spectacle of themselves. "Honey, please. Let's walk for a bit. Look at that sky. Isn't it beautiful?"

She reached for him and was relieved when he took her hand.

Wayne said nothing, but seemed calmer. They passed the abandoned shanties. Light flickered inside the Morrisons' home. The street was empty, and the twilight silent. Even after fifteen years, she had never quite reconciled how haunting mountain stillness could be.

"You cold?" he asked.

"I'm fine."

"You shivered."

She laughed. "I didn't notice." He held her gaze. "Really, it's nothing."

The concern was fleeting. By the time they turned to retrace their steps, she felt him pulling away again.

As they neared the gate, she remembered the wreath. Rushing to the truck, she pulled the box from behind the seat. "I thought I'd make one for your mother too, if I can find the time before she arrives."

She heard the knock as she turned. He'd plunged ahead like always.

She scurried onto the porch as George Dalton opened the door. "Whoa, the mercury is plummeting! Please, come in."

Olympia appeared as he took their coats. She had outdone

herself . . . hair up, pearl earrings and necklace. "I'm just finishing up. Goodness, George, take them in by the fire."

"I'm working on it," he assured her, gesturing them into the parlor.

Elisabeth handed her the gift.

"Should I?" Olympia asked, and Elisabeth nodded.

Olympia seemed pleased when she opened it. "It's pretty. Look, George."

"Can I help with anything?" Elisabeth offered, but Olympia waived her off as she retreated toward the kitchen. "Don't you dare. Katie and I have it covered."

"Hi, Mrs. Hunter," she called out.

"Evening, Katie," she echoed back as she took a seat near the hearth.

They exchanged pleasantries. Soon George and Wayne were deep in conversation, rattling on about a recent brawl at one of the logging camps by the river. "They have to stop that flow of moonshine," she heard George say as she took in the room.

The furnishings were ornate, stately mahogany pieces and a plush sofa with an intricate pattern of red and gold. Picture frames rested on the mantle.

In one photograph Olympia sat in a studio, an infant Katie in her arms. In another a young Olympia with flowing locks stood beside another girl on a white-railed porch, scrub oaks and a marshy glade behind them. The one of George was taken outside a gothic brick building. He was clutching a trophy awkwardly so as not to block his fraternity sweater.

Katie appeared at the doorway. "The wreath is lovely," she whispered. George looked up. "Mother says dinner is ready," she announced.

Elisabeth rose. Katie had always been a nice girl. Somewhere along the way she'd become a young woman.

"Are you joining us?" Elisabeth asked.

"Oh, no. I'm off to see Louisa Jenkins. Mother wanted time for you all to visit on your own."

George started toward the entry. "I'll walk you . . ."

"Pa, it's three doors down. I think I can manage."

George caught Elisabeth's eye, and she laughed. "What can you do?"

*   *   *

The dining room was as fine as the parlor, if not more so. Velvet draperies framed the windows. A delicate lace runner adorned the glossy table, which glistened in the glow from three large oil lamps with ruby red bases. The place settings consisted of fine silver, bone china and Fostoria crystal.

"I hope the ham is moist," Olympia explained after they were seated. "I've been known to overcook it."

"It looks perfect," Elisabeth offered. "Everything does."

"Grace?" Olympia asked, looking to George.

He said a few words about old friends and new family before blessing the meal. Then he smiled. "Now let's eat. I'm famished." Wayne chuckled, seeming to have warmed to the occasion. Then again, he might just have been hungry.

The ham was a tad dry though the maple glaze was flavorful, as were the beans and sweet potatoes. As they dined, light conversation gave way to weightier topics. At one point Olympia blasted the rise in crime. "It's disgusting. They come into our communities, claiming they want work. Then they prey upon locals when they get themselves in a bind."

She gorged herself on anger for several minutes as they looked on.

When she paused for a sip of tea, Elisabeth saw her chance. "Katie's grown into an impressive young woman. Her new hairstyle is so poised."

Olympia beamed. "Yes! I finally convinced her to trim those schoolgirl bangs. She resisted, but I think she rather likes it now. The girl can be so obstinate, and her mind goes everywhere. Lately she has it in her head to become a teacher."

George winked at his wife. "She takes after someone else I know."

Olympia pursed her lips, but softened when he touched her hand. She set her glass down and launched anew. "Speaking of ideas, Katie and I have been discussing the wedding."

Elisabeth sighed inside, realizing she'd changed only the subject, not the format, of the conversation. Still, hearing about the nuptials was better than enduring another political diatribe.

It seemed Katie, or rather Olympia, had made a few decisions. The wedding was set for the fourteenth of June in Churchville, at the McGuintys' home. The ceremony would be outside, under a large tent. A reception would follow inside the home. Olympia then pinned them down on their expected attendees, visibly pleased at the small number, as they anticipated a large following on their side of the aisle.

The June date worried Elisabeth, but she said nothing. Wayne was hellbent that no one was to know of the "lying" doctor's prognosis. If he had no objection, what was she to do? Glancing over, she saw his scowl had returned. He paid scant attention, stewing as he devoured a second helping of ham.

"Have you been to The Hearthstone Inn?" Olympia asked, drawing her back.

Elisabeth took up the slack. "No, we drove down that way years ago. We picnicked at Warm Springs, but didn't make it further.

"Well, it's delightful. I know it's a bit expensive, but they really ought to consider it. A young couple should have something to remember, something special. George and I honeymooned in Charleston for a week, my family being from South Carolina originally."

"Is that where the photograph was taken, the one on the mantle?"

"Yes, my sister Dottie and I used to summer on Hunter Island. That was taken at my grandparents' cottage."

Elisabeth turned to George. "Is that where you met?"

He started to respond, but Olympia was on a roll. "No, George and I met in Richmond. My family moved there when I was sixteen."

She skipped a beat, glancing at her husband. "My father was a surgeon, and he opened a new practice."

George cut in. "My family owns a dry goods operation in Richmond. After learning the business, I wanted my own store." He sighed. "My father wasn't keen on the idea. I have four older brothers, and he holds certain notions. Olympia convinced me to strike out on my own."

"We're starting small, but we have big plans," Olympia added.

George eyed his wife, then changed the subject. "Olympia tells me you hail from Alabama. What part?"

Elisabeth nodded. "Adeleine. It's a tiny crossroads outside Eufaula."

"Is that where you met Elisabeth, Wayne?" George asked.

Wayne set down his fork. "Yes, in Eufaula. She was at the market." He grinned, more to himself than to any of them. "She had the prettiest eyes I'd ever seen."

Elisabeth clasped his hand, confused by his shifting moods all evening.

"So you're from Alabama as well?" Olympia pressed.

"No. I was born and bred in Vermont."

"You're a Yankee!" Olympia exclaimed as if she'd discovered an imposter. "But your accent?"

"Been south of the Mason Dixon over twenty years. Guess I acquired it."

"I believe the war ended some decades back," George teased his wife.

Chastised, she throttled back. "I simply hadn't realized. So how'd you come to be in Alabama?"

Wayne leaned back. "Well, it started out as Florida. None of the mills in Colchester were hiring, so a buddy and I had the idea of heading south. We figured if we had to be out of work, might as well be someplace warm.

"Our money ran out before we made it to Miami. A man in Jacksonville was headed west. He said companies were hiring in the panhandle so we tagged along." He leveled his gaze at Olympia. "We joined a logging camp outside Apalachicola. Sometimes a man has to go where the jobs are."

Elisabeth squeezed his hand hard as Olympia's eyes widened. Between her mouth and his temper, the whole evening threatened to unravel.

George interceded. "So how did you wind up in Alabama?"

Wayne looked over. "Well, my buddy and I stayed on the crew a year. We made money, did some fishing, even swam in the gulf." He chuckled. "It's like bathwater, only saltier.

"The next summer a hurricane blew in, and wreaked havoc on the operation. The newest men were let go, including us, so we decided to head home." He winked at Elisabeth. "But we parted ways in Eufaula. He went on north, and I found a reason to stick around."

Elisabeth smiled, recalling his dogged pursuit all those years ago. "Wayne can be charming when he wants to be," she chided. "Pa chased him off at first, but eventually he warmed to him. My father was the most successful cotton farmer in the county."

"I hear the Chattahoochee is a beautiful river," George commented.

"Oh, it is. And the bluffs are dotted with old plantation homes." She lost herself in the reverie. "Our home wasn't near as grand, but perfect in its own right. It was a fine farmhouse built of yellow pine. You could see for miles from the wrap-around porch. Sweetbay magnolias dotted the yard."

"Like that twig up by your house," Olympia poked.

Elisabeth bit her tongue. At least she'd rejoined the conversation. "Yes, Wayne brought a seedling back last time we were there."

"To visit your parents?" George asked.

She glanced down at her plate. "For my niece's wedding. When I was nine, my mother died in childbirth, along with the baby, a little boy. So it was just my father and me. He had a stroke the year Wayne and I married." She fell silent. Perhaps she'd said too much.

"If you loved it so, why did you leave?" George's tone was gentle.

She caressed Wayne's hand. "Farming didn't suit Wayne. We learned of opportunities here, so we sold." She forced a smile. No doubt they knew the rest anyhow. People liked to talk. Why dwell on the deceit, or the partners who'd left them hanging? Another failed mine. Theirs wasn't the first; it wouldn't be the last. They managed.

"The boll weevil made a real mess of things after we left. So it all worked out for the best."

George nodded. "It always does." Then he turned to Olympia. "Dear, why don't we take coffee in the living room? Wayne and I will have cigars, and let you ladies have some time."

Elisabeth couldn't retreat to the kitchen fast enough. Even Olympia seemed to breathe easier as they cleared the dishes. Afterward, Olympia made coffee and sliced a walnut cake while Elisabeth prepared the tray.

"You know," Olympia began, "I wouldn't presume to intrude, but it might do you a world of good to get out more. Hadley can be dreary enough, but it must be mighty lonely up there on the ridge. Other than at service or in our store, I never see you. Why, I haven't seen you socially since that Daughters of the Confederacy gathering at your place. That's been nearly five years."

Elisabeth sighed. If Olympia Dalton was offering sympathy, she must have said too much. "I have no complaints. Wayne and the boys keep me busy."

"But your boys are nearly grown," she asserted. "You know, it's not too late to join the fight for national prohibition. The Women's Christian Temperance Union is in the thick of things now. Our success in Virginia may yet extend across the land, Lord willing. It all boils down to a handful of states. We could use another strong voice to bring pressure on state legislators."

Fortunate to be facing away, Elisabeth stifled a laugh. So it wasn't sympathy at all. With Olympia there was always a motive. "Well, I am busy right now, with Joshua on the mend. Orders at the quarry always slow in the winter, so I've taken on more sewing. But I admire your work on women's suffrage. Perhaps I could help come spring?" She turned with the tray. "I think it's ready."

"Thank you, Elisabeth. That'll do nicely." She eyed her warily. "With prohibition so near at hand, suffrage has taken a back seat for the moment. But our efforts have taught me that real change will only be sustained when women have the vote. Men can be strong on war, yet so meek on matters of humanity."

Olympia placed the cake on the tray and started pouring the coffee. "You mentioned Joshua's recovery . . ." she began, letting the sentiment hang.

"Yes?"

"His color is much better now, and I scarcely notice his limp. I take it he's in good health, other than the scars?"

Facing her now, Elisabeth maintained a tight mask. The context was plain, and the query understandable. Olympia wanted grandchildren. "Yes, the doctor assures me he's good as gold."

Olympia nodded. "That's so good to hear." And with that, she picked up the tray. Elisabeth held the door, and they breezed into the parlor to join the men.

*   *   *

Elisabeth set her empty cup on the saucer. Dessert was nearly done. It was time to put the evening to bed, lest any other tangents lead them astray. "Thank you for inviting us. Your home is charming."

Olympia perked up. "We've made the best of it. At least it's not a shanty, though our house in Richmond was much larger. After nearly a decade, I still can't bear to part with any furnishings. Memories, you know."

She caressed the arm of the sofa. "We thought we'd own a new home by now. But given how things have panned out, the lease has proven a blessing."

George shifted. "Olympia," he started.

"Yes, dear."

He shook his head. "Nothing."

"No time like the present," she muttered. "Would anyone like more coffee?"

Elisabeth demurred, watching George. For the first time all

evening, he appeared rattled, even perturbed.

Wayne wasn't as coy. "Time for what?" he asked, handing Olympia his cup.

Olympia filled it. "George?" she prompted.

All eyes upon him, he gave a strangled look. "You know we think highly of Joshua. He's a fine young man."

Elisabeth's heart skipped. "And we feel the same. Katie's a lovely young woman," she blurted.

"You misunderstand," George continued. "It's nothing bad. But has he mentioned our recent conversation?"

Wayne stiffened but said nothing.

Elisabeth shook her head. "No."

"Well, it's just I've asked Joshua to consider helping at the store. Our new store, that is, in Churchville. We've kept the news under wraps, but we'll be opening it soon. We offered Joshua a position." He stammered. "More than a position; we'd teach him the business."

Elisabeth exhaled. It was an opportunity, a fresh start, the answer to a prayer. But seeing the fury in Wayne's eyes, she tempered her response. "He hasn't said anything. I imagine he's thinking it through. Joshua is deliberate in his decisions."

"It's not only his decision," Olympia interjected. "He has Katherine to consider."

Wayne grew agitated, nearly spilling his coffee.

Elisabeth jumped in before he said something they'd regret. "Joshua understands that. He respects Katie."

"Of course he does!" George exclaimed. "And I've asked him to consider your family as well. Our offer is genuine. We respect it's his decision . . . his and Katie's," he added with a nod to his wife.

Wayne fumed. Olympia, suddenly quiet, began gathering their plates.

Elisabeth scrambled to patch things up. "It's a kind offer, Mr. Dalton. We appreciate your confidence in our son."

Her eyes pleaded with Wayne, but his words were raw. "I cut work short for this. We're heading home."

She put on her best face. "It is getting late, and we have the drive." She reached for Wayne, but he was already half way to the door.

The goodbyes were awkward, and iciness engulfed them when they stepped outside. "Tell Katie we said goodnight," she inserted as the door closed.

She tried to engage Wayne on the way home; but he said nothing, his eyes glued to the road.

After a while she turned away. There was nothing to see. The sun had long set, plunging the forest into darkness.

21 – Heading to Paris

"I can't believe you have to stay! Tommy groused. *"The sergeant's out of line on this. You ought to speak to the lieutenant, Wolfie. I'll do it if you want."*

Joshua paused from cleaning his rifle. *"No! I don't need you to do anything. I'm just meeting one of the French snipers. Sergeant had nothing to do with it. I asked to speak with him."*

"Before you knew we'd have leave! Why can't you talk to him next week?"

"I want to hear from someone who knows what it's like before we move up. He's one of their most experienced, and he speaks English. Just leave well enough alone, will ya?"

Tommy pursed his lips like he did when he felt betrayed. He grabbed his duffel and fished out a scrap of paper. *"Here's where we'll be staying. Nico knows someone. They're holding a room. They say everything will be full so don't lose it."*

"I doubt I'll make it. Maybe I'll stick around Toul."

He regretted the words as soon as they escaped.

Tommy exploded all over again. *"I don't understand! You've been talking about seeing Paris since we shipped out. Well, here's your chance. Four days! Now suddenly some village in the shadow of the front is fine?"*

Joshua shrugged. He was a horrible liar. *"I'll try to make it,"* he said, feigning concentration on the rifle.

Nico and Buster rounded the corner. *"Well, if it isn't the sergeant's pet,"* Buster called out. *"Nico didn't mention you were tagging along."*

Joshua kept his cool. *"I'm not,"* he said flatly.

"Nico said he could," Tommy countered. *"But he says he isn't coming."*

"Figures," Buster groused.

Joshua ignored him. The sniper training had created a separation with the other men. Most didn't care. But a few, Buster among them, resented it. He turned to Nico. "So what all do you have lined up?" Nico was more interested in himself than any unit squabbles so the quicker he started talking, the better.

It worked. Nico launched into a description of clubs, and mused on where to find the best prostitutes, which Tommy pretended to ignore. Soon enough the trio were on their way.

"Don't lose the address," Tommy huffed as they departed.

Joshua finished cleaning his rifle, then paced about as more men shuffled through. Once the coast was clear, he scurried to gather his things. There was no way of knowing if he'd be back before Tommy so sticking with the pretense that he'd lingered in the local villages was his best bet. He felt a knot in his stomach, already anticipating Tommy's griping when they returned.

The thought nagged him as he made his way out of the reserve trench. Perhaps it was disloyal, but he was done second-guessing himself. If anything, he worried something would intervene. He'd run into men from the unit. Or Aiden would think better of the invitation, and he and Claire would board the morning train. Panicked at the thought, he picked up his pace.

Beyond the supply depot, he lit a cigarette. Aiden was right. The rest of the men had cleared out early. Still, he cut across the nearest field to avoid the main route. By the time he stumbled upon a secondary lane, he'd begun to question his decision. The few vehicles he encountered were heading toward the front. If he couldn't hitch a ride, he might not make it.

He ran for a while before flagging down a French officer. Mangling his way through rudimentary pleasantries, he pleaded for "le gare dans Toul, s'il vous plaît!" The officer nodded and accelerated.

Even so, it was nearly 2:00 when they cleared the village checkpoint. Moments later the officer pulled up in front of a narrow house with carnations in the front window. A blond in a robe peeked through the drapes, then recoiled upon seeing Joshua. The officer pointed to where the street dead-ended at the tracks. Joshua offered a rushed "merci" then ran.

He traced the edge of the train yard and scrambled up the end of the platform, where a crowd had gathered. Sprinting, he entered the depot and snaked through the packed interior, wondering if he should purchase a ticket. He glanced toward the main doors, where a trio of British soldiers was entering. That was all. There was no sign of Aiden or Claire.

He raced back onto the platform and continued on, shoving his hand in his back pocket. After all this, had he even brought Tommy's note?

A woman pulled a child from his path.

Locating the scrap of paper, he rotated slowly, scanning the crowd once again. His heart sank at the sight of the arriving train. Folks began edging closer to the track.

Just then he heard a woman's voice. He swung about, noticing the narrow walk alongside the depot. He raced over and peered around the corner.

There they were, together near a side window. Claire, still in her nurse's uniform, was chattering. Aiden stood by the window, smoking a cigarette as he scanned the interior. Claire stopped mid-sentence, drifting toward him. An instant later, Aiden squashed the butt against the wall and flicked it over the edge into the bushes.

He looked up, relief in his eyes. "I've been watching the entrance the entire time. How did you . . .?"

"I didn't arrive out front," he blurted. Claire tugged his hand, urging him over. "I came up the platform on the far side. I'm sorry."

Aiden smiled as he pulled a ticket from his pocket. "It doesn't matter. You're here now."

*   *   *

The train filled up quickly, forcing them into the dining car. They joined an old woman seated in a booth for four.

"I'm glad we have seats," Claire observed after a few stops. "By the time we reach Paris, it will be standing room only."

"This is all for the Fourth?" Joshua asked.

"Yes," she laughed. "Last year the celebration was larger than Le Quatorze Juillet. I was describing it to Aiden earlier. American flags lined the Champs d'Élysées. The crowds were tremendous. It was fantastic, even by Parisian standards."

Joshua had heard as much that morning, but hadn't believed it. Nico had a tendency to exaggerate.

Aiden smirked. "Not even the Paris Gun can keep them away! So much for Germany weaponry defeating the French joie de vivre." He'd spoken little during the ride, letting Claire take on the lion share of the talking. If she minded, it didn't show. If anything, she seemed to relish her part.

She spoke of recent efforts assisting American medical teams as they set up in Lorraine. "Colonel Stevens says I have a home with them should I ever tire of the hospital." She paused. "Those nurses from the states . . . I admire their courage in travelling so far for their men.

Joshua nodded, wondering if there was anyone she couldn't charm.

Suddenly she jumped up. "We should switch seats."

Joshua went along, noting the stern glance of the old woman as he nestled in beside Aiden.

"We'll be staying with my friend Lily," Claire resumed. "I think you will like her. She's an artist."

"Among other things," Aiden muttered beneath his breath.

Joshua felt a swift kick. He winced, splashing tea on his shirt. Aiden burst out laughing.

Claire's eyes grew wide. "I'm sorry. That was meant for him." She leveled her gaze at Aiden.

Joshua chuckled, unsure whether to wipe the stain or rub his shin. Aiden offered a napkin so he opted to clean up. Claire and Aiden were like kids together.

Claire continued. "Lily's not yet established as a painter so she works as a waitress at Le Chat de Minuit, which has performers.

Aiden thinks she's an exotic dancer, or something." She volleyed again at Aiden. *"And what if she were? She's pretty, and they make good money."*

The old woman glanced up from her book, eyebrow arched.

"If only Claire were wearing a habit," Aiden whispered.

Claire leaned forward. "What did you say?"

"I said you're pretty enough as well, if only you weren't a nurse, and such a capable one at that."

Claire was peeved. "You're impossible! You know what Lily went through with that bastard Max."

The woman slammed her book shut and turned toward the window. With Claire squared off against Aiden, Joshua's grin went unnoticed as well.

Aiden straightened up, chastised. "You know I do." He glanced over. "Lily is an excellent painter, a natural."

Claire seemed partly mollified. "And improving each time I visit. Her mentor thinks she will be ready to show soon."

The passengers from the latest stop filtered in. Joshua noticed more buildings along the tracks.

"You've never seen Paris, have you? Aiden asked. "Do you want by the window? We'll be arriving at the Gare de l'Est station, but you might get a glimpse of the Eiffel Tower as we approach."

"I can see plenty. I just like seeing the buildings. The architecture is so beautiful."

"Then you'll love the arrondissements along the Seine. We'll be there tomorrow." He turned to Claire. "Is Lily at the café tonight?"

"Yes. She'll be working every night."

"Then we'll head there after we're settled. If we can get in?" he asked, still easing back into her good graces.

"That would be nice. I'm sure Pierre will fit us in, when he sees you." She cast a fleeting glance at Joshua. "I might dress up, if I can find something of Lily's," she mused before observing the passing streets.

Joshua studied her. She might have a heart of gold, but a sharp tongue defended it. He had no intention of crossing her. And who was Pierre?

He lost the thought when she shifted, again drawing his attention to her ring. It still didn't add up. He'd have to ask Aiden.

He gazed outside. The buildings were continuous now, row after row lining cobblestone streets.

Aiden jostled him, pointing to a domed structure rising from an imposing hill ahead. "That's where we're heading . . . Montmartre."

*   *   *

The steps were the longest Joshua had ever seen. Framed by trees on the left and ornate homes on the right, they appeared to rise clear to the top. He began to memorize the leafy pattern weaving up the lampposts. Climbing higher, the city unfolded beneath them. Nearby rooflines and chimneys gave way to sweeping views of the avenues beyond. Aiden glanced back occasionally, offering a wink or a smile.

It had taken nearly an hour to clear the Railway Transit Officer, so they had chosen to walk rather than brave the crowd entering the Metro. Claire had explained it would still have been a hike, the subway lines running on either side of the large butte upon which the village sat.

Though eager to ride the Parisian marvel, he enjoyed seeing the streets. They were stately and brimming with activity. Every building boasted elaborate stone and brick facades adorned with intricate detail.

To think the city stretching before them was filled with such creations thrilled him. Then there was the shrine above, demanding attention. Its large dome glowed in the afternoon sun.

"The Basilica of Sacré-Cœur," Aiden said, answering his unspoken inquiry. "The Catholic Church's attempt to reclaim the village of Montmartre from communist hordes and other undesirables. They completed it just prior to the war."

Claire smirked. "They haven't chased away all the radicals. Some have joined in. Lily says one of the priests is a regular at the café. Apparently he has a roving eye and hand."

Aiden chuckled. "Why do I not find that surprising?"

Joshua imagined Mom would have nodded if she could hear them, but the idea shocked him. Could it really happen? And he knew nothing of communists in France. He'd always known Hadley was small. Yet even now he found it hard to imagine just how far the world stretched beyond it. He might as well be on Mars. Things operated so differently.

Finally they reached the top, pausing in a tiny park beside the basilica.

Claire sighed. "The funicular would have been packed as well so it's good we took the steps."

"The funicular?" Joshua asked.

"A tram built into the hillside," Aiden explained. "Locals take it up and down from Montmartre. It's on the other side if you'd like to see it."

"Sure."

"Go ahead," Claire suggested. "I need to catch my breath."

"It can wait," Joshua offered.

"No," she insisted. "Go. See. I'll watch our things."

Joshua looked at Aiden. "Can we?"

They took off, passing before the imposing dome.

Aiden laughed. "You should see yourself. You have that same wide-eyed look as that first day."

Joshua shrugged. "Can't help it. Things overwhelm me sometimes. I've never been any good at hiding it. It's embarrassing."

"No need to be embarrassed. It's refreshing." He paused. "Attractive."

Joshua averted his gaze, but glanced over a second later.

"I'm glad you came, Wolfie. I wasn't sure you would."

"I wanted to." He was afraid to say more.

Aiden nodded. "Paris is amazing. As for Montmartre, well, it can be rather eye opening. Sitting up here over the rest, the village is unique, both of the city and beyond it. Heck, they still have farms and vineyards, not to mention a colorful cast of characters. You'll see things here you won't see in the rest of Paris.

"But if you find yourself uncomfortable at any time, simply tell me. We'll find plenty to entertain ourselves. Is there anything particular you want to see?"

Joshua felt butterflies as he looked across the city. "I'm up for anything. Take me wherever you'd normally go." He could feel Aiden's eyes upon him. "I suppose there is one thing."

Aiden leaned in. "Yes."

"I want to see the Eiffel Tower. I want to stand at the top."

Aiden threw his head back. "Oh, that. Of course. Who doesn't? I have to warn you, it'll be crowded. Still, I guess everyone wants to see the tallest structure in the world."

Joshua studied its curving form on the horizon. "I just find it amazing they could build something so strong yet so graceful."

Aiden looked as well. "I suppose it is, isn't it? It'll be a pleasure, Wolfie. We'll explore it together." He tapped Joshua's arm. "And that's the funicular," he continued, pointing as a crowded tram rose into sight.

They walked over to watch the operation up close. Aiden grew animated, pointing out various landmarks on the horizon. Joshua scarcely heard a word, enjoying the warmth of his presence. Neither of them heard Claire approach.

She dropped the bags behind them. "We need to move on, boys. I have to speak with Lily's landlord."

"Sorry," Joshua explained. "It was my fault. I could stand here all day gazing over the city. It's fascinating."

She laughed. "I have a feeling about you, Joshua. You won't be content simply to watch. Not for long."

Joshua looked at the skyline again, then over to Aiden. "Maybe." The butterflies were back.

22 – Christmas Tree

Flurries whipped about in the gray sky, darting through the branches of the bare oaks. Still, they hadn't amounted to anything more than slivers of white in rocky crevices and among the crinkled leaves blanketing the ground.

"Are you sure you're gonna want to drag it back all this way? I'm not the one with the trick leg, you know," Scott groused as they crunched along.

"Mom would like a spruce. I heard her talkin' with Grandmother."

"Not sure that warrants a crusade to the next county. There are healthy pines steps from the house. And what about those spruces over the ridge where you've been running off to?"

"You can head to the truck anytime. It's what she wants. And as for the ones closer to home, they're all too large. So this is it unless you know of some hidden stash, in which case I'm all ears."

"Damn, Josh. I thought engaged fellas were supposed to be happy. You're as sour as vinegar. And good luck hauling the tree after you chase me off."

Joshua was poised to strike again but relented upon seeing his brother's saucy grin. "I suppose you can stick around," he muttered.

When Joshua had been eight, Dad had gotten the idea to find a red spruce for Christmas like the ones he'd known growing up in Vermont. The occasion had been a secret outing to cheer Mom, who'd been bedridden with some unexplained malady.

Joshua had been so eager he'd risen early to hook up the wagon by himself. The search for the perfect tree had always been a thrill. The prospect it might also boost Mom's spirits had made him positively giddy.

He could recall Scott pouting on the porch as they pulled away, and the fear in his eyes when Dad halted Butterscotch.

Dad had bolted over. With uncharacteristic tenderness, he'd scooped up Scott. The universe had righted itself when Dad tossed him into the bed of the wagon, threatening to tan his hide if he made a single peep about being tired.

As it turned out, they were all tuckered out by the time the deed was done. The trek to the Laurel Fork had been long. Finding a suitable tree in the mist had proven tricky, with Dad eventually resorting to topping out a taller specimen. It had been nearly dark by the time they returned to the wagon.

Back home, Mom had scolded them something fierce, though seeing her on her feet again had made it all worthwhile. They'd all stayed up past midnight to decorate the tree.

It remained Joshua's favorite childhood memory. He'd never seen his parents as happy together, before or after. So if Mom wanted a red spruce for Christmas, a red spruce she'd have, even if it took all day. Given the logging in the years since, he suspected it might.

"At least you didn't bring the guitar," he poked, still itching to retaliate.

"I thought about it," Scott muttered.

Joshua shot him a scowl.

"Not up here. I'd have left it in the truck. What do you have against my playing anyhow? Why does it matter to you?"

"Cause I have to hear it," he spat back.

Scott said nothing.

He'd struck a nerve. "I shouldn't have said that."

Scott brushed past him. "You got that right," he growled, his eyes burning a line along the frozen ground.

"I was kidding . . . really. I just want to do this for Mom. She doesn't ask for much."

"You think I don't want to help Mom?" Scott yelled over his shoulder. "I helped plenty while you were off fighting the noble cause. But not everyone can be a hero, I guess."

Joshua started after him. "I didn't mean . . ."

Scott cut him off. "I know what you meant. You think I'm stupid."

Joshua shook his head, speechless. Scott got flustered at times. Reading had always been tough for him, so he struggled at school. But he wasn't dumb.

Scott spun around. "Do you even care why I bring it everywhere?"

"I'd wondered," Joshua lied, realizing he hadn't considered it at all, so wrapped up in himself. "Why?"

Scott measured his words. "When I play, people . . . other people, that is. Well, they listen. You know I hate talking to strangers. Nothing ever comes out like I want. But with the guitar, it's different. When I play, I don't have to say anything to be heard. It comes natural."

Joshua nodded. "You taught yourself. I could never do that." He hesitated. "Maybe that makes me stupid."

His brother stared into the woods for a moment, saying nothing. Then he looked over, throwing up his dukes playfully. "You're not stupid, Josh. You're my sparring mate." He pointed at the patch of evergreens above. "Now let's go steal us a tree from heaven."

*   *   *

Later, after shaking the ice from the fresh cut spruce, they surveyed the hillside, contemplating the route down.

"I was telling you about my playing," Scott said out of the blue.

Joshua looked over, noting his furrowed brow. "Yeah?"

"I wish I could play at home. Don't know why Dad won't let me. I thought maybe it was because it was his guitar, but that doesn't add up."

"Has Dad ever made sense?"

Scott kicked at the ground. "True enough. Guess I just thought he'd ease up about it eventually."

Joshua shrugged. There was nothing to add. It had always been the blind leading the blind trying to figure out their father. He nodded toward the piles of slash over from where they'd ascended. "I say we avoid the forest altogether. Nobody's out here anyhow."

Scott nodded. "I'll lift the trunk. Just carry the saw and guide the tip."

Joshua began to protest, but stopped. His brother was right. It would go faster. Still, he needed to set one thing straight. "Scott?" he began.

"Yeah."

"I'm not a hero."

Scott looked baffled, but then cracked a smile. "If you say so. You'll get no argument from me." His laughter rang out across the hillside.

23 – Sultry Montmartre

Claire laughed as she led the way up the narrow stairwell. "I think the nurse's uniform helped."

"How's that?" Aiden called out.

Claire stopped on the landing. "He demanded an explanation for the two of you staying in the studio. Lily warned me he often subjects visitors to an inquisition."

"So what did you tell him?" Aiden asked.

"I said it was doctor's orders, that you were shell-shocked after a rescue mission at an orphanage."

"You didn't!"

Claire smirked. "No. I said you were my husband, and that Joshua was her cousin from Iowa. Then I stood there wearing my 'whatever you think is best, doctor' expression."

"He believed you?"

She rolled her eyes and trudged up the next set of stairs. "I have no idea, but we have the key."

They stepped into a dim hall on the next floor. The window at the end was nailed shut, and half the lights were burnt out. The air was stale. Underfoot, the ornate rug was worn bare in spots.

Claire shoved open a door near the middle, and they tumbled in behind her.

Aiden's jaw dropped. "Not bad," he breathed.

Claire snickered. "It is unexpected, isn't it?"

Joshua nodded. Crossing the threshold was like slipping through the looking glass. The tiny studio, taller than it was wide, was painted pale blue. Opposite them a wall of windowpanes framed in white was adorned with silky yellow draperies. The branch of a mature elm hung across the lowest rows. Above it the Eiffel Tower beckoned on the horizon, glowing in the late afternoon sun.

Inside, a curvy red chaise, mahogany wardrobe and two silver end tables rested upon the ebony wood floor before them, while a kitchenette occupied the corner beside the entry. Beyond it a door opened into a nook containing a second wall of windows. He supposed it was large enough for a bed, but instead it housed a hodgepodge of art supplies, crates and a miniature desk.

"The shared bath is down the hall. I imagine she's cleaned it better than anyone has in years, but don't expect it to have the same Lily flair." Claire shook her head. "You should have seen the filth when she moved in."

*   *   *

Joshua was watching evening revelers ascend the hillside when Aiden returned from the bath. Humming a tune, Claire grabbed a dress and a bottle of perfume from the wardrobe before rushing out. She'd allowed them to freshen up first in order to consider all her options. "Lily said to pick something I liked," she'd explained at the start of her quest.

Aiden went to shut the wardrobe. "Ladies and their clothes," he muttered, then shook his head. "Lily can't have purchased all this."

"Do you think?" Joshua asked, hesitant to finish the question.

Aiden shrugged and joined him at the window. "I best not get into trouble. They've been friends since they were little. Claire thinks Lily can do no wrong. I'm not so convinced."

"Who is the man Claire mentioned? Max, I think?"

"The devil. Claire is right about him. He would have killed Lily if she hadn't divorced him. Probably still would if he knew where she was. I helped David when he went to retrieve her."

"David?"

Aiden sighed and glanced at the door. "I know this is Claire's business, for her to share or not as she sees fit. But he was my friend too. David was Claire's husband." He hesitated. "We served together in the legion. I was with him when he died in Verdun. That's how I met Claire. He made me promise to look in on her should anything happen."

"I'm sorry I asked. I'd noticed her ring, but I wasn't sure."

"You did nothing wrong, Wolfie. I'm just protective of her. Claire's been through a lot." He opened the French windows, and they leaned against the rail. "It's not only protection. I'm not sure she even needs that now. I respect Claire. She does whatever she sets her mind to, and can convince anyone of anything. Claire's a survivor." He glanced inside. "Apparently Lily is too, in her own way."

Joshua nodded then peered into the narrow garden beneath them. A gray cat beneath the tree eyed them warily. "I'm glad you asked me to come. I was nervous."

"Nervous?"

He couldn't hold his gaze. "It's just . . . well, I guess I don't know what to . . ." He was unable to finish.

"What to do?" Aiden scooted near. "Just be yourself. I'd like to know you better, Joshua. I've wanted to since the beginning, since that first day."

"But why?"

"Who knows?" He shifted. "Oh, that's not fair. I know why. I saw you there in the hallway. You looked so lost, and so earnest, like you were trying to do everything just right. I know what it's like to mold yourself to suit everyone. That used to be me. But you can only do it for so long." He paused. "Am I right?"

No one had ever spoken the truth so plain before. He didn't even let himself. "Is it that obvious?" he pleaded.

"For me, maybe. For most people, no. I saw something familiar. At first that was all. I thought I'd keep an eye on you, make sure you were alright."

"What do you mean?" The gears clicked. "You asked to be in our company?"

Aiden nodded. "You have to understand. Command was in turmoil, and I'd been lost in the shuffle. The day after class, I went in and requested a direct assignment, said I knew where I wanted to be. The clerk nearly chased me out, but took down the information. Next thing I knew, I had orders."

Joshua digested the confession. "You said 'at first.' What

changed?"

Aiden cocked his head. "You really don't know?"

Joshua studied the foreign landscape before him. He didn't have words. He'd never dare conceive them. "I'm here," he breathed. "I don't know what comes next."

Aiden said nothing. He touched Joshua's face, turning it so their eyes met. Then he leaned near.

Joshua trembled, feeling Aiden's breath.

"One step at a time, Wolfie," Aiden whispered. "It's enough that you're here."

Joshua jumped at a noise in the hall.

Aiden released him. "It's alright. She knows."

The door burst open. Claire tossed her things on the chaise and spun around. "Will this do?" she asked, her eyes leaping back and forth between them.

Aiden whistled. "Fantastic. Magnifique!"

Joshua let himself breathe, then nodded in agreement.

The nurse had blossomed into a lovely mademoiselle. The lavender dress she'd selected was fresh and flattering, with lace accents and sleeves. A white velvet hat dotted with stitched flowers fit snug over her head, pushing her dark bangs into teasing curls about her face. Light rouge brought out the sparkle in her eyes. Claire looked as if she'd stepped out of a fashion house.

"Good!" she exclaimed, reopening the wardrobe. "Lily even has lotion . . . I saw it earlier." A moment later she latched it shut. "Are we ready?" she asked, admiring her earrings in a small hand mirror.

Aiden moved toward the door. "We'd better be. I'm famished."

Outside the night was warm, though cooler than when they'd arrived. Street musicians serenaded the throng flowing through the tight weave of streets. Soon they ventured down a narrow lane to Le Chat du Minuit. A crowd had gathered, enjoying the tunes of a mandolin player. Joshua joined them while Aiden and Claire stepped inside.

A man with slicked back hair tipped his hat. "Bienvenue à Paris," he greeted. The young lady with him plucked a red rose from her bouquet and pinned it to his uniform lapel. Their friends laughed.

"Merci." Joshua blushed, his already slim vocabulary vanishing in the presence of an audience. Fortunately Aiden emerged.

"We're in," he whispered, and they bid adieu to his new admirers.

"How?" he started to ask, but Aiden had already plunged into the cramped interior, sliding up to the maître d', a tall blond man.

They waited as Joshua squeezed through. The maître d' appraised him with pursed lips then led them through the candlelit maze of diners. They arrived at a round table nestled into the corner. The maître d's eyes lingered on Aiden before he turned to Claire. "Lily va vous rejoindre tout de suite."

Claire squeezed Joshua's hand as he departed. "Pierre is harmless. He's just a bit smitten with Aiden."

Joshua leaned back, watching as the man retreated to his post.

Aiden winked. "Do you need help with the menu?"

Joshua shook his head. The French was daunting, but he recognized a few dishes from a book he'd seen. "coq au vin," he said, somewhat as a question.

"Excellent choice," Claire complimented. "You'll love it." Then her gaze moved passed him. "Lily!" she exclaimed, jumping to her feet.

The boisterous greeting was but a taste of what followed. Claire scurried around Joshua. The two shrieked and embraced. Claire stepped back, and Lily gushed over the dress in a rapid French Joshua had no hope of following. A tray of drinks arrived, and Aiden thrust one into his hand.

Finally he was introduced to the benefactor for their stay, a striking woman with piercing green eyes and full auburn locks. "Enchanté!" she gushed, kissing him like he was family.

Lily and Claire chatted in calmer tones. Then Lily took their order and vanished.

"I like that," Aiden observed after sipping his drink, a lemony concoction with a pale blue haze and a cherry at the bottom.

"Lily knows I love my aperitifs," Claire explained. "The

bartender likes to surprise us." Lifting her glass, she touched Joshua's hand. "To good friends, old and new."

24 – At the Cabin with Pete

Joshua hitched Butterscotch to the cart, which they'd piled high with stone and materials. "We'd better stop or it'll all wind up in the hollow."

Pete tossed a handful of tools into a bucket. "I'll carry these."

"You want to ride Butterscotch? He won't mind."

"Nah. If you lead, I can keep an eye on the cart."

"Good idea. There's not really a trail."

"Figured as much."

And so they began. The trek was slow going beneath cloudy skies. The weather had threatened for days, but it hadn't amounted to anything. Still, the farmer's almanac called for snow by Christmas, so he was eager to get supplies to the cabin while the ground was dry.

Partway up the ridge they took a break, leaving the cart while they descended to Sully's spring with their canteens. Joshua filled a pail for Butterscotch while Pete climbed onto an outcropping of rock.

He swung around to let his legs dangle. "Scott'll be mad he couldn't come. He's about had it with school."

Joshua scooted alongside him, ignoring the twitch in his thigh. "Mom'll have his hide if he gets it in his head to drop out. Be plumb foolish this near graduation. As for this, I doubt he'd be up for it. He'd rather wander off with his guitar."

"Can you blame him? If I had his talent, I'd play hooky all the time."

Joshua rubbed his chin. "Is he really that good? I've heard him picking at the strings a bit, but none of it sounds like music. The only time I heard any songs was at Thanksgiving, and that was only a couple."

"He was nervous, 'specially with you there. Scott can play popular tunes, but where he really shines is playing what's in his head. All that tinkering is him figuring out the melody, gettin' the rhythm right.

Once he puts it together, it's somethin' special. I ain't never heard a man work a guitar like your brother. Heck, I want to sign him up for a talent contest down in Monterey next month. But I can't afford the entry fee, not with the piddly hours I'm workin'."

"Still picking up shifts, huh?"

Pete leaned back. "Yep. It's why I'm home this week. But that'll change come January. We're starting a new tunnel. Mister Tuckerman thinks we'll find a thicker vein, not as broken up." He took a gulp from his canteen. "Damn well better, or I'll be out of a job come spring. How about you? Scott says you've been helping your dad in the quarry."

"Some, but orders are few and far between. No one's building in the mountains these days. If folks are buying stone in the valley, they're getting it local. No need to get pocono from the ridge when there's a quarry of bluestone down the lane."

He slid off the rock and wandered over to Butterscotch. "Still have work in Head Waters though. The old farmer hails from Pennsylvania, so guess the pocono reminds him of home. I'm finishing their fireplace next week. Now his wife wants a larger icehouse."

"You must like the work, seeing as you're fixin' up an old cabin in your spare time."

Joshua stroked Butterscotch's neck. "I suppose," he mumbled.

Pete jumped down. "Heck, I don't mind. I know what it's like to want to get away. After we got the news about Nate, I ran off whenever I could. What with my mom goin' crazy and all, it was better than sticking around the house. Still is, I suppose. I breathe easier over at my uncle's."

They started again, moving across the ridgeline and onto the northern face. The sky grew darker as the clouds thickened. "She doing any better?" he asked.

Pete shrugged. "Hard to tell. She doesn't weep all the time now. Or scream. The doctor gave her something. Mostly puts her to sleep, but she's doing small things. She dresses herself. She eats. We even decorated for Christmas, so I suppose she's learning to cope."

Joshua paused, contemplating the steeper incline and the boulders. He hoped they could manage. It'd take forever if they had to lug the stones piece by piece.

He glanced back at Pete. "Guess that's the trick, isn't it? Figuring out how to cope."

*   *   *

"Just a bit more," Joshua urged. Given a final shove, the beam scraped up the face of the top stones. With a snap, it popped into place atop the wall cap.

Pete stepped back. "I wasn't so sure that was gonna work."

"Neither was I." Joshua massaged his thigh, then ran a hand over their handiwork. "Seems stable. I'll need to beef up the rafters, now that the corner's back together."

"Should last 'til another spruce clips it." Pete wiped his brow as he poked around the interior of the cabin. "You mentioned framing the fireplace. You aim to fix the windows too?"

"The broken sash, at least. Maybe replace the cracked panes."

"We have old sashes in our cellar. You could use the glass if you want."

"Sure, if your father won't mind."

"They're just gatherin' dust. Hangin' sashes is tricky, 'specially by yourself. If you want, I can help next I'm in town."

"There's no need. I feel bad you wasted a day out here."

Pete shrugged. "It's no trouble. Didn't have nothing planned anyhow. Besides, I was glad I ran into you the other day. I wondered how things were going. Scott mentioned the engagement."

Joshua tossed a fresh log onto the fire, sending a splattering of embers across the hearth.

Pete kicked a glowing chunk back into the firebox. "I've been meaning to talk to you."

Joshua jostled the logs with the poker. "About what?"

"Somethin's been buggin' me, and you're the only one I knew to ask."

He looked over. "Yeah?"

Pete's words came slow. "When you were there, were you scared?"

Joshua set the poker aside. He took a seat on the dusty floor. "Why do you ask?"

"I dunno. It don't change nothing. But the whole time we were growing up, I can't remember Nate being afraid. Not that he let on." He fidgeted. "I was the one scared of my own shadow."

Joshua rocked in place. "Nate was pretty fearless."

"That he was. But when he got to the front he sent a letter. It was different. Before he never really talked about the war. He wrote about the men, things he saw, funny things that happened. But that was all. I figured it was on account of Mom. She's always been, well . . ."

"Nervous."

"Yeah, even at her best Mom's pretty wound up." He sighed. "But this letter was serious. He told me to make Dad proud, said he wanted Mom to be happy. And he said he was scared. Then, not a week later, came the word. Word that he was gone. Ever since, I can't shake the feeling. Like maybe he knew. Maybe he had a sense, but didn't come right out and say it."

Joshua rocked harder. "I don't know, Pete. When we were on the front, it didn't feel real. We ate. We slept. We did what we were told to do, what we had to do. But the men didn't talk about it. I was the same. It was like I pretended it wasn't happening." He felt Pete's eyes upon him.

"And the battle?"

He jumped up. Pacing about, he ended up at a window. He stared out at the spruces. "I can't remember the battle, Pete. I mean, there are parts. Sometimes I see things. Feel things. But it's all jumbled. The doctor said it's the shock, from being buried and all.

"But as for being scared, all I know is this. There was no stopping the war. There was no harnessing it. You couldn't keep it from coming. Even if you could have seen something bad before it got to you, nothing would have changed. It would have still kept coming."

He made himself face him. "Pete, I'm not sure what you're

asking. But I don't know that it meant anything, Nate's letter that is. I was scared the whole time . . . every minute. Any man who says they weren't is plain lying." He shrugged. "Maybe Nate needed to say it. Maybe it just came out. I doubt it meant he knew he'd die. I don't think it works that way."

Pete said nothing. He turned toward the fire.

"Sorry, Pete. I know that doesn't help."

Pete sounded wounded. "No, it does. Really." He dusted off his pants. "I don't know why it matters. It's just I dunno what he was thinkin'. And I'll never get to ask." He shuffled toward the door. "You were there so figured I'd ask you. It's the closest I'll get."

Joshua slumped. There was nothing more to say. Words didn't help. He knew that.

Pete opened the door. "You wanna lug the rest inside?"

Joshua joined him. "Suppose I oughta, else I'll be digging it out of a snow bank come next week. Let's get it done and head on back."

*　　　*　　　*

The talk was breezy on the way home. Pete groused about his cousins, but recounted their antics with a smile. "I can act like I want when I'm there," he joked at one point. "No need to worry about steppin' on eggshells if everyone else is throwin' dishes."

Joshua felt peppier too. He hadn't crumbled. The war still weighed heavy on him, but the voices were softer. Sometimes he could even silence them.

"How much is the contest, Pete?" he asked as they descended toward the house. "The one over in Monterey."

"Three dollars. But first prize wins twelve. I went last year, and I think he'd have a shot. There was a man with a good voice, but Scott could've outplayed 'em all. Second place gets six, and third gets his entrance fee back. They sell tickets at the door. The whole thing's a benefit for the school."

"What if Katie and I go in on it with you? He wouldn't chicken out, would he? Scott can be skittish."

"Not with his guitar he's not. You'd be surprised. He played in front of everyone at the school last week. I snuck in to see him. He didn't flinch none at all."

"I had no idea," he breathed. "Alright then, I'm in. Katie suggested we get gifts together for the families. She had some ideas for Mom and Dad, but we'd been stumped on Scott. I'll get you the money."

Pete beamed. "I'll take care of it. The contest is the end of January. I might be full up at the mine, but you should go."

"We'll see. Maybe I'll take Katie, that is if he wants us there."

"Oh, he will. He talks about wanting you to hear. He wants to make you proud."

The thought chafed at him, though he couldn't say why. He was still pondering the matter as they neared the clearing. Hearing a stranger's voice, he slowed Butterscotch to a halt.

Two men were with Dad down by the shed. One was a large man, balding on top. The other was a young negro. He was tall, with short-cropped hair. When he turned, Joshua could see his left arm was missing.

"What's goin' on?" Pete asked.

"I don't know. Can't make out what they're saying."

"Should I head on?"

"Maybe. It's probably nothing, but you never know with my dad."

"Alright then. Tell your folks I said to have a good Christmas."

"Will do, Pete. Yours as well. Thanks for the help. I'll bring the money down tomorrow. Maybe pick up an old sash too."

"That'd be fine. I'll head over to Monterey before leaving for my uncle's. Now you let me know if you need more help."

Joshua watched him disappear down the ridge before turning his attention to the men by the shed. Abandoning Butterscotch, he inched over to an oak along the tree line.

The balding man was talking. "Sir, we know it's your land. We just need an inventory of the ridge. Your property extends all the way to the top. It's the only parcel we haven't seen."

Dad cut him off. "If I'm not selling, why do you need to see it? I don't need a bunch of government men traipsing over my land, noting my comings and goings. Last I checked, property owners still have a few rights."

"Sir, we're gathering information on forests across the whole county. Harrison and I could start right now. If we hurry, we'd be done by dusk."

Dad seethed. "Now listen here. Don't you take me for a fool. I know how this works. First, you want an inventory. Then you come back, just wanting a couple photographs or a survey. Next thing you know, the government wants it all lock, stock and barrel for pennies on the dollar. So you listen up, and you listen good. That over there's my home. This quarry here is my livelihood. And contrary to what you've been told, folks up here don't need savin'.

"Between here and Staunton, all those mills and mines and farms. Those were carved from this land. That's what progress looks like. If the government had left well enough alone, we'd have had ourselves a railroad by now. And all of us would be doing a heck of a lot better."

Dad glanced up, his gaze zeroing in on the oak. He hesitated, but continued. "Now I know you're only doing what you've been told. But folks don't take kindly to strangers walking up and asking to poke around their land." He looked at the negro. "You, young man . . ."

The negro nodded. "Yes, sir?"

"Did you lose your arm in the war?"

"Yes, sir, I did. Battle of Soissons."

"Well, that over there's my son. He just got back from the war as well. This here land is his future. It'll be his when I'm gone. Those aren't just pretty trees up there. I own that land and every stinkin' mineral, ore and rock beneath it. I'm not giving that up for anyone. A man's got to feed himself, and his kin."

Having been called out, he emerged from behind the trunk.

The balding man tried again. "Sir, we need to finish our inventory."

Dad's temper flared. "You just got your answer!"

"Our boss will send us back."

"Not if he knows what's good for you. Or him. Now get off my land!" His final words took on the threatening growl Joshua recognized from every beating he ever received. It still had power over him. Its meaning was unmistakable. The discussion was over, and the men knew it.

The man trudged by Joshua. "Good day," he nodded. The negro followed, shooting a fleeting glance in his direction.

Dad's anger wasn't spent. "I could have used you this morning," he barked after they'd gone. "Not to mention that cart. So you gonna help me get caught up?"

He wasn't asking.

"Yes, sir. I'll tend to Butterscotch and be right down."

"You do that," he snarled before stomping away.

25 – Christmas Eve

"It's a lovely tree," Katie observed, walking over for a closer look. "These ornaments are so intricate. They're Bohemian, aren't they? I've never seen so many on a single tree, even at my grandparents' store in Richmond."

Mom beamed. "Yes. They were my mother's. When I was a little girl, I used to get so excited when she brought the boxes out. The oldest ones were her mother's from a year she spent in Europe. She collected the animal figures. There's a bird in a cage up near the top. My mother preferred geometric ones. She liked the mix of shapes and colors."

Katie touched the delicate glass beads of one shaped like a star. "I think I do too," she concluded, then stepped back to join Joshua.

Grandmother gave him a pat. "They look nice on the spruce. Scott said it was quite the quest to find it."

Joshua blushed. "It wasn't that bad, just a bit of a climb."

He felt her penetrating gaze. "Is it easier now, with the leg?"

He shrugged. "It gets stiff sometimes, but I manage."

Though she'd aged since her last visit, the summer he turned twelve, her laughter was as hearty as ever. "Oh, I know all about that. Believe me, it's worse when it's cold. If you're hiking mountains in December, you'll be fine come spring."

He nodded. "I hope so."

"Are we opening presents now?" Dad interrupted.

Everyone looked to Mom. "Well, we could, while Katie's here."

Katie chimed in. "There's no need. You already moved your meal to Christmas Eve on my account. Don't open presents early too."

Mom shook her head. "Foolishness. We're glad you could join us. And it's good you'll be with your aunt and uncle tomorrow. I'm sure that means a lot, especially this year." She looked over at the fireplace. "Scott, could I get your help?"

"Sure, Mom." He scrambled from his perch by the fire and began distributing the small collection of packages.

It was a sparse Christmas after a hard year, but everyone had a couple of gifts. Mom had sewn a few items - shirts for the men, a shawl for grandmother, a scarf for Katie. Grandmother had brought tins of candies and cookies with her, as well as the finest gift, though Joshua had the benefit of giving it.

"Oh my!" Katie exclaimed after Joshua prompted her to open the carved wooden box. "How beautiful."

"Grandmother wanted you to have a proper engagement ring," Joshua explained. "It's better than anything I can afford."

"It's yours?" she asked, looking over her shoulder.

"No, dear. It's yours. It's been in need of a proper home. Elisabeth and I spoke with your mother. It should fit."

Katie slid the ring on her finger. "It's perfect. Thank you. Thank you both." She gave Joshua a hug then leaned forward to give Grandmother a closer look.

Dad took an interest. He studied the craftsmanship of the decorative silver band. The deep lavender stone was round in shape and buffed smooth, with a tiny pearl inset. Having her hold it to the light, he even managed a compliment. "That stone is near flawless. It's a pretty amethyst."

"Is that all the gifts?" Mom asked after the hoopla faded.

Katie nudged him. "Katie and I have one more," he announced, "though we don't have a package. It's for Scott."

Scott had drifted back to the fire, but raised an eyebrow. "Huh?"

"Would you rather?" Joshua asked Katie. When she demurred, he continued. "Well, it was Pete's idea. But we all went in together on it."

Scott edged closer. "On what?"

"There's a musical contest in Monterey next month, a benefit for the school. We paid your entry fee."

Scott looked stunned. "That's three dollars!"

"Yes. Pete went down this past Sunday. We can ask if they'll refund . . ."

Scott laughed. "No, it's not that. I want to play. It was just the fee. I never expected. Thank you." He bounded over. "And you'll come?"

"We'd like to," Katie offered.

"Please. And you as well, Mom?"

"We'll see, son." Her eyes were following Dad, who'd risen. He was shuffling around the kitchen.

Grandmother wasn't coy. "You should all go. Music's a gift. I loved hearing you practice when you took your mother and me into town the other day."

"What are you doing?" Mom called out.

"Getting more pie," Dad gruffed. "Didn't seem anyone else would."

She grimaced as she rose. "I'll get it. Would anyone else like more?"

Scott gave up. "I'll bring you a piece, Grandmother."

Katie moved toward the window. "The snow's heavier now. You should take me home before it gets worse."

He eyed the twirling wet flakes. "I suppose you're right."

Mom rushed over when she saw them at the closet. "You're leaving so soon?"

"Yes. We're heading out early tomorrow, and I promised Mother I'd help wrap gifts tonight."

Mom glanced outside. "And in this weather. You tell your father to drive careful." She helped her tie the new scarf. "It's been wonderful having you. Come and see us, anytime at all."

Dad and Scott said their goodbyes from the kitchen, but Grandmother joined them. She squeezed Katie's hand. "I'm so glad I was able to meet you."

Katie showed her the ring one more time before slipping on her gloves. "Thank you again. I couldn't have dreamed up a prettier setting." She gave her a hug then looked to Joshua. "I guess we're ready."

"I guess we are." He gave assurances to Mom before she could fret. "I'll drive slow and head right back."

*   *   *

The snow was light but persistent on the way home, the wet flurries firming up as the temperature fell. By the time he made it back, an inch had collected atop the couple from the day before. Pulling into the open shed, he shut off the engine. The motor pinged as it cooled. Big fluffy clumps floated around the eaves, skittered across the hood, then vanished into small puddles.

His thoughts drifted, and he lost time like he sometimes did. Next he knew the hood was flecked with ice.

Shaking off the cobwebs, he clamored out. Walking up the hill, he noticed Grandmother on the porch swing. She sat perfectly still, her eyes on the forest.

She jumped when he reached the steps. "Oh, dear! I must not have heard you drive up."

"I, um, got back earlier. Are you cold?"

"Not with my new shawl," she chuckled. "Come. Join me."

He stomped up the snowy steps, then plopped down beside her, ignoring his own chill.

"Katie's real nice," she observed after a moment. "Sharp as a thorn too."

"Yes, she is. She was at the head of our class."

"And she does like the ring?"

"She does. And she loves family heirlooms so it suits her. But you didn't have to, Grandmother. I would have figured something out. I got my bonus check."

"You'll need that to get settled, and it won't go far. This country doesn't do enough for its veterans. It never has." She shook her head. "Maybe we could if there weren't so many. I'll never understand it, the business of war, that is. It isn't that I'm not proud of you, dear. I couldn't be more so."

"I understand."

She leaned back to look him over. "You've matured so much.

Scott has as well. I see your father in both of you."

"You do?" He didn't see Dad at all.

"Certainly. Scott has his music. And you're as headstrong. I saw that the first time I visited, when you were but a tyke." She smiled. "That's a good thing. Your father, he was like a train once he decided something. Bright . . . driven. No one could tell him any different once he figured things out."

He nodded, still not seeing it.

Her green eyes locked on his. "It's the figuring out that's tough."

"Maybe that's it," he muttered, turning to watch the snow.

"It is. And it doesn't get easier." She let out a little laugh. "If anything it's easier when you're young."

"How so?"

"Well, I can only speak for myself so it's just an old lady rattling. But when I was young, I thought I knew how things would be. I didn't have the music like your father, yet I'd always fancied myself an artist. As a child I used to draw, capturing the world . . . and the worlds inside my head.

My life was much the same. I harbored these images, fantasies of how it would all play out. I thought I had angels on my side."

She sighed. "It was a lie, of course, but a convincing one. Even when things went off track, and did they ever, I clung to those pictures. They blinded me for so long."

He struggled to make out the tree line, shrouded in thickening snow. The sketches in Lily's studio crossed his mind. "Until?"

"Until I lost my son."

He looked over. She wasn't making sense.

She didn't acknowledge him, absorbed in her thoughts. "Well, didn't so much lose him as chase him off. I made his life so hard that he found it easier to run than to put up with me."

"I don't understand."

She shivered. "Your father's a capable man. But I raised him to cling to me. As he grew, I corralled his every dream. I shamed him into staying at home, giving up his music, starting at the mill.

"I dug at him. And for a long time he let me. He cared that

much. He stayed home longer than any man ought to, especially one as gifted as your father."

She clinched her jaw. It wasn't clear she'd go on.

"So what happened?"

"Life happened. The more I clutched at my delusions, the more life caught up with me. When the panic hit in '93, folks in Colchester thought we'd weather it. We always had before. But it wasn't like the others. Farms failed. Banks failed. Even the millwork dried up. They let him go, and like a fool I blamed him for it." She shuddered. "So your father left. Thank goodness he still had the gumption.

"After he was gone, I had all the time in the world to think it through. To see what I'd done, how selfish I'd been."

He tried feeling sympathy for Dad, but couldn't. The anger was too thick.

She patted his leg. "I know it's hard with your father. I see how he is with you boys. But there's more to know, Josh. There always is."

He looked over. "I know you're trying to help."

"I don't know about that. I just know the ideas you have now aren't etched in stone. Life's more random. It can be horrible. I imagine you've already seen more than your fair share of that. But it can be wondrous too.

"For over half my life I tried to force the world to fit me. I lost my husband in some godforsaken swamp. I chased off my only child. It was only when I thought my life was over that I found everything I needed. I had possessed it the whole time. It was in me."

He looked away, unable to face her.

The porch swing moved. Grandmother rose and walked to the rail. She fidgeted, running her fingers along the top. A clump of snow tumbled off. "An old woman should know to keep her mouth shut."

He joined her. "It's not that. I appreciate the advice."

She sighed. "And I appreciate the sentiment. But truth is my mind does wander. I spend more time these days looking back than forward. Sometimes I ought to be alone with my thoughts, or keep them to myself."

"Is that why you came outside?"

"No. I figured your father needed some breathing room. I think it chaffed him to hear me praise Scott. He certainly never heard any from me.

"I was too bitter then, angry at being wronged, furious at how God had taken my Arthur. When what I should have done was cherished what I loved in him, and shared it with our son."

She rocked in place. "Not much I can do about that now."

She paused a moment then looked up. "That's not the only reason I ventured out. I do love a snow, even now when it aches in my bones."

He studied the lip of the quarry. It was nearly dark. The snow was heavier, but he could still make out the jagged surfaces. "I do too . . . always have."

"My goodness," she breathed. "You remind me of your grandfather standing there. You have the same look in your eyes."

The thought startled him. He'd never considered what his grandfather looked like. There weren't any photos, and Grandmother had rarely spoken of him at any length. But now he pressed. "What was he like?"

She tilted her head, reflecting. "Arthur? Well, he was handsome, lean like you and Scott. He had a real gentle nature. He lived up to his name, hunting whenever he could. He told me he found it calming, said being alone in the forest gave him time to think."

He grinned. "You don't say."

"And he loved the wintertime." She laughed. "I remember the two of us on a walk one season. We came upon a barn that had burned the summer before. The snow was fresh, and the sun had just come out. Arthur was a few steps ahead. When we came upon the ruins, he stopped in his tracks. I came up beside him and asked what he was looking at."

"What was it?"

"Well, he simply pointed to the old barn. Snow had buried the burnt parts. What was still standing looked majestic, capped in all that powdery white. Your grandfather let out a little laugh. He said, 'Ruth, there's nothing like a fallen snow to open your eyes. It shows you the beauty all around, hiding in plain sight.'"

The image comforted Joshua. "Grandfather was right. Even the quarry looks pretty. See how a crown's forming along the crest?"

She squinted. "I do indeed."

They stood in silence, watching the drifting currents. The wind rustled the last clinging leaves while snow gathered like a blanket. They didn't hear the door open behind them.

Scott poked his head out. "There you are! Mom was getting worried. She's insisting on a few carols before Dad heads upstairs."

"We'll be right in," Joshua assured him.

Grandmother waited until the door shut. "Thank you for spending time with me, dear. It occurs to me you share something else with your grandfather."

"What's that?"

"You're a good listener. Arthur was always patient with me and my moods."

"I wish I could have known him."

She shook the snow from her shawl. "I wish you could have too. I surely do."

"Grandmother?"

"Yes, dear."

"Could you ask Scott to get out his guitar for the carols?"

She looked puzzled. "What do you mean?"

"Scott never plays at the house. Dad won't let him."

She pursed her lips. "I'd wondered. Are you sure I ought to? I nearly set him off earlier."

Joshua shrugged. "None of us dares. I know Scott would like Dad to hear him play. Not sure why it even matters."

"Oh, it matters. You always care what your parents think, even if you convince yourself otherwise." She touched his arm before he opened the door. "I'll ask, but I can't make any promises."

"I know, Grandmother. We never know just how things will play out."

She gave a little laugh. "You're a quick study, young man. A very quick study."

26 – Parisian Heat

One cocktail became two, and wine arrived with their meals. Laughter was plentiful as well. Joshua found it easy to let go, comforted at being a stranger in a strange land. Even his French improved as the evening wore on, or at least he grew bolder speaking it.

Claire encouraged him, correcting his accent and teaching him new expressions. She shared funny anecdotes from her childhood, as well as gossip about Lily's artist friends. Montmartre, it seemed, kept her tethered to a world beyond the front.

Aiden also talked of Paris. He explained its history and culture, and shared his favorite haunts. He touched Joshua on occasion, either to make a point or simply to tease.

Joshua basked in the attention, which Claire observed. She winked at one point, smiling her approval. Lily stopped to chat a few times, and Pierre sought Aiden's eyes each time he ventured near. But mostly they were left to themselves, enjoying their reprieve and each other's company.

It wasn't until dessert that Joshua noticed the gradual adjustments of the room around them. Tables began to disappear, revealing a small stage along the main wall. As more diners departed, new guests arrived, ordering only drinks. A few were seated but most gathered along the walls. With a final shift of the lighting, the transformation from restaurant to club was complete. A man in tails stepped onto the stage to introduce the evening's performances.

Claire tapped his arm. "After midnight is when Montmartre sparkles."

Aiden laughed. "Some would say that shine is moving to Montparnasse."

"You can have the Rive Gauche, Aiden," she shot back. "To me this is what a night in Paris will always be." She leaned into Joshua.

"The music's better here. That is the air I need to breathe."

The debate was lost on Joshua, but it hardly mattered. His thoughts were muddled from the alcohol.

To keep the room from spinning, he focused upon the mandolin player, who had moved inside to kick off the evening. After a few songs, a portly man with a deep baritone joined him. Their upbeat songs pleased the crowd, which shouted accolades between the numbers.

Aiden twisted to watch for a while, before moving his chair between Claire and Joshua. Claire rested her head upon his shoulder while Aiden nuzzled his leg against Joshua's. "That's better," he whispered.

Joshua looked around, but no one paid them any mind. The audience was a diverse mix. Couples puffed up in finery sat beside men in work clothes. Young men cradling their dates stood shoulder to shoulder with aging spinsters. It seemed everyone had found a place in the café.

Aiden leaned near. "Are you having a good time?"

"Yes. It's incredible."

Aiden glanced about the room. "It is kind of special. I'm glad you're here."

Joshua met his gaze. "Me too."

The song came to an end, and the emcee returned. Though he'd found the song lyrics indecipherable, Joshua could follow the host. The man introduced the next performer, Gabrielle Dupont, in glowing terms. He said she sang of truth, with a voice from her heart.

A mature woman with dark wavy hair stepped onstage. Unlike the jovial baritone, she neither smiled nor interacted with the patrons. Her presence was like a shadow passing over on a sunny day, yet enthusiasm bubbled through the audience.

Claire sat up. "I've heard of her. Lily said her voice is mesmerizing. Apparently she'd been in the cabaret years ago, before becoming a shopkeeper. Most of the villagers didn't even know she sang. But when her son was killed, she began to perform again."

The woman gestured to an old man at a small piano near the bar.

He leaned over the keyboard and began to play.

The first notes were soft, aching chords, each line a shifting echo of the one preceding it. With deliberate pacing a melody emerged, a simple tune that sounded both new and familiar, like a lullaby one barely recalls. Joshua found it entrancing, a stark contrast to the lively performance moments earlier.

After a time the piano faded, and the woman began to sing. With a powerful alto, she launched a variation of the haunting composition. Her gaze journeyed over the crowd, caressing each individual.

Closing his eyes, he grew lost in the melody. He saw forests and streams and fields. He stood above the deadly pond then inside the bombed-out church.

At the time the encounter had been fleeting, just part of the exercise. But now, given freedom to hover, he pondered its fate. The battle must have been savage, reducing centuries-old walls to rubble and pitting the belfry. He wondered if men had died. And the parishioners, were they all gone, part of the exodus from the front? Would they find their way home, someday when the war ended?

Until now, he'd dismissed such glimpses of destruction. It had all come before him, and somehow that lessened the impact. But come next week, it would be his war. He would move from witness to insurgent. He'd be responsible for his decisions, his actions. There'd be no one to blame, no one to answer for him.

The realization startled him. His eyes flew open, and he found himself back in the dim corner of the tiny café. He glanced about, self-conscious. He noticed the piano had begun again. The playing intertwined with the woman's voice until the tunes joined, reaching the closing in unison. The final note hung in the air.

The room was silent for a moment before erupting in applause. Joshua didn't join, stunned from his strange journey. He was still recovering when Aiden jostled him.

"Come now," Aiden pleaded, turning to Claire.

She wiped her cheeks. "I'm fine. It simply caught me off guard. Such a moving expression of loss." She drew a deep breath. "That and I drank too much."

"And you've been up since your shift last night. I'm surprised you lasted this long. We should get you to bed."

She adjusted her hat. "No. All I need is a bit of water. The evening's young."

Joshua reached over. "Aiden's right. We have other nights."

Reluctantly she agreed. Aiden pulled out his wallet. Lily gave Claire a parting hug. Then they made their way through quiet streets to the studio.

*   *   *

Aiden found extra linens in a cabinet while Claire changed. She returned, still apologizing. Collapsing onto the chaise, she pulled the blanket close. "You should go back out," she mumbled. In minutes she was fast asleep.

Aiden refilled her water and gave her a peck on the cheek.

"You take good care of her," Joshua observed.

Aiden shrugged. "She keeps an eye on me too." He glanced at the quilt Lily had left near the windows. "We could walk for a while, unless you're ready to turn in. I know a place down in Pigalle. It's kind of hidden."

Joshua contemplated the starry sky. "If you're sure. I still can't believe I'm in Paris. I could probably wander all night."

Aiden checked Claire again. "Lily said she'd be home soon." He grabbed the key from the counter. "So let's wander."

They descended from the village and then traipsed along cobblestone streets at the base of the butte. Dim figures appeared down side streets, but they passed no one. Aiden seemed intent on reaching the destination, reminding Joshua of the drive into the village the week before.

After several blocks, including doubling back at one point, Aiden sighed. "This is it. I couldn't recall at first."

They crossed the street and entered a narrow alley. Opening a side door, they stepped into a dingy hall. Aiden exchanged words with a large man, who pointed to a narrow staircase.

In the stone and brick basement, a trio of men looked up from a small bar. A man playing a piano acknowledged them. The room was dim, a cluster of bulbs above the bar providing the lion's share of the light.

It was a space that demanded whispers, so they complied. "I'll get us a drink," Aiden breathed. "You can go on in."

Joshua let him go ahead, puzzling over the comment. Then he realized the heavy draperies along what he thought was a wall instead shielded a separate space.

He pushed through the nearest panel and was met by eyes from tables in the shadows. Only a few had candles, but all were occupied. In addition men lined the walls, using the stone cap of the foundation to hold their drinks.

He paused a second then moved toward a gap where the wall intersected the line of draperies. As he neared, two older men appraised him. One with silver hair whispered "bonsoir" before sliding down.

Joshua looked at the ground, unable to respond.

After a minute the room began to murmur, confirming that conversation had ceased when he'd entered. Breathing deep, he garnered the courage to look around. A few men still eyed him, but most had gone back to their conversations. The crowd was diverse – businessmen, workers, men of all shapes and sizes. Many were older, but some were near his age. One young chap winked then whispered to his companion, who burst into laughter.

The far curtains parted. Aiden appeared, a cocktail in each hand. He scanned the room. Joshua waved, willing him to move faster. The young couple devoured Aiden with their eyes as he moved alongside the draperies.

"I don't know what this drink is. It was on the house."

Joshua took the glass and downed a third of it. His throat burned.

Aiden grinned. "But it is mostly brandy, so I was going to say take it slow."

Joshua nodded vigorously. "I felt a little on the spot."

"Sorry. I shouldn't have sent you ahead. You're new so everyone *has to have a look."*

"Which means you aren't?" he teased, eager to ease the tension.

Aiden glanced away. "I've been here before, but I'm hardly a regular." He propped himself against the wall. "We don't have to stay."

Joshua looked around, struck by the humor of the situation. He tilted his glass toward the young chap, who was still staring. "If you find yourself in unfamiliar territory, you might as well take a look around."

Aiden eyed him quizzically. "So is that your philosophy?"

Joshua chuckled. "Actually I think it's something you suggested the day we met. As for this, I don't think I have a philosophy. But I do have a drink." He clinked his glass against Aiden's then took another gulp.

The ice broke after that. The man with the silver hair struck up a conversation, slipping into English when he realized it would be easier. He was a banker from somewhere in the city, though Joshua failed to catch the details. His companion hailed from southern France. They asked about the war, concerned about recent German advances. "We are honored the Americans have come," his companion said at one point, with such sincerity Joshua blushed.

The two men left a bit later, but not before buying another round.

When they'd gone, Aiden explained. "We don't have to finish them. They'll only keep coming if we do." He laughed at Joshua's reaction. "Not just here, but everywhere. You'll see. Parisians can be magnanimous when they want to be. At times they may be condescending, and they are. Still they're grateful to have troops on the ground."

Joshua nodded, nursing his drink as he surveyed the room. Try as he might to distance himself, he found the jovial anonymity comforting. He never knew such places existed.

Everything was subtle, but the messages were clear. He recognized men who were together. Some were clearly chums, out having fun. Still others pursued a more active dance. Aiden let him be. Though they stood close, they didn't touch. He was grateful for that.

Men came and went. None caused a stir. Maybe they were locals. He wondered if he'd exaggerated the initial reaction in his head, though he knew better. It was as if somehow they knew, though he suspected his expression had given him away.

The far drapery opened again, and another man slipped inside. This time it was no stranger. It was Pierre from the café. Joshua turned to Aiden, who'd already noticed.

He took Joshua's drink and set it down. Then he took his hand and pulled him through the curtain behind them.

*   *   *

The night wore a foggy sheen, and a crescent moon played peek-a-boo above the darkened rooflines. Joshua wanted to ask about Pierre, but hesitated. Having secured his mask, Aiden forged along the narrow street.

"We can take the path," he announced, turning onto a street that ended at the foot of the bluff.

Joshua caught up to him as they began their ascent. "Wait," he whispered.

Aiden glanced over. "Sorry."

"You seem bothered."

"It's nothing," Aiden scoffed, but he drew to a halt. "Maybe we shouldn't have gone."

"Don't say that. It was . . . it was fine." He stepped nearer. "I take it this is why you and your father don't speak?"

"Me liking men, you mean?"

Joshua reached for him. "Yeah. That's what I meant."

Aiden looked at Joshua's hand on his arm. "The easy answer is 'yes.' But the longer it's been, the more I think it was convenient. If not this, it would have been something else."

"What happened?"

"He found out about me. It was my second year of medical

school. *Apparently he scheduled some meetings in the city and made a surprise visit to the apartment, on purpose I think. I was with a friend when he showed up."*

"*That was all?"*

Aiden bristled. "*Yes. It was nothing tawdry!*" He resumed walking, slower. "*I apologize. I didn't mean to snap.*"

"*We don't have to . . .*"

"*No, it's alright. I'm just not used to talking about it . . . with anyone.*" He shook his head. "*Besides, that was how it ended. It began earlier, with a classmate. I didn't know him well though I had seen him out once, in a bar on the lower east side. He was brilliant. From the beginning it was clear he'd be at the top of the class. But shortly before first term ended, he was suspended from the program.*"

"*Why?*"

"*Because he was caught, or turned in. The program was cutthroat so it wouldn't surprise me. The school dismissed him on moral grounds. My father heard about it. He made some crude comment while I was home. I confronted him, told him they were fools for kicking the man out. So he already had his suspicions.*"

"*You could've denied them.*"

"*He made the accusations. I simply refused to lie.*"

"*Your father told the school?*"

"*And ruin his reputation? No, cutting me off was neater.*"

"*So you joined the Foreign Legion?*" His tone betrayed his doubt.

"*Not immediately. I began an internship at a brokerage house. I figured I'd make some money, pay my own way. But when my father found out, he put a stop to it. One day my mentor called me into his office. He told me to report to the lead partner the next morning. He said the firm had questions regarding my personal affairs, that some reservations had been expressed.*

"*I pressed, and he mentioned an associate of my father's. So I knew. I left the office and wandered around lower Manhattan. I heard the news that night over a drink.*"

"*What news?*"

"The classmate kicked out of the medical program. It seems he fell into the East River. Actually, he jumped."

Aiden said nothing while they climbed a steeper part of the trail, but spoke again as they entered a small vineyard. "I walked into the partner's office the next morning and quit. Later the same day I contacted the legion."

Joshua nodded, trying to comprehend.

"Maybe it was my own death wish."

"You shouldn't. Don't ever say that!"

Aiden turned to face him. "I was only kidding."

"Well, it isn't funny."

He reached for Joshua. "Please. It's just I don't know why I joined, not really. So I joke about it now." He sighed. "Besides, it was a lifetime ago. I wouldn't change a thing. I learned who I am here. The war gave me a purpose."

"And when the war ends, what then?"

The question seemed to catch him off guard. "I don't know. I'd still like to be a doctor, I guess. If I can find a way." He turned the question around. "And you? What will you do?"

Joshua had never looked beyond it. He gazed at the heavens. "I have no idea. And I haven't a clue who I am."

"You don't need to know, Wolfie. Not yet. But you ought to ask yourself every once in a while."

They continued up through the vineyard. The crescent moon climbed with them, and a low glow hovered above the eastern horizon.

Joshua decided it was safe to ask. "And Pierre? What's that about?"

"Oh, hardly worth all the subterfuge. I just didn't want to see him." He looked over, choosing to be blunt. "Pierre's a player. Last time I visited, he locked onto me, flattering me." He shrugged. "We ended up together. It was a mistake."

Joshua averted his eyes. "I may be naive, but I kind of figured that."

They kept climbing. When they reached the trees above the

vineyard, they paused. This time he held Aiden's gaze. "And me. Would I be a mistake?"

Aiden shook his head. "No. Not if you were sure."

He took Aiden's hand. "I'm sure," he breathed, moving into the shadows.

27 – Confrontation

Elisabeth flung the unfinished dress aside. She closed her eyes and pressed her fingers against her eyelids. Her neck was tight as well, which was understandable. She'd been sewing since dawn.

She glanced outside. With some relief she noted it wasn't simply her failing vision. A cloudbank had rolled in. She added another log to the fire. Then she moved to the window, attempting to will away the throbbing ache.

Maybe it would snow. The wind had shifted, and she could feel the moist chill. They'd never reached January with so little on the ground. By now they'd normally have a standing foot or more. Yet she could still see bare earth, and lingering patches from Christmas had turned black and dingy. At least Joshua had been able to keep working, as had Wayne. One had to be thankful for small graces.

There was movement at the shed. The truck wasn't visible, and she figured Wayne had already left for the delivery. But squinting closer, she could see him fiddling around.

With a start she flew into action, grabbing her shawl and snatching the basket from the counter. He never ate enough these days so she took advantage of any opportunity.

Outside the wind was stronger than expected. She pulled her shawl close as she made her way down the bluff. Reaching the lane, she saw him emerge, threatening to disappear into the quarry before she could catch him. "Honey! Wait!"

He didn't react at first, then gave a halting glance over his shoulder. She waved the basket. He shook his head, but started back toward the shed.

"I'm running late," he snarled when she reached him.

"You need to eat something. It's roast chicken on rye. Five minutes at most."

He took the basket and set it atop the cluttered tool bench rather than stepping under the eave. Taking a bite, he chewed, staring the whole time.

She stood firm, watching. Seemed everything was a contest, a show of how rough he had it, like a petulant child. She was in no mood for it.

Still, she gave conversation a shot. "How's it coming?"

He finished chewing before mumbling his response. "Slow. The stone's inconsistent recently, all blasting to gravel. Might have to dig out the lower end soon."

She shrugged. "There are worse problems. The mild winter's been a blessing. I remember years there weren't any orders come January."

He finished another bite. "Suppose so. Ol' McCullough's not much good to me these days. His rheumatoid flared up, same as last winter. Frankly I'm not convinced it'll be any better come spring. His wife's been urging him to head on back to Carolina."

She suspected where he was heading, but followed anyhow. "She's been egging him on that for over a decade. Hasn't come to anything."

He looked her square in the eye. "This year might be different, though it'd be just as well. I'd rather not have to let him go. Josh'll be back to full speed by then."

Wayne had been at it since that evening at the Daltons . . . bullheaded, refusing to see anything but his own intentions. She'd let it slide, what with the holidays and his mother's visit. But that was over now. They had to stop pretending, about lots of things.

"Josh might be busy elsewhere," she said, matter of fact.

He dropped the half-finished sandwich onto the ground. "Don't have time for this," he growled, shoving the basket aside. For an instant he looked as if he might throw it. "Some members of this family need to get their heads on straight."

She eyed the chunk of rye in the mud. Never an ounce of appreciation. Never a thought to what she'd given him, what she gave every day. She shook her head. "Has it ever entered your thick skull that maybe Josh doesn't want any part of your damn quarry."

She regretted the words as soon as they escaped.

"My damn quarry! You love saying that, don't you? You've been waiting . . ."

She tried to yank back the errant words. "No, I . . ."

He exploded with the knifing tone that frightened the boys and made her blood run cold. "Oh no you don't! You meant it! You sit up there watching me work myself bloody, all to keep a roof over our heads. And you, with your spells, curled up in bed fretting your lot in life. You're just giddy at the prospect of our son deserting what I built so he can wear aprons and smile at the ladies."

This time he did toss the basket. It bounced, threatening to skitter over the edge. She shuddered, and it only encouraged him.

"Don't tell me you didn't know what was coming. You were all but pushing for it, telling your sob story and batting your eyes at George Dalton all evening. Are you hoping maybe he'll take you along too? Is that what you want?"

At his worst, it was what he always went for, some insinuation of betrayal. Yet he had no problem leaving them to rot on this godforsaken ridge, like that was a good idea. She wouldn't stand for it, not anymore. "What I want," she screamed, "is for our boys to have a chance. He's my son too!"

He moved for her, and she flinched. She'd told him early on that if he ever laid a hand on her, she'd be gone. It was true then, and it was true now. He stopped short, but the blood burned in her veins.

"It was your idea, old man, so don't you point your grimy fingers at me. You had to go prove yourself like some damned fool. When the others wanted out, I warned you not to let 'em. I warned you!"

She walked over to the basket, still seething. Retrieving it, she turned. "I've kept my end of the bargain. My inheritance bought this land. I feed you. I keep this family together. I raised our sons. But I won't have them slaves to your pipedream any longer."

She hadn't meant to say it, not like that.

Wayne clinched his hands and shook in silence. He took a few steps. Their eyes met, and she saw fear. He turned and shuffled toward the edge.

"Wayne, I'm sorry," she called out.

He wavered, then collapsed to his knees as his body buckled. "Eli!" he squealed in a voice she'd never heard before. Then he fell face first into the mud.

28 – Lunch with Katie

Katie was nowhere to be seen when Joshua entered the store, but he heard boxes shuffling in back. A moment later Mr. Dalton emerged, adjusting his spectacles.

"Joshua. What a surprise! How's your father, young man?"

"Better, but Doc say's he'll need another week in bed. He instructed my mother to make sure he eats regular."

Mr. Dalton looked skeptical, but Joshua stuck to the story. Mom had insisted. "Your father's proud," was all she'd say when he pressed the matter.

"Is Katie around?" he added, changing the subject.

"Not now, but she's on her way. She's helping me with the inventory." He wiped his hands on his apron. "Some days it never ends. So what brings you to town on a Friday?"

"Finished early. I need more stone, and Scott can't help 'til tomorrow. I thought Katie might want to have lunch."

Mr. Dalton winked. "I suppose I could spare her for a visit with her fiancé." He glanced at the clock. "She should be here any moment."

Joshua backed toward the door. "Thanks, Mr. Dalton. I'll keep an eye out for her. Promise we won't be long."

Outside the fresh snow was melting, and icicles along the eaves dripped in the sunlight. He lingered on the stoop for a bit then ambled on up the street. Normally he wouldn't have minded a chat with Mr. Dalton, but the job offer had been gnawing at him. Though neither Katie nor her father had mentioned it, given the turn of events at home, it was bound to come up eventually. He had no desire to hasten the matter.

Katie appeared ahead. She quickened her pace upon seeing him and gave him a quick peck when they met.

"I spoke to your father. He says I can borrow you for lunch."

"That sounds wonderful! I ate with Mother, but I'll have a soda."

They made their way to Buck's. The diner, if you could call it that, wasn't much to look at. Ingrid Buck had begun brewing coffee some years back to help make ends meet. After a time she'd added a hand painted sign pointing to the side porch of their shanty. A chalkboard behind the screen listed a handful of breakfast and lunch items. The food was sufficient, suitable for bachelors or workmen with little to spare.

As they approached, Joshua noticed a negro in the vacant lot adjacent the shanty. The amputee ranger he'd seen with his father was wiping snow from a crate.

Joshua studied the man's movements as he dragged over another crate. He managed well with one arm. Of course, it was the least of his handicaps. Hadley didn't take well to strangers, particularly negroes. Having a negro working for the government . . . well, the scorn was nearly unfathomable.

Distracted, he nearly ran Katie into the man's companion at the gate. The older ranger stepped back, tipping his hat. "Pardon, ma'am," he muttered. Katie slipped inside, and Joshua let the man pass.

Emerging with a couple sodas and a sandwich a few minutes later, he saw the men at their makeshift table. He tapped Katie on the arm as they got situated on the bench by the porch.

Katie confirmed his suspicion in a whisper. "The Bucks won't serve him."

He finished a bite of the chicken salad. "So how was your week?"

"Good. Busy prepping the new store. I've been thinking of you. Is your father any better?"

"He's back to snarling all the time, so guess that's a good sign."

"Your father means well."

"You been talking to my mom? You sure sound like her."

"Maybe she says it cause it's true."

He fidgeted. "Can we talk about something else?"

"Well, I suppose. Let's see. Mother's driving me crazy over the wedding."

"How so?"

She took a sip of her soda. "Oh, just everything. She wants to invite more folks, for one. Pa finally drew the line on all her temperance friends. Some of them are nice, but most are just plain busybodies. I can do without all their judgments, especially on our day." She touched his hand. "Do you have any thoughts on the ceremony?"

"Can't say that I do."

"Figured as much. Most men don't give a wit about such things. Do you even want to hear about it?"

"Sure," he offered.

She launched into the details. "Well, by June we'll have roses, which got me thinking. Mother has a couple of white hybrids that bloom early. There won't be many, but we can supplement them with lilies. I'd really like the colors to be sky blue and white, though Mother insists its common. She keeps pushing all these purple shades. Frankly I find them gaudy, but she says it'd be more stately." She snickered. "Like we're royalty or something."

He tried to listen, but the details soon blurred. As she continued, he found himself eavesdropping on the men, catching snippets of conversation.

The topics were routine. Work assignments. Complaints about a new boss. But his ears perked up when he heard mention of the Garth parcel.

The older man shook his head. "I tell ya, Harrison. That there's a lost cause. The son's going to sell to the highest bidder, and it ain't going to be the purchasing unit. Logging companies will jump all over the chance to get at that forest."

The black man leaned back. "I know. But it's a shame. Other than the Ramsey parcel, those might well be the last untouched ridges in three counties. I even heard rumor there's a stand of red spruces on one of them, though damned if I could find it." He shrugged. "Of course it's impossible to inventory that much acreage in one day."

"Well, there you have it. He'd have given us more time if he was serious. Mark my words, it'll all be clear-cut in a few years."

Joshua studied the ridge above. It hardly seemed right. Weren't some things meant to be wild?

"Joshua! Did you hear me?"

He jolted. "Sorry. I was distracted. It is nice of the McGuintys to open up their home."

She shook her head. "I knew you weren't interested. I was asking about The Hearthstone. Could my parents pay for a few days? Mother says the honeymoon could be their gift."

The truth slipped out. "Is there anything your mother doesn't want her stamp on? She gonna name our children too?"

Seeing the hurt in her eyes, he tried to ease up. The effort fell short. "It's all too much. First your father offers me a job. Now your mother's taking over the wedding. Suppose I ought to be thankful she likes the ring, else I'd have to send it back to Vermont."

She bristled. "I like the ring! That's all that matters. You know my mother's opinionated. She always has been. I can handle her. But as for Pa, you've no right to question his motives. He wouldn't have asked if he didn't think you'd be good for the store, and he's been patient. He knows your family needs you now."

She squeezed his hand. "Josh, I'm fine either way. It's your decision. I want you to be happy. I want us to be happy."

"I'm not gonna take over the quarry," he spit out. "I know that much."

"I hear you, Josh. I understand."

"Katie, I can't promise unless I'm sure. I do appreciate his offer." He sighed. "Your father likes me, unlike your mother."

Her response was swift. "Mother likes you, too! She just has her ways."

"No, she doesn't. She barely tolerates me."

Katie grimaced. "She doesn't know you like I do. She doesn't see how kind you are. You've always been kind. Quiet. Thoughtful. You were never like the other boys. I can be myself with you."

She stopped talking, but her expression betrayed her. She was wrestling with something.

"What is it?" he asked.

"It's nothing."

"Katie?"

She pulled her hand away. "It's just . . . it's just she says things that aren't right, and I don't know how to respond. Not on this. She is still my mother."

"About what?"

"You can't mention it," she pleaded, "even if it makes you angry."

"What?"

"Promise you won't hold it against her."

"What did she say?" he demanded. Then, realizing she needed to hear the words, he relented. "I promise."

Her shoulders fell. "Mother says she doesn't trust you. She says you're the kind of man who can't be trusted. 'A man with secrets,' she keeps saying." Doubt flashed across her face. "She says I'll never really know you."

He turned away, feeling the burn inside. "Your mother should keep her thoughts to herself."

Katie persisted. "That's what I mean! It's foolish. She doesn't know what she's talking about."

He grew flush, suffocating beneath the weight of her faith. He could never tell her, and it was behind him. What more could he do?

When he turned, their eyes met. All the right words escaped him. "I won't say anything," he blurted instead.

They sat in silence, fishing for a way out.

After a moment, she glanced at the men. "Mother was funny when he came into the store."

"The negro?" he whispered.

She nodded. "She tried to act all egalitarian, telling him of course he could buy a few things. Then she yanked me into the back and made Pa go out to keep an eye on him. Now she won't leave me in the store alone."

He shook his head. "Can't believe they'd send him here, as if folks weren't angry enough."

She leaned closer. "Thing is, he's the one with the degree. Chuck stopped by the store last week. He says the man attended some negro university up north. He fought in the war too. That's how he lost his arm. Apparently he gathers all the forest inventories, but isn't allowed to go out on his own. They're afraid he'll be chased off. Or worse."

Joshua thought of the men's conversation. "What do you think about it? The government buying up the land and all."

She pondered a moment. "I don't rightly know. Mother's upset. Everyone who comes into the store claims to be. Then the ones who own up and sell. Pa says we'll be alright with the new store. I suppose it hurts Chuck more than anyone. Loggers have to find more trees, I guess."

She took another sip of soda. "You know, I used to despise him in school. He was always so full of himself. But he's turned out to be quite nice."

"What about the ridges?" he pressed.

She gazed up. "Be a shame to see them laid to waste like those along the river. The Bible says we ought to be good stewards, but seems to me men forget that when there's money to be made." Her eyes found his again. "You're not like that, Josh. I don't want you to be."

He sighed. Sometimes it wasn't suffocating at all.

"Besides," she continued, "I have a lot of memories of you and me up there."

She was right. They'd wandered high and low together, and she'd trusted him from the start. He had watched over her, helped her. Maybe that could be enough.

He nudged her. "You were so afraid of the forest when you first came to Hadley. Do you remember?"

She leaned back, a smile creeping across her face. "Yes. Then again, I was frightened of most everything back then. I'd been so pampered in Richmond. The first time you suggested we leave the lane for a climb, you might as well have suggested we explore the moon. I was terrified."

"But you took to it. You're not afraid now."

She breathed deep, still taking in the sky. "No, I suppose I'm not. And as for the ridges, I rather like them. So I guess I'd rather keep everything just as it is."

"Me too," he said.

She took his hand again. "I know, Josh."

She finished her soda. "Well, I suppose I ought to be getting on. It'll take Pa twice as long to do the inventory without me."

They rose and acknowledged the men, then made their way up the street.

"Blue," he said as they neared the store.

"Excuse me?"

"I want the wedding to be blue. I hate purple."

She drew back. "I never knew that."

He winked. "Cause it isn't true. But there's no need for her to know."

Her laughter made it seem alright.

29 - Roses along the Seine

Claire tapped his arm. "Another coffee?"

Joshua jolted. "Oui, s'il vous plaît." He watched the waitress place a fresh cup before him, disappointed it wasn't larger. Across the table Aiden came into focus, his brow furrowed as he scanned the newspaper. Joshua waited for him to look up, but the headlines of Le Temps proved too great a distraction.

"Someone didn't have enough sleep," Claire teased.

Despite his embarrassment, he grinned. "Nothing this can't solve," he muttered, taking a sip. Setting the cup down, he took stock of the morning. The sky was clear. The sidewalk was damp with morning mist, though it was burning off fast. All in all, the weather for the celebration looked promising.

By the time he finished his second cup, the caffeine had performed its magic, reviving his eagerness to explore. "So when do we head out?"

Aiden folded the newspaper. "I'm ready if you both are." He glanced skyward. "Should we walk or brave the Metro?"

"I want to see the Metro," Joshua interjected.

Claire nodded. "Then we should go. It'll be madness later."

Joshua grabbed his hat and stretched. Between the hillside and the hard studio floor, his muscles were sore. After a block Aiden backtracked to the café to retrieve the blanket, the sole remnant of abandoned plans for a picnic lunch. Then they descended cobbled streets on the far end of Montmartre.

The Metro entrance sat in the center of a small square. Folks were arriving from all directions, but the crowd was tolerable. As they approached he admired the cast iron and ceramic structure. "Abbesses," he breathed, pondering the name.

The lift was full so they took the staircase. After a couple of spirals, he began to wonder how far it descended. Aiden settled in beside him, as if reading his thoughts. "'Abbesses' refers to the local abbey. It's one of the deepest stations. When the Nord-Sud Company extended the A Line prior to the war, builders had to dig through abandoned mines beneath Montmartre."

"This entrance is different than the one we passed yesterday," Joshua observed.

"Different companies, different designs. The Nord-Sud entrances aren't as ornate as those of the Paris Metropolitan Company. They lack all the curvy flourishes. But I like the Nord-Sud lines. The stations are lined with intricate tile. Their train cars are impressive too. You'll see."

"You really love Paris, don't you?"

Aiden shrugged. "How could anyone not? So much thought goes into everything . . . every façade, every street, every nook. Nothing escapes notice, nor should it. Details matter." He paused. "Maybe it's that Paris has been my refuge from the beginning, so different from everything else."

Joshua felt the shield go up. Aiden's expression hardened. It was the mask he wore with the men.

"I understand," he uttered quickly, hoping he'd stay.

Aiden's face softened. At the platform he held Joshua's elbow, letting Claire lead. "How are you feeling?" he whispered.

Joshua blushed. "Good."

"Me too." Then he pointed to the arched ceiling, explaining the mechanics of the structure. They continued their exploration until they heard the rumble of the train, when they moved to rejoin Claire.

*   *   *

Aiden strained to view the stage as the crowd erupted at the end of another speech. He seemed content to watch the entire line-up, but Joshua had lost interest.

Half the speeches were in French, though it hardly mattered. They all sounded the same – acknowledgment of the hardships, gratitude for the sacrifices and confidence in a glorious outcome.

Even the rhythm was predictable, and he'd taken to clapping on cue from changes in cadence and tone. One speech would have been sufficient, but apparently all the dignitaries needed a moment in the sun.

The morning had been more interesting. A display of captured German armaments had greeted them as they'd emerged from the Metro at Place de la Concorde. They had exchanged bemused looks at the sight of children climbing the instruments of war, some mangled from battle. Afterward they had watched row after row of soldiers march beneath the American flags along the Avenue des Champs-Élysées.

But now, baking in the midday heat, Joshua found himself envious of Claire, who'd wisely retreated to the shade.

Aiden noticed his discomfort. "We can go," he conceded with some reluctance.

"Please," Joshua admitted. So they retreated from the crowd to the comfort of the trees. After scouring for several minutes, Joshua discovered her on a sheltered bench, chatting with an old woman.

Claire glanced up. "Have we won yet?"

Joshua laughed. "Several times, I think."

Aiden wasn't amused, and she clasped his hand. "I know. It all matters." She spoke to him like a mother consoling a fretting child, acknowledging his disappointment while refusing to dwell on it. Then she turned to the old woman. "Madame Chapelle, ce sont mes deux amis Américains, Aiden et Joshua."

The woman nodded, and Claire continued. "Madame Chapelle was telling me about her late husband." She looked at Aiden. "Seems he would have liked the speeches too. They were why she came down today. But the crowds were too much, and she couldn't find her friend."

Aiden knelt to speak to the woman. After a moment she offered him her frail hand. "Que Dieu vous bénisse."

He helped her stand, and they walked arm in arm toward the Avenue. Claire eyed Aiden approvingly as she and Joshua tagged behind. Entering the crowd Aiden approached a man seated on a bench. The man rose, and Aiden helped the woman situate her umbrella. Then he kissed her hand and rose, making his way back.

"She'll be fine," he explained. "She said she met her husband after his return from Algeria. They'd been married sixty-two years when he died last spring."

Claire nodded. "Did she mention her grandson? He's in Lorraine as well."

"Yes. She grilled me on conditions. She understands the situation better than most."

Claire sighed. "I imagine she has plenty of time to read, and worry."

Joshua watched the woman as they spoke. She shot an admonishing glare at the couple chatting beside her before leaning forward to hear the speaker.

"Shall we find something to eat?" Claire asked.

Aiden pointed at the food carts along the next block. It seemed others had the same idea. "I can get us something, but it'll take a while."

"If you don't mind." She gazed off the avenue. "And you want to show Joshua the Eiffel Tower, is that right?"

"Yes. Why?"

She glanced back. "I thought we might find a quiet spot near the Seine. You have to cross anyhow. Unless you'd rather watch more speeches."

"I think I'm finished." He gave a knowing grin. "I suppose you want to go on ahead."

She smiled as if caught. "Maybe. You know where?"

"I know."

She looked to Joshua. "Care to escort me, or are you two inseparable now?"

Joshua laughed. "No. I'd like that."

Aiden shrugged. "I'll muster up what I can. See you in a bit."

*   *   *

Joshua drank in the sights as they strolled. The Eiffel Tower rose ahead. Nearer sat a building domed in glass. Claire explained the Grand Palais exhibition hall had been converted into a hospital for the war.

Paris was even grander than he'd imagined, photographs failing to do it justice. But while he appreciated Aiden's observation about the details, he found the formal areas intimidating. He preferred the functional parts – the stations, the markets, the neighborhoods. They felt more human. He shared the thought with Claire.

"Oh, I agree. The neighborhoods are so lively. Of course, being from Lorraine, Paris is new to me as well. Before the war I had only visited once, though it left an impression, memories I'll cherish forever." She squeezed his arm. "Now I enjoy visiting Lily, and sharing the city with friends."

Joshua sighed. She made it easy to feel comfortable. Otherwise he might have pondered the evening, giving in to guilt. He considered thanking her for letting him join them, but doing so ventured too close to the reason he had. He wasn't that comfortable. "So what parts were so memorable?" he asked instead.

"I'll show you one." She released his arm and dashed across the street, entering a park on the far side.

Joshua checked for traffic then followed. Trotting along a curving path, his eyes were drawn to the river. A series of bridges stretched clear to the horizon. Ahead, Claire drew to a halt beside a rose garden. She was still catching her breath when he reached her.

"I'm on my feet constantly, but I never run anymore," she explained. "When I was little, I used to race all over our village. Mother would scold me, warning it was unladylike. But I loved it so. I felt free."

He chuckled. "I mostly hiked. It was easier."

"Aiden said you grew up in the mountains. That must have been fascinating."

"It was. I dream about them sometimes." He shrugged. "All the time, I guess."

Her eyes grew wide. "I know what you mean. Every night, no

matter how exhausted, I drift to sleep imagining the fields outside Remenauville."

She took the blanket and started along a path among the roses. "Mother says the places you love become a part of you, and you a part of them. Your mind takes you back, even if you leave. In her case, Remenauville was all she ever knew."

"Where is she now?" he asked.

"In Bordeaux, with her sister. We stayed in Paris a short while. But it was too large, and too expensive. We spent all our savings, which wasn't much. Everything else we left behind." Claire surveyed the landscape, selecting a grassy spot shrouded in yellow blooms. "Mother hates it. Her letters are filled with talk of going home."

He helped smooth the blanket atop the grass, recalling Aiden's description of the destruction. "And you?"

She seated herself. "I'm not nearly as confident. When I arrived in Toul, I made inquiries. Recently I asked Aiden. He was evasive, but I've seen the front. I doubt anything remains."

"So would you live in Paris?"

"Perhaps. I haven't thought that far. I do well to get through each day." She met his gaze. "Aiden said you asked about David."

"I didn't mean to pry. I had noticed your ring."

"It's fine. I don't hide it. Aiden said you were observant. I hope you don't mind me saying, but you're like a young pup . . . poking around, figuring out his world. I think that's why Aiden's drawn to you."

He averted his gaze, thankful when she didn't press.

"As for my ring, I like wearing it. I refuse to live in mourning, but I do miss my David. It's why I come here when I visit Paris."

"I don't understand."

She retreated into memory, a smile creeping across her face. "This garden is special."

"How so?"

Her story tumbled out. "I had known David my whole life. When we were children, he used to tease me. But we had a connection, even then.

"My father was an Englishman, much older than my mother. He was a kind man, encouraging and often spoiling me. I was seventeen when he died, and David was there for me. After that our bond deepened, yet we never rushed. It didn't seem necessary.

"When the war began, David was at university. At the time we thought it a bump in the road. We knew it was war. But no one expected it to last, not then. Nevertheless, we changed our plans. David enlisted, like many young men. He asked me to meet him before he reported. I told Mother I was visiting Lily and her husband, and travelled to Paris. One afternoon David brought me to this garden, where he gave me this ring. We married a week later."

He admired the sparkle in the sunlight, unsure what to say. "It's beautiful."

She adjusted the band. "It is, isn't it? Such a promising start." Her eyes watered.

"I've upset you."

"It's nothing you have done. It simply overwhelms me sometimes, even now." She plucked a nearby bloom. "You know, I find it strange. Everything about my life is defined by what it was before . . . where I lived, who I married.

"I imagine it will be different someday. Someday I'll find a new home, a place where I'll build a new life. Not now. Not yet. But I can see the possibility." She hesitated. "Not long ago, I feared I wouldn't survive at all."

"No," he breathed.

She looked up. "Oh yes. You have to understand. My husband was dead. Mother and I were refugees. By the time we reached Bordeaux, we were destitute. My aunt kept telling me I had to go on. But when everything is stolen from you, those words mean nothing."

"So what changed?"

She sighed. "Me, I guess, with help. I had my family, people who loved me. In time I could hear them. Eventually I was ready to live again. I found a purpose; I became a nurse." She sniffed the rose. "That, and I held onto the days."

"The days?"

"All my days with David. I thought of special days, like when we came here. I imagined the early days, growing up in Remenauville. Our first kiss . . . our first fight. I spent hours recalling days, lingering over details, crying over them. It was painful at first, but that changed. I began to recall others, casual ones . . . days that hadn't seemed special at all at the time. Looking back, I realized they were. They were filled with life, and we were together." She caressed the petals. "Being together made them special."

He looked around them. The sun dappled through the trees. The scent of warm grass mingled with the sweet smell of the roses. For the first time he had a glimpse of the man he was, the man he might become. "Today's a good day," he observed.

She laughed softly. "It is. The secret is they all are. Every day has potential, no matter how dark. You have to hold onto that promise."

They heard the approach of footsteps. "Where are you?" Aiden called out.

Claire jumped up. "Here," she announced. "And we're hungry."

Aiden hurried over. "It's the best I could do," he explained, tossing Joshua a wink as he distributed croissants and sacks of roasted nuts.

30 – Pete after the Snow

"You got it?"

"Almost. There, that should do it." Pete tugged on the sash chain then shoved the counterweight back into the pocket.

Joshua slid the sash into place, raised it a few inches, and released it. Without benefit of a stop, the sash wavered but hung in balance. "Perfect! Just like the others."

Pete punched his shoulder. "Told you I could fix windows."

Joshua stepped back. The newly cut panes were crisp, and had proven easier than expected. He ran his finger along the glazing. "Thanks, Pete. They look good."

Pete glanced about the room. "It's mighty cozy here. You get the trim back up and give it a good sweeping, and we'd be just about ready to move in."

Pete had been in high spirits all day, telling jokes and teasing him. His mood was contagious. "Guess I'd have to own it first," Joshua responded with a laugh. "Katie thinks I'm crazy. She keeps bugging me to bring her up."

Pete ambled over to the fireplace. "Why haven't you?"

Joshua shrugged. "I dunno. It's been kinda nice having a place to wander off by myself. Guess I'm not quite ready to give it up. You're the only one who's seen it since I started."

Pete grabbed the ladle from the mantle and stirred the cast iron pot above the flame. "I think it's ready. Hand me the tins there?"

They took their stew and cornbread outside. Though the air had a bite, sunlight bounced off the fresh snow. It was about as bright as it ever got among the spruces.

Perched against the trunk of the fallen one, they ate in silence. It wasn't 'til Pete grabbed a second piece of cornbread that he spoke. "You know, I been thinking about this place."

Joshua reached for his canteen. "How so?"

Pete gazed about. "Just pondering on how it came to be. My dad remembers the farm down in the hollow. He said the family kept to themselves, though he saw it once when he was little, at the elder daughter's wedding. Seems she moved away, and the rest of them . . . well, the cholera got 'em. So I get it, the tie to the man who built the cabin, that is. But why here? Why build a place no one can get to?"

Joshua studied the spruces and the boulders on either end. "It is kinda pretty."

Pete cocked his head. "I seen a lot of pretty places. I ain't never hauled a pile of rocks out to build a cabin at one of them."

"Well, you've got me there. Though I have an idea."

Pete pulled a small flask from his coat. "I thought you might. You tend to mull over things, Josh."

"Oh, do I?"

Pete took a sip and shoved the flask in his direction. "Yeah, nearly as much as me. So I want to hear this here idea of yours."

Joshua took a swig then handed it back. The rush hit as he ambled over to the engraved stone. When he glanced back, Pete was waiting. He decided to play it light.

"Well, as I see it, Anna grew up around here, at that farm below I guess. It would have been mighty lonesome. No Hadley. Just your place and the ranches down by the river. So I reckon she wandered all over this ridge, on her own or with her siblings. Probably played among these spruces. Maybe she used to sit out there on the ledge, staring over the valley, wondering what her life would hold."

Pete nodded. "'Tis likely."

Joshua spun about, ignoring the tightness is his thigh. "But then a young man wandered through one day, and took a fancy to her." He tipped an imaginary hat in Pete's direction.

Pete took another swallow then dipped his head. "The young Mister . . .?"

"Garth. His name was Garth."

"That's right. Mister Garth."

"Yep. And, well, Mister Garth was a big shot back east . . . steel baron, industrialist, something powerful like that. He'd come here looking to acquire some land, and found love along the way. When he left, he took Anna far from her beloved spruces. But he promised they'd return someday, probably said he'd build her a little cabin. I imagine it was a sincere promise, one he intended to keep."

Joshua returned for more moonshine.

"So what happened?"

The alcohol burned on his lips, and he felt a twinge of guilt. There was no glossing over it. "She died, out of the blue, like the rest of her kin. That's what happened." He handed the flask over and retreated toward the cabin. "So Mister Garth traveled out here to keep his promise. Best he could anyhow."

He wore a convincing smile when he turned. "More stew?"

"Sure, if you're getting it."

In the cabin, he collected himself. Maybe it was best to be straight about it. Anything less seemed disrespectful.

When he returned, he tried again. "You see, a nurse I met in France, she believes places get in your blood. They stay with you. So I like to think this was Anna's place. She found it special, and this Garth fellow knew how important it was. So when she died, he did what he could. He kept a promise."

Pete met his gaze. "That sounds about right, Josh." He dunked a chunk of cornbread in the stew and then popped it into his mouth. He chewed slowly, deep in thought.

"You know," he said when he finished, "maybe everyone has a place, or needs a place, someplace where they know who they are."

Joshua looked back at the cabin. "Maybe."

Pete opened the flask again. He poured a dash of moonshine into the cap and handed it to Joshua. Then he raised the flask skyward. "To Anna and her cozy cabin," he announced.

"To Anna," Joshua echoed.

*   *   *

They worked a while longer, putting the jambs back in place and reinstalling the trim. Pete talked of his mother and how she was getting out a bit. He said it made coming home easier.

"You seem chipper too," Joshua observed as they wiped the panes. "Tons better, really."

Pete sighed. "I am. I still miss Nate something fierce, but I don't dwell on it. Not all the time, that is. Some days I feel real good."

"He'd have wanted that."

Pete nodded. "Besides, I got no complaints. Work's going well. The new tunnel's coming along. We hit a decent seam, and it's growing as we go deeper. Mister Tuckerman's eager, so there'll be more shifts from here on."

"I know you've been wanting the work."

"I have. Though there's no way I'll make it over to Monterey to hear Scott play. You plan to go, don't you?"

"Yeah, I'm gonna drive Katie over. Might bring Mom if Dad's doing better. She's been shy of leaving him, but Scott would like her to come."

"Sure hope she can. You know, it's a good thing you're doing."

"It was your idea, Pete. We just helped." He tossed his rag into the bucket then grabbed the broom. "Scott's lucky to have a friend like you."

"Like to think I'm your friend, too," he teased.

"Goes without saying." He tried to read Pete's expression but came up short. "What's going on?"

"Can I share something with you, as a buddy?"

"Sure."

"Well, there's another reason I'm doing better."

Joshua propped himself against the broom. "What's that?"

"I think I'm in love."

"Huh?"

Pete had been holding it in, and the words bubbled forth. "Her name's Mara. Mara Brosmer. She lives down the way from my uncle's."

Joshua nodded, trying to catch up. "How long?" he asked. "I mean, how'd you meet?"

"Well, that's the thing. I been seeing her my whole life.

Whenever we visited my uncle, that is. But we were just kids, and it would only be for a short while. We never had much to say. But being down there most all the time, it was different."

Pete laughed as he paced the room. "When I first went to stay with them, I was so blue. And my cousins, they're so loud and all at each other. So I had to take walks just to hear myself think. I'd see her up on her porch or doing chores, and I'd nod and go about my business.

"So one day I'm in town, and she was there with her mother. I was all dingy from work, but they came over to say hello and to offer their condolences about Nate. We chatted for a bit, and I was struck. That's the only way I can describe it. I saw her in a whole new light. I realized she was just quiet like me. That's why we never talked."

Joshua set the broom aside. He opened the door. "Have you told her?"

Pete bit his lip. "Not in so many words, but I been seeing her nearly everyday. I stop by after my shift, and we chat by her fence. We never run out of things to say. Just telling her about my day feels good. And she has the prettiest eyes. I could look at them all day."

He sucked in a deep breath. "I'm happy for you, Pete."

"I was always envious of you and Katie, how you were together. I used to wonder how it was. Now I understand. I feel I can tell Mara anything. It's like she knows me better than I know myself. Yet she likes me anyhow."

"That's how it ought to be," Joshua whispered.

Pete had calmed his pacing, but was still bouncing. "Mom's still a might fragile so we're gentle with her, even good news. And with Scott in school, well, I just had to tell someone."

Joshua stepped outside, and Pete followed. "I'm glad you did. But I'll let you tell Scott yourself. He'll be tickled."

"Yeah, I want to surprise him. Want him to meet her too. Scott's good at reading people. I know he'll like her, though. She's special."

"No doubt she is. So when do you see her next?"

"Well, that's the thing. I'm heading back this evening instead of tomorrow. We're going to spend the day together, and for once I won't be all covered in dirt. We plan to take a drive in my uncle's buggy if the weather's nice. It's funny. I see her all the time now, but it'll be our first real outing."

Joshua squinted at the afternoon sun. "Sorry I took your only day in town."

"It's no trouble, Josh. Told you I'd help. Besides, we're nearly finished, aren't we?"

Joshua glanced toward the cabin. Nothing more had to get done, yet he could feel himself sinking. He'd only drag Pete down too. "Why don't you head on? I'm gonna touch up the trim while there's still light."

Pete seemed puzzled. "I can stick around. You've another brush, haven't you?"

Joshua made a show of thumbing through the cart. "Maybe. But the windows are small. I'll handle it. You get going now." He forced a grin. "You have to follow when love finds you."

Pete laughed. "I suppose. But, hey, I'll see you next time I'm home. You tell Scott to break a leg, though not a word about Mara."

"Not a word . . . promise."

Shortly after, Pete ambled off, taking his spark along with him. Joshua watched him disappear behind the boulders before wandering over to Butterscotch.

"You have enough water, buddy?"

The pail was low, though not empty. He went to the cart and returned with the last of the cornbread. "We'll get you some oats when we get home," he whispered.

Brushing the crumbs from his hands, he moved toward the cabin but stopped short. He shook his head. It was no use.

Weakness overcame him. His knees buckled. Then came heaving sobs and the sudden, unstoppable tears.

31 – A Walk in the Clouds

Claire tossed aside the sack of roasted nuts. "That's enough salt for me."

Aiden shrugged. "Sorry. The cart I chose had run out of most everything."

She launched a walnut at him. "I'm teasing." She peered over the rose bushes. "Though I am thirsty. There's a fountain by the river."

Aiden retrieved the nut from inside his collar before it could disappear down his shirt. "Should we move on then?"

Sensing her hesitation, Joshua chimed in. "What if Aiden and I walk over and come back afterward? If you'd rather stay, that is."

Claire flashed a grateful smile. "That would be nice. I'll walk with you to the fountain, and then you two can go ahead. I'll be around here somewhere."

And so it was decided. They left the blanket among the roses and emerged into the surrounding park. After taking turns at the fountain, Claire wandered back beneath the trees. He and Aiden set an angle toward the nearest bridge.

They walked in silence at first. Joshua was hesitant. He sought Aiden's eye when they paused to watch the rippling current beneath them. The water shimmered in the sunlight.

Aiden flicked his cigarette butt over the edge. "What is it?" he whispered.

"I was thinking."

Aiden grazed a finger along the back of his hand. "I imagine. Listen, if you need time alone, I'd understand. When I first, um, ventured out, I'd flee afterward. Then I'd pretend nothing had happened. I was quite good at denying it."

Joshua bristled. "I don't deny anything. It just feels different."

"So you want to figure it out. I'd tell you it's a waste of time, but it wouldn't stop you. If we were in New York, I could give you the books I found. I used to think I could fix it if I understood." He pushed back from the rail. "But the explanations were all bullshit, so I gave up after a while."

Joshua pondered his words as they continued on. He didn't understand much, but knew it wasn't a clinical matter for him. When they reached the opposite bank, he touched Aiden's arm. "I don't know about all that. I just know I like you," he began before words failed him. "I hope that's alright," he stammered.

Aiden glanced about. "I like you too. Besides, Wolfie, I shouldn't act like I have anything to teach you, not on this. You might be way ahead of me."

Joshua frowned. "How so?"

He tapped Joshua's chest. "Seems you already know it's what's in here that matters. It took me forever to accept that. I still struggle with it." He hesitated. "What I'm saying is I have to take one step at a time. That's all I can promise."

"I understand."

"You sure?"

"Yeah. I'm sure." Then, determined to make it so, he started again toward the tower. "Let's get moving. We've still got a ways to go."

*   *   *

Encountering large crowds beneath the tower, they opted for the steps rather than wait for an elevator. Other souls had braved the climb as well. Joshua had a brief scare, thinking Tommy was among a descending group. After that he remained on alert.

When they reached the second platform, they took a break, wandering about the observation deck.

"It is amazing," Joshua observed, studying the elaborate weave of metal. "A true marvel."

"And after two decades, still nothing compares to it. No wonder the Germans want it so bad."

He scoffed. "They want the Eiffel Tower?"

"No, but they do want dominance. The Kaiser aims to end Britain's influence over Europe. Everything else is a means to that end. France is merely a field of play, a deadly one. Millions of lives lost for vanity, for power."

"Why do people accept it? Ordinary folks, I mean."

"Why do people do anything? The French are fighting for their homes, their culture. The real question is why are we here. I joined the Foreign Legion to spite my father." He glanced over. "And you, why did you join?"

Joshua looked across the Seine. Montmartre rose in the distance. Nearer, he sought the rose garden. "I told myself it was for people like Claire. When the war started, I used to read articles, anything I could get my hands on. I remember this photograph of a bombed village. The journalist had spoken with a woman fleeing the countryside with her baby. I told my brother that maybe I ought to help."

"Knowing you, Wolfie, I believe it. You're so damned earnest about everything. But is that all, the only reason?"

He sighed. "I guess I saw a chance . . . a way out." He'd never really admitted it before. Not even to himself.

"Marching to war is a heck of way to seek a new life. There are easier routes. Still, as reasons go, it's better than some. Outside the draft most men couldn't tell you how they wound up here. Yet they'll be changed forever."

"So what's one supposed to do? I'm here now. We all are."

"Survive. Do your duty. Maybe you can do some good. The important thing is to leave wiser than when you arrived. And never forget you have a lot of living left when it's over. This isn't your life, Wolfie. It's just a part of it."

"How can you be so sure? You never show doubt. It intimidates the men."

Aiden smirked. "You said it. Never showing doubt doesn't mean I don't have it. Men only make it through if they believe they will. Even then there's no guarantee. But without believing, you're already lost. A friend taught me that."

Joshua caught his eye. "David?"

"Yes." He looked away. "Joshua, I arrived in France angry and with nothing to lose. Men like that are dangerous, to themselves and anyone around them. I know that now. David was my platoon leader. He set me straight."

"How?"

"By confronting me. That is, once he knew. See, I was a wreck. But I kept it hidden. At night I'd shiver in my cubby. By morning my nerves would be worn raw. I'd spin delusions, convince myself nothing could harm me. I went on like that for weeks, until it all came to a head.

"One evening we set out on a raid. No sooner than we'd cut the barbed wire than a man tripped a mine. A blast of mud and blood rained over me. I nearly heaved. After that, everything went blurry. We kept moving. Somewhere along the way my fear turned to rage.

"The raid was a disaster. When we reached the German trench, they were waiting. They mowed down a third of the squad in the first seconds."

"David ordered a retreat, but I refused. I ran straight toward the gunfire."

"How did you survive?"

"David tackled me from behind. A couple of men held position, risking their own lives. Somehow we managed to scramble out.

"When we got back, I thought he'd have me court-martialed. Or at least beat the hell out of me. But he was kind. He helped me clean up. Afterward he walked with me. He asked why I was here, why I'd come to France.

"I gave him offhanded answers, the lies I told everyone.

"Each time he'd listen, then ask again. He wouldn't let go. It was a battle of wills, one I was in no condition to fight. Eventually I broke down. I told him about medical school, my father. Even myself."

"What did he say?"

"It didn't matter to him. He told me hatred, whether directed inside or out, could destroy a man. He said I should think about that. But he gave me a warning too. He said if I ever let my hatred possess

me, if I ever let it endanger anyone again, that he'd shoot me himself. Then he told me to get some rest." He chuckled. "And I did. I slept all night, for the first time since we'd reached the front."

"And from that you became friends?"

"Not at first, but it was a start. He understood me after that. Guess I knew myself better too. One day he asked about my studies. He suggested I teach the other men. Later he told me about Claire, asked me to check on her should anything happen. I suppose that's when I knew we were friends."

"He must have been quite a man, to hear you talk. Claire too . . . she spoke so highly of him."

"David adored her, but how could he not? Claire's special. Then again, so was he. He remains the wisest man I've ever known."

Joshua watched a pigeon pace back and forth atop a lower beam. "Can I ask you something?"

"Sure."

"How did he die?"

Aiden clinched his jaw. "A random shell, early one morning. I had just seen him. He'd been in the shelter when I stopped to bum a cigarette. He joined me out in the trench. The shell struck after I left. I knew it was close. Sometimes they were. But it didn't occur to me it had been a direct hit, not at the time. As it turned out, he was struck right where I left him."

Joshua shuddered.

"All those battles, and he was killed in the trench on a quiet Sunday. If I'd stayed, I would have been killed too. And if I hadn't come by, he wouldn't have been there at all."

He wiped his face before continuing. "There's not a damn thing you can do if it's your time. David understood that. He used to say you were only alive if you were learning. The only real death is giving up, letting fear paralyze you . . . deceiving yourself into thinking you're living when you're just passing time."

"I wish I could believe that. It sounds good. But I don't want to die."

Aiden looked away. "Neither did he. It's a war, Joshua. People die."

"I'm sorry. It's just I'm not strong like you. I get so scared."

"Everyone gets scared, Wolfie. You're stronger than you think."

"I want to be."

"You are. You'll see."

"How do you know? Drills are easy. I've never been in battle."

"Wolfie, I've watched you for weeks now. The drills aren't easy. Captain's made sure of that. Other men get frazzled, but you don't. So tell me. What are you thinking in those drills? How do you keep your head on?"

He shrugged. "I don't know. Guess I block things out. Once I know what's expected, what's necessary, I don't feel anything. I simply react. It's what I've always done."

Aiden nodded. "Seems to work. No reason to think it won't on the front." He jostled him gently. "Now come on. We still have a ways to go."

Joshua studied the pinnacle above. He recoiled. The rules had changed. He did feel . . . he felt lost. "It looks lonely up there. Can we go find Claire instead?"

Aiden glanced about before patting his cheek. "Sure. Then we'll head back for a nap. You look tired." He held his gaze. "I'll hold you," he whispered.

Joshua felt himself choking up. "I'd like that."

"It's alright. I'm here. Tomorrow we'll have a picnic on the hillside, just the three of us. How's that sound?"

Joshua pinched his eyes, shaking off the moment. "A real picnic this time?" he teased. Then he sighed. "I don't care what we do. Let's just go."

32 – Sweet Elisabeth

Elisabeth was winded, and her shoulders ached. So much for lifting her spirits with a walk into town. It might have been fine if she hadn't stopped for the groceries. She'd intended to send Joshua in the morning but changed her mind, not wanting to rush preparations for tomorrow's dinner. They were finally returning the courtesy the Daltons had extended to Wayne and her a month earlier.

She slowed to negotiate an icy stretch. There had been another reason she'd made the purchases. Truth was she feared Joshua might well disappear at dawn, like he used to. In one sense the possibility came as a relief. Normal was something she hardly recognized these days, what with Wayne's condition.

At least Joshua was improving. His walk was more natural, and his hair thicker. Though flecked in silver, which gave her pause, it mostly covered the scar. She knew she should count her blessings, but his behavior gnawed at her. He had a job and a fiancé now. It was time he stopped gallivanting all over the ridge.

She jostled the bags. That wasn't it either, not really. Who should care if he liked getting out on his own? He was a fine young man. She just resented having to defend him. Olympia Dalton's comments at the store, though mild on the surface, carried a cutting edge, steeped in judgment. Joshua didn't need to give her any cause for doubt.

Oh, how she dreaded another evening with the woman. To start it felt plumb foolish purchasing food for guests from their own store. Not that she had a choice. Hadley was a meager town. Options were for other folks.

She breathed a prayer. It did no good to dwell on petty gripes. The important thing was the gesture, the ritual of joining families. Their backgrounds and values might be different . . . *were* different, she chuckled. But they'd make the effort. It was expected.

She thought back to the first dinner, in that other time before

Wayne's collapse. The friction remained vivid. Between Olympia's pontificating and Wayne's sulking, it could have been worse. Not that she'd been much better, droning on about her childhood. And still nothing was resolved regarding George Dalton's offer to Joshua. How ever would they get through another night?

It'd be best to avoid the matter altogether. For one she could applaud Olympia's efforts on prohibition, seeing as a final flurry of state legislatures had passed the amendment in recent days. Pa would have called the whole lot of them busybodies, which they were. But then he'd known how to say his peace without remorse, a trait she'd failed to inherit.

Or had she simply forgotten how? She hadn't always been meek. Growing up she'd been bold. Eager. Where had that gone?

Losing Mother had been the start. Pa had been so broken. Mindful of him, she'd never spoken of it, burying her own pain. By the time Wayne had come along, she'd convinced herself she was fine. He'd been strong, and he'd made her feel special. That had sustained her a while, until the move.

When things got rough, she'd lost her way. Blue days became blue weeks. Wayne had plunged ahead, dragging her along. Leaning on him had proven easier than standing on her own. She saw that now. Was it too late to set things right?

She shook off the doubt. A soul had to start somewhere. She still had a voice. Perhaps something small? A bottle of Pa's favorite scotch lay stashed in the attic. She could fish it out to toast Olympia's success. She cracked a smile, imagining the scene. It was a fantasy, though a pleasing one.

Drawing a breath, she took on the steeper grade. The particular thorn of Olympia Dalton would work its way out with the wedding. Joshua and Katie were bright. They'd strike a balance with the families, though it hardly helped now. June was still months off. Would Wayne even . . .?

She shuddered. It was too late for discussion. The Daltons were footing the bill, and plans were set. Wayne hated ceremonies, and this one sounded more like a highfalutin show than a celebration of family. Not that she was surprised. With Olympia, it was all about appearances. The way she carried on, you'd think they owned Kirven's department store, not a roadside grocery. People were funny like that, always making more of themselves than they actually were.

Elisabeth had given up such airs. No one cared. In these parts she was the quarryman's wife, end of story. Their road together had been no garden path, yet they did share a love. Not everyone could say that. It was plain to see, even in church. She'd witnessed the distance, and outright slights, when couples thought no one was paying any mind. She'd had her share of frustrations. But marriage was for keeps, and Elisabeth Hunter was a woman who kept her promises.

"Better to be poor and loved than rich and tolerated."

Pa had made the observation after seeing how Marty Tomkins, a wealthy suitor, treated her. At the time she'd been entranced by the trappings of romance. Now she could see his wisdom. She sighed. Romance . . . like that mattered in the long run.

Still, the thought tugged at her. Did Joshua and Katie have a spark? Maybe you needed that in the beginning, before the winds began to blow. It had never been a problem with her and Wayne. Pa had even threatened to chase him off once, irked at how he hovered about the farm.

Joshua wasn't like that. She understood he was working. Wayne had been as well; it hadn't deterred him. Something didn't seem right about a young man not spending more time with his bride to be.

Reaching a sunny gap, she paused to warm herself. Even on a mild winter's day, frigid pockets hung in shadows along the ridge. Having nowhere to sit other than atop the packed snow, she stood motionless, facing the sun. At least she could see the house now, which helped.

She was struck by the silence. Wayne hadn't worked in the quarry since that day, and the McCulloughs were visiting family. Even the sawmill over by the river was quiet. Perhaps it was the recent snow. Maybe there were no more logs to cut.

Sometimes she thought about that. In the early years, they'd practically seen fortune racing their way. Wayne had been encouraged. She'd been comforted. It seemed the hurly burly of mines, mills & logging operations had to bode well. Even absent the coal, orders for stone had risen. But ultimately the boom left them dry. The wave receded, taking everything, even the trees in the valley.

Shivering, she sought signs of life. A distant hammering started, then stopped. A light breeze rose and fell. For a moment she heard something else. Music. Well, not so much music, more like chords chopping at a melody. She strained to hear, but it faded quick as it began.

She resumed walking, anxious to get home. As she proceeded, she pondered the tease of a tune. Familiar, but the snippet had been short. And who would be playing? Scott was at school. Even if he weren't, she wouldn't have heard him. Other than the carols on Christmas Eve, Wayne still forbid his playing near the house.

Her pulse quickened. Surely he wasn't ditching school again? Other than the autumn after Joshua left, it hadn't been a problem. Scott was a free spirit, but he was honest. When he'd promised to stop, she'd believed him. She hoped her faith hadn't been misplaced.

By the time she reached the porch, she'd convinced herself it had merely been the wind, or a trick of the mind. But then she heard it again, beyond the far edge of the quarry. It had to be Scott.

Tossing the sacks onto the swing, she stormed back down the steps. This close to home, within earshot of Wayne. What was he thinking? She'd tan his hide herself.

The playing continued in fits and starts as she trudged above the lip of the quarry. She'd hear a few notes, then a pause. Despite her anger, she found herself following along, piecing it together.

At the tree line, she heard it again, beyond the wooded knoll. She made a beeline through the brush. As the melody resumed, smoother now, she began to hum along.

Her heart skipped.

It had been years, but she knew the tune. Scott wasn't playing. Wayne was.

Topping the crest, she saw him. He sat facing the valley, perched on an exposed rock. After a moment he paused to study the strings. Then he leaned his head back, letting his fingers find the memory on their own.

She couldn't recall the last time she saw him play. But she remembered a sticky summer day in Alabama, out on a Sunday stroll. They had ducked inside an old barn during a thunderstorm. For a while he'd played familiar tunes. Then, with a wink, he'd adjusted the tuning. "One of my own," he'd teased.

He had called it "Sweet Elisabeth." She slipped into the memory as he began again, playing the tune all the way through.

Somewhere over the years he'd stopped, banishing the guitar to the attic. Hard living had consumed them, and they'd abandoned superfluous things. Now she returned, remembering the youth she'd been and the young man who'd charmed her.

When the final notes faded, the warmth of a distant summer yielded to the winter chill. Wayne turned and cocked his head, peering through the branches. Then he scooted around to face her.

Patting the stone beside him, he offered a weary smile. "Care to sit a spell with an old man, my sweet Elisabeth?"

33 – Lily

Joshua toweled off quickly then slipped on the clothing Lily had scrounged up for him. She'd found civilian clothes for Aiden as well, resulting in another knowing nudge to Joshua. He almost wondered if Aiden's suggestion to forego uniforms on their final day was simply to prove his point.

It didn't matter to him. Lily was nice, and a kind host. She'd even prepared them dinner before her shift the previous evening. This morning she had spirited Claire away for a private chat over coffee.

He glanced in the mirror. The pants were snug but comfortable. The shirt hung loose and light, perfect for a summer day. He felt pampered – sleeping late, a bath and fresh clothes. He rubbed the scruff along his cheek, electing not to shave. It was about as close to rebellious as he got. Then he smirked; maybe he was the rebellion.

The knock startled him. "You ready?" Aiden asked.

He gathered his things and opened the door. "Yeah."

Aiden appraised him. "Not bad. You going to try to pull off being a Frenchman today?"

Joshua brushed by him. "Sure, a mute one. I'll gesture."

"Hey, that's my gimmick!"

"But your French is better. So you get to do the talking."

Aiden grabbed him from behind, tickling him. "Not to worry. We're going to disappear today. I doubt we'll be running into anyone."

The door to the stair opened, and an old couple carrying groceries entered the hall. Joshua pulled free and stepped aside, letting them pass. The man nodded while the woman cast an accusing eye.

"Not going to run into anyone, huh?" he whispered after they'd gone.

"Oh, I'm sure they're accustomed to the company by now."

Aiden gestured at his outfit.

Joshua didn't take the bait. "I wanted the striped shirt," he grumbled.

"It fits me better. You're too scrawny."

Joshua started to balk, but melted when he saw the teasing grin.

"You look fine," Aiden breathed. "Did you sleep well?"

Joshua leaned against the wall. "I did. Between our nap yesterday and sleeping in, I think I'm rested."

"Good, because I'm going to need your help. We're going to set up above the vineyard, and I promised Claire we'd take care of the cooking. You have any skills?"

"I can boil water." Aiden rolled his eyes so he relented. "My brother and I used to camp while hunting up on the ridge. Nothing fancy, but I've grilled game. We'll figure something out."

"You don't talk much about your brother. About all I know is that encounter with the mountain lion. What's he like?"

"Scott? I don't know. He's my brother. He's a good kid I guess, kinda quiet until he gets to know you. Then watch out."

"You've been gone a while. I imagine he's grown."

"Mom says he's filling out. He was already bigger than me when I left." He shrugged. "I wasn't real pleased about that."

Aiden laughed. "You ever write him?"

"I write Mom. I'm sure she shares the news. Why?"

"It's just good to have a sibling. You should cherish him."

Joshua nodded. "I suppose you're right. He has always been there." He cocked his head. "Is this about your sister?"

Aiden looked startled. "Not intentionally, but perhaps. I have been thinking about her lately . . . not sure why."

"Maybe you just miss her."

"I suppose so." He picked at the peeling wallpaper. "We never hunted," he chuckled. "Or grilled for that matter, but we had our own outings."

"Picking blueberries?"

Aiden shook his head. "You and your memory. Yes, on summer holiday. But even in the city, we found adventures. There may not have been mountain lions, but we had our own wilderness. It's called Central Park."

Joshua studied him as he spoke, seeing the twinkle in his eyes as he recounted epic hide and seek games beneath summer skies and sledding excursions after winter snows. He could almost imagine a young Aiden traipsing around, little sister in tow.

"Anyhow, we had our fun," Aiden finished abruptly, embarrassed. "All I'm saying is don't neglect your brother. It's good to have someone who knows where you started."

He nodded. "Maybe I'll write him a note, though he'll find it strange."

"Perhaps. But he might like it, even if he never admits it. Siblings are like that too." A shadow crossed his face.

"What is it?"

Aiden shrugged. "Oh, thinking. I wish I could have known Sarah when we were older. When she got sick, we were at an awkward stage, picking at each other all the time. I thought I was too big to have a kid sister. She was changing too, so the irritation was mutual. But it would have passed.

"After the fever all I could do was sit by her side." He sighed. "We still went to the park, though. Her hospital was nearby. Even after my parents moved to Boston, I'd visit her. If she were having a good day, they'd let me take her over. It seemed to calm her. I like to think she remembers, deep down."

Not hearing anyone, Joshua dared to rub his back. "Maybe she does."

Aiden straightened up. "We should get moving. Claire and Lily returned while you were bathing."

"Is Lily joining us?"

"No. She said she needed to work, finishing sketches or something. I wasn't really listening. She has a shift tonight, so we'll have Claire to ourselves. They were able to visit a bit. I suppose that's good."

"Maybe Claire thinks of Lily as a sister," he offered.

Aiden considered the idea, and his face softened. "You could be *right."* He tugged at Joshua's collar. *"You ready, François?"*

"Oui, Jacques," he replied, looking forward to a day in disguise.

*   *   *

The meal was a success. The sliced potatoes were a bit undercooked, but tasty. The salad was simple. Joshua's grilled chicken was delicious, if he said so himself.

The day proved to be another scorcher so they retreated from the fire, settling in under the trees. *"I should have brought more wine,"* Claire mused after a bit. *"There's another bottle at Lily's."*

Aiden, sluggish upon the blanket, ignored her. Joshua sat up. *"I could go get it."*

"Oh, I didn't mean that. It was merely an observation."

He'd already risen. *"I don't mind. It won't take long. That way we can linger."* He surveyed their little haven. The breeze felt good, and the view of the vineyard pleasant. There was no reason they couldn't stay until dusk, or later.

Aiden tugged at his pants cuff. *"You sure? I can go with you."*

"Nah, I know the way. It'll be a nice stroll."

Aiden rolled over. *"Alright, then. I'll take a nap."*

"Who's the sleepy one now?" he teased.

"The word's 'comfortable.' There's a difference."

Joshua nodded. *"Sure . . . comfortable."*

Claire rose and moved toward the bushes where they'd left the basket. *"Hold on. I have some money. Could you buy some cheese? There's a market across from Lily's apartment. Anything will do."*

"Make sure to knock at the studio," Aiden whispered when she was out of earshot.

Joshua kicked at his ribs. *"You're mean."*

"Yeah," he winked. *"Just don't be long."*

"I won't." He turned, accepting the coins from Claire.

The walk was refreshing. In a small square he encountered artists displaying their works. He browsed for a few minutes, and greeted a pair of young women as he departed. Feeling their eyes upon him, he *wondered if his accent had fooled them or if they were laughing behind his back.*

There wasn't any question at the market, where the chatty owner tripped him up. Nevertheless he muddled through, purchasing chèvre, some jam and a fresh baguette.

At Lily's apartment he gave a light tap, then listened at the door, hoping not to prove Aiden right. Hearing nothing, he stepped inside. Lily was on the chaise, dozing before her shift. He couldn't blame her; her hours were strange.

He retrieved the bottle of wine, and poured himself a glass of water. Taking a sip, he admired the little jewel box studio and its view of the city. No wonder he found himself defending her. Lily did what she had to do, and why shouldn't she? Life in Montmartre had to be fascinating.

He eased toward the window. Their presence had disrupted things, but Lily had swept the room and folded the blankets. Peeking into the workroom, he saw it remained as unkempt as the main room was organized. Crates stuffed with paper and canvas were strewn haphazardly across the floor. She had set up an easel during the day, positioned to allow a view outside as well as to sketches tacked upon the wall. The tiny desk beside it was covered with paints, brushes and additional sketches.

A rustle rose from a box near the window. A silken gray cat emerged and jumped onto the windowsill. The feline sprinted toward the opening but paused at the moment of decision, glancing back.

Feeling the appraisal, Joshua stood still. "It's alright," he whispered. Then he averted his gaze and moved parallel along the wall, keeping his distance. As he hoped, the cat hesitated and then sat, choosing to remain.

Joshua stopped at the desk. He thumbed through the smattering of loose sketches, suppressing a laugh when he came across posed studies of men on the chaise in the other room. His loose shirt and Aiden's striped one both made appearances, among other items of men's clothing. Perhaps Aiden wasn't the detective he thought he was.

After a moment he turned toward the easel. An unfinished painting of a small boy with pale blond hair greeted him. In the image the child knelt on the curb of a flooded street, reaching for a toy boat caught in the torrent. Golden locks framed his face, and his blue eyes showed fear as the craft evaded his grasp. He looked vulnerable as only a child can, and Joshua found himself wanting assurance the toy had been saved.

His gaze shifted to the floor, where another canvas had fallen. Joshua picked it up. This one was complete, a portrait of an elderly man sitting on a bench. The tree beside the bench was bare, and a cloak shrouded the man's face. As with the other painting, the figure's brilliant eyes drew Joshua in. Though the man looked ragged, his stare was firm, set upon some unseen object out of view.

Joshua's discomfort at the image eased when he realized the figure's gaze flowed past him toward the window. "Maybe he doesn't like you," he whispered, but the cat failed to see the humor.

He laid the painting on the desk, then thumbed through another stack. Some were fully realized images, rich in detail. Others were spartan, a few strokes outlining a vague background accompanied by a detail or two, a face or object.

There were dozens, all on pages from the worn leather satchel Lily kept by her side. She probably took it everywhere, pulling it open to capture scenes as she proceeded through life. He felt jealous, his undocumented journey seeming trivial by comparison.

Behind him the cat dropped to the floor, interrupting his musings.

He turned to find Lily in the doorway, rubbing her temples. "Mon Dieu!" she sighed. She looked at Joshua and then the cat. "You meet Felix? Le chat . . . cat?"

"Oui. We're becoming friends, kind of." He grinned. "Il est mon ami maintenant."

The cat cast another wary glance then moved to Lily. She bent over and extended her hand. Felix sniffed then nuzzled her fingertips before retreating again to the windowsill.

"Not mine," she explained, rising. "Peut-être le vieil homme . . .

avant." She pointed at the tree. "When I come, he sit. I feed. He come. He go." She shrugged.

"I guess it's his way," he commented.

Lily looked puzzled.

"His manner. Sa nature?" he offered, wanting to say more but not having the words.

She nodded, seeking a few of her own before continuing. "He knows me now. Maybe he stay longer, for more than the food and the warm." She laughed softly, then joined Joshua by the desk.

"You like?" she asked.

"Oui! Très beaucoup."

She cocked her head. "Things I see. C'est tout." She sighed. "Many artists in Montmartre. So many and so good. I learn."

"Ils sont bons," he assured her, realizing his opinion hardly mattered.

"Je dessine ensuite je peins," she explained, confirming his suspicion. "Regarde." She pointed at the painting on the easel, then at a sketch tacked to the wall. The sketch held the essence of the nearly finished work. The boat and boy's face were clear. A straight line and squiggles represented the curb and flooded lane. "Je me souviens . . . I remember," she explained.

"I understand . . . je comprends."

"I show you!" she exclaimed, disappearing from the room. Felix recoiled at the sudden movement, but remained.

Joshua waited, listening to her shuffle with the satchel and then move to the kitchenette. Just as he considered she had intended him to follow, she returned. She held a small bowl in one hand and a piece of paper in the other. Felix straightened up, sensing food. He jumped to the floor as she set the bowl down. She grazed his neck before turning to Joshua.

"Hier . . . yesterday?" she said as she thrust the paper in his direction.

He expected something from Montmartre. Instead he was startled by an image of Aiden and himself.

The sketch was rough, but their faces clear. Aiden, uniform

unbuttoned, sat reclined against the window. His eyes were open, and his arm was draped around Joshua.

As for himself, he was resting against Aiden's chest, holding his torso.

The rest was a blur, intersecting lines to represent the windowpanes, hash marks to indicate the chevrons on Aiden's sleeve. The image was both innocent and intimate at the same time.

"You want?" Lily asked.

Joshua's heart leapt. But then he frowned. He couldn't show it to anyone. Where would he keep it? What if someone came upon it?

He looked up to find Lily eyeing him expectantly. She might not understand. He patted his heart. "Très beau. But you should keep it." He pointed at her. "You could paint it. Tu peins?" he finished, gesturing toward the easel.

Lily studied the painting of the boy before turning her gaze to the stacks of waiting sketches blanketing the desk. Taking the sketch from him, she set it upon the shelf at the back, placing a jar of paint atop it. "Maybe. I remember." Then they shared a laugh and retreated to the main room, leaving Felix to his dinner.

34 – Montmartre Dawn

The studio was dark when Joshua woke. He nestled against Aiden, but the hard floor and anxiety over their departure put an end to sleep. Frustrated, he rolled over to face the window.

Clouds had moved in during the night, bringing a light drizzle. The windows were misty, and a cool moistness crept in the open ones. He considered shutting them. But soothed by the earthy scent wafting in, he chose to let them be.

After a time the shower passed. The sky lightened. He rose.

Lily lay sprawled across the chaise. Claire was curled upon the floor nearby, having shrugged free of her blanket. When he adjusted it, she pulled it close. Wavy locks slid across her face.

He tiptoed across the room, noting movement in the studio. Felix poked his head up from a box of sketches, appraised him and then slinked back down.

Lifting his clothes from the counter, his belt fell loose, the buckle clanking hard against the surface. He turned to check the sleeping trio, but no one stirred. His gaze lingered on Aiden's face. Even at rest he looked intense.

He dressed quickly and grabbed his boots, lacing them in the musty hall.

Shuffling down the stairwell, he emerged outside. A line of clouds marched west, morning stars emerging in its wake. Obeying a vague inclination, he proceeded toward Sacré-Cœur. Rather than follow the cobbled streets through the village, he cut across a small field straddling the bluff. The damp grass dotted with hawthorns reminded him of the old farms below Hadley.

It felt like the start of a morning hunt. Though a continent away, the sensation of the land emerging from night felt familiar.

Sunday morning back home. Mom would be in church by now. Scott, defying her again, had probably retrieved his satchel of tobacco from the hollow oak. By now he'd be along the ridge with his rifle. Dad would be growling over some task at the house or down in the quarry.

On occasion Mom would shame Dad into joining her. If so, he'd be slumped beside her in one of the rear pews. Katie would be with her parents, second row on the right, praying for the men at war. He bristled. Katie might pray for the others, but she'd be thinking of him.

He pulled out a cigarette, sidestepping the matter. What good was prayer anyhow? If God used war to mete out punishments, the preceding days had sealed his fate. He might as well accept the consequences.

Then again, why would God care who he loved, much less condemn him for it? Joshua had never feared God, but he did fear death. He pictured his body rotting in some muddy hollow.

They'd been told remains littered no man's land, bodies too remote or too dismembered to retrieve. But he'd never let himself consider his might join them. Surely loved ones had prayed for men slain all across northern France. It hadn't been enough. They were still dead.

He lit the cigarette and took a puff. It was a cruel truth. Prayer might comfort those offering them, but it wouldn't change a thing. Angels with tote boards didn't determine the ranks of the dead. If he were to live, he'd have to be sharp, fast and fortunate.

Thoughts of battle lingered. During drills he pictured unseen bullets, dodged imagined explosions and slashed at phantom attackers. But so far no actual bayonets, gunfire or grenades had delivered the ultimate test. He could only hope Aiden was right when he judged him ready. He could hope that was enough. And he supposed, in the end, he could pray. Perhaps God would show mercy. Maybe angels could still hear him.

Reaching the edge of the field, he hopped a fence and joined the stone lane leading up to the basilica. Arriving in front, he climbed the steps. Then he sat, staring out over the city. A cool breeze pelted his face. He felt alive.

The pink sky had given way to orange when he noticed the figure on the lane. Claire joined him.

"I thought I might find you here. You'd mentioned the view when we first arrived." She pulled the blanket close. "There's a bit of a nip," she observed.

"I think a front passed," he replied. "I couldn't sleep."

"I barely remember lying down. Too much wine, I suppose."

They sat in silence, gazing across the city. A flock of starlings rose from the hillside, swirling and shifting like a melody. As they evaporated into the distance, Joshua looked over at her. She was beautiful . . . graceful and warm. Despite everything, she remained defiantly positive. He never knew people, real people, could be that way. Yet here she was.

Still gazing ahead, she spoke. "Aiden says you're moving to the front line."

"Soon as we return, apparently."

"Be careful. And trust that you will be fine." Then she shook her head. "That's not what I mean, not exactly."

"I understand."

She turned to face him. "No, there's more. You need to know, Joshua. Men do survive. At the hospital, I see men die, but I see them pull through as well. I see it everyday. What you believe matters.

"When Mother and I fled Remenauville, the war terrified me. But I don't fear it now. It took David. I refuse to let it take me as well." She sighed. "You must believe you will make it. It's important. Especially now that you have each other."

Joshua stiffened. The emotions were still raw. It'd taken his whole life to get here, to admit the feelings. He couldn't conceive what followed.

Claire continued. "Aiden loves you, Joshua. He so hoped you'd come. Then yesterday he told me he was happy. I used to fear he'd never meet someone. I doubted any man worthy of him. But you are good for him. He's at ease with you, and Aiden's never at ease. I see how he looks at you, and you him. I think you love him too. So you must find a way. You must stay alive, for each other."

He frowned. He couldn't make that promise. No one could. "I'll try," he whispered.

She grasped his hand. "I'm no fool. I know one can't escape death. I know all too well. But the other afternoon, in the rose garden, I spoke only of the past.

"Beautiful days aren't all in the past. You have to believe new ones await you. You must go after them, and create them. Please, Joshua, hold on to the days. Trust that you and Aiden will share them, together."

He nodded. It's what she needed, and he didn't want to disappoint her.

35 – The Contest

Katie wasn't on the porch when they pulled up on their way to Monterey, though she answered on the first knock. But it wasn't until the steps that she noticed the truck. "Your father's coming?" she whispered.

He leaned in to take her arm. "It caught us all by surprise. Scott's too jittery to drive, so you'll be sharing the back. I made it as comfy as possible."

"Morning, Mr. & Mrs. Hunter," Katie called out as he helped her up. She gave Scott a pat on the leg.

Scott scooted across the tarp-covered bench. Setting the guitar aside, his darting glance found Joshua.

Joshua winked before climbing into the driver's seat. Then he opened the throttle.

The going was slow at first. The roads were slushy, particularly the rutted stretch near the sawmill. But heading west on the Parkersburg pike, they made up for lost time.

Dad dozed, and Mom's idle chatter ceased. They passed the old Confederate battle works, followed by the trenches above McDowell. His eyes were drawn to the patchy forest rising from the ruins. France would be like that some day, on a larger scale, as nature healed the ravaged land.

Mom squeezed his arm, but said nothing. During his first weeks home, she had hinted at questions, which he'd ignored. Still it comforted him that she noticed, that she knew.

They arrived at the wood-framed hall shortly after noon. A crowd had gathered outside, which surprised him until he considered the matter. It was winter; there wasn't much going on.

Dad jolted awake. "My word," he mumbled, his voice gravelly. "They're all here for Scott?"

Mom leaned in near. "Him and everyone else, honey.

Remember, it's a contest. They'll be others." She twisted about. "How many are there?" she called out.

Scott shrugged. "Haven't the foggiest." He grabbed the guitar case and rose, scanning the crowd. "Guess I'd better go find out," he breathed as he helped Katie descend.

"Now relax," she advised, brushing off her skirt. "There isn't a thing to worry about."

Joshua held the guitar while Scott leapt down. It seemed his earlier nervousness had edged a notch toward outright fear. "She's right, little brother. Just have fun."

"I can do this," Scott muttered, more to himself than to them. He retrieved the guitar then ambled toward the main steps. A moment later, he yelled back. "I'll find you right after."

By then Mom had climbed out the driver's side and moved back around. She was talking low with Dad, who'd yet to budge. He looked pale and panicked. "Your father and I are going to stay out here," she explained when they joined her.

"You'll meet us, though?" Joshua asked, puzzled. "Inside."

Mom's whisper had an edge "We'll see."

"Should we save a seat?"

"It doesn't matter. Now go." She pulled a handful of soda crackers from her bag.

Katie intervened. "Come on, Josh," she urged. "We'll see you in a bit, Mr. Hunter."

Making their way up the steps, he glanced back. "He looks lost."

"Is he like that a lot these days?"

He shook his head. "Not that I've seen. Most days he's ornery as ever. He even worked a bit last week, gave Mom a real cussing when she tried to stop him." Then it dawned on him. "Of course, some days he doesn't come downstairs at all."

"Your father's proud, Joshua. It has to be tough on him, his body faltering. He's a fighter."

"You're right on that. He fights everyone."

"That's not what I meant."

"But it's true. Except you. He's liked you from the start, since we were kids."

She spun across the wide porch. "What's not to like?"

"I'm not gonna indulge you, young lady," he teased.

She held his gaze. "I wouldn't mind a little indulging. We are engaged, after all."

"Katie!" he scolded, glancing about as he opened the door.

She sauntered in, giggling. "Nobody heard me. You are a funny one, Joshua Hunter."

The rotund woman at the ticket table answered the question of the hour. "Seven total, two songs each. And you all have come the farthest. It's only our second year, but word's getting out. You'd better grab seats fast. It'll be standing room only by the time we start."

They pushed forward, with Katie squeezing through to snag two seats along the aisle, warding off a potential conflict with her smile. Joshua joined her a moment later. "We'll switch when they get here," she suggested.

Joshua nodded as he took in the audience. It was comprised of country folk, mostly farmers and sheepherders. Highland County occupied the thin ridges and elevated valleys nestled against West Virginia's Allegheny Mountains. The inhabitants were chatty, given the bubbly conversation bouncing off the wood paneling.

Katie noticed as well. "Happy bunch, aren't they?"

"Isn't Churchville like this? I figured valley towns were all the same."

She shook her head. "It's social, but nothing like this."

As if to make the point, a young woman grabbed her arm. "Howdy! I don't believe we've met. I'm Nancy Green, and this here's Logan O'Malley." A tall man with dusty brown hair dipped his head. "You're not from around here," she continued.

Katie smiled. "Katie Dalton, and this here's Joshua Hunter. He's my . . ."

"Fiancé," the woman finished. "I saw the ring. Me and Logan just got engaged as well." She lifted her own hand for inspection. "Wedding's in March. So what brings you to Highland County?"

"My brother," Joshua injected before she could go on. "He's

performing."

"Oh my goodness! I know now, from over the mountain." She nudged her fiancé. "You remember, Logan, that young man who came by last month. What was his name?"

"Pete," Katie offered.

"Yeah, Pete. Nice fella. He braved the snow last year, just to come watch. Said he had a talented friend, a guitar player. It was to be a surprise, right?"

The rapid-fire piston of her voice grated. Joshua stifled a smirk, figuring her beau probably never had to utter a word. Just then the young man turned and locked eyes.

"Yes, a Christmas gift, from Pete and us," Katie explained.

"Well, guitars are popular this year. There's another. Then there's a fiddler and a man with a dulcimer. Also we have the Clancy twins. Those girls have great harmonies. Mrs. Nichols will sing her hymns, of course, and another woman plays the piano. Does your brother sing, or just play?" she demanded.

Though Joshua had averted his gaze, he could still feel Logan's eyes upon him. "I, uh . . . I don't rightly know."

Nancy shot a look of disbelief. "You don't know?"

Katie saved him. "Well, he mostly plays. But he has a good voice too, a rich baritone. We're just not sure what songs he's performing today."

"Oh," Nancy said, pausing for the first time, probably stumped at the concept of a person not sharing every thought that crossed his mind.

Logan jumped at the opportunity. "You play too?" he asked Joshua.

"No . . . no talent here." He grasped Katie's hand.

Nancy recovered in force. "Look!" she shrieked. "Leanne made it!" In a flash of awareness, she noticed Katie pulling back from the piercing. "Sorry, dear. I just didn't think she'd come. She's about ready to burst. Leanne!" she screeched at a blond woman making her way up the side aisle. The description, though blunt, sized up the situation well. "I've got to see her," Nancy finished, already on the move.

"Nice meeting you," Katie called out. "You too, Logan."

Logan gave a nod and proceeded to glance back not once, but twice, as he rushed after her.

Katie shook her head. "Poor Logan. Fortunately he won't be able to hear her cackle by the time he's thirty."

"I don't think he hears her now," Joshua observed, his stomach churning.

"Something bothering you?" she asked.

"No. Simply recovering." Another shriek carried across the room, and they burst into laughter.

*   *   *

Mom and Dad still hadn't entered when the school principal rose to welcome everyone. He introduced the three judges – the mayor, the school music teacher, and a local choir director.

He announced the line-up. Scott would be last, and Joshua felt for him, knowing he'd be a bundle of nerves in back. Playing had to mean a lot for him to put himself out here like this. He hoped Pete was right. It would ache something fierce if his efforts fell flat.

He glimpsed Nancy and Logan standing in the far aisle, their pregnant friend seated beside them. When Logan looked over, Joshua shifted his gaze, vowing to avoid him from then on. Fortunately, the performance began.

The first player was the young fiddler, a boy in his early teens. He showed potential, but fumbled through a section of his second piece. The twins were talented enough, their voices blending well on a version of "Down by the Old Mill Stream." Clearly they were a crowd favorite, boosted by an extended clan up front.

As for the others, the second guitar man was stoic, proficient but making no connection with the audience. Conversely, the lady after him delivered her hymns more like a scolding than an expression of joy. The dulcimer player was friendly, a crusty man who cracked jokes between his tunes.

If there was a surprise among the bunch, it was the piano player, who wielded confident and expressive hands. Her rendition of "Keep on the Sunny Side" received a particularly favorable reception from an audience steeped in Scotch-Irish roots.

As she finished, Joshua saw Mom slip through the rear door. He stepped into the aisle and lifted an arm. She acknowledged him, but shook her head. She moved farther in, tugging Dad behind her. His color was back. Katie beckoned them forward, and they again waved off the offer. Folks in the back shifted to allow a view.

Joshua turned his attention to the stage, where his brother had emerged, shifting his weight as he waited for the principal.

"And now I'd like to introduce our first contestant ever from outside Highland County, Mister Scott Hunter."

Scott picked up a stool and plopped it down center stage. "Howdy everyone," he said, a little soft. "I play better perched up, like on a rail fence. Still getting used to playing inside, for people," he added louder, with a wink. A few folks smiled.

"My first is a tune most of you will know. It's a song I grew up hearing, though it might be a bit more popular on the far side of the mountain."

He propped himself against the stool and looked around. His eyes widened, but he held steady. Breathing deep, he let his shoulders fall. Then he began.

Joshua recognized the song from the first notes. He'd heard it his whole life, down by the logging camps and from the old men who used to hang outside the tavern before it closed. They even sang it in service on occasion, though it was hardly religious. Then again, the song was from the heart, about a lonely soul far from home. So, in a way, it fit.

O Shenando' I long to hear you,
Away, you rolling river
O Shenando' I long to hear you
Away, we're bound away, across the wide Missouri

O Shenando' I long to see you
Away you rolling river
O Shenando' I long to see you
Away, we're bound away, across the wide Missouri

'Tis seven years since I have seen you
To hear your rolling river
O Shenando' I long to see you
Away, we're bound away, across the wide Missouri

O Shenando' I'll not forget you
I'll dream of your clear waters
O Shenando' you're in my mem'ry
Away, we're bound away, across the wide Missouri

His brother held the last note, his smooth baritone fading softly into the still air of the room. When he finished, he shrugged, back to being bashful. The crowd loved him for it, rewarding him with hearty applause. He beamed for an instant. Then he wiped his hands on his pants and set about making adjustments of the strings.

More confident, he explained himself. "This next one, well, it's my own. You see, I started with the guitar a couple years ago, after my brother left for the war. I kinda felt my way for a while, 'til I got a songbook. Even now, when I'm with my buddies or out wandering, I tinker. This one doesn't really have a name. It's just something I play sometimes while waiting for school. So I guess I'll call it 'Morning.'"

He looked down at the guitar then began. A few notes then a pause, followed by a few more. The tempo started slow, but quickened. Soon it was like the strings were chattering back and forth, striking up a conversation. Joshua leaned forward, watching Scott's hands, wondering what was next. He'd never heard anyone play like that. It was as if his brother, not taught the convention, had been freed. He'd learned to make his own melodies, discovering them as he went along.

Katie was mesmerized, as was the audience. Glancing back he

saw Mom, her mouth agape. Beside her Dad wore a sly grin, like he knew an inside joke. Joshua squinted, trying to understand.

By then the tune had grown, the chords stronger. Scott's name for the tune fit. It felt like the sun was rising in the room, burning hot behind him. Turning back, he was astonished at the speed with which his brother's hands flew along the neck of the guitar.

It was more than talent. His brother had a gift, like the woman in the Montmartre café the previous summer. Then Joshua hadn't known the words, but could feel the pain in her voice. With his brother, the guitar was his voice. And when it spoke, you felt alive.

He recalled how Claire had been overcome that distant evening, moved by the performance. And he pictured Aiden, tending to her as always . . . ever the protector.

His heart caught, pain surging as the song reached its crescendo. When the crowd leapt on the thundering final chord, he couldn't. It took everything to keep it inside.

Katie touched his shoulder. "Wasn't he wonderful?"

He gathered himself. "Yeah. He did well."

"More than well. That was amazing! I had no idea."

He drew a deep breath. "Me neither." He forced himself up and glanced back, just as Mom made her move.

She seized the open aisle, pulling Dad. He looked more like himself now, only happier. They reached them as the principal took the stage.

Mom hugged him. "Whew," she breathed. "I'm so proud . . . of both my sons."

The principal reminded everyone of the dance later, and said awards would be given within the hour. Folks clogged the aisles so they decided to linger rather than fight the tide.

Scott appeared shortly after, strangers glad-handing him as he made his way through.

Mom squeezed him tight when he reached them. Then Dad shook his hand. "You did good, son," he said.

Scott looked shaken but held strong, like he'd been taught. "Thank you, sir. I'm glad you came."

The moment passed, and Dad withdrew. But it was alright. It was just fine.

*   *   *

Mom stroked the ribbon on the way home. "Can't believe he won," she whispered so as not to wake Dad. "Too bad you and Katie couldn't have stayed for the dance."

"It'll be dark by the time we get back, as it is."

"I know. But I'd have liked to see you two out there together."

A while later, she spoke again. "Those ladies were all so nice. They were glad to hear you'd come home, back to your brother."

"They complimented you, too. Dad even seemed to enjoy himself." He sighed. "It's been a good day, hasn't it?"

"Yes, son. The best." Then she chuckled.

"What is it?"

"Oh, they asked about his musical training, like I had anything to do with it."

"Well, you are his mother. You raised him . . . raised us both."

"Yes, I suppose. But the way he played. He didn't get that from me." She adjusted Dad's blanket. "That's all him, and a bit of your father."

It was hard to imagine, but maybe she was right. He'd seen something that day, something new in Dad's eyes. *Pride.* It seemed one of them had finally done something right, in the unlikeliest of ways. How was that possible?

He pondered the matter all the way home.

36 – The Front

Joshua heard a rustling outside his cubby. "You awake?" Tommy whispered, fear in his voice.

He loosened his grip on the knife, rousing himself. "Yeah."

"I can't sleep . . . thought I smelled gas earlier."

Joshua lifted the blanket and climbed out into the trench. "It's the latrine, or the maggots, or heaven knows what. If it were gas, we'd know it."

Tommy eased back. "I shouldn't have bugged you."

"It's fine. I couldn't sleep either," he lied.

"McKenzie said nights like this are perfect for raids, with the fog and all."

"Phil McKenzie says a lot, mostly to get under our skin."

"But it's true. The raid the other night was in the fog, not near as thick."

"And it failed. The Frenchmen on lookout killed half the bunch. None of the Huns even reached the trench, except that poor soul who fell in after they shot him."

Tommy said nothing. He crossed his arms and rocked in place.

"It takes some getting used to. But you have to rest."

"I know," Tommy muttered. "I'm trying." He looked lost, beside himself. "Wolfie, if something happens, promise you'll tell Mary and my parents. Tell them . . ."

"We agreed never to talk about that," Joshua snapped. But he eased up. All the brave talk in the world wouldn't help. "Let's keep an eye out for a while . . . just in case."

Tommy sighed. "I'd appreciate it."

"Didn't help that it was right after we moved up, did it?"

Tommy shook his head. "Sure as hell didn't."

The firefight that first evening had jarred them all, yet Tommy seemed consumed by it.

Joshua tried to get his mind on something else. "Tell me about Paris. Was it all you expected?"

Tommy looked puzzled at first, like he'd been asked about someone else's travels. But then he spoke. "Yeah, it was huge. Tons of people, statues and buildings. I didn't see everything I wanted, not even the Eiffel tower. Nico kept dragging us to the brothels. Buster didn't seem to mind . . . so much for his wife." He rolled his eyes. "You should have come. We would have done some exploring."

Joshua looked away. "Maybe." A rat scurried toward him along the wall. It looked up then shot beneath his legs, vanishing in the dark. They were fearless among the men.

"Why didn't you?"

He figured the less said the better. "Wasn't up for it. Had some thinking to do."

"About Katie?"

He recoiled. "No. Why?"

"You don't talk of her these days. Don't write her either."

"Since when do you keep track of my letters?"

"I didn't mean nothing by it. I just noticed."

"We're not engaged. We never were." He stiffened. Katie still sent notes on occasion, but he hadn't found words for her. "I can't talk about it."

Tommy nodded. "I understand. Makes sense now. If you ever need . . ."

"I appreciate it," he spit out. Then he tried another tack. "So what did you do, while Nico and Buster were, uh, busy?"

Tommy shrugged. "I waited."

Joshua cracked a smile. "Really? You just waited?"

"What was I supposed to do? I couldn't wander off, and I sure as heck wasn't going to partake." He grinned. "A couple of them were real nice places. At one they served me bourbon. One of the ladies knew English. She asked if I had a girl. We talked a while, before she had to, well, you know."

Joshua dissolved into snickers. "Work?"

Tommy laughed. "Yeah. Work."

After that they breathed easier. Tommy even drifted off, right there in the trench. Joshua tried, but it hardly seemed worth it. Soon enough they'd have to stand to.

After the company orderly passed, Tommy spoke again. "Are you with Lee today?"

"Yeah." Lee was in second battalion. He and Joshua had been training as a sniper team for weeks. "I wish they'd go ahead and send us out. We need to get to it."

"Sergeant said as much. He was looking for you yesterday. Did he find you?"

Joshua nodded. "He caught up with me before chow."

"You were right about him. He's been downright decent since we moved up. Guess he did just want us to be ready."

"Guess so."

The other men had tumbled into the trench by then. Tommy punched his arm. "Thanks, Wolfie. I owe you."

Joshua shrugged. "Don't worry about it. But stay alert today. Get some coffee in you."

Tommy winked. "Will do. You too, buddy."

37 – The Spruces

Joshua gave the pebble another high toss. Snagging it as it fell back to earth, he glanced toward the Daltons' store. No one had come or gone in the twenty minutes he'd waited. The same was true of their house farther down, though their automobile was gone. He wouldn't mind seeing Katie, even her father. But he didn't want to run into Mrs. Dalton. He was in no mood for her.

With a shrug he hauled off and launched the pebble toward the creek. It arced high but fell short, a puff of white marking its impact on the crusty snow.

He'd been out of sorts in recent days. The job in Head Waters was done, and there were no quarry orders to fill. He knew he ought to help out at the store. Katie had hinted as much, going on about how they were in over their heads in Churchville. He hadn't bitten, allowing her to believe he was still busy.

He shook his head. An omission was no better than a lie.

He kicked at the Morrisons' fence, cringing as the throb tingled up his leg. He was sick of feeling like an invalid. The leg had stopped improving, and the scar looked horrible. So much for thinking he could go on like it was nothing. He'd have a limp the rest of his days, no matter how he sought to disguise it.

About the time he gave up on seeing anyone, the negro forest service worker appeared on the opposite end of town, notebook in hand. As Joshua expected, he passed the diner and entered the store.

Joshua edged closer, moving to within a dozen paces by the time the negro emerged. By then he had tucked the notebook under his arm, pressed against a box of soda crackers. In his hand he held a tin of sausages. "Morning, sir," he muttered before ducking his head and rushing by.

Joshua turned to see him climb the snowy steps of an abandoned shanty.

The man let the crackers and notebook tumble onto the porch. Then he crouched and placed the tin of sausages between his boots. He pulled a bull's head can opener from his pocket and proceeded to pierce the top.

He opened the box of soda crackers next. Feeling Joshua's eyes upon him, he glanced up. "Yes, sir? If you want, I'll move along."

Joshua retraced his route, stopping in the street out front. "Nah, it's fine. I'd just been wondering how you'd handle your lunch there."

The man paused from situating himself. "I do alright, sir."

He'd never really had a conversation with a negro, having only seen them on occasion, mostly on crews laying single rail track for logging companies down by the river. He understood the reasons why, but the formality chafed. "I'm Joshua . . . Joshua Hunter. I saw you with my father a while back. You and that other man."

The man nodded. "Yes, sir. I remember." He looked down at the crackers.

Joshua gave up on the name for the moment. "Please, have your snack."

The man fished out a sausage and placed it atop a cracker. He popped it in his mouth, chewing as he prepared another.

Joshua stood awkward for a few moments, studying the ridge and stealing glances back toward the store. When the man was nearly done, he spoke. "Say, was there a young lady inside when you got your lunch?"

The negro lifted his head, but finished chewing before he responded. "No, sir. I didn't see the young Miss Dalton. Her mother was at the counter."

He chuckled. "Did she growl at you?"

The man shook his head warily. "No, sir. Can't say that she did."

"It's just Katie, the young Miss Dalton, she had said . . ." Thinking better of implying the man was a menace, Joshua stopped short. "Never mind."

The man rose and placed the box of crackers on the inside sill of a broken window. Seeing Joshua's confusion, he explained. "If the critters don't get them, they'll be there tomorrow."

Joshua nodded. "What's your name?"

"Carver. Harrison Carver, sir."

"Please don't call me 'sir.' I'm Joshua. I'm younger than you, least I think I am. I heard you went to university. And we were both in the war."

The negro looked him up and down. "If you want . . . Joshua," he drawled.

"It's fine . . . honest. Listen, Harrison, a few weeks back Katie and I were over at Buck's. You and the other man were having your lunch nearby."

"Me and Maloney. I know."

"Well, I overheard you say there weren't any stands of red spruce in the county."

Harrison brushed the crumbs from his pants. "Yes, sir. Sorry, it's how I was raised. We've seen a few individual trees, but no stands."

"I know of one."

Harrison studied the ridge with a questioning eye. "It couldn't be on your father's land. It's all southern exposure."

"No. The stand sits on the far side, on the Garth parcel. There are only a couple dozen trees, but they're sizable. It's kind of hidden. I could show you if you want."

Harrison glanced about nervously. "I don't know. We only received permission to walk that land for one day. My boss would have my hide if he knew. And I'd be out of a job."

Joshua pressed. "You're up on the porch there," he began, nodding at the shanty. "That lands no different. I've wandered those ridges my whole life and never encountered another soul. One of the logging companies took a few liberties with the far border some years back. But other than that, it's been left alone."

Harrison rubbed his chin. "The forest is remarkable. Some of the oaks are older than those over on Hardscrabble Knob. I didn't even detect any prior fire damage."

"I could take you now. If Katie wasn't around, I planned to go for a hike anyhow." He shrugged. "It's where I go when I have the time."

Harrison looked toward the valley. "I'm supposed to head down to the river. They have me working on the seeding plan."

Joshua nodded, embarrassed. "Of course. I shouldn't have asked."

Harrison stopped him. "No. It's not that." He scrutinized Joshua's face. "You're sure about this? We won't run into anyone?"

"I'm sure. That land's about as isolated as you can get. I just . . . well, I figured you might want to see the stand. You sounded interested that day. But you have your work."

Harrison smirked. "The seeding plan? There's no hurry on that. It's just something for me to do, seeing as I can't deal with folks on my own in these parts. Things get worse the longer I'm here."

"So you're up for it?"

Harrison took a final look around before giving a cautious nod. "Sure, Mister Joshua. I'd be up for seeing this here hidden forest."

*　　　*　　　*

They didn't talk at first. Joshua avoided the lane toward home, crossing to the far end of town instead. At the creek, they filled their canteens. Then they picked up the original Indian trail, all grown over now. It made for a longer ascent but ensured they'd go unnoticed.

At one point Joshua realized he'd drifted ahead. Looking back, he saw Harrison off to the side, inspecting a chestnut tree. After a moment he propped his notebook against the trunk and scribbled. Joshua had a feeling he knew why.

"Is it the blight?" he asked when Harrison caught up with him.

"No signs on the trunk, and there are healthy husks beneath the canopy. But it won't be long. There's no stopping it now. They're all afflicted just thirty miles east."

Joshua's heart sank as he studied the towering giant, and the others nearby.

Harrison looked like he wanted to speak, but said nothing.

Later Joshua paused in a gap along the trail, tossing back a grin.

Harrison froze. "What?"

"You might want to get out that notebook again." He eyed the surrounding oaks then pointed down the ridge. "I believe that's my father's quarry over yonder."

Harrison shook his head, but Joshua caught the hint of a smile.

They took their time after that, Harrison taking notes along the way. It was past noon when they crossed the ridgeline. The air chilled as they approached the boulders. Undeterred, Joshua trudged through the deeper snow.

Emerging among the spruces, Harrison spoke first. "My Lord!" He observed the rocky face rising above. "No wonder I didn't see them. Unless you knew that path, or tumbled in, you'd never think to look. Even the boulders are camouflaged up in here."

"That's not all," he explained.

"What do you mean?"

He motioned for Harrison to follow, watching his reaction as they proceeded. He sensed a kindred spirit, justifying the instinct to bring him.

"Well, I'll be," Harrison breathed as the cabin came into view. Pausing, he observed the spruces and the surrounding geology. Though he still held the notebook, he made no move to write in it. Finally he walked over, hesitating at the door.

"Go on," he assured him.

Harrison stepped inside. Joshua let him be, taking a moment to glance about. The air was crisp, and snow blanketed the dense branches. An idea came to him, but he dismissed it. Still, he was moved to join him.

When he entered, Harrison was at the mantle, scribbling. He finished and looked up, his expression somber.

"What's wrong?"

"Well, I'm getting all this down, but it feels more a history than a live record. This will be gone when the loggers get at it, cabin and all." He eyed the pile of materials. "Are you the one who's been working on it?"

Joshua nodded.

Harrison said nothing. They walked out and made their way to the fallen trunk. Settling against it, Harrison lifted the canteen strap over his head.

He took a swallow then gazed around, sporting a toothy grin.

This time Joshua was puzzled. "What is it?"

"Reminds me of the mountain above my parents' farm in New York when I was little. The spruce forest was peaceful, like a cathedral." He shrugged. "Before they chopped it down and carted it all away, that is."

"Is that how you got interested in forestry?"

Harrison reflected. "Suppose it has something to do with it. Though my degree's in botany. When I got back from the war, my options were limited." He gestured down. "The arm and, well, all the rest. But my mother read the forest service was hiring veterans. So I applied."

Joshua chuckled. "Then they sent you here. How's that been?"

"For a negro, you mean?" He was no longer smiling.

Joshua felt chastised. "Yes, that's what I meant."

Harrison took another drink. "Not the best. The men I work with are mostly fine. But I can't really do my job so what's the use?" He shrugged. "I'm hoping they'll send me out west before they find reason to fire me. Then maybe I could do some good. Out there it's not too late. The damage is done here. It'll take generations for the forests to recover, if ever."

He glanced about. "Even what's left is likely to be logged. The forest service is no savior. The mission is flood and fire prevention, not conservation. Besides, hardly anyone sells 'til the land's all spent."

"But there'd be a chance?"

Again Harrison looked baffled. "Not for this ridge. The owner intends to sell to private investors. He's coming to town next week, and the purchasing unit's putting in an offer. But he hasn't agreed to meet, which is never a good sign. As for the rest of the ridge, you know where your father stands."

The comment cut to the quick. "I suppose I do."

Harrison cocked his head. "You shouldn't blame him. Times are tough. People are barely holding on. There's no getting ahead these days, not for working folk."

Joshua rose and ambled toward the cabin. So it was useless.

"Can I ask you something?"

He turned. "Sure, Harrison. What is it?"

"Why are you doing this?"

His gaze fell. "I don't rightly know, not entirely. I heard you talking that day. And Katie said things weren't going well for you around here. Guess I thought I could help."

The smile returned. "Not that. I appreciate it. Truly I do. But I meant *this*." Harrison pointed at the cabin. "Why work on something that's not even yours?"

He felt even sillier than when Pete had danced about the question. There was no denying it was a foolish undertaking. It made no sense at all. Still, he tried. "I don't know. The cabin was just up here falling apart. After everything over there . . ." He shook his head, not finding words. "Then I came home, and everything was a shambles here too. If not the war, it was the flu. Hell, between the saws and diseases, even the forest is dying."

He kicked at the snow. "A man has to try, doesn't he? To put things right."

Harrison studied him. "The war hit you hard, didn't it?"

The observation punched at his gut. No one ever asked, though maybe he just hadn't let them. "Didn't it you?"

Harrison drew a deep breath. "Yes, sir . . . Joshua. You could say that it did. Not that anyone gives a damn." He stared at him, defiant. "I was a member of the 93rd Division, 369th Infantry. You ever heard of us?"

Joshua shrugged. "No."

"That's because we were black. Commanders didn't know what to do with us. Either that or didn't want anything to do with us. The other negro division, the 92nd, got caught between rival colonels, both white. The men were ill trained, sent into battle prematurely, then trashed by the brass who gave the orders."

"We were luckier in the 93rd. With us they didn't even try. No sooner than we landed than they armed and equipped us as a French unit."

"I heard General Pershing wouldn't let Americans serve under a foreign flag."

The comment uncorked a bottle of fury. "Well, I guess you heard wrong, cause they made an exception when it came to us." He jumped up, his voice rising. "Not that I ought to complain. The French treated us decent, like equals. I'm proud of what I did, of what we did. We turned the tide at Soissons. We stopped the German advance and pushed them back. I fought for my country, as sure as any white man did."

"I'm sure you did," Joshua insisted. He hadn't meant any harm.

By then Harrison was beyond hearing. He stomped back and forth. Several times he started to speak but nothing came out. It was painful to watch. Finally he drew to a halt, closed his eyes and stood motionless for several seconds. Joshua could almost see the throbbing.

When Harrison opened his eyes, he was calmer. "I should know better. My mother says anger's an acid in your blood. It'll eat you alive if you let it."

Joshua swallowed. They had little in common, but when it came to the emotion, it was like he'd been handed a mirror. So that's what people saw, when it overtook him. "I understand," he offered.

Harrison pursed his lips. "I think you do, at least a little." He hesitated for a moment then looked up expectantly. "But I do have an observation, on you that is, if you'll let me."

"I'm listening."

"So you got clobbered by the war. We all did. But you're not dead, not by a long shot. I see your limp, but you have all your limbs." He shrugged the shoulder of his missing arm. "Sounds like you have a girl, too. The young Miss Dalton is mighty nice. She's decent. I'm a good judge of that . . . I have to be. So don't be wasting your time fixing up someone else's broken home. Go build your own. Start a family. My mother says the only thing that can stop you is yourself."

Joshua grimaced, kicking again at the snow. If it were that simple, he'd have done it already.

"Sir?" Harrison asked, edging closer.

"It's still Joshua," he breathed.

Harrison nodded, relieved. "If it helps, my mother also says I talk too much."

He grinned in spite of himself. "Your mother sounds like a wise woman."

"That she is," Harrison mused. "All I'm saying is you're still here. I know men who aren't. No doubt you do as well. You have to make the best of it."

Joshua sighed, reaching a decision. "I'm trying." He pointed at the etched stone.

Harrison crouched to study it. "Who's Anna?"

"If what I've been told is true, Anna was the owner's mother. Seems her husband built the cabin after she died. The heir would have been a boy. Probably doesn't know it exists." He looked around. "Too bad someone can't show him. Maybe it'd give him pause."

Harrison gazed about, pondering. "I could talk to Maloney. He's persuasive. But it'd be a long shot."

Joshua caressed the stone. "The whole undertaking's a long shot, isn't it? Saving a forest that's damn near wiped out."

"I'll try, Joshua. I surely will." Then he rose and disappeared behind the structure. Joshua heard him tap the rear windows. When he reappeared, his smile had returned. "You do good work," he observed.

"Thanks." He averted his gaze. The sun had slid back behind the ridge. "I suppose we should head back."

"Yep. I'd best not be out wandering after dark."

It had never occurred to Joshua, living like that. "We'll head to the lane," he suggested. "You'll get back faster."

Harrison glanced at the sky, gaging the light. "That might be wise."

38 – First Kill

Nico eased down from the loophole. "Fog's so thick I can barely see. It'll be the same for them. You ready?"

Lee gave a thumbs up. In the shadows beyond him stood Aiden, who'd come to see them off.

Joshua met his gaze. He nodded. "Let's go."

And so began their first day of sniping.

He scrambled over the top and fell to his stomach. The fog was indeed dense, and the sky dark beneath a new moon. Conditions were the best they could have hoped.

His heart pounded, yet he felt calm. He and Lee were ready. The scouting forays in the preceding weeks helped. Plus they'd practiced moving out and back twice the night before, varying the route. He'd grown numb to the shock. Last evening he'd even noted a rotting corpse as a fallback position, perched as it was above a crater, likely from the explosion that killed the man.

It was impossible to navigate no man's land in complete silence, particularly with a rifle. Still, he imagined drifting like the fog across the broken surface. If anything, Lee was more skilled than Joshua, so quiet that early on he used to wonder if the lanky Iowan was still behind him.

After glancing repeatedly during early drills, Joshua no longer felt the need. His shadow followed with no conscious thought. Lee was no different.

They maneuvered through the barbed wire more smoothly than the previous night. As they scrambled on, he listened for shells and launching flares. The light breeze was a concern, suggesting nature's shroud might soon vanish.

They arrived at the predetermined position among a stretch of craters facing a short jog in the front. The bend offered more opportunities, though it left them more exposed as well. He unfolded the handwritten map, then covered the edges with dirt. He'd long since memorized the main targets. Still, he felt better having the sketch. Laying it out was his ritual.

He wouldn't call it superstition. Unlike some, he refused to believe silly tricks would keep him safe. But maybe it was. All he knew is he'd done the same on every practice run. He had no reason to stop now.

The waiting began.

Lying prone, he watched the fog lift. At first it was nearly imperceptible. The breeze had lulled again so the erasure was slow, from the ground up.

A few inches became a few inches more. He could sense rather than see the pile of rocks twenty steps ahead. He knew their positions from morning watches. He studied the largest one, natural though shaped like a brick. It wasn't gray like the Pocono stone from the quarry back home, more of a dirty brown instead. The color appeared only in his mind at first. But as the sky lightened, the image and the object became one.

Lee tapped his belt. "Let's get two," he signaled.

Joshua winked. They'd joked earlier that they might as well face the pressure of a first kill by taking out two Huns instead. Of course, the French sniper who'd helped train them had said it might take weeks. He warned them not to rush. As he put it, "Impatience will only kill you. Each mission you survive is a successful one."

Lee went back to studying the enemy trench with his binoculars, and Joshua began another visual scan. He could see better now, though they'd agreed to wait until daybreak. As long as they didn't create a shadow or stir up dirt, the glare of the rising sun would obscure them. With luck, they might find a target during the morning hate.

He imagined a clock ticking in his head the way he used to while hunting. Back then he awaited bucks moving along the morning ridge. Now he sought men arriving on post, who in turn stalked them.

The need to view the enemy is what provided opportunities. He practiced sightlines on the enemy loopholes. The breeze picked up, and Lee tapped again.

Three knots.

He closed his eyes an instant, noting the pressure against his cheek. He wanted to memorize the sensation, to grow attuned the way a musician must know the precise touch even absent his instrument.

A flare went up.

His every nerve snapped taut. He and Lee were outfitted to be invisible against the hellish landscape. They were caked with mud and dried grass, and their faces and hands were painted. A dirty cloth shielded the rifle sight. Even so, he breathed shallow until the glow faded.

If they'd been seen, they wouldn't know. Not yet. Maybe never if the Germans were well trained, which they were. A bullet slicing through one of them would be the other's fateful notice.

The minutes stretched. He felt the sun creep up from behind, starting with his calves. He noticed the stench, stronger than during the evening drills. No doubt the subtle warming unleashed the scent of decay.

Lee didn't need to tap this time. Five knots. Joshua filed away the sensation and scanned again. It was time to hunt.

*   *   *

Several minutes ticked by, maybe ten. Movement. He teased the rifle over and checked the sight. Nothing. It wasn't a loophole, at least an identified one. The angle was acceptable, barely. Any more direct and a shot would be traceable. He glanced at Lee.

Three knots.

Was it a ruse? He shifted his focus to each noted loophole, then back to the new spot. He imagined the projection of a shot, figuring a delay of half a second. Then he waited, trusting instinct.

A moment later he saw it. Dust. Just a smidgen, but it caught the light as it rose above the lip of the trench.

The scope confirmed it, as did Lee's tap. Perhaps a team had *begun a new loophole during the night. If so, they'd be rushing to finish. Some of the others might be fake, or go unused. But if the Huns were carving a new one, there'd be two or three men. One slip, and he might have a shot. They'd already been careless twice.*

He flexed his hand. The sun inched higher, and the breeze picked up. Another waft of dust flitted above the lip. Someone was definitely hollowing out the top edge.

Seven knots.

A tiny gap appeared in the sandbags beneath the lip. He could see an orange dot of light striking the rear trench wall. A shadow moved across it, then away. Then back again.

He held his breath. This was it.

Gap follows shadow. Gap follows shadow. Gap. Fire.

A plume of dust rose, and the shadow stuck. The man had slumped against the hole.

Seconds later, he heard faint yelling. More dust rose, then the orange dot reappeared. They'd pulled the man down.

He had a hit, possibly a kill given the lack of movement. Lee made eye contact, but gave no signal. What was there to say?

One seemed enough, but they stayed at the ready. Rushed reactions might provide another opportunity.

The firing started up. A decoy they'd created past the rocky rise was strafed by a machine gun. Shells exploded too, near enough to give them a shake, but random enough that he breathed easier. The Huns were guessing. Within minutes both sides were ablaze with the morning hate.

They held position all day, baking in the sun. Only after nightfall, but before the rise of the moon, did they retreat. Absent the fog, they eased back gingerly along the route with the best cover. He understood how a wanted man must feel.

Back in the trench, the scout officer took their report. Aiden waited, walking with them after they were done.

"Good job, men," he said at the tunnel split.

Lee shrugged. "I'm beat. Never been so tired."

Joshua shook his hand. It seemed appropriate.

He faced Aiden when Lee had gone. "I'm alright." He didn't want to talk.

Aiden touched his arm. "Get some rest." Then he vanished.

Tommy was on lookout so he had solitude. He leaned his rifle against the trench wall and collapsed beside it. The night was quiet, save for distant bursts of artillery. The sound was comforting. He knew he ought to climb into his cubby, but couldn't. Not yet. He needed something.

Gazing up, he followed the shaft of stars above the trench. He recalled a summer's night when he was little, sitting with Scott on the crest of the quarry. They'd been counting stars between two oaks on the far end. Scott had grown excited, like he'd figured something out.

"I bet they're all angels," he'd blurted. "One for every person who ever walked the earth."

"Angels," Joshua breathed, searching in vain for the new one.

39 – Dad

Though light bathed the southern face, the sun was sinking fast. Harrison would need to hurry to reach the ranger cabin before dusk.

Joshua angled lower along the ridge, emerging down the lane from the house.

Harrison spoke. "Thank you kindly, Joshua. Today was decent. I almost felt like a ranger again."

Joshua shook his hand. "Hope you get your transfer."

Harrison looked up the ridge. "Me too. In the meantime I'll see what we can do about the parcel. Maloney's a good man. He's the only one who's had any luck with the owner. If anyone can convince him to meet, it'll be him."

"Thanks."

"You're welcome." Harrison's gaze drifted to the lane, his face tightening. "Damn," he breathed.

Joshua looked to see what had alarmed him. "It'll be fine. Though you'd best get on now."

Harrison had already stepped back. "You take care, sir."

Joshua watched him retreat before turning. Dad had vanished, but he knew better. He might as well get it over with.

Sure enough he was waiting. "What the Sam Hill are you doing with that negro?" Dad snapped as Joshua passed the shed.

Joshua walked over. There was no need to draw attention. This didn't concern Mom. "Showing him the Garth land."

Dad shook his head. "That isn't your land to show. And you know good and well I don't want them up here. You defyin' me, boy?"

"Had to get over the ridge somehow," he mumbled, eyeing the quarry. "You'd have thought these old hills had been hacked at long enough. Maybe folks ought to let 'em be.'"

There was a time Dad would have struck him simply for having an opinion, and that would have ended the conversation. But truth was, he looked worn.

Not that he was finished. Dad had to have his say. "You've always thought you were too good for the quarry. Afraid to get your hands dirty, running off any chance you got."

Joshua shook his head. "I've never been afraid of the work. But you're right on the other. Hell, I marched into a damn war to get away. Then again, you know all about running off. Maybe I got that from you."

Dad took a step, but didn't lift his arm. "It'd be easier if you could rile me. I see that now." He sneered at the quarry. "And I own my mistakes. But I make no apology for being rough on you boys. Weak men get crushed in this world. So if you want to hate me for it, you go right ahead."

Joshua glared. "I don't hate you. I'm just tired of jumping every time you take a swing. It's always about you . . . what you want, what you decide, what you think everyone ought to do. Well, I don't want what you want. I never have. And you can't beat me over it anymore."

Dad smirked. "So I hear. You're all set now. Got a girl, and a job to boot. Soon, you'll be wearing an apron and smiling at the good folk down in Churchville."

The words stung. "It's not . . . it's not like that." He clutched for anger, but it evaded him. "I haven't given an answer." He lowered his gaze. "I don't know what I want," he admitted.

Dad's disgust remained, but he eased up. "Boy, any fool can see that, even this one. I see you moping around, pouting when you think nobody's paying any mind. It might feel good gunning at me, but seems to me you're only running from yourself. If I thought you'd hear, I'd offer some advice."

Joshua looked up. "I'm listening."

"Son, get off your backside and do whatever it is you're gonna do. Because the way you are now, you're no good to anyone . . . not your mother, not your girl, not even yourself. It's time you made up your mind."

Joshua looked away, not reacting. He wouldn't give him the

satisfaction.

Not that Dad would have noticed. Having said his peace, he'd already stomped off toward the house.

Joshua lingered a moment then stumbled back toward the lane. He pulled a chunk of coal from the ice and chucked it over the lip. It ricocheted below, breaking in two.

He really hated it when his father was right.

40 – Approaching Thunder

Joshua tossed another sandbag onto the pile before wiping his brow. The mercury was the highest since they'd arrived in Lorraine. It didn't feel like September.

"You're not going soft on us, are you, Private?"

He stifled a grin. "No, Sergeant. Not at all."

"Good! Because the Germans aren't easing up, and I need to speak with you."

Smitty rose from his shoveling. "Afternoon, Sergeant."

"Afternoon." Aiden glanced about, then winked. "Looks like the heat's getting to you too. Why don't you head out and get some rest before tonight."

"Thanks, Sergeant!" Smitty replied. He tossed the shovel aside and trotted off fast, as if Aiden might change his mind.

Joshua waited until he rounded the bend. "Hey," he breathed.

"Hey yourself." Aiden leaned in. "Follow me, and act like you know what you're doing." Without another word, he began walking.

They navigated the support trenches for a time. Then, shortly after passing Buster and the lieutenant, Aiden darted into a communication trench.

"Where are we going?" Joshua whispered.

"Are you packed up for tonight's rotation?"

"Yeah, I was scheduled all day so I prepped this morning."

"Then hold tight. I'll explain in a bit."

Aiden's voice had an edge so he didn't press.

He didn't recognize any men they passed, though Aiden exchanged words with another sergeant. They crossed through the reserve units, then cleared the trench system entirely. Aiden quickened his pace but avoided the road, stomping directly into the brush. He proceeded several hundred feet, skirting the back edge of a sparsely wooded hill. Eventually he descended lower, stopping beneath a sycamore.

Turning to face him, Aiden put his finger to his lips. They stood in silence for several minutes, listening for movement. Finally he grazed Joshua's hand. "Wolfie," he breathed.

Joshua grasped for his hand, but Aiden pulled back. "It's risky enough already. But I needed to talk with you."

"What's happened?"

"In a minute. First off, how are you holding up?"

Joshua shrugged. "Sick of grunt work, but good."

"And the others?"

"Well as can be expected. Everyone's beat, but getting along. Even McKenzie's been half decent."

"So everyone's ready for the rotation?"

"I guess. Not like we have a choice. The new sector won't be a problem . . . we know the drill."

Aiden glanced away. "Kind of."

When it came to the war, he'd never seen Aiden nervous. "Are the rumors true?"

Aiden cocked his head. "This week's rumors?"

Joshua nodded. Aiden had a point. Each week brought new ones.

"Essentially, yes. I spoke with a bud. Fresh troops are arriving, and not just Americans. British units have returned from Italy and Palestine. With the Germans pushed back from their spring offensive, the brass feels the time is ripe."

"When?"

"Still to be determined, but St. Mihiel's been a thorn from the beginning. They'll want to clear the salient early on. I expect orders within the month."

Joshua's confusion grew. "We knew it would come. Why bring me out here? If you're worried about Lee and me, you shouldn't. We're ready. The terrain's different. Heck, it's easier in a way. With the forest blasted clear, there's a hell of a lot more debris than over at those old farms. We've plenty of cover."

Aiden's brow furrowed. "That's the thing, Wolfie. You won't be with Lee. You'll be with the unit when we launch. Lee was struck last *night."*

"He just rotated up. Is he . . .?"

"He'll be fine. It was during a raid. A grenade blast threw him . . . broke his arm. Others weren't so lucky."

"Have you seen him?"

"This morning. Then I spoke with the commander. It was his decision."

"Can't I have another spotter?"

"Under normal circumstances, yes. We'd rather have you out there, especially before the launch. But there isn't time. You and Lee know each other, can read each other. It's the same with the other teams. No one wants to mess with that, not now."

Joshua's stomach churned. He supposed he ought to be relieved. It wasn't that he liked the sniping. But when he and Lee went out, their actions were what counted. Matters lay in their hands alone.

He put on a brave face. *"Lee will recover?"*

"Yeah. It's a clean break, though he tore some tissue. That and he got his bell rung. His ears are still ringing." Aiden smirked. *"He's convinced he disappointed you."*

"Yeah. I'll have to give him hell." He picked at the bark on the sycamore. *"So that's it?"*

Aiden shrugged. *"Once battle plans are set, there'll be scouting missions. But that would be all."* He looked him in the eye. *"Wolfie, you need to be alright with this, and thinking ahead. Prepare yourself."*

He snapped. *"I got it. Battle coming. Message received."* He regretted the words soon as they escaped. *"Sorry. I'll be ready. Thanks for telling me in person."*

Aiden looked stung. *"You know that's not the only reason."*

He glanced about, then took Aiden's hand. *"I know."*

Aiden stiffened.

Joshua's laughter was uneasy. *"This isn't Paris, is it?"*

Their eyes met. *"I wish it were. I've thought about it."*

Joshua nodded. Neither of them had a clue what came next. But they had to get their first. He released Aiden's hand. *"We should get* back."

Aiden understood.

They moved with caution, looking and listening. Near the road, they paused to let a convoy pass.

Joshua studied Aiden, his gaze drifting up his muscular back, catching glimpses of his face whenever he turned. He wanted that life too, wherever it might lead. He recalled Claire's insistence they had to survive for each other. That's when it dawned on him. "When you visited Lee, did you see Claire?"

"My word, yes. It slipped my mind. She's settling in." He shook his head. "I never thought they'd allow an exchange, even temporarily. But the American nurse was willing. Together they convinced that Colonel she befriended." He squinted. "She had a message for you. Something about days. I can't recall exactly."

"Hold on to the days?"

"Yeah, that's it. What does it mean? She wouldn't say."

"Something she talked about in Paris. It means there's always hope."

Aiden nodded. "That is Claire, isn't it? You know, she really took to you, Wolfie."

"The feeling's mutual." He glanced ahead. The convoy drew to a halt, and a crew of men swarmed to unload supplies. The activity would provide an opening.

Aiden was of the same mind. "Remember, I'll do the talking."

He dared to brush his hand one last time. "I'll let you."

41 – Letter from Claire

The bridge was slushy so Joshua slowed. It wasn't like he was in a hurry. Mr. Dalton had made the offer two months earlier. Recently he'd assured Joshua to take the time he needed, given his father's condition. Five minutes more wouldn't matter.

Coming to a halt outside the store, he looked to the heavens. The sky was overcast, and high clouds streamed west. Hadley hadn't experienced a real storm all winter, but that looked set to change. He and Katie should have time for their trek, but they'd need to keep an eye out.

He stepped out of the truck, but didn't enter the store. Instead he lingered, taking in the strip.

The Morrisons' house at the end was the only structure with an air of permanence. Nearer, the abandoned shanties were sagging. By now mold had likely eaten away the insides. Eventually the roofs would cave in. He noted the cleared spot on the one porch. Chances were an opened box of crackers sat waiting behind the broken window.

When the store closed, the decay would quicken. Other residents would leave, including the Bucks. He looked beyond their diner toward the Daltons' home. He wondered about the roses. Perhaps some would grow wild.

What happened when a town died? Did it vanish forever or would a wanderer shuffle through someday, hearing echoes? How long would their trappings remain? He might have given the cabin a few years. But it too would disintegrate, if not knocked down by loggers first.

His life was no different. He'd do the expected then die. That's what people did. It's why he'd come down the ridge. The time had come to accept his lot.

Mr. Dalton caught him before he could follow through on his

own. "Joshua!" he exclaimed from the doorway. "How long have you been standing there?"

"Morning, Mr. Dalton. Only a moment. Is Katie around?"

"No, she and her mother had to head to Churchville at first light. But they'll be back soon." He opened the screen door, and Joshua joined him inside. "I understand you plan to walk the ridge. Are you sure that's wise? A storm's expected."

"It's her idea, sir. But I brought the truck so we could drive up. It'll save us time. We'll keep watch."

"Alright, if you say so. We trust you, Joshua. You know that, don't you?"

The query seemed strange, but he didn't dwell on it. "Yes, sir. I appreciate that. Actually it's why I'm here. I'd planned to speak with you both, but it's really you I need to see."

Mr. Dalton pursed his lips. "Hold that thought, young man. We'll get to it." Joshua followed him to the counter.

"Have I ever told you about Mrs. Dalton?"

Joshua shook his head, trying to decipher the question. "No, sir. I don't believe you have."

Mr. Dalton sighed. "It's no secret Olympia is opinionated. Some would call her headstrong. Others, well, they might say something else."

He nodded, but said nothing. There were only wrong responses, as far as he could tell.

Mr. Dalton gave a sympathetic wink. "I'm not blind to your particular situation with my wife. I'm not blind to a lot of things." He let the words hang. "But here's what you should know about my wife. I don't give a wit what people think because they don't know her. They'll never know her like I do. They have no idea what we've faced together.

"Olympia is a woman driven to build a better life for her family. She has a passion to make this world more like the one hereafter. And she has an eye for beauty. I fell in love with the whole of her years ago. So she can be demanding. She can have her moods. None of that matters, not to me.

"When I see her with her roses, weeping when she thinks no one is watching, I know I'm glimpsing the soul of the woman I married, the woman I vowed to honor and cherish. That's what love is, Joshua. Seeing everything in a person, the good and the bad. It means being devoted mind, body and soul.

"Do you understand what I'm saying?"

"I think so." More was expected, but words evaded him. He pushed through the awkwardness. "I want to do right by Katie, sir. I thought about your offer, and what's best for her."

Mr. Dalton held his hand up. "I've got a package for you, son." He turned and walked to the back.

Joshua was baffled. Mom was expecting new patterns, but he couldn't imagine anything else. What could it possibly have to do with Katie?

Mr. Dalton returned, handing him a packing tube. He eyed Joshua and looked ready to speak when his gaze shifted. Joshua heard two automobiles thunder by. "What the heck?" Mr. Dalton asked aloud, brushing past him.

Joshua glanced down, seeing the stamps and postmarks. He knew before he read the name. It was from Claire.

His mind reeled. Why a package? An image flashed, one nearly forgotten. Could it be? Maybe, but it could be anything. Claire had promised to write. Then again, so had he.

The screen door slammed as Mr. Dalton stepped outside. For the first time he wondered about the commotion. He joined him on the stoop.

Mr. Dalton took note of the package and of Joshua, but said nothing before turning back. The automobiles had stopped in front of the Morrisons' house.

Joshua took advantage of the distraction. "I'll be back," he muttered as he descended the steps.

He walked up the street in the opposite direction. After several steps he glanced over his shoulder. Mr. Dalton was still preoccupied with the goings on, so he turned and traipsed toward the creek. He wouldn't be hidden, but no one would come up on him either.

Stopping among a patch of sumacs, he pulled out his pocketknife and sliced the top edge of the tube. Tearing it open, he tipped it over. The letter slid out first. He held it while he went after the main contents, a rolled up canvas.

The tube fell to the ground as he unfurled it. He knew the image as soon as saw the row of windowpanes across the top. But he wasn't prepared. The letter flittered to the ground.

Lily had painted it after all.

There they were, resting in her jewel box studio in Montmartre. The painting was vivid and flawless, like a window through time. The city glistened beyond the elm. But what captured him was Aiden. He was awake . . . head back, gaze distant. His arm lay draped over his own sleeping form. Protective. Tender. Joshua hungered to feel that touch again, just once more.

He wasn't sure how long he stared, but the letter was damp when he retrieved it from the snow.

Dearest Joshua,

I have been meaning to write you for some time and regret not sending a Christmas note as I had intended. It hardly seems possible four months have elapsed since you departed. You cross my mind nearly everyday.

I must confess my writing you now was prompted by the painting, which I imagine you have already observed.

Lily, you see, has had her debut. I journeyed to Paris to join her for the opening. Her works are exhibited in a small but respected studio in the heart of the village. The show, "Le Moment de Relâchement" / "The Unguarded Moment," has been well received. Still, you can imagine my surprise at encountering the painting, for I had no idea she had captured your image last summer.

Seeing it was like glimpsing a past life, of which I have had far too many. I must have stared for twenty minutes, recalling our time on the hillside, along the Seine and in the cafés of Montmartre. The memories are fond ones, good days all, and all too fleeting.

And that, mon ami, leads me to the reason I have been remiss in contacting you. You see, after you left France, I reflected on the burden I had placed upon you. I look back now with some shame at my behavior on the morning of our departure from Montmartre. I shudder at my insistence that you had to survive, that you and Aiden had to be together. It was an unfair, cruel expectation, one I pursued even after your trauma.

The morning they found you was horrid. I knew something had gone wrong from the moment your friend had been brought in without Aiden. I had even prepared for the worst.

Yet when you arrived days later, pale but alive, I allowed a moment of hope. That is, until I saw the medal. Then I knew he was gone. After that, I went a bit mad I suppose, turning my focus to you. Perhaps something in my pursuit was noble, but it was selfish as well.

Just as I had insisted the two of you share the lifetime love David and I had been denied, I wanted you to live, not on your own terms, but in place of my friend.

I didn't fully understand my actions until you were gone, leaving me to face my loss alone. The realization left me embarrassed and without adequate words to ask forgiveness.

Lily and I spoke after the opening. She gave me the painting, widely regarded as her finest effort. Even now I covet it, though I have no doubt it belongs with you.

All I ask is should you not wish to possess it, please return it to me so I may cherish the memory of my dear Aiden during one of the happiest times of his too short life. You may send it, and any correspondence, to Lily at her studio in Montmartre.

As for you, mon ami, I wish you nothing but the best for all your days, which I pray will be long and joyous. I appreciate the brief time we shared, and would feel honored should you ever wish to renew our acquaintance. If you see fit to do so, I promise to be a friend first and to grant you freedom to discover who you are, and what you desire, without pressure.

With that, alas, I must rush this to the poste before I lose my nerve. Tomorrow I return to Lorraine. Though the war has ended, many men remain scarred. In that regard I fear our work may never end. Come spring I hope to transfer to a convalescent hospital outside Paris, close enough that I might enjoy the city, far enough that I might yet encourage Mother to join me. Sadly my fears regarding Remenauville were correct. It has been destroyed, the ground poisoned. We will never again call it home. But we shall find a new one, of that I am confident.

Be well, mon ami. May you always hold tight to the days.

Claire Laurent
Montmartre, January 1919

He stood in the slushy snow for a long time. He might well have stayed until he froze had it not been for the scream.

It was a blood-curdling one.

He turned to see Mrs. Morrison stumble out onto the porch. "No!" she shrieked. The automobiles, which had circled around to depart, halted. Mr. Morrison jumped out of the first vehicle and raced back toward the house.

A woman Joshua didn't recognize emerged from inside. She began tugging at Mrs. Morrison, who locked her arms around the porch railing, crying and wailing.

Mr. Morrison joined them, but it was a tussle. The hysterics had made Mrs. Morrison strong.

"No!" she shrieked again, even louder than before. "Not Pete! Not again!" Then she let go, and both she and the woman went flying backwards, slamming into the front of the house.

Only then did he realize he'd retrieved the tube and was moving toward the spectacle. He stopped to roll up the canvas, returning it and the letter to the tube. "Not Pete," he breathed aloud. What the hell had happened?

He reached the street and began to run. By then Mrs. Morrison had collapsed into a sobbing heap. Mr. Morrison gathered her in his arms. The other woman held the door, then disappeared inside after them.

Joshua approached the men in the first automobile. He didn't have to ask.

The driver's face was ashen. "There's been an accident at the mine. A new tunnel collapsed."

"Is he dead?" Joshua demanded.

The man shrugged. "He's missing, along with another man. They're digging, but it'll take a while. They've already pulled one body out."

A thunderclap exploded in Joshua's head. His ears began to ring.

He didn't notice when Pete's father returned, but he stepped back when the car bolted forward. Turning, he watched them race down the street and out the far end of town.

Joshua staggered toward the store, tossing the tube into the truck. "Pete," he mumbled, unsure what Mr. Dalton was asking. "The mine," he added as he fumbled with the crank.

He sped home without another word.

*   *   *

Upstairs, he pulled out the canvas and draped it over the hutch. It was happening again. Everything was spinning wild.

Shaking, he opened the drawer. He retrieved the cigar box and fished out the Saint Christopher medal. Clutching it tight, he stared at the image of Aiden.

"Josh!" Mom called up. "It's Katie and her mother. They're out front."

He glanced about, dazed. He'd left without her. Slamming the bedroom door behind him, he moved to the basin. The cold water struck his face, pulling him back.

From the top of the stairs, he caught a glimpse of Katie in the doorway. She looked frightened . . . vulnerable.

42 – St. Mihiel Eve

Tommy gave the folded note a quick peck. "Hope it gets out," he mumbled when he realized Joshua was watching.

"If not, you can deliver it yourself," Joshua teased. Though they'd both been trying to keep things light, it was useless. The day's raid had been a disaster. The platoon had made it back, but others hadn't. Artillery had taken out half the squad providing them cover.

Tommy shrugged. "I'd best get it to the lieutenant. You have anything?"

"No. I wrote my mother yesterday." Tommy didn't ask about Katie anymore.

When he'd gone, Joshua checked his gear again, then gave up. He was as ready as he'd ever be. Plopping onto the ground, he eyed the swath of sky above.

He cursed the clouds rushing over. The rains had fallen all week. More might obscure their advance, but would make a sloshy mess as well. It was bound to breed confusion, not to mention they'd be on their own. The squadrons wouldn't launch in poor weather.

More men streamed by. They were bringing all the units up now. No one spoke. In the end the trenches were nothing more than rat holes, endless channels of mud, rot and darkness.

A figure moved against the tide. It was Aiden.

He started to rise, but Aiden shook his head. "I'll sit," he called out.

"Hi," Joshua breathed once he was situated.

Aiden glanced about. "Where's Tommy?"

"Dropping off a letter. He'll be back pretty quick." Men were crowding near so he kept his answers brief.

Aiden didn't seem to care. He scooted close. "I'm checking in with all the platoon leaders, but wanted to come by."

Joshua imagined touching him. "Wish we could start now. They know we're coming anyhow. Even I won't sleep tonight."

"You need to," Aiden scolded. "It's gonna be a long day."

Joshua nodded. "How's Lee?"

"Good. He's keeping busy in support, though he tried to convince me he's battle ready."

"Still haven't forgiven him for leaving me hanging."

"You can get onto him later." He bounced off Joshua's shoulder. "And you . . . are you alright, with the unit and all?"

Joshua shrugged. "Tommy's pleased. Buster still glares at me, but that's nothing new. As for the others, I doubt they care. They have more on their minds than me." He shook his head. "Today was bad."

"I know. Tomorrow could be worse so keep your head clear." He brushed his hand. "I'll check in after we get settled."

Aiden's certainty was unnerving, but he let it slide. Tommy had appeared.

"Evening, Sergeant," he greeted, eyes darting to Joshua.

Aiden stood. "Evening, Tommy. I was just giving Wolfie an update on Lee."

Tommy's voice wavered. "He's still out, isn't he?"

"Yep."

"Lucky devil. Though it's good having Wolfie back." He pulled out his tobacco. "Have time for a chew, Sergeant?"

Aiden took a pinch.

Joshua waved off the offer, listening as Tommy pressed Aiden on the day. "Is it true things went better up the line?"

"Yeah. The offensive's going well. The divisions to the west advanced deeper than expected. And we did our part, keeping the Huns from breaching the flank. Tomorrow will be our day. We'll take the front . . . you'll see."

Joshua saw the gears turning, but Tommy didn't press. None of them spoke at all for a time, 'til a gust of wind penetrated the trench.

Tommy sniffed. "More rain's on the way. If I could block everything out, it'd almost be like a night in the barn."

Aiden studied the sky. "You plan to start your own farm someday?"

Tommy shrugged. "I suppose. It's what I know, and what Mary wants. Haven't really considered the matter as of late." He shook his head. "How about you, Sergeant? Josh said you'd been in medical school. Would you go back?"

"I might. Have to see how things pan out." He glanced over.

"To New York?" Joshua asked. He'd pictured being there, if not Paris.

"Probably. You ever been, Tommy?"

"Nah. I've been to Pittsburgh. And Paris was pretty, from what I saw of it. But city life doesn't suit me . . . crowds everywhere, bickering all the time."

Aiden nodded. "It can fray your nerves, for sure, though there's nothing quite like it either. Everyone jostled together, forced to get along. My sister and I used to sit in Central Park watching people. Been thinking about that a lot recently. Maybe it's time I went home."

He looked at Joshua. "How about you?"

Joshua held his gaze. "I don't know. You make New York sound appealing." He leaned back. "Though I guess I'd head home first." He felt himself along the ridge, wishing they could tag along. "There's nothing better than sitting under the oaks on a summer day, breathing sweet mountain air while eating peaches." He chuckled. "Or plums. They're good too."

Aiden smiled. "Definitely plums. They'd be better."

They went silent after that, each lost in thought. Then Aiden spit out his chew and pushed off the wall. "I should get going. Thanks for the tobacco, Tommy."

"Anytime, Sergeant."

Aiden leaned over, extending his hand.

Joshua gripped it tight as he rose, holding on an instant longer than necessary. "Goodnight, Sergeant," he breathed.

Aiden retreated, continuing down the trench. Joshua watched him disappear into the men before looking to the sky. Distant lightning lit the clouds.

Saying nothing, he reached for the tarp. Tommy grabbed the other end. The storm was coming.

43 – At the Cabin with Katie

Mom was setting Scott's guitar case aside when he descended the stairs. "The mine? My Lord!" she finished, eying him strangely.

Katie reached for him. "Oh, Josh! First Deek and now this. I just don't know . . ."

Though numb, he hugged her

"Mother's outside. She'll drive us over to his uncle's. Pa hears that a girl he's been seeing is there as well. I was just telling your mother. Chuck's taking his crew to help dig. Scott went with them so he gave me his guitar."

He shuddered as an image flashed. He couldn't be there when they pulled out the body. "No! I'm going to the cabin. I'll go on my own."

Katie recoiled, but it was Mom who spoke. "Josh! Why? The last place you need to be today is wandering the ridge."

"It's alright, Mrs. Hunter. It was my idea," Katie defended though her eyes carried doubt. "I'll speak with Mother."

He followed her down the porch steps then veered behind the house toward the tree line, ready to head out if she changed her mind. From there he watched the pantomime at the automobile. Words were exchanged. Mrs. Dalton grew apoplectic with fury. Still Katie joined him, umbrella in hand.

Joshua turned as she drew near. The going was tough, the snow thawed just enough to be slippery. The wind picked up, bringing heavier clouds.

They hiked in silence. At the ridgeline he stopped, his eyes drawn to the mist drifting through the upper branches. It felt familiar.

"What is it?" she asked.

"Nothing, I guess." He couldn't face her. "I should have let you go."

She grabbed his arm. "With my mother?"

He pulled free.

"Do you mean with my mother?" she repeated.

He couldn't do it. "Yes," he breathed.

They began their descent. The snow on the northern face was deeper and firmer. Each step crunched through the crusty glaze.

Approaching the boulders, he offered his hand. She looked determined but flustered . . . confused. He couldn't blame her.

They emerged among the spruces, and he guided her to the cabin. "There," he said.

Katie propped the umbrella against the fallen spruce. Then she walked to the door, hesitating. "Join me?" she asked, plaintive.

He moved closer but stopped short. He couldn't.

She opened the door and stepped inside.

When she emerged, she appeared pale. Moving toward him, she glanced back. "It's cozy," she muttered.

They stood in silence.

After a moment, she looked up at the spruces. He followed her gaze, struck again by the mist moving through the branches. He'd been on the ground, and there had been yelling. He remembered it from the nightmares.

"Josh?"

"Yes."

"This is about more than Pete, isn't it?"

He couldn't think of Pete. It hurt too much.

"Josh," she pleaded.

He looked at her.

"Pa said you got a letter, a package from France . . . from a French woman."

He shook his head. "It's not that."

"If it is," she breathed, "I could understand."

"It's not," he insisted.

"I didn't think so." She turned toward the cabin. "Not sure it even matters."

"What do you mean?"

She stared ahead, weighing her words. "You know, I've been

carrying around this fantasy that all of this was about me. You fixing up a cabin, building a home for the two of us. I even asked Chuck. I wanted to know if you'd spoken with him about buying it once they acquire the land." She shrugged. "I knew it didn't make sense. There isn't even a road."

She took a few steps. "Guess a girl can convince herself of most anything . . . when she's in love."

She turned to face him. "But this isn't about us at all, is it? It's about you, or someone. Or something." Her eyes were pained. "Pa said it'd take time. He said battle could change a man. I kept trying to give you room."

"Katie, I . . . I shouldn't have . . ." The words caught.

"Shouldn't have what?" Her gaze grew steely. "You're as icy as this damned ridge right now. Would you care at all if I weren't tugging at you, constantly? Cause I can't keep at it. I can't spend my days trying to make you love me."

"I care. I thought I was doing what you wanted . . . what I'm supposed to do."

"You asked to marry me out of sympathy? Is that it?"

He shook his head. "No. But people expect . . ."

"People!" she snapped. "This isn't about anyone else. It's just you and me. What do you want, Josh? Do you want me?"

He felt sick inside. "What I want doesn't matter. Not anymore. I can still take care of you."

She stepped back, reeling as if struck. "You believe that? You think it's enough." She eyed him like a stranger. "I used to think I knew you. I thought you were the nicest boy I'd ever met."

He had no defense. A coward deserved this.

She moved to a nearby spruce. Facing away, she ran her fingertips along the needles of a low branch. Clumps of snow hit the ground. "It's not too late. We'll say we made a mistake." She gasped. "It happens to be the truth."

He stepped toward her. "If you want."

There was fire in her eyes when she turned. "Just stop! This isn't about me. Don't make this about me! Don't use me like that!"

He reached for her, but she waved him off.

"Don't touch me!" She crossed her arms, bracing herself. "I should go," she whispered, like she was convincing herself.

"I'll walk you home," he offered. "Whatever you want."

"There's no need!" She brushed past him. "I wandered these hills for months, Josh. Trying to understand, feeling like a fool, wondering how I couldn't have known. When your letters stopped, I hiked all the way to Churchville. My uncle had to drive me home!"

She composed herself. "I know the way back," she finished, resolute.

"Katie, I . . . I'm . . ."

"Don't you dare say you're sorry!" She pulled the ring from her finger and flung it at him. It bounced from his coat into the snow.

She grabbed the umbrella. "There's a storm coming, Josh. You do whatever it is you need to do, but I'm going home."

She hurried away, not looking back. He watched her disappear behind the boulders.

He stood motionless, his ears ringing. The air was thick now, and damp. His gaze fell to the surface of the snow.

Spotting the hole, he knelt. He lowered his hand, waving his palm gingerly side to side until he felt the ring.

Afterward he moved to the ledge. Stepping onto the rocky lip, he stared down through the tortured oaks. They vanished into the gray, like ghosts in the fog.

He contemplated joining them.

After a while he dropped to his knees. The images were close now . . . so near. He chose to wait for them.

The wind gusted. Sometime later, a freezing drizzle pelted his face. He began to stitch it together, the day he lost everything.

It too had begun in the rain.

44 – Racing into Hell

The rain fell in sheets all night. Just before dawn Tommy and he clamored from beneath the tarp, grabbed their gear and followed the others to the jump off point.

The artillery had begun their barrage by then, and the sound was deafening. He never even heard the order. Instead he followed the man beside him when he propelled himself over the top.

The sniping missions were silent and precise, crawling and scurrying. Even raids were launched during lulls. Everything about the assault was different. It defied all reason, like racing onto a live firing range.

Expecting to be struck before his feet hit the ground, he felt a strange relief when he wasn't. The platoon moved fast, squeezing through gaps in the barbed wire cut the evening before. Explosions lit the raindrops, and his ears rang. He moved by instinct, feeling the ground more than seeing it. The puddles were large, joining to form small ponds and misshapen lakes. At one point McKenzie sank to his waist in a murky crater, forcing Joshua to divert around him.

The maneuver put him in the lead for a time. The unobstructed view gave him a rush. He could see distant flashes, and hear the whir of bullets and shells. The sulfur haze burned his nostrils. Explosions vibrated through his body, but he kept running. Twice he glanced back to see if his team was still with him. They were.

They reached the German defenses. As crews started in on the barbed wire, Joshua hit the ground atop a low rise. Only then did he realize he was shaking.

Being in position helped him focus. It felt like sniping, only easier. The targets were plainly visible. He picked off two men in the first minute. They had been on the run . . . retreating.

"Move in, Hunter! We're taking it!" the lieutenant yelled.

"Yes, sir!" he acknowledged, rising. It was then he saw McKenzie clutching his arm. There was blood.

Joshua stepped toward him, but the lieutenant shoved him through the gap in the barbed wire. "Keep going!"

And so it went. They battled through the enemy trenches, securing them. While others remained, their unit pushed forward. The terrain softened. Aside from fresh bodies and craters, the forests and fields lay relatively unscathed. The sky grew lighter, yet still the rain fell. The explosions came fewer as the Huns retreated. After a time the assault felt more like a chase than a confrontation.

In one hollow they smelled chlorine, but removed their masks when it became apparent there was no threat. The scent was bitter but the potency spent, a diluted pocket trapped beneath low clouds.

Shortly after noon, they paused to regroup. The lieutenant received word McKenzie was bandaged and on his way to rejoin them. The corporal had tumbled into a German trench, breaking his back. No one else had received more than a scratch. Joshua studied the faces of the men, seeing wide eyes and stunned expressions.

Tommy appeared beside him. "So far, so good," he muttered.

Joshua nodded. The morning couldn't have gone any better.

45 - Mountain Trash

Elisabeth lingered on the porch. She watched Joshua disappear around the corner of the house. She saw Katie approach the automobile and the scowl on Olympia Dalton's face. No doubt that damned woman was badmouthing her son again. A minute more and she'd have found herself facing a less accommodating adversary.

The action proved unnecessary. As usual Katie's gentle persuasion working its magic. Her mother handed over an umbrella, even as she shook her head in disgust.

After they'd gone, she whispered a prayer for Pete. When she gazed up, she noticed the clouds streaming over. A stab of fear pierced her gut. They shouldn't be going.

Rushing off the porch, she raced to the corner of the house. They had already entered the forest so she scrambled up to the tree line. She cried out for them, but heard no response. With neither coat nor boots, she had no hope of catching them.

She called out once more. Then, feeling foolish, she made her way back to the porch, cursing at the slippery snow.

Inside, she tried to settle into her daily rituals. She checked on Wayne, bringing him a bowl of broth. He was sleeping so she covered it with the saucer.

Returning downstairs, she forced herself to sew. Until the new patterns arrived, the work was piecemeal. Had Joshua brought a package in with him? She wasn't sure. He'd rushed through so fast, heading straight upstairs.

The sinking feeling returned. It bothered her . . . the look in his eyes, his refusal to go to the mine. The scars must be deep, and not a thing she could do. The few times she'd tried, he'd only pushed her away.

Of course it worried her. He'd always be her boy. But it seemed all she could do was watch.

Eventually she tossed the sewing aside. She added a couple logs to the fire then jabbed at them, taking out her frustration.

Watching the flames normally soothed her, but today provided no comfort. She stared a while longer, praying. Then she put on her coat and moved onto the porch. Damp flakes of snow had begun to mix with the steady rain.

Perched on the swing, she watched it change over entirely. There was still no sign of them. She dug at the notched wood on the arm, waiting . . . for something. She wasn't sure what.

The automobile was moving too fast for the icy lane.

That was her first thought when she saw it. Roused from her trance, she stood. But it wasn't Chuck as she'd expected, bringing Scott and news of Pete. It was Olympia Dalton.

The automobile skidded to a halt. Olympia hopped down and bolted toward the house.

Fear gripped Elisabeth. "What's happened?"

"Your boy is what's happened! Where is he?"

"I don't know. He and Katie are . . ."

"He and Katie aren't anything! Katherine's at home, soaked to the bone. She's in her room and won't come out."

"But he wouldn't have . . ."

"Wouldn't have what? Left her alone in the wilderness? Disrespected her? Still be getting gifts from his French whore?"

"Don't you talk about my boy . . ."

"Oh, but I will! My daughter is a mess now. But the best thing ever to happen to my Katherine is ridding herself of your scab of a son."

Her mind reeled. "The engagement?"

"There is no engagement! Damn near the only thing I could get from her. I swear if he so much as touched her, I'll have him hung."

Elisabeth stormed down the steps. Enough was enough. Nobody attacked her family. "Now you listen here! My son would never harm Katie. Never!"

Olympia snorted. "Oh, he wouldn't? Not the brave soldier! Everyone patting his back. Coddling him. Seems to me he had plenty of time for other things while he was gone, leaving my Katie to pine over him like a fool.

"And you, with your genteel upbringing, bragging about your precious farm, courting some filthy Yankee. Well, you got exactly what you deserved. You're nothin' but mountain trash now. You and your whole family. It's all you'll ever be."

Elisabeth stepped closer, eyes narrowing. She was done apologizing for their existence. She knew Olympia's type. Hell, she'd grown up with them. Olympia was accustomed to folks cowering in her presence. She wasn't used to anyone standing up to her.

"You know, Olympia," she began, her tone even. "I learned a lot from my Pa. It wasn't all teacakes and parasols. Pa was a drinking man. He loved his scotch."

Close now, she leaned in. "And Pa loved his guns. I didn't have my mother, so he raised me as he saw fit. He taught me to shoot. And you know what, Olympia. I was *good* at it."

She nodded back toward the house. "He left me his Remington when he passed. I got it inside. It's in the pantry, handy, in case something wild wanders in off the ridge. Us mountain gals know how to take care of ourselves, *and our families!*"

Olympia took a step back, her eyes wide. "You wouldn't," she hissed.

Elisabeth took another step. "You just try me."

She let the words hang, then pointed to the automobile. "Now you be on your way. Get off of our land!"

Olympia wasn't done. "Don't you ever again set foot in our store, and don't you go pouting to my husband either," she scowled. The threat came off weak, given how she was slinking away.

Elisabeth walked up the steps. Turning, she saw Olympia fumbling with the crank. She went inside, slamming the door behind her.

From the window she watched Olympia climb into the automobile, glancing up twice. The wheels spun in the wet snow until she managed to turn. Then the automobile shot forward and disappeared down the ridge.

Only then did the rush fade.

The sense of dread returned. Olympia had to be wrong. Josh and Katie fit, like two halves of a whole. She couldn't imagine them fighting. Had they ever?

Wayne was calling her, and had been for a while. "Wait a cotton pickin' minute," she yelled as she climbed the stairs.

The rest of Olympia's tirade came back to her. *French whore?* What the heavens was that about? She hesitated outside her son's room, making up her mind.

She turned the knob and pushed. The door swung open, and she saw a glint of silver atop a loosely rolled canvas.

46 – The Mission

As the day stretched on, the thunder of artillery continued to recede in the distance. Meanwhile the rain grew patchy, showers mixed with periods of mist. Still, they set up tarps, in case the deluge returned.

Joshua looked up when he heard the roar of the squadron overhead.

Tommy spit out his chew. "Now they join the fight."

"Not much they can do about the weather."

"Neither can we. No one canceled our launch."

Joshua didn't bite. They'd gone round and round about the use of air power. He figured Tommy was jealous of the pilots. Joshua certainly was.

It didn't matter. Standing there was enough. No one knew what tomorrow would bring, but they were safe for now. They were out of the trench and clear of no man's land. The trees were intact and leafy. Grass in the adjoining field grew lush, glistening.

Joshua looked around, hoping to spot Aiden. No luck. He had rushed through a bit earlier, preoccupied, not even glancing up, which was fine. The men needed him, and it wasn't like they could talk. Joshua just liked seeing him.

"Jones! Hunter! Get over here!"

They scrambled over to the where the lieutenant had gathered a half dozen men. Buster scooted aside so they could squeeze in.

The lieutenant began. "We've been ordered to stay put for now. We met our objectives, as has the 90th. The sense is the Germans may cede the salient back to the Hindenburg line. They've had four years to fortify positions there."

Tommy nudged Joshua, as he'd suggested as much earlier.

"Still, we have to be ready. Units to the east remain under heavy fire. If the Germans have set a trap, things could flare up at any time."

"So what do you need, Lieutenant?" Smitty asked. It wasn't impertinence. If the lieutenant were giving an update, he would have assembled the whole platoon.

"We've been given a mission. Just because the Huns are retreating doesn't mean they're making it easy. There have been sniper strikes. Inspectors clearing the fortifications have found booby traps."

"Members of the 90th reported hearing rifle fire in a patch of forest to our west. One man's been shot, and another's missing. A sniper team could be holed up in there. We've been asked to check it out."

"Why don't they deal with it?" Tommy asked.

"The lead units have pressed well beyond the position. They have their hands full. So it's our responsibility now."

"Lieutenant?"

"Yes, Hunter."

"If it's a sniper team, why not send me? I'll find them. No need to risk anyone."

"I appreciate that, but reports are sketchy at best. Could also be a squad, or nothing at all. Since we don't know, I've asked Buster to assemble a team. That's Corporal Higgins now. Captain just promoted him. You're to sweep the area before nightfall."

"But, Sir?"

"No more questions, Hunter. This isn't a discussion." He opened his map.

Joshua studied the geography as the lieutenant spoke. The wedge of woods straddled a shallow glen between two fields, maybe a quarter mile across at its widest point. A stream meandered down the center. He'd never questioned an order, but this felt wrong. It didn't make sense for the Germans to leave behind a squad. If they were retreating, it didn't make much sense to leave a sniper team either, though it was possible. But if they were dealing with a sniper, sending a team was a bad idea.

The lieutenant handed the map to Buster, who gave them five minutes. Joshua trotted back to prep his rifle while Tommy left to *take a piss.*

"Hunter!" Buster called out after he'd gone.

Joshua finished removing his bayonet and rose. "Yeah."

"Good thinking. That's why I suggested to the lieutenant that you join us. If a sniper team's in there somewhere, you'll know what they're thinking."

Buster had never complimented him, and he wasn't buying it now. "I know one thing. Eight men can't sneak up on a sniper."

"Well here's another thing you should know. I'm leading this mission, and I won't have you second-guessing me. Now finish with your scope and grab your gear." With that, he stomped off.

Tommy brushed his shoulder after he'd gone. "And I thought McKenzie was bad." He rolled his eyes. "Buster gets the first field promotion, clear out of the blue. Sure as hell didn't see that one coming." Then he slid his helmet on.

47 – A House of Cards

The snow was heavy as Joshua made his way back, a steady cascade of flakes blowing in from the northeast, collecting fast. He felt frozen, inside and out.

Emerging from the trees he could barely see the house. The solid gray sky fused with the white in front of him. It would be dark soon. Thoughts of Pete came with guilt. He couldn't dwell on it without the demons tugging . . . sharp, jagged memories that tore deep.

On the porch, he caught his breath. He pulled out the ring. He'd have to tell Mom, but he'd head upstairs first. Then he'd figure it out.

He hadn't counted on her waiting for him.

She was staring at the fire, but turned as soon as the door opened. He could see it in her eyes. She knew.

He opened the closet and placed his hat and gloves on the shelf. Hearing her walk over, he left the ring as well. She was facing him when he turned.

"What in God's name have you done?" she demanded.

He closed the closet. "Katie and I . . ."

"I know. That's not what I'm talking about."

His heart stopped. Glancing up, he saw the bedroom door ajar. "I need to clean up," he mumbled.

"Was this his?" She raised her hand and released her grasp. The medal swung free, confronting him.

He reached for it, but she pulled back. He saw her eyes. She'd never looked at him like that. It was more than disappointment. Far more. It was disgust.

"You had a chance, Joshua! A fresh start, with a good woman. The Lord won't keep giving you chances. Not when you spit in his face."

He crumbled. "I tried."

"It's not a matter of trying," she seethed. She held his gaze, refusing to let go. "My boy . . . a heathen. Taking up with some . . . some . . ."

"His name was Aiden," he stammered. "I loved him."

The slap came fast and hard. "You animal!" she screamed.

The room wavered, and his face stung. Dad bellowed from upstairs.

Mom brushed past him. He heard her footsteps on the stairs then the pause. Feeling her eyes upon him, he turned.

The medal landed at his feet. "Get rid of it, along with that trash upstairs. I nearly burned it, but this is your mess. Fix it!"

Retrieving the medal, he sensed she'd stopped again.

This time she didn't bother looking back. "And change before you catch your death. You're never to speak of this again. I won't have you shaming your father."

Then she was gone.

*   *   *

Like a wounded beast, he clawed for escape.

He shoved the medal into his coat pocket and fumbled with the door. Bolting out, he slipped on the steps. Grasping the rail, he felt splinters and saw drops of red in the snow.

A memory flashed. *Seedlings flecked with blood, bodies scattered among them.*

He tried to run, but the snow was too slippery. It grew heavier as he slogged through the forest. By the time he reached the ridgeline, he could barely see.

All he knew was to keep going, trusting the compass in his head. He had to reach the cabin. It was the only home he had left, the only place he felt safe.

He thought of the pain in Katie's eyes and the judgment in his mother's. He'd never regain their trust. He didn't deserve it. They wanted things he could never give, but he'd lied to them. He'd deceived everyone, even himself.

On the northern face he felt the full force of the gale. The roar was deafening. Branches struck his face as he plowed through a patch of mountain laurel. His cheeks burned from the lashing, then numbed again. He fell once and picked himself up. Then he fell again.

Emerging into the broader forest, he sought the refuge of large trunks as he trudged on. At one point he sheltered behind an ancient giant. Looking up, he realized he could no longer make out the canopy. Night had fallen.

The ridge grew steep as it did near the fault line. He slid down. Five feet, maybe ten. Regaining his footing, he tried to edge back up, to no avail. He was too weak.

What was the use? The life he'd dared to want had died in France. Why hadn't he?

Pushing off of a trunk, he lurched forward. His good leg sank through the snow. Pain shot though his injured thigh as it stretched awkwardly. Then he fell backwards, tumbling . . . plummeting.

He fell through branches before his chest struck a boulder. Sliding down, he felt his face scrape along the edge. Then he dropped again, hitting feet first. His ankle caught, then twisted. He landed face first on a hard layer of snow.

He felt pain everywhere at once . . . torso, leg, ankle and head. Rolling onto his back, he felt the world spin. He grew lightheaded. The last thing he noticed was the relative quiet, how the roar of the gale was muffled.

48 – In Need of Angels

Her heart skipped a beat when she heard the door slam.

Wayne heard it too. "What the hell is going on?" he asked. "There's never been such a ruckus."

From the window she saw a figure in the snow, a blur moving fast. Dear God, what was he doing?

"Eli! What is going on?"

She told what she dared, bending it a bit. "There's been an accident at the Tuckerman mine. Men are trapped. Pete Morrison's over there now, you know. Everyone's worked up. Scott . . . and Josh, they've gone to help."

"In this weather? They ought not be out."

"Scott says it isn't bad once you get down the ridge a piece."

If he had suspicions, he let them slide. "And Pete? Is he alright?"

She chose to lie. "I think he's helping. Josh mentioned something."

There wasn't time for guilt. Not about that. Her mind raced. She needed to go after Josh. She'd been harsh, but it was necessary. His soul was at risk.

Lord knows they'd never spared the rod, but Wayne had wielded it. She had been the soft heart because she could be. But she had to set their son right. It was all on her now.

"You're not telling me something, Eli."

She spun around, realizing he'd been watching. She was no good at this. "Honey, I'm worried about Pete. Truth is, he's missing."

The partial confession saved her. He held out his hand, and she grabbed it. Even battling affliction, he had strength to spare.

Winds buffeted the eaves as she stared out, watching for a break. None came. If anything, the storm had grown.

After a time, Wayne sat up. "Eli, I need to head to the outhouse."

"Honey, it's bad out there. We have the bedpan."

"You know I hate that blasted thing. It . . . it's . . ." He didn't finish. He didn't need to. No man wanted to face that his body was failing, especially her husband.

"You sure you can make it?" she asked, gears turning.

"With your help," he muttered, a concession.

Ten minutes later the storm was indeed worse, and they were in it. The twenty paces to the outhouse were sheer torture. "I'll wait," she assured him.

Closing the door, she made her way down to the shed. The truck was there, but no sign of Joshua. Her face grew numb in the raging gale.

He'd run off? In this weather? It took all she had just to make her way back to the outhouse. He couldn't be on the ridge. Could he?

Her heart caught. She already knew the answer.

Wayne emerged. By the time they fought their way back to the house, both their faces were red. He couldn't tell she'd been crying.

She kept up appearances, breathing prayers underneath. Back in their room, he wanted her near so she lingered.

Eventually he tired. She lit a second lamp, promising to return. "Hope to God they're hunkered down," he breathed, another admission, worry he'd never show the boys.

It was the only time she nearly faltered in his presence.

Closing their door, she stood in the hall. The house creaked. Lamplight flickered on the beams. "Dear Lord, my boy needs you," she whispered. "And I need you too."

The door to Joshua's room was ajar. She drifted toward it, then stepped inside.

The canvas was on the floor where she'd flung it. Reaching down, she noticed loose stationary beneath the hutch. It must have fallen as well.

Rising, she unfurled the canvas, pinning one corner with the globe and the other with the lamp. The bottom hung free over the edge. It was enough. The image confronted her, and she made herself look.

Joshua was unmistakable. He lay curled on his side. His eyes were closed, and his hand . . . well, it clutched at the man's torso.

As for the man, he wasn't much older. He was wearing the medal, that saint's medal. His eyes were open, his stare intense. His arm was draped over Joshua. *Aiden* . . . is that what Joshua had said? Was he Irish? Did it matter? Whatever they'd done was wrong . . . unspeakable.

Joshua had called it love. Dear God . . . how?

Eyes burning, she read the letter. After, she stared again at the painting. It didn't make sense. Still, she wanted him back. He was her son.

The stomping on the porch startled her. She nearly knocked over the lamp.

She rolled up the canvas. Returning it and the letter to the tube, she placed it on the floor beyond the hutch. Then she flew down the stairs.

"Josh," she breathed as the door opened.

But it wasn't Joshua. It was Scott.

*   *   *

"Don't look so happy," he chuckled, still brushing off snow. He was covered in wet soot. "It's horrid out there. I started in a snow shower and practically had to feel my way the last stretch."

He hugged her before she could speak. "Pete's alright, Mom! He's shook up, but he's fine. We got both him and the other chap. They'd been digging from the other end."

She pulled back. "You shouldn't have been out in this. Why didn't Chuck . . .?" Unable to get at the real matter, she grasped at small things, unimportant things.

"Oh, he tried. The lane's too slippery so I walked the last half. Now I'm wet, filthy and nearly frostbitten. I'm so sorry, Mom!"

She could see he was giddy over his friend. "It's fine. I don't mind . . ." Then her voice caught, refusing to go on.

"What's wrong?" His eyes flew around the darkened room. "Where's Josh? Katie said they'd be following, but they never showed."

She looked out the window.

"How long?"

She forced the words out. "Not Katie. She's home. I guess. But Josh, he left. I don't know . . . an hour, maybe two."

It wasn't registering with Scott. Why would it? She tried again. "He and Katie . . . the engagement's off. He came home. And, well, I . . ."

He reached for the door. "I know where he'd go," he insisted.

She grabbed his arm. "Son, No! You said yourself. It's too harsh."

"Mom, I can find him. I know where's he heading."

Nothing she said mattered after that. She clutched at him as he stepped outside.

On the steps he pulled free. "Mom, calm down! I'll be back . . . with Josh! He's the only brother I have. I thought we'd lost him in the war, and there wasn't a thing I could do. I'll be damned if I'm gonna lose him in some fool snowstorm."

Then he vanished into the gale, leaving her more alone than ever.

49 – Sitting Ducks

The wind had picked up by the time they reached the glen. Low clouds mixed with smoke grazed the land, but the rain had ceased. At first there were no trees at all, just grasses and thorn bushes between the fields. A stream trickled toward them, draining the wedge of forest ahead. The Germans had left this particular stretch untouched during their long occupation.

They had passed an abandoned bunker in the preceding field, along with two men from the 90th returning from the lead advance. They said they'd passed right by the glen, unaware and with no incident.

Joshua wasn't comforted. The wooded patch was a sniper's paradise, offering sightlines onto both fields and endless hiding places in between. Moving forward, he scanned the deepening layers. He'd see clearly a bit then another cloud would drift in from the field, engulfing them in momentary fog.

His heart pounded. It wasn't no man's land, but could be just as deadly. He didn't sense the same caution in the others. They seemed dazed, lulled by the assurances of the men and the receding battle thunder. What they were doing made no sense . . . clustered too close, ambling up the middle. They'd been taught better.

Smitty started to speak, but Buster shushed him. He then looked to Joshua, who nodded. The two of them veered to the outside, opening up some distance. The others failed to follow suit.

After a bit it became too much. Joshua drifted back.

"Buster," he whispered, keeping his eyes on the forest.

"Yeah."

"We should fan out."

Buster slowed, and Joshua stepped closer. The other men weaved forward.

"What?" Buster hissed.

"I said we should fan out. We're sitting ducks here."

Buster spun around. "Damn it, look at me when you're talking!"

Joshua diverted his eyes. If he hadn't, he wouldn't have seen the bullet slice through Buster's neck.

From there all hell broke loose.

Buster seemed suspended in place for an instant. Then his body hit the forest floor with a thud.

The men dove, as did Joshua. Nico scurried to Buster's side. It was no use. There'd be no stopping the blood.

As the men yelled back and forth, he closed his eyes to ponder the angle. From where? He reopened them. It had come from the middle. Distance was another matter. The sound was a blur, lost in his shock. And he'd missed the flash entirely.

Nico bellowed as the futility sunk in. "Oh God! Oh God!"

"Quiet!" Joshua yelled. "Did anyone see the shot?" he demanded as another cloud drifted across. The sniper team might be retreating, or preparing for another target.

Not all the men answered. Those that did couldn't say.

With few options, he took position, slipping his helmet off. It was the easiest thing to see . . . he knew from experience. "Nobody move! Not one inch!" he yelled.

The air cleared again. He swept the glen, focusing on the middle. Some parts were too exposed, given the better options. He concentrated on rocky areas and denser thickets. If the sniper team had ducked out of sight, he'd never see them. But if they intended to strike, he might have a chance, a slim one.

Seconds ticked by. Nico was sobbing, soft but audible. He blocked it out, considering the moment of impact again. Middle right. The bullet had come from the middle right. He narrowed his focus. Where would he be, if he'd taken the shot?

His own position was horrible, lying prone in a shallow dip, a cluster of seedlings obscuring his view. Still, he could see the gradual rise of exposed stones, blanketed with brush. Not the best spot for firing into the fields, but perfect to target a bunch of fools wandering up the middle of the glen.

Another cloud drifted through, lighter this time. It worked to his advantage. Using the rifle sight, he zeroed in on the rise. He'd been right. There was movement. The sniper team was on the ground, edging back with each passing cloud.

To his left someone moved, but he let it slide. It wouldn't matter if he got his shot off.

The fog thickened. He shifted the barrel a fraction, tracing the projected movement. He gauged the breeze as best he could.

The air cleared to a haze, even as the next cloud rushed in. He saw the slightest of movements, right where he expected.

He fired.

Just as he pulled the trigger, he saw a blur. Then mist obscured everything. Some twenty paces ahead, he sensed movement. He started to lift his head, but drew back. The cloud cleared too fast.

He saw another flash. Startled, he returned fire, twice for good measure.

The forest grew silent. Another cloud drifted through. This one carried large drops of rain. They fell fast yet stopped as soon as they began.

He felt moisture on his scalp, and a sting. Sliding his hand up, he touched his ear and pulled back. Blood.

His mind raced. Fingers. Toes. Eyes. He felt his ear again then his scalp . . . more blood and a narrow crevice. He traced the length from above his temple to just behind his ear. It would bleed like hell, but it'd be fine. He'd only been grazed.

The gunfire had silenced the men. He scanned the rise. Nothing. He felt alone on the forest floor, except for the rustling that didn't fit.

He planned it out. Buster was gone, but it meant they had time. He'd verify the kill. That, and get the other man.

"Stay put!" he yelled. "I'll move up," he added, softer.

A cloud drifted through, and he scrambled forward. He tried to identify the rustling. Ahead he saw a man on his side, rocking among the seedlings. Tommy.

He crawled faster. "Tommy!" he breathed. Then he froze as the air cleared.

"Tommy!" he repeated.

The response was a low whine. "I think I've been hit."

"Yeah, buddy. Maybe." He didn't wait for the cloud. He checked the sight again then closed the remaining gap. "Nico! I need you," he whispered back.

Another wave of fog covered them as Nico crawled up from behind.

"Let's see what's going on, buddy." There was a bit of blood on Tommy's face. His eyes were closed. "Can you look at me?"

Tommy opened his eyes. "I see you, but I can't right myself. I saw the sniper and went to fire. Did you get him, Wolfie?"

"I think so. But let's check you out first."

He waited for the next wave of fog. Nico reached them. His sleeves were soaked with blood.

"You were hit too," Tommy said, staring at Joshua's head.

"Just a graze." He noticed an awkward bulge on the side of Tommy's helmet. It didn't make sense. "I'm going to roll you onto your back now."

Reaching around Tommy's neck, he felt blood. Then his fingers slid across a hole. His heart caught. The bullet had entered from behind, beneath the lip of Tommy's helmet. The blur on his first shot hadn't been fog. It had been Tommy, moving into position.

Nausea overtook him as his world unwound.

50 – The Chase

Joshua heard Nico speak but lost the words. "Huh?" he asked as another wave of fog covered them.

"What's the matter?" Nico repeated.

He didn't answer, realizing Tommy was watching. "You'll be fine," he assured him. He finished easing him onto his back, then squeezed his hand. "Can you feel that?"

"Yeah," Tommy whispered. "But I'm dizzy. Everything's hazy."

"That's just the fog. Now stay with us, buddy. We're gonna get you out of here."

"Nice try, Wolfie." Tommy reached for him. "Tell Mary . . ."

"Tell her yourself," he insisted. Then he looked at Nico, who was studying the helmet.

Nico started to speak but stopped when his gaze met Joshua's.

"Get him back," Joshua pleaded. "Keep him talking. Smitty runs fast. Send him ahead for Sergeant Reynolds. He'll know what to do."

Nico glanced at the rise. "The sniper."

He was right. They might be waiting. But there wasn't time. Joshua drew a breath. The air was clearing.

Nico grabbed his arm, but he pulled free.

Joshua rose and sprinted forward. The expected bullet never came. "Go!" he yelled as he pressed forward.

Another wave engulfed him, bringing more raindrops. He stumbled crossing the creek but held his footing. Nearing the position, he scanned the ground.

They were gone.

He glanced back. The men were on the move. Three carried Tommy; the others had Buster. Smitty had taken off across the field. The incident began to replay in his head, but he blocked it. He couldn't. Not now.

Sweeping the forest floor, he saw flecks of blood. He'd hit one, *but was it the sniper or the spotter? A fresh clip lay on the ground, probably dropped as they retreated. No doubt they had others.*

He moved cautiously but scrambling for cover made no sense. If they had planned to fire, he'd already be dead.

He followed the sparse trail of blood to a row of briars. Pushing through, he descended into a small hollow. Another wave swept over, failing to penetrate the sunken cavity. Ahead he saw the body . . . the first one.

Beyond it lay others, scattered among knee-high seedlings.

He edged closer. There were over a dozen, all German. They lay askew, some atop each other. They'd been shot in the head and stabbed. None had helmets. Or rifles.

It hadn't been a firefight. The men had been executed.

Blood was splattered across the damp seedlings, leaving nothing to track. Standing motionless, he sorted it through. Something was missing.

Turning toward the field, he moved out of the hollow. From the crest, he scanned the forest edge. He saw helmets beneath a tree, along with a couple of Mauser rifles. The executioners should have taken them all. With a start he spun around. Somewhere there was another rifle.

He saw it farther along, shoved into the leaves before the last cluster of bodies. With his finger on the trigger, he crept forward. The first were lifeless. Their bodies lay face up, bullet holes visible. The other, a few feet over, was sprawled face down. The torso was bloody, as was the exposed shoulder. The latter wasn't bleeding much. But it was bleeding.

He pressed the barrel into the soldier's back. "Don't move!"

The soldier flinched. "Bitte! Bitte!" he whimpered.

One bullet. An easy target. The easiest. Then he could walk away.

He thought of Buster and Tommy. He studied the soldier's blond hair, and the empty gaze of the nearest body. Another rain cloud passed over.

When he hadn't fired even after it cleared, he used the barrel to nudge the man's hands away from his body. He stepped on the man's wrist, ignoring the resulting wail. Reaching down he felt for a knife. There wasn't one.

"Roll over!" he demanded, prodding the man's ribcage.

The man complied. The fear in his eyes was real, as was the pain. Still, it would be dangerous.

He backed away. Slowly he lowered his rifle to the ground. Then he pulled out his knife.

The man pushed back, wincing.

Joshua dropped the knife and shook his head. "No! Nicht!" His gaze drifted to the man's torso. "Let me help . . . helfen."

The man froze.

Edging closer, Joshua unbuttoned his shirt and tossed it aside. He showed his empty hands. "Easy," he breathed.

He knelt.

The man twitched when Joshua touched his abdomen, but kept his hands pressed to the ground. It wasn't trust. It was a truce.

*   *   *

Joshua waited until the soldier was out of sight, making his way north. The shoulder was shattered, but sufferable. The two bayonet stabbings were another matter. Though the bleeding was staunched, a ripped undershirt could only do so much. The soldier had already bled out a great deal.

Even if the man survived his wounds, he might well be shot crossing temporary lines in the night or while trying to surrender.

Joshua supposed it should matter to him, but it didn't. All his thoughts were of Tommy.

The rain had returned by then, light but steady. He retrieved his uniform shirt and gathered the rifles. Along the way, he tossed the Mausers into a patch of thistles.

Midway through the field he saw two figures on the lower edge. He moved toward them, breaking into a sprint when he saw the body on the ground between them.

51 – Saint Christopher

Aiden looked up as he approached. With a word to the medic, he raced over. This time neither hesitated. They embraced in the open field.

"I thought I'd lost you," Aiden breathed, turning his attention to Joshua's scalp.

Joshua brushed his hand away. "It's fine." His gaze drifted to Tommy. He looked peaceful.

"I'll get a rag," Aiden said. "Stay here."

"I need to speak to him."

"You can't, Wolfie. He's unconscious. Please, just wait."

"How is he?" Joshua yelled. Receiving no response, he edged nearer.

Aiden returned with a rag and some gauze.

"How is he?" he repeated. "Tell me."

"He's breathing. The medic managed to bring ice, but not enough. It's not always the blood loss. Sometimes it's the swelling. That's what happened with my sister."

"Does he have a chance?"

Aiden began to wipe his wound.

"I need to know. Is there a chance?"

Aiden looked him in the eye. "Wolfie, I don't know. The body's resilient, but has its limits. The bullet tore through his shoulder blade before penetrating his neck. It passed through the back right side of his head, clear through his skull. I'm surprised it didn't penetrate his helmet."

"So what does that mean?"

Aiden's silence spoke volumes.

"Then he'll die."

Aiden stiffened. "He will if he doesn't reach the field hospital. I sent Smitty to the clearing station. I told him to look for Claire. She can convince them to send an ambulance."

The medic fell to his knees, crying out. Aiden handed Joshua the gauze and rushed over.

Tommy began shaking. Aiden urged him to hold on while the medic adjusted the cradle around his neck.

Joshua's gaze fell to the damp grass. The rain was heavier now. His heart sank. Aiden's force of will couldn't fix Tommy.

His rifle hit the ground with a thud. He started toward camp, hearing the men's voices, seeing their accusing looks. The gunfight looped in his head. If only he'd waited. "No!" he breathed, veering into the field.

He slowed when he reached the bunker.

It was unfinished, the top partly exposed. Wood scaffolding rose within a concrete shell. Peering into the dim interior he saw assorted construction materials, discarded crates . . . and a man.

The startled inspector aimed his flashlight at Joshua.

Joshua considered retreating but didn't. The hole was deep. He imagined sinking into it forever.

The inspector protested as he leapt onto the scaffolding.

Joshua brushed passed him and squeezed by a concrete mixer blocking the middle of the top platform. He climbed the series of ladders down until he reached the muddy base.

Collapsing against the wall, he wiped his face. Rainwater had diluted the blood. He fumbled with the gauze, then dropped it.

The bottom ladder rattled. He looked up, expecting the inspector.

"Wolfie?" Aiden asked. "I can barely see."

It crossed his mind to say nothing. "Here," he whispered.

Aiden joined him. "You wandered off. A second later and I wouldn't have seen you."

"What about the ambulance?"

"Smitty came back. They're sending one, but I have a few minutes." He wiped Joshua's face as he gathered the gauze.

Joshua said nothing for a time, reliving the moments in the glen. Finally he spoke. "It wasn't a sniper. He'd been stabbed. The others were dead."

Aiden paused from his wiping. "You were right to kill him."

"I didn't," he admitted. "I could have. I stood right over him. I've done it before . . . it's what I do."

Aiden leaned in, so close Joshua could feel his breath. His voice was even. "That's different."

"Is it? I don't see how." He squeezed his eyes shut, trying to erase it, erase everything. "Tommy . . . I . . ."

"Nico told me."

He went limp.

"Look at me, Joshua."

He could see Aiden's face in the dim glow. The inspector moved above. Light bounced off the wet walls.

"Listen to me. It wasn't your fault. Nico said you saved them."

Joshua looked away. "That's a lie."

Aiden turned his head back. "No, it's not. You're hurting. Anyone would be. But you can't torture yourself. Now let me finish."

He succumbed, feeling the gauze tighten around his scalp. He wanted to cry but couldn't. It'd be selfish.

Aiden pressed against him as he worked. "You did this for me once. You remember?"

Joshua nodded. "At the hospital . . . that first day."

"You're a better patient than I was." Aiden scooted back. "There, that does it."

They sat for a moment, then Aiden moved. His lips brushed Joshua's cheek as he rose. "I'd better get back."

Joshua looked up, holding his gaze.

Aiden hesitated. He fished the Saint Christopher medal from his shirt.

"I can't have you getting lost again so maybe you'd better wear this from here on." He knelt, placing the necklace over Joshua's head. "I love you, Wolfie."

Joshua clutched the medal.

"Pull yourself together then head back to camp. I'll check on you later. Promise me you'll wait. You hear me?"

He nodded.

Aiden moved toward the ladder.

Joshua found his voice. "I love you too," he whispered.

Aiden winked, then began to climb.

Joshua followed his progress up the second ladder before his gaze drifted. His eyes had adjusted. The concrete walls were finished, but the scaffolding was old. No one had worked on the bunker for a long time. The Germans must have abandoned their plans.

On the highest platform, the inspector had stopped Aiden. They moved to opposite sides of the mixer.

Something wasn't right. Even if the Germans had left it, why would it be sitting there?

He screamed just as the explosion blinded him.

52 - A Brother to Lean On

Aiden's breath was soft on his cheek. "Wolfie, you have to get up," he whispered. "Don't make me tickle you."

Joshua smiled, his eyes still closed. He was sore from the hillside. "Is it even daylight?" he murmured.

Aiden laughed. "It was daylight when we fell asleep. Now we have to go. Claire will be waiting."

"I'm so tired," he protested.

"You can rest later," Aiden insisted. He rubbed his morning stubble against his cheek. "Come on. The day's calling. You have to get moving."

Joshua shivered as Aiden's warm hand slid across his torso, rousing him. He sighed. Aiden was right. It was time to wake up.

*   *   *

He opened his eyes.

For an instant he thought he was in the bunker. Lying on his back, wracked in pain, staring into darkness. It had been like that, for hours . . . for days.

But there was no rain. He was cold, and bitter air moved over his body. The dark forms of the boulders came into focus, nudging him into the present.

He sat up, taking stock. His chest and ribs were bruised, but nothing felt broken. The wetness on his face might be snow or blood, or tears. Whatever it was didn't seem serious.

The ankle. Now that was a problem. It was sprained, if not broken. Either way, he wouldn't be putting weight on it. The leg felt like it always did, a dull ache he ignored best he could. He could still flex it.

He'd fallen between two large boulders. They didn't form a cave exactly, but they had sheltered him. A bluish glow revealed a gap to his side.

He crawled through and emerged outside. His shivering started with the first gust. But the storm had cleared, and moonlight bathed the snowy hillside.

Where were the spruces?

He gazed around. The ledge was illuminated above. Though he had reached the fault line, he'd slid and tumbled to a position beneath the cradle.

He thought of the memory, or dream . . . whatever it was. He knew the mind could play tricks. Panicked, he reached for the medal. It was there, safe in the recesses of his coat pocket.

Pulling it out, he studied it in the moonlight. Now he knew.

He slipped it over his head, then went to work. Ascending the ridge wouldn't be easy, but he had to try. Now that the front had pushed the storm through, it would get colder, much colder. He had to reach the cabin to start a fire.

Unable to climb the ledge, he slid down another dozen feet to where the outcrop had a lower profile. Still, crawling over the jutting rocks proved painful.

Back among the trees, he began clawing his way up. He pushed with his good leg and pulled at roots and trunks where he could.

It was slow going. A few times he slid back. All the while he grew colder. He couldn't believe he'd come all this way only to fail. But he had his doubts. After a while they became serious ones.

"Please, God," he whispered. It was his first prayer in months, since those first hours in the bunker. He could remember them now.

He kept climbing. But as his hands grew numb, his progress slowed. His vision began to blur.

He'd paused to regroup when he heard Scott. He was higher up, possibly in the cradle itself. "Josh!" he yelled. "Josh!" he repeated.

"Scott!" he screamed. The wind gusted as he called out, so he rolled over. "Here!" he yelled louder when the gale eased.

"I'll come to you. Keep yelling!"

He laughed until he cried. He'd yell all night if that's what it took.

*   *   *

He sat as near the fire as possible, hungry for warmth. His clothes were drier now, which helped.

After a bit he shifted to warm the other side. Movement was painful. He'd taken quite a tumble. If he had struck his head or had fallen differently, he wouldn't be sitting there.

Scott had stayed by his side at first, holding a snow-filled rag to his ankle, telling him about Pete. Now he was up, poking around the inside of the cabin.

He returned to the fire. "So this is the project, huh?"

Joshua shrugged. "Yeah. This is where I've been knocking about . . . working through things. Do you remember playing *Cowboys and Indians* here, back when we were little?"

Scott plopped down. "I remember. It wasn't as nice then."

Joshua wanted to say more. His brother had grown up. He could probably talk to him if he dared.

Scott gave an opening. "Mom told me about you and Katie."

"It's my fault. I treated Katie wrong." He stared at the fire. "Seems I've been a coward about lots of things."

He looked at Scott. "Sorry about not coming to the mine. I thought he'd be dead. I've seen that before, someone else I loved."

Scott studied him, warming his hands. "Josh, when you came home, I wanted you to be the same as when you left. But I've been watching. And, well, it seems I'm not the only one. Seems everyone keeps expecting you to be the same. But you're never going to be, are you?"

Joshua shook his head. "I had to figure that out too." He measured his words. "I'll spend the rest of my days making up for what I did in the war. It won't be nearly enough."

He looked up at the frosty window. "And there's more, something I'm not ready to say. Something my heart says shouldn't matter, but my head knows it does."

He met his brother's gaze. "Scott, I can't stay. I don't belong here anymore."

Scott said nothing for a moment. Then he nodded, like he'd sorted it out. "I can see that," he began, "but you have to come home on occasion. Mom will want you to."

Joshua shuddered. "I'm not so sure about that."

Scott was firm. "I am. She'll need you to, especially after Dad passes. I want you to as well. You're my brother. Always will be."

Joshua finally understood why Scott didn't have to talk much. People who say the things that matter don't need too many words. "I will," he promised.

He reached down to feel the swell of his ankle. It'd be purple for weeks. "Thanks for coming after me."

"You took care of me once. Just returning the favor." He rose. "Think you can make it home? Mom will be beside herself . . . almost had to drag her along."

"I'll need a walking stick. I left one outside a few weeks back. And I'll have to lean on you."

"Figured as much." He gestured at the ankle. "Is it broken?"

"Hope not. I'll wrap it when we get back. Might need your help with that too."

"You'll have to show me."

Joshua sighed. "I can do that. It's something I learned in France."

53 - Moonlight

She was with Wayne when he woke.

In the moments after Scott vanished into the snow, she'd been frantic. Outside for too long, she'd grown hoarse calling out against the gale. Inside, she couldn't stop shaking, from more than the cold. Finally she got a grip on herself. She chose to believe they'd make it home.

Rising, she worked on the fire, nursing it to a roar. She brought in more wood and coal, and started the stove. Then she pulled out the pots, filling them with snow. If they needed hot water, they'd have plenty.

Checking the porch once more, she headed upstairs to gather dry garments and to check on Wayne.

It was in their room she realized the snow had ended. She walked to the window. The gale was strong from the north, and the snow was drifting. But the sky was clearing. Big puffy clouds passed beneath the brazen moon.

"Elisabeth?"

She turned. "I'm here."

Though groggy, he propped himself up. Some days he was confused. She wondered what he'd remember from earlier.

But he could be sharp too, like the man she'd married. "Are the boys still out?"

She nodded. "They're down at the Morrisons'," she lied. "Pete got out safe."

Wayne squinted at the window. "The storm has passed. Still, they ought to be getting on home. The ridge'll be icy."

She grimaced, unable to disguise the pain.

"I'm sure they're fine, Eli. They're just a bit rash at times." He clinched his jaw. "They get that from me, I suppose."

Setting the clothes on the chest of drawers, she moved to his side.

"But they're capable. They got that from you, too."

He looked addled for a moment, wracking his brain. "You saying that brings it back. Eli, I had the funniest dream."

She perched on the bed. "What was it? Tell me."

"Well, let me think now. It was two dreams really, kinda running into each other. But you were all there. You and Scott, and Joshua.

"The first part was in a room, like that hall over in Monterey. Scott was playing his guitar. People were happy. You were wearing a pretty dress with lots of flowers. But you were young, like when we married. I was watching your eyes while you laughed." He looked at her. "They're still as pretty."

She glanced away. "Not when I'm weeping, they're not. What was the rest?"

He pondered a moment. "'The other part was different. Josh was in the woods somewhere. Well, I guess it was woods, maybe a big park. He was building a stone bridge. Behind him I could see men playing ball on a stretch of grass. But there were tall buildings too, in the distance." He chuckled. "I thought I was only watching, like in the first part. But then Josh stopped for a moment. He spoke to me."

She nestled nearer. "Whatever did he say?"

"He said, 'Look at all the trees, Dad. Just look at them.' Then he smiled."

She shook her head. "Oh my. It does sound like something he'd say."

"It does." He placed his hand over hers. "Josh is just different, that's all. But he's stronger than he knows, stronger than I give him credit. They both are."

"We did good, I guess. Best we could anyhow."

"You did. I was hotheaded, like always."

"Don't say that."

"Eli, you don't have to defend me anymore. I know I made a mess of things. You know it, too." He squeezed her hand. "But I'm trying to make it right. I've been working at it."

She looked at him funny. "What do you mean?"

He shrugged. "They'll buy the land."

"What? Who?"

"The government. I spoke to them. Well, once anyway, a couple weeks back. I had Scott talk to them too. He was the one who picked up the papers."

"What papers?"

"Purchase papers. A contract for sale, Eli. I asked them to draw one up, and had Mr. Dalton look it over. He's smart on things like that. He suggested a provision. You could stay in the house long as you need."

"But the quarry? And the McCulloughs?"

"Ol' McCullough knows. They're heading back to Carolina. And the quarry isn't worth anything to anyone, not in the long haul, like you always said. The offer isn't much, but it's fair. It'll leave you free and clear, with a little extra. You can find a place."

"But where will we go?"

He cupped her cheek. "Eli, *we* won't be going anywhere. You know I won't be joining you. Go wherever you want . . . wherever you'll be happy."

She broke down after that. The boys were still out there, and now this. "You didn't mess up. You did what you had to do. I chose you, knowing that. We did it together. I'd have lived in a shoebox, just to be with you."

He held her a long while. He let her cry 'til she was done.

*　　　*　　　*

Later he faded. "Have Scott get out his guitar when they get home. Ask him to play something nice," he whispered as he drifted off.

Downstairs she added more logs to the fire and rekindled the stove.

Putting on her shawl, she wandered outside. The brisk wind battered the sweetbay. Moving off the porch, she kept an eye on the tree line.

Another puffy cloud passed over, then the moon burst forth

again. It hung above the treetops, bathing the quarry in soft light.

She looked around, taking it all in. She was alone, just as she'd always feared, staring out over a lonely heaven.

She trembled. Maybe love was all she had. Maybe it was all anyone ever had. It was everything.

"Dear God," she breathed, not finding words.

The wind calmed, as did she.

Two figures emerged from the forest, one leaning on the other. She wanted to run to them, but they'd be inside soon enough. She walked back to prepare for their arrival.

54 – The Fallen Snow

Joshua checked the wrapping, appraising his brother's efforts. "Not bad," he muttered to himself.

The fire was warm, but he was antsy . . . unsure what to say to his mother. Before heading upstairs, Scott had brought him the cane. It wasn't a crutch, but would do. Joshua made his way to the window.

The fresh snow glowed bright in the moonlight. Grandmother would have appreciated the grand display.

He wondered what she'd say about him. Maybe she'd understand. Then again, maybe she wouldn't. It would be like that from now on. He'd have the make the best of it.

He didn't hear his mother approach.

"You alright?" she asked.

"I will be."

"What are you doing?" Her tone was gentle.

"Looking at the snow. Thinking."

"About what?"

He sighed. "Figuring things out. I remembered something Grandmother said at Christmas. She said a fallen snow could open your eyes, help you see the beauty in the world."

She stepped closer, and he saw she'd brought some tea. Together they gazed upon the snowy landscape.

"I couldn't see it earlier," she said after a bit. "Now I can."

She offered the mug, and he reached for it. She clasped her hand around his. "Maybe love's like the fallen snow."

He looked up.

"I put it away . . . upstairs," she breathed.

She let go and retreated to the kitchen.

Scott came back down, and he heard her ask about the guitar. A few minutes later the playing began. The tune was soft, like a lullaby.

He stared into the night, feeling the warmth of the mug.

55 – Spring Thaw

Snow still lingered in the shadows of the trees, and ice on the edges of the creek. But a haze of pale red floated within the canopy of the budding ridge. Passing the Morrisons' home, he saw their spicebush had begun to bloom. The delicate white flowers were ablaze in the morning sun, defying the chill. He took it as a good omen.

He'd said goodbye to Dad the night before. They knew it would be the last time, but didn't speak of it. Still, they'd had more to say to each other in the past month than they'd managed over two decades.

His father would never know everything. But he knew enough. He had wished Joshua well.

Mom had made eggs and hash for breakfast, taking the opportunity to again ask why Scott couldn't drive him to the station.

"And have him miss school?" he'd teased. Then, seeing her teeter, he'd explained himself once more. "I want to walk out on my own, and see it like I always have. Besides, I'm taking the coach. It's not like I'm hiking all the way to Stokesville."

After that she let the matter go. It had only been filler for all she didn't ask.

With hugs out of the way, he'd set out with his cane. Between the old injury and the tender ankle, he'd given in. Still, he planned to ditch it after he reached New York. It wouldn't look good when seeking work.

He shifted the duffel to his other hand as he approached the store. It was closed now, the Daltons having moved on to Churchville shortly after the canceled engagement. The two weren't related, not directly, though he hadn't seen her since that day at the cabin.

Peeking through the window, he saw empty shelves. Strange how a place so associated with one's life could vanish so fast.

Proceeding on, he saw the Daltons' automobile. It sat alongside their old home, obscured by the rose bushes.

He was studying the house when he heard her whisper his name.

She was sitting on the bench at Buck's. Her hair was different, kind of a wave; and she wore a new coat. It looked as if she'd been waiting a while.

"Katie," he breathed.

She approached the fence, bringing an answer. "Scott came by the new store last week. He said you were leaving this morning." She looked over at their old house. "Pa's packing up some things. Mother refuses to return so I've been helping. He knows why I wanted to come today."

"How did you know I'd walk?"

Her smile was warm but uneasy. "I wasn't sure, but figured you would. I was counting on it really."

He nodded. She still knew him better than most anyone. That hadn't changed.

The words he'd been mulling for a letter tumbled out. "Katie, I know what you said. But I am sorry. I was wrong . . . selfish." He wanted to say more, but didn't. Anything else would have been for him, not her.

"I appreciate that, Josh. I do." She glanced about. "You have good weather. It's a fine day to leave Hadley."

He surveyed the sad strip. "What's left of it, anyhow."

"You have that right." The silence was awkward before she spoke again. "Maybe the forest will reclaim it. I understand it'll have a foothold up on the ridge."

"A bit of one. Scott must have told you my father sold."

"As did the elusive Garths."

He sighed. It had been inevitable. "So Chuck's father purchased it."

She eyed him intently. "No. The forest service did. I thought you knew that."

He couldn't suppress a grin. "I hadn't heard."

Suspicion confirmed, she gave a knowing nod. "Chuck's none too pleased, but he'll get over it. As for me, I rather like knowing our ridge won't be ravaged."

"Me too."

Katie pulled her coat closed. "I should get back. Pa's been on his own for nearly an hour. Mother will be furious if any of her china gets broken."

"I'd best get on as well . . . can't miss the coach."

"Pa could drive you," she offered, then caught herself.

"No, I told Mom I wanted it this way. This is my doing . . . my decision." Their eyes met. "Katie, you deserve to be someone's everything."

She couldn't hold his gaze. "Don't you be lonely in the big city."

She left after that, and he waited 'til she went inside.

Descending toward the river, he considered her situation. Katie deserved to be happy. Women had so few options, no matter how bright they were. He could move on. A man could do that. No one would think anything of it.

He thought of how Claire had managed. He'd finally written. The note had been short, with the promise of another when he got settled. He told her it had been rough, but that he was coping.

He recalled how she had talked of her days with David, and how they sustained her. The idea had been heavy on his mind as of late. He and Aiden hadn't shared many days. Most of them had been on the front.

But he had a handful. He had them, a Saint Christopher's medal and a captured moment in time. It wasn't much, but it was something. He wouldn't forget. He'd carry them always.

.

Epilogue

Elisabeth dried the final plate and placed it in the cupboard. Then she walked into the sewing room. The two new dresses she had pinned for Ellie Meeks were waiting where she'd left them the night before. Though she had stayed up late working on them, she'd risen early as normal to prepare breakfast for Scott.

He'd be heading off to work soon, and she'd have the place to herself.

Streaming sunlight beckoned her to the window so she obliged. She enjoyed how the morning rays lit the room, one of the many reasons she liked the little house. Still, it wasn't the same as being outside.

The air had a bite, but the grass was still green. Beneath the window the black-eyed susans remained bold and yellow. The frosts were coming, but they hadn't reached them yet.

She sighed. Maybe she could do some mending out by the creek to start the day. That way she could enjoy the morning before delving into more intricate work.

She gathered the items and her sewing kit. At the door she hesitated. There was one more thing.

Walking over to the desk, she retrieved Joshua's letter. It didn't matter that she had read it while standing in the store in Monterey the day before. If she read it again, she could almost feel like she was visiting, his descriptions were so vivid.

The screen door slammed behind her. She made her way across the yard, passing the gazebo. Reaching the bench, she seated herself with her back to the stable so she could listen to the gurgle of the creek while gazing at the house and the ridge beyond it. The view was her favorite on the tiny farm.

She had described it to Wayne near the end, when he could still talk. At the time he'd promised to see it with her. Some days she felt he'd kept his word.

The mending could wait. She pulled the letter out instead.

It hardly seemed possible six months had passed. Of course it had been a hectic time for all of them. And Josh had returned once, in May for the funeral.

That was when he and Scott had constructed the gazebo, designed to serve as a greenhouse as well. Window-paned slats were stashed up underneath, ready to be slid into place for the winter. Joshua said he got the idea from one he saw in a riverside park shortly after his arrival in the city.

Time would tell if the sweetbay would survive, though it was healthier already, even after the transplanting.

She smiled when she pulled out the little extras he'd included. One was a map of Central Park marked with projects. Between the menagerie and the boathouses and the bridges, there seemed plenty to keep his crew busy. That came as a relief, the bonus being he seemed to enjoy the work.

He'd also included a sketch of his apartment, which from the looks of it wasn't much bigger than his old room. But he said he could walk to the river and to work and to most anywhere else he got it in his mind to wander.

She was curious how he was getting on, and imagined there were things he'd never share. She was fine with that. It was possible to love him without fully understanding. Wasn't it like that with anyone for whom you cared deeply?

He did mention volunteering with a local medical institution. He said he'd convinced the administrator to bring patients to the park on occasion. Apparently he and one of the groundskeepers helped, sharing cuttings of flowers and plants. He said the outings helped soothe them.

That he would have been so bold struck her. Not that he would be interested. He'd always had a charitable soul. But that he'd put himself out there, engaging folks so readily. Perhaps the city was good for him after all.

Saint Sebastian's . . . a Catholic institution, no doubt. She shook her head. All those silly prejudices, and the way she had clutched at them like a blanket. They hadn't shielded her from her fears.

Nowadays she didn't have the time for such foolishness, having wasted so much already. People were people, most doing the best they could.

As for Joshua's next visit, she'd have to wait until Pete's wedding. Money was tight, and he owed time from the funeral. Plus he said there was one trip he had to make. It seemed the Pennsylvania farm boy Josh had befriended in the service was still struggling. Josh promised to tell her all about it someday, in person.

Scott wandered up. "You're not chilled out here, are you?"

She set the letter upon the table. "Not at all. It's just a little crisp."

"I take it that's from Josh?"

"Yes. He says he hopes you're enjoying being an amateur farmer when you're not grinding away at the grist mill."

"The city boy's become quite the joker, hasn't he?" He glanced at the small field. "Besides, I think we did well, considering how late we planted. You be sure to tell him it makes ends meet until the guitar can feed us. Which brings me to ask, have you decided if you're coming tonight?"

She laughed. "As if I've missed a concert yet. Will she be there as well?"

He blushed. "I have no idea, but I'm kinda hoping."

She nodded. "She will be if she's smart."

He changed the subject, as she figured he would. She didn't push. Scott would find love when he was ready. Perhaps both her sons would.

"I was thinking I might put the slats in the gazebo on Sunday. Do you think it'll work? I know the sweetbay means a lot to you."

"Of course it will." She shrugged. "If it doesn't, we'll plant something else, something beautiful. Or I will, when you move on."

He shook his head. "I told you, Mom. I'm not going anywhere. You see that hill over yonder? That's where my house will be, once I find the right girl."

"We'll see about that. She might have her own ideas on where she wants to live, and it may not be next to her mother-in-law. And you'd best hear her out."

"Alright, alright. I'll be sure to keep that in mind when I have that particular dilemma. For now my main concern is getting to work on time." He gave her a quick peck then ambled off.

She watched him crank the truck and climb into the cab.

As the truck disappeared into the valley, she reflected on how they had ended up in Highland County. It was funny how people touched each other, in ways large and small. Not even a year ago her son had returned from the war, and flu and disease had gripped them all.

Now he was in New York. Wayne had passed, and she and Scott were here. Even Katie had moved on, studying to become a teacher and being courted by Chuck if what Pete told Scott was to be believed.

Tragedy had come and gone. No doubt it would come again someday.

In the meantime you could only do what you could do, and be good to each other. She understood now. But it wasn't until that snowy night on the ridge that she had learned to see what was right before her eyes all along.

Just then a pair of finches flitted into sight, bounding from branch to branch on the tall maple by the creek. They only lingered an instant before they disappeared again, vanishing into the field.

It didn't matter. She had to get started anyhow. Still she took another moment, simply to look around. *A good place on a good day, and loved* . . . a soul couldn't hope for any better than that.

A Special Thanks

Thank you for reading *The Fallen Snow*. The residents of Hadley and their kindred spirits in France have floated about in my head for years. Now, having finally found the words to awaken their world, I am understandably eager to share it with ours.

If you have enjoyed or been touched by the tale, I would welcome your recommendation of the novel to friends, family and avid readers you may know. Please visit www.thefallensnow.com for more information on the characters and setting, as well as suggestions to help ensure *The Fallen Snow* reaches a wider audience.

Thank you again for taking the time to read my debut novel. I hope you found the experience worthwhile.

May you hold tight to the days . . . always.

John

Historical Notes

World War I – Called "The Great War" at the time, World War I began in July 1914 and ended on November 11, 1918. It involved every major global power, resulting in over 30 million military and civilian casualties. The Great War saw the rise of modern weapons, including machine guns, poisonous gas, tanks, airplanes and missile precursors such as the Paris Gun. As military tactics lagged behind advances in lethal technologies, the war quickly bogged down into trench warfare, the horrors of which scarred a generation of men.

After originally maintaining a neutral stance, The United States entered the war on April 6, 1917. Upon entry a national army was organized, aided by the largest draft in US history up until that time. General Pershing, the American Expeditionary Forces (AEF) commander, insisted troops be trained stateside before deployment. As a result few US troops were deployed before 1918, though their numbers swelled thereafter, aiding in decisive allied victories later that year. Despite suffering tremendous losses, the US was spared the annihilating devastation experienced by allied forces during the initial years of the war.

The 82nd Division was organized in August 1917 at Camp Gordon, Georgia. Comprised of men from all 48 states, the division became known as the "All-American." In May 1918 the 82nd arrived in France and trained with British instructors in the Somme. Transported by troop train to Lorraine in June, units soon began to integrate into the front lines. In September the division participated in the allied offensive to retake the St. Mihiel salient.

1918 Influenza Pandemic – From 1918 to 1920, three waves of influenza caused by the H1N1 virus swept the globe, triggering one of the deadliest pandemics in human history. Between 50 and 100 million people died globally, most of the victims young and healthy. The deadliest wave of disease swept the globe between September and November 1918, during the closing days of World War I.

Historical Notes

Weeks Act - Signed into law by President Taft on March 1, 1911, the Weeks Act permitted the federal government to purchase private land in order to protect eastern watersheds and to support fire prevention efforts. It also allowed the federal government for the first time to establish and maintain national forests in eastern states. Though controversial when passed, the Weeks Act is now regarded as one of the most successful pieces of conservation legislation in US history. Its passage allowed eastern forests to begin their long recovery from abusive logging practices employed at the turn of the twentieth century.

Shenandoah National Forest - Later renamed "George Washington National Forest" so as to avoid confusion with Shenandoah National Park formed sixty miles east, the Shenandoah National Forest was established May 16, 1918. Using Weeks Act provisions, government purchasing units began to identify, examine and recommend land for acquisition starting in 1913. Over subsequent years, decades and to a lesser degree through today, the contours and range of the national forest emerged as parcels were cobbled together.

Most initial purchases comprised lands denuded by the destructive logging practices of the time. Other parcels consisted of mountain farms, spent mines or dying settlements. A few contained native forests, often fire damaged or inaccessible. Inclusion of these coveted parcels did not ensure their preservation. To this day fierce policy disputes rage over the best use of lands managed by the US Forest Service. Still, the existence of renewed forests and rare old growth in eastern states is only possible due to these early efforts.

Hadley is a fictional community, as are events portrayed in actual locations. Yet the unique history of forests in Virginia's western Augusta County and eastern Highland County is real. The remote wilderness areas surrounding Shenandoah Mountain are a haunting reminder of the lands that inspired a nation of pioneers.

Acknowledgments

Writing is a reclusive process . . . until it's not. One day you realize the time has come to share your work with others. So you start with trusted friends and colleagues, not simply those likely to praise your efforts but also those ready to challenge your instincts.

I've been fortunate to receive both types of support, often in powerful combination. I begin of course with Jim, the love of my life and my greatest advocate. Without him none of this would be possible – physically, financially or emotionally. The greatest gift I have ever received is his faith in me, coupled with an undying patience. Only he was besieged with a dozen variations of short segments on countless evenings, each time listening with care though I know they must have sounded the same after a time. Still, he let me so I could hear the words aloud until convinced they'd hit their mark . . . only to change them again the next day on my own.

Thanks go out as well to those who dove deep into the novel, finding rare insights. To Doug for delving into Joshua's emotional state, his journey and his relationships. To Janet for recognizing the larger spirit at work on the page. To Ilinca for her keen edits and pointers on the French and their customs. To Bill Gracie for giving me confidence right when I most needed a boost. Applause as well for my clan of fellow writers – Meg, Ellen, Kalen. Thank you for your sage advice. A nod to novelist Susan Coll, as well as Bill and David of Politics & Prose, for helping me believe I could do this. And one additional toast to Dave, Rocky and Ron, whose insights came unexpected, both in their detail and their depth.

I'd also like to thank the circle of friends who gave me hope the tale might find a receptive audience. First to Jayne, whose own special beauty found its way into the book. Then on to Rod, Robbie and Patience, who share the distant spark that awakened the novel. To Darrin and Bruce, who remain my angels. To Kate and Mia, whose wisdom and grace amaze me always. And then to Emily and Tony, for their eagerness to explore lingering traces of old Virginia, and to

Renea and her parents, who first welcomed me to the ridges. That, in turn, leads to Lou Ann, my Highland County host. The escapes to your cozy cabin sustained my inspiration in every season.

My family deserves special recognition. To my father, who taught me a love of the wilderness. To my mother and sister, who nurtured my love of words and worlds beyond. And to my grandmother, whose presence I felt on many a day, memory being the gift that it is.

Another gift is music, so I'd like to close by acknowledging two guitarists – William Ackerman and William Coulter. Their evocative tunes carried me each morning from my condo in DC to the ridges and hollows of rural Virginia, providing a haunting score for opening my mind. Perhaps the rhythms found their way into the tale after all, as I often imagined they would.

While it is true that writing begins as a reclusive process, it very much ends with an act of sharing. So my gratitude goes out to each and every one of you for sharing in this experience with me.

With love,

John

About the Author

John J Kelley is a fiction writer crafting tales about healing, growth and community. Born and raised in the Florida panhandle, he graduated from Virginia Tech and served as a military officer. After pursuing traditional careers for two decades, he began writing.

John is a member of The Writer's Center (www.writer.org). He lives in Washington, DC, with his partner of eighteen years and can often be found wandering Rock Creek Park or hovering over his laptop at a local coffee shop.

John recently completed his debut novel, a work of historical fiction set at the close of the First World War. *The Fallen Snow* explores the emotional journey of a young infantry sniper returning to a remote mountain community reeling from war, influenza and economic collapse.

For more background on the novel or to learn how you can help recommend the novel to others, please visit *www.thefallensnow.com*.